MIDNIGHT BETRAYAL

Also by Melinda Leigh

Midnight Exposure
Midnight Sacrifice

She Can Run
She Can Tell
She Can Scream
She Can Hide

MELINDA LEIGH

MIDNIGHT BETRAYAL

Montlake
Romance

Text copyright © 2014 Melinda Leigh
All rights reserved.

Published by Montlake Romance, Seattle

www.apub.com
Amazon, the Amazon logo, and Montlake Romance are trademarks of Amazon.com, Inc., or its affiliates.

ISBN-13: 9781477824238
ISBN-10: 1477824235

Cover design by *theBookDesigners*

Library of Congress Control Number: 2014903120

Printed in the United States of America

For Granny,

For a lifetime of unconditional

love and support.

CHAPTER
1

Two weeks ago

She died faster than I'd expected. In fact, the whole abduction and killing scheme was easier than I'd anticipated. I'd allowed several hours for tonight's task but finished well ahead of schedule.

I shifted the dagger in my grip. The light from the camp lantern shone on the engraved hilt, and blood gleamed wet and thick on the silver blade I'd honed for the occasion.

She'd been easy to lure. A simple offer of drugs had been enough to entice her into the car. Once I attained the privacy of this abandoned house, the rest of the steps proceeded as planned. I'd been keeping her for several days, but tonight was the grand finale. Remembering the hours spent perfecting my scheme and the clockwork precision of its execution, adrenaline raced through my veins. Though dampness lingered below ground, I wasn't cold. The event had gone off beautifully, and success was always a thrill. But for the culmination of a daring plan, the conclusion had been decidedly anticlimactic. I'd planned this for so long, envisioned every moment of each step along the way. How disappointing.

What had I done wrong?

The human body was appallingly fragile.

Size, fitness, strength. None of that mattered. One slice to the neck was all it took to turn a living being into a pile of connective tissue and bone.

Standing tall, I surveyed my work. She was naked. Her jeans and shirt, sliced from her body on day one, were folded neatly beside her. Her last-minute struggling had loosened scabs over the punctures on her thighs. Fresh blood dribbled in thin rivulets across her skin. The wounds had ceased bleeding now that her heart had stopped.

I'd anticipated that the killing would be messy business, but I hadn't appreciated the sheer violence of dying. The cut had been perfectly placed for a quick death. I'd like to claim I'm not entirely without mercy, but that wouldn't be true. My decision was based on practicality and the necessity of adhering to my schedule. After all, it wasn't the first time I'd used a knife on her flesh, but it was definitely the last. The first few heartbeats after the knife stroke had produced rhythmic spurts with decreasing trajectory. The concrete slab wasn't perfectly level. The remaining blood that flowed from the wound had run downhill and pooled against the cinderblock wall. Once her heart stopped, gravity allowed the body to leak for several minutes postmortem. Thankfully, I'd stood well back from the red river, sparing my clothes and shoes from contamination.

Leaning over, I switched to a reverse grip on the handle and used the knife point to draw a spiral on her abdomen. Even on an utterly still subject, precision took care. What I'd give for the spirograph of my childhood. There. Done.

I wiped the blade on her T-shirt and placed the knife in a plastic bag inside my kit. Now for the finishing touch. I'd brought everything needed for a proper funeral pyre: paper, kindling, gasoline. The match was struck and tossed. Fire whooshed, flames embracing the body with greedy fingers. I made my exit, not waiting to see if anyone noticed the fire—or the smell of burning flesh. Even if they did, this wasn't the sort of neighborhood where anyone rushed to call the police. Grabbing the camp lantern, I hurried to my car and stowed my bag in the trunk. I checked the dashboard clock. An hour to spare. I'd counted on her putting up a better fight. Instead of thrashing and resisting death, she'd acquiesced with a few minor struggles, surrendering the moment she saw the knife. Perhaps the puncture wounds had been too deep.

Did some people hang on to hope longer than others? Were physical condition, age, and strength major factors in a person's survival instinct, or did mental stamina play the largest role? Did a happy student with a bright future have a greater desire to fight death, a stronger will to live, than a homeless runaway? Or was the survival instinct an inborn trait as independent of life events as eye color?

All interesting questions, but before they could be analyzed, the next step of my plan needed to be executed.

Another girl waited. Another death. Another fire.

CHAPTER
2

Today

The collection storage room of the Livingston Museum of Archaeology maintained the optimal temperature and relative humidity to stabilize the deterioration of the artifacts stored on its shelf-lined walls. Filters and vigilance reduced exposure to light, pollution, and pests. At a long stainless-steel table in the center of the twelve-by-twenty-foot space allocated to the European collection, Louisa examined the Iron Age Celtic short sword with gloved hands. With a sixteen-inch blade, the two-thousand-year-old weapon had been light and deadly in the close-quarters combat the Celts had favored. She returned the ancient piece to its open acid-free box. Moving to a second container, Louisa unpacked the newly arrived reproduction and held it next to the original, the length of shiny steel a sharp contrast to the artifact's heavily corroded blade.

It was perfect.

Displayed side by side in the glass case beneath the battle mural, the juxtaposition of old and new swords would help museum visitors envision Celtic warriors charging into combat with the Romans. In the far corner of the room, life-size figures frozen in battle would reenact the deadly clash in 3-D. If Louisa closed her eyes and pictured the exhibit room as it would look in a few weeks when the new renovations were complete, she could hear the sounds of screaming men and the *thunk* of heavy blades on metal shields, smell unwashed bodies and sweat over the coppery scent of fresh blood.

She was hopeless, stuck in the past, living in her imagination. Even as a child, she'd had more books than friends, especially after her mother died.

No. She wasn't going to be that person anymore. She'd left her old life behind.

No more hiding in history to avoid the present. Being fired from her last position was a stain on her résumé—even though she'd recovered the artifacts that were stolen under her watch—but like a cat free-falling from a high-rise, she'd landed relatively unscathed. Yes, in order to get a job, she'd had to take the blow to her ego and accept a demotion to assistant curator. In Maine, she'd curated an entire small museum. But she was grateful to work in the field she loved again, and that she'd been forced to leave the painful family entanglements of her hometown. Being away from home gave her an exhilarating sense of freedom that compensated for her lower salary. It was a good thing her trust fund enabled her to do as she pleased.

Regardless of the drawbacks, Philadelphia was still her fresh start. Nothing was perfect.

Someone knocked on the door behind her. She set the knife down, crossed five feet of gray speckled linoleum, and opened the door for the department administrative assistant. April followed her back to the table. "Oh, the reproduction is lovely."

"It is." Louisa leaned back and studied the gleaming new weapon. "I hope it's as effective in wowing visitors as it is beautiful."

"Don't underestimate the glitter effect. People are like fish. They're drawn to shiny objects." April cocked her head as she watched. "The new exhibit is going to be spectacular. Visitors are going to feel like they're in the middle of an epic battle."

"That's the idea. Just give me one minute. I'll be right with you." Louisa repacked both boxes.

"Take your time." Respecting Louisa's concentration, her assistant waited, but the toe of her practical flat shoe tapped an incessant beat.

Satisfied the weapons were secure, Louisa placed the artifact on the shelf. Peeling off her gloves, she removed her glasses and slid them into the pocket of her suit jacket.

April got down to business. "Director Cusack wants to see you in his office."

"What's wrong?" Louisa turned toward her assistant.

At fifty-five, April was small and slim with bright red hair styled in a short, spiky cut that suited her energetic and quirky personality. She'd been with the museum for decades. April knew everyone and everything that went on inside its glass-and-brick exterior. Nothing slipped past her experienced scrutiny.

"I'm not sure what he wants." April's frown and narrowed eyes conveyed her displeasure. "But the police are with him."

"The police?" As if being summoned to the director's office wasn't enough to stress her out. Louisa tucked the boxed reproduction under her arm and followed April to the hallway. The door locked automatically behind them.

"I suspect it's about Riki."

"I hope it isn't bad news."

Riki LaSanta, a second-year intern working with the Egyptian collection, had gone missing a few weeks before. The police had questioned the staff when the girl first disappeared, but with no evidence of foul play, the case hadn't garnered much attention. Though she didn't work directly with Riki and hadn't known the young woman very long, every time Louisa saw one of the MISSING flyers posted around the museum and university, her chest ached. What could have happened to her?

"I don't know, but the police look grim." April's eyes misted. "I was hoping Riki had just needed a break. I know her grades were shaky this semester."

Louisa gave April's forearm a supportive squeeze. "That's what everyone is hoping. It's a valid theory. Graduate school is tough. The pressure can get to anyone."

They walked down the corridor in silence. Louisa's heels tapped on the tile, echoing the staccato beats of her heart. At a junction in the hall, they stopped.

"Do you want me to take the reproduction up to the prop room?"

"Would you? That would be great." Louisa handed her the box. "I already cataloged it. It goes along the far wall with the other props for the *Celtic Warrior* exhibit."

"I'll take care of it." April lowered her voice. "Watch yourself in there. Cusack will be looking out for his own hide, not yours."

"I will. Thanks."

She and April parted ways in the center corridor. Louisa paused outside the director's door to button her jacket. Composed, she walked into the outer office. The blonde receptionist talking on the phone waved her through. Two sharp-eyed men sat in the guest chairs that faced the director's antique mahogany desk. Behind his desk, Dr. Hamish Cusack, director and chief curator, stood, prompting his guests to do the same.

"Dr. Hancock, come in." Lured from a museum in northern England seven years before, Director Cusack's accent was as impeccable and British as his manners. In a tailored charcoal suit that contrasted with his guests' off-the-rack attire, he was tall and fit for his fifty years. Cusack gestured to the men one at a time. "These are Detectives Jackson and Ianelli."

Detective Jackson was a wiry African American in his mid-fifties with a shaved head that reflected the overhead light like

7

polished walnut. Ianelli was younger, perhaps forty, with dark hair and olive-toned skin that suggested Mediterranean ancestry. The buttons of his blue dress shirt strained against the bulge of his belly.

"Let me get you a chair." Cusack rounded his desk, picked up a wing chair in the corner by the seat back, and angled it between his desk and the detectives. Louisa was no genius at reading subtle human body language, but her boss's position was blatant. He was declaring his neutrality. He'd neatly put her between him and the police and distanced himself from the situation.

She shook the policemen's hands and perched on the chair. "What can I do for you gentlemen?"

The older detective, Jackson, cleared his throat. "We'd like you to look at a few pictures, Dr. Hancock. But I need to warn you they might be a little . . . disturbing."

Louisa touched the pearls at her throat.

"We've found a couple of symbols that look strange. Director Cusack thinks they're Celtic. He says you're the expert." Jackson's shrewd eyes watched her fidget.

She lowered her hand, interlocking her fingers on her lap to hold them still, and glanced at her boss. He avoided eye contact. The rat. The museum Cusack ran in England was full of Celtic artifacts. "Where did you find the symbols?"

Jackson's response was abrupt. "On a murder victim."

She flinched. *They couldn't want her to . . .* She met the detective's unwavering gaze. They did. Despite a silk blouse and suit jacket, a wave of damp cold rolled over Louisa's arms like fog across the bay. "You want me to look at a dead body."

"Not exactly," Jackson said in an equally flat voice. "Photos."

Pictures were a better option, but not by much. She took an unsteady breath. Someone had to help the police, and it was obvious that someone wouldn't be her boss. "All right."

Jackson slid three photos from a yellow clasp envelope and spread them out on the director's desk. The images were zoomed in so closely that at first she wasn't sure what she was seeing. Plus, the skin was dark . . .

Louisa put on her glasses. *Oh God.* That was a person's skin.

"The marks are hard to see." Jackson pulled a small magnifying glass from his pocket. "They're very small, and the body was burned."

The graphic mental image that followed his statement dimmed her vision for a fraction of a second. Knife wounds. Charred skin. She was accustomed to seeing blade marks on bones that had been buried for a thousand years. Time provided distance. But this . . .

These wounds were here and now. They screamed pain and fear and violence.

Jackson hovered the glass over the tiny purplish blotches. "These bruising patterns are what we're interested in. They look like spirals and something else."

Louisa closed her eyes to the gruesome images and took a single deep breath. She lifted her eyelids and studied the marks, trying to detach herself from the pictures as if studying a recently unearthed bone. It didn't work. This was too recent, too fresh, too real. She still saw a person, charred skin, and suffering. Determined, she cleared her throat and focused. "Those look like typical Celtic symbols: spirals and knots. This one might be a horse."

"What can you tell us about them?"

"Celts decorated their weapons with symbols of their gods and beliefs, whatever they thought would give them an edge in battle." Louisa fought the nausea gathering beneath her sternum.

"What type of weapon might leave marks like this?" Jackson asked.

"We have a few Celtic daggers with engravings." Louisa knew she'd seen a similar pattern.

"Are the weapons here?" Jackson stacked his photos and slid them back into their envelope.

"Yes, they're in the collection storage room. We're in the process of building a new exhibit of Celtic weapons. The artifacts are locked away until the renovations are complete."

He fastened the metal clasp. "Can we see them?"

"Certainly, but the blades aren't sharp enough to kill anyone." Louisa shuddered. To leave bruises around the wounds, the blade must have sunk to the guard. Great force—or great rage—would have been required. "They're between eight hundred and two thousand years old."

"No one is claiming that the weapons have anything to do with a murder." But Cusack's voice sounded hollow.

Louisa and the policemen ignored him.

Swallowing a wave of sickness, Louisa walked toward the door. The three men followed her back to the artifact room. She unlocked the door with a swipe of her ID card. Inside, she pulled on white gloves and scanned the shelves for the boxes she wanted. The first three she checked held Iron Age daggers. Only one was engraved, but the carvings didn't match. She grabbed the next box containing a Bronze Age specimen. She moved it to the center table and raised the lid. The corroded blade was encased in a thick patina of verdigris and rust. She pointed to the curved guard that separated the blade from the handle. "It's hard to see on the original piece, but the engravings were spirals and knots. May I see the photo again?" Though that was the last thing she wanted to do.

Please don't match.

Jackson pulled out the picture and held it next to the artifact. "All I can see is rust."

She slid a magnifying lamp from the center of the work-table and positioned the flexible gooseneck over the dagger. Worn down by time, the engravings were faint, but her experienced eye visualized a mirror image of the marks on the victim's skin. She compared the symbols to the marks in the photo in Jackson's hand. Not every symbol had made a distinct impression, but the ones that were visible matched those on the ancient weapon.

With questions whirling in her head, she stepped aside.

Jackson leaned over the magnifier. He stiffened, then straightened and knuckle-slapped his partner on the arm. "Take a look."

Ianelli stared through the lens and grunted. "Damn. That looks close, but like Dr. Hancock said, there's no way in hell that blade killed anyone. Looks like it would crumble if you touched it."

Dread flooded Louisa's belly. Her blood chilled, flowing through her limbs like the Atlantic in January. "The museum commissioned a reproduction of this dagger."

"You had it copied?" Jackson asked.

"Not exactly. The reproduction is made to show how the knife would have looked when it was new." Louisa returned the artifact to its box and shelved it. They left the collection storage room and walked down the hall to the elevator.

"Collection storage space is always an issue," Cusack explained as he pressed the button for the third floor. "Maintaining a controlled environment to protect artifacts from deterioration is quite expensive. Items not of historical value are stored separate from artifacts."

The elevator dinged, and they emerged from the elevator into an empty industrial-looking hall of ugly green paint and scratched gray linoleum. The museum spent the majority of its budget on the parts of the building that were accessible to the public. The third floor was a hodgepodge of small rooms. Halfway down the hall, Louisa opened the door and swept her hand over the wall next to the doorframe. Overhead florescent lights flickered and then held their brightness.

It has to be here.

Rows of metal shelves held the objects the museum used to round out displays, like the prop room of a movie studio. Like a studio, the museum portrayed slices of life throughout time. A dozen six-foot-tall shelving units formed aisles, and the shelves were packed full of items.

Louisa walked to the last aisle. A tag on the shelving affixed to the wall read CELTIC WARRIOR EXHIBIT. She scanned the labels on the containers and pulled down the correct box. "The dagger came in a few weeks ago. Here it is."

She lifted the lid. The box was empty. Her knees weakened, and she nearly dropped the container. "It's gone."

Surely the weapon was simply misplaced. But where was it? The new *Celtic Warrior* exhibition was scheduled to open in three weeks. She replaced the empty box. Picking up a clipboard, she flipped pages of the computer printout. Her finger stopped on the line for the dagger replica. "It's on the log sheet. It should be here."

"How many copies of this dagger were made?" Jackson asked.

"We had one made." Louisa wrapped her arms around her waist.

Ianelli scratched his forehead. "Could there be others?"

"I don't think so, but it's possible," Cusack answered in a grim voice. "I'll get you the name and number of the maker."

"Is this replica sharp enough to kill someone?" Jackson asked.

"No." Louisa pulled out the sword replica that arrived that morning. She handed it to Jackson. "The edge was dull like this one, but it could be sharpened like any other blade."

Jackson ran a finger along the edge. "Is it valuable?"

Cusack shook his head. "Not particularly. We had to pay a design fee, but the actual value is nominal. You can buy museum replicas online for under a hundred dollars."

Jackson pulled a notepad and pen from his jacket pocket. "Who has access to this room?"

Blood rushed in Louisa's ears. External sounds dimmed. Eyes riveted on the empty box, she vaguely heard Cusack answering the detective.

"The items stored up here aren't of high value. Security on the third floor is minimal. Most of the staff has access. We have a senior curator, three assistant curators, museum security, two curatorial administrative assistants, one intern . . ." His voice trailed off as he listed the people who had access to the weapon.

The detective scanned the ceiling. "Are there security cameras in here?"

"No," Cusack said. "There's a camera in the elevator."

It appeared someone was killed with an item stolen from her museum. An image of Riki's MISSING flyer popped into Louisa's mind. Louisa had seen the pretty brunette in the corridors. The girl had always smiled in passing. Sadness filled her at the loss of a young, promising life.

"Who is the victim?" Louisa asked quietly.

The men stopped talking and turned toward her.

Jackson's face tightened. "We can't say at this time."

"But do you *know* who it is?" Louisa gave Jackson a direct stare.

His lips flattened, and he crossed his arms over his chest. "We have a suspicion of who she is, but we're waiting for confirmation to make an official ID."

"The victim is female?" Louisa's mind traveled back to the photos, then to her memories of Riki.

"Yes." Detective Jackson frowned. "All I can tell you is that the victim is a Caucasian female, probably in her early twenties.

A homeless man found her in the basement of an abandoned building a few hours ago. We were lucky to get a jump on the press, but the stories are breaking now."

In the weeks since Riki disappeared, seven bodies had been discovered in the Philadelphia area. After the first three, museum employees had stopped speculating each one could be Riki.

"Do you suspect the victim is our intern?" Louisa pressed.

But Jackson's eyes gave away nothing but irritation.

"Do you have photos of the dagger replica?" he asked, ignoring her question and leaving her to assume the worst.

"Yes, I have pictures."

The detective gave her a pointed look. "We don't give the press all the details of the case. We would appreciate you keeping our discussion in confidence."

"Of course." Louisa crossed her arms.

Next to her, a grim-faced Cusack nodded.

Jackson handed them each a business card. "Please call us if you remember anything or if you notice anything unusual."

The police took drawings, measurements, and photos of the dagger reproduction so the medical examiner could determine if the museum replica was the likely murder weapon. As soon as the detectives finished with her, Louisa retreated to her tiny office and sank into her chair.

Dear God, not again.

She couldn't believe this was happening. For the second time, items stolen from her museum had been used by a killer. Six months ago in Maine, a madman had used stolen museum pieces in bizarre Celtic rituals that killed several people. Now it was happening again.

Conor Sullivan had pulled her into the investigation. He'd connected the missing artifacts to an elaborate mass murder attempt, and she'd gone with him to help solve the case. Conor, and her reaction to him, had been nearly as disconcerting as being swept up in a violent murder case.

She opened her bottom desk drawer, pulled a folder out, and set it on the desk. Opening the cover, she spread newspaper articles across the blotter. The last story wrapped around a black-and-white photo of Conor escorting her to her car after the police had finished with her interview. She was barely visible in the picture. The angle of his big body blocked most of hers from media intrusion. Looking at it now, she could almost feel his protective stance, his powerful body touching hers. Her toes curled at the memory.

From the moment they met, he threw her off-kilter. She'd just lost her job. In the two days they'd worked together, his fear for his brother, the horror of being involved in a murder case, and her inexplicable response to him compounded into complete confusion in her already-turbulent life.

He wasn't the sort of man she dated: cool, polite professionals with backgrounds and interests similar to hers. No, there was nothing cool about Conor. She hadn't wanted to be attracted to him, but just looking at the picture now sent heat swirling low in her belly. She took off her glasses and slid the picture a few inches farther away on the blotter, as if distance between her and the photo created a like chasm in her emotions.

It didn't.

But all that was behind her. Six months ago had been a difficult period in her life. Now that she was settled again, she'd have better control.

That would be easier to believe if Conor didn't live in Philadelphia.

And if she didn't keep his picture in her desk.

The door opened, and she jerked upright.

"Relax." April closed the door behind her. She carried a brown paper bag in one hand and two large coffees in a cardboard

tray in the other. "You haven't eaten all day. We're having a dinner break. No shop talk."

"Thanks." Louisa glanced down at the newspaper articles.
Shoving them hastily into her desk would be obvious. She forced
her hands to move slowly gathering up the papers. "You're the
best."

April set her bounty on the desk. Louisa took the coffee with
an *L* written in black marker on the side.

"I know." April fished two wrapped deli sandwiches from the
bag. "Turkey or tuna?"

Louisa sipped the coffee and selected the turkey club. She
took a tentative bite, and her stomach begged for more. "This is
great."

"There are cupcakes for later." April produced a small white
bakery box. "Cupcakes make everything better."

"No argument from me." Louisa took another bite of her
sandwich. The deli had been generous with the bacon. Her taste
buds applauded.

April spied the photo before Louisa could push it into the
folder.

"Honey, you don't have to hide that. Everyone in the museum
knows what happened at your last job. Those articles were passed
around the break room. In fact, it's one of the reasons Cusack
hired you." April dropped into one of the two leather club chairs
facing the desk.

"I don't understand."

"I sort of *overheard* Cusack telling one of the board members that it'd be an opportunity to get a top-notch curator at a
bargain-basement price. He also said that you were replaced with
someone far less qualified. The Maine museum probably needed
to cut its budget."

Louisa's heart dropped. But then his decision made sense. Museums, especially smaller ones, operated on very limited funding, and the recent economic downturn had affected donations and grants. Who would ever have thought the situation that brought her to Philadelphia could happen twice?

"I'm pretty sure your father's reputation helped too."

Her assistant's answer was yet another blow. Louisa hadn't even gotten this entry-level position on her own merit. Currently living in Stockholm, her father was a renowned expert in Viking burials, and she was inadvertently borrowing his academic success. The events in Maine, and now here in Philadelphia, were out of her control, yet her career was in jeopardy. She suppressed the surge of self-pity. How could she feel sorry for herself when a woman had been violently murdered?

April picked up the article. "I saw this picture before. *Who is he?*" She brought the red-framed glasses hanging on a chain around her neck to her nose.

In the photo, Conor's lean face was turned away from Louisa and toward the cameras. He'd been furious at the macabre story-lust of the media. Anger hardened his angular features. With his unshaven jaw, he looked more than a little dangerous. The motorcycle boots and leather jacket contributed to his bad-boy persona.

"His name is Conor Sullivan. His family owns a tavern in South Philadelphia."

"*He* lives *here*?" April pursed her lips and raised a single brow. "Please tell me you're seeing him and then give me all the details."

"No. I'm not seeing him." What would it be like to be with him again? Heat crept up Louisa's neck.

April raised her eyebrows and considered Louisa from over the half lenses of her reading glasses. "Is he an asshole?" she asked with her typical bluntness.

"No."

April made *mmm, mmm* sounds at the photo. "Scorching."

Conor's hotness wasn't in question. "We don't have much in common, and we met under such bizarre circumstances. I'm sure he doesn't have any interest in seeing me."

April studied the picture. "Louisa, he might not be looking at you, but his body language is all about you. He's practically wrapped around you. If a man like that was paying me that kind of attention . . . Wonder how he feels about older women."

Louisa couldn't hold back a short laugh. "I admit. He is good-looking."

She bit into her sandwich. April's distraction had allowed Louisa's stomach to settle, which undoubtedly had been her assistant's intention. Louisa struggled to connect with people, but April's honesty and humor, along with Louisa's determination to be less of a loner, had eroded Louisa's resolve like the persistent drip of water on rock.

"Honey, calling that man good-looking is like calling Michelangelo's *David* a nice statue." April fanned herself.

"I don't usually go for the bad-boy type."

April shook her head. "That is no boy. *That* is a man."

The door opened again, and Louisa's intern hurried into the office. Though she'd just turned twenty-one, Zoe's long body retained its youthful slimness. With her long brown hair tied back in a ponytail, she looked younger than her years. Her brown eyes were open wide. "The police asked me a bunch of questions. Why would anyone steal a replica? Its dollar value is relatively low."

Louisa replaced the picture of her and Conor and returned the folder to her drawer.

Zoe's face paled. The freckles popping against her fair skin lent a frightened cast to her complexion. "They wouldn't tell me anything, but it must have something to do with Riki's disappearance, right?"

"I really can't say what the police are thinking," Louisa said. "April and I are going to stay tonight and run a complete inventory on the European exhibit." It would likely be an all-nighter. "We could use a hand."

"I have a date."

Louisa looked up from the sandwich. "Really?"

"You don't have to act so surprised that I have a boyfriend." Zoe grinned. "Though, honestly, even I'm shocked he asked me out."

Louisa smiled. "I'm only surprised because you never mentioned him before."

Zoe was several years younger than her graduate student peers and suffered from the social awkwardness that often accompanied brilliance. She was an excellent intern, though, except for some habitual lateness. No doubt both those issues would resolve as the girl matured.

"He's new. Tonight he's taking me to a hockey game." Zoe sobered. "But I guess I could cancel if you really need me to stay."

Louisa and April shared a resigned smile.

"No, you enjoy your date." Louisa knew exactly what it was like to be desperate to fit into the social environment when you were different from everyone else. "We'll manage."

"Thanks." Zoe grinned. Excitement radiated from her brown eyes.

"Be careful." As Louisa knew from experience, boys knew how to take advantage of naïveté like Zoe's. Her settled nerves tightened at an old memory. No. Not the time. She put the old pain back in the dark corner of her mind, where it belonged.

"Don't worry. I'll be fine."

"Have fun," Louisa said as Zoe bounced out of the room.

Louisa's thoughts turned to the gruesome photos the police had brought. Was the body Riki or some other poor young woman? Whoever she was, had she thought she was safe? Where and how had she been taken?

And most importantly, would the killer strike again?

CHAPTER
3

Would this night never end?

In the basement of the South Philadelphia bar he owned with his three siblings, Conor set up a new keg of brown ale. The old brick floor dug into his knee. Finished, he climbed the steep wooden staircase, passed the kitchen, and went back into the main room.

A cheer erupted at the far end of the bar. A half-dozen college-age hockey fans circled around a table, all dressed in Flyers jerseys. They'd painted their faces with orange and black stripes in support of their team. Conor didn't recognize any of them, and unlike the usual Sullivan's crowd, these boys had been overt about flashing their cash since they came in an hour ago. One raised his hand and snapped his fingers for the waitress. The sound didn't carry over the din, but the superior attitude came across crystal clear. An aura of privileged aggression hovered around the group. While Conor appreciated the dollars in the drawer, this bunch set off his well-developed troublemaker radar.

Conor lifted the hinged partition and moved behind the bar. Tilting a glass under the tap, he tested the flow of ale.

The part-time bartender, Ernie, was at the register, ringing up a customer.

"Is Terry still here?" Conor asked. His old friend, now a beat cop, had been nursing an off-duty beer when Conor went downstairs.

"He just left," Ernie said.

"Figures." Just a ten-minute walk from the Sports Complex, Sullivan's was a postgame stop-off for fans either commiserating a loss or celebrating a win. He nodded toward the college crowd. "Are they behaving?"

"So far." The lighted Heineken sign reflected off Ernie's bald dome. At seventy, Ernie had been supplementing his social security a couple of nights a week at Sullivan's for years. "But while you were in the basement, they downed another pitcher of beer and a round of Jägermeister shots."

Ernie wiped a condensation ring from the worn-smooth wood.

"Hopefully they're barhopping, and they'll move on soon." Conor checked the head on the ale. Perfect. He poured the test beer in the sink. "If not, we'll cut them off."

"Hey, get back over here." The voice was irritated, male, and drunk.

"I said no, Heath." The lone girl in the bunch, a slim brunette in painted-on jeans, squirmed her way off a drunken college boy's lap. Her ponytail and the scattering of freckles across her nose made her look painfully young.

"Don't be a tease." Drunk Boy grabbed her with both hands by the waist and tugged her back. With short, dark hair and blue eyes set too close together, his face was predatory, hawkish.

"Stop it." She spun and swatted at his chest.

"Crap." Conor set the empty glass down and headed toward the ruckus.

"And here we go," Ernie muttered.

Conor waded into the spat. "Is there a problem?"

"Yeah." Drunk Boy's face reddened. "You butting into my personal business. That's the problem."

If the kid had been a regular, he would have backed off at Conor's glare. But he was full of belligerence, beer, and himself—the trifecta of stupidity.

Conor gave diplomacy a try anyway. "The lady would like you to let go of her."

"I think I know what my *lady* wants more than some old dude."

"Kick his ass, Heath," one of his friends yelled from the table.

"It's time for you to leave, boys." A headache started in Conor's temples. Longest. Day. Ever.

"Fuck you." Drunk Boy pushed the girl off his lap and stood up, his posture combative.

Physically, they were well-matched. Drunk Boy was a couple inches over six feet tall and had the lean, athletic build of a lacrosse or soccer player. But size wasn't everything. At six-two, Conor ran regularly and lugged kegs and cases of beer every day. He'd given up boxing years ago, but he worked out on the heavy bag a few times a week. Plus, Conor had been bouncing his own bar since his twenty-first birthday. He'd introduced a hundred obnoxious drunks to the sidewalk on the other side of the door. If Drunk Boy's brain cells weren't pickled in Jägermeister, the younger man would have thought hard before he threw a punch.

But pickled they were.

The punch was slow and sloppy. Conor slapped the kid's hook out of the way and fired a punch neatly into his jaw. Drunk Boy crumpled on the wood floor as if his bones had evaporated. Shocked silence filled the bar for a solid minute. Then the friends got up and stumbled over.

Ow. Pain rolled through Conor's knuckles. He was sick and tired of dealing with young assholes.

Drunk Boy blinked and sat up. His nasty squint caught on the brunette. "You're such a bitch."

Conor tucked the girl behind him. He addressed the group. "Pick up your friend and get out of my bar. Don't come back."

They didn't argue. Two buddies hauled Drunk Boy to his feet and dragged him out.

Conor turned to the girl. "What's your name?"

"Zoe."

"I assumed you didn't want to leave with them. Can you call someone to pick you up, Zoe?"

"I'll call my roommate." Nodding, she pulled a cell phone out of her purse.

"Next time, don't go out without a couple of girlfriends for backup. Being alone with those guys isn't smart."

"I didn't know they'd turn into such jerks after a few beers. We go to school together." Big, brown eyes blinked innocently up at Conor. God, she was a pretty thing. But much too young for him. Much, much too young.

Even if she weren't, he'd sworn off jumping into bed with women he barely knew since the Barbara I-forgot-to-mention-I'm-married McNally episode three years ago. For a relationship that had only lasted a few months, it had left a damned big impression. Being deliberately lied to and used had soured his attitude toward dating, as had the ease with which she'd manipulated him.

"We close at midnight on Mondays," he said.

"My roommate should be home." Texting furiously, she slid back into the booth. Conor cleared away the booze, brought her a Diet Coke, and left her watching ESPN. She was still there an hour later when Ernie and the kitchen staff were clearing out.

"Did you get your roommate?"

She shook her head. "No. I'll take the subway."

She is not your responsibility. Conor backed away. He needed a pretty college girl about as much as a rash. Both tended to hang around long enough to make life uncomfortable. "And there's nobody else you can call? Do you want me to call you a cab?"

She shook her head and batted those thick lashes again. "No. I take the subway all the time. It's fine."

He glanced out the window. In the light of the streetlamp on the corner, a figure in a hoodie hunched against the rain. South Philly was generally safe during the day. A working-class neighborhood, people looked out for each other. Families tended to stay generation after generation. But a young girl alone at midnight . . .

"Do you want me to drive you to the station?"

"Would you do that?"

"Sure." Because he was a giant idiot genetically incapable of minding his own business. He'd parked his car illegally in the alley. He had to move it anyway. And that guy on the corner gave off the wrong vibe.

Besides, the sooner he got her out of here, the sooner he could go to bed.

"Oh, thank you."

"Come on. My car is out back." Conor locked the front door to the bar and led her out into the back alley. The rain had settled into a steady, soaking drizzle. No sign of anyone or anything that shouldn't be here.

Conor patted his pocket. "I have to run upstairs for my key. Wait here."

But she was right behind him as he jogged up the stairs to his apartment over the bar. Conor flipped on the light. His keys were usually on the table by the door. Not there.

Zoe sidled behind him. "I didn't want to wait in the dark by myself."

"OK. Wait here. I have to find my keys." Conor did a quick surface scan. Nothing. The kitchen counters were clear. In the bedroom, he went to the nightstand, moved some books, and shuffled some papers before finding his key ring on the dresser under a stack of junk mail. When he came out of the bedroom, Zoe was standing in the kitchen leafing through an advertisement circular.

"Sorry it took so long." Conor motioned toward the door. "Let's go."

He grabbed an umbrella on the way out, then put Zoe into the twenty-year-old Porsche he'd bought as a junker and spent most of last year restoring. The SEPTA station was only eight blocks down. He pulled to the curb behind a transit bus.

"'Night." She got out of the car and turned away.

"Good night." Remembering when his sister had been assaulted in a parking garage years ago, Conor glanced in his rearview mirror. Standing on the sidewalk, digging something out of her purse, Zoe looked so young and vulnerable. *Damn it.* He jumped out of the car and ran around the back end. "Wait." He tapped her shoulder.

She whirled, jumping backward, her eyes wide in alarm. She pressed a hand to her chest. "God, you scared me."

"I'm sorry. Are you sure I can't get you a cab?"

"No, you've done enough." She backed up a step.

He dug a business card out of his wallet. "Do me a favor? Give me a quick call when you get home."

She took the card. "Sure. Thanks again."

A horn blared. His car was blocking a cab. The driver leaned over the passenger seat and gestured between Conor and the Porsche with irritation.

"Be careful." He returned to his car and pulled out into the street.

And that was that.

He drove back to the bar and found a parking spot down the block. The guy in the hoodie was gone when Conor circled the bar and went into the alley. At the base of his apartment steps, a faint whimper carried over the sound of traffic on Oregon Avenue. He turned his head and listened. Another thin whine emanated from the darkness under the stairwell. Crouching, he squinted into the shadows.

A dog cringed in the space between the brick building and the wooden stairs. Plenty of strays roamed the city streets, but something about this animal's posture was off. He ran upstairs for a flashlight and a couple slices of cheese. Back outside, he shined the light into the dark crevice. It was a pit bull or a pit mix, blue-gray in color, and injured.

"You hungry?" Conor squatted and tossed a piece of cheese a few feet in front of the dog. The dog shuffled forward, sniffing the air, body tense and postured for flight as it licked at the aged provolone.

Numerous old scars, fresh cuts, and oozing abrasions criss-crossed the dog's skin, mostly around its head and face. A meaty collar encircled the neck, and a short piece of heavy chain hung from it, all signs that the pit bull could be from a dog-fighting operation—and a bad one at that. The poor beast was razor thin. Pit bulls were naturally muscular dogs, but this one's skin was stretched taut over visible sinew and bone. How the hell could a skinny dog fight? Not that this one looked like much of a fighter. There wasn't anything aggressive about its posture.

Raindrops splattered on the asphalt. Thunder crashed, and a bolt of lightning streaked across the sky. The dog flinched, cring-ing toward the stairwell.

He should go upstairs. Picking up strays was not his responsibility, and with his current luck, the dog would bite him. He'd spent the last eighteen years of his life helping to raise his younger siblings. Now his family was settled. Business was up. Some debts had been paid. Conor finally felt like he could relax.

Maybe he'd take a vacation.

Alone? Yeah, that was lame, but he hadn't even had a date in ages. Not that he was really trying. He couldn't get that curator he'd met in Maine out of his head. Something about pushing the cool blonde's buttons heated his blood and made the women who tried to pick him up at the bar seem . . . too easy. Dr. Louisa Hancock would be a challenge.

God, there must be something wrong with him. He was thirty-eight. It was time to settle down like his siblings, not go looking for extra work.

Thunder cracked again, and the dog went flat on the pavement. He tossed another piece of cheese on the ground closer to his feet. The dog moved forward, one eye on Conor, one eye on the food. He squatted and held a chunk toward the dog. The rain intensified, soaking Conor's hair and dripping onto his nose. The dog moved forward and took the food from his hand. A drop of blood dripped onto the blacktop and swirled pink in the eddying runoff. He looked up at his apartment door, then back at the dog. Big, brown eyes blinked at him with a thoroughly pathetic, soulful, woe-is-me expression.

"Just for tonight. In the morning I'm taking you to the animal shelter. I'm not home enough to have a dog."

The pit licked his fingers.

"Come on." Holding the remaining provolone in front of the tentative dog's nose, Conor led him—he glanced back—*her* up the stairs and into his apartment. He filled a bowl with water and spread a fresh towel on the old linoleum floor. "I'll be right back. The first-aid kit is in the bar."

He jogged downstairs. He was halfway to the back door of the bar when footsteps and the metallic echo of a garbage can being knocked over put him on alert. A teenager was making his way down the alley. He stopped, squatted, and inspected behind the Dumpster. Conor sidestepped toward the door without taking his eyes off the kid.

"Hey." The kid shuffled into the light. Under a black zip-up hoodie, he wore a wifebeater, saggy jeans, and Air Jordans. "You seen a gray dog?"

The kid didn't look familiar, but the mean glint in his eyes— and the condition of the dog upstairs—set Conor on edge. He shook his head and lied. "Sorry, no."

The teen postured, spreading his arms at his sides, puffing out his chest, and leaning his upper body toward Conor rooster-fashion. "Guy across the street says he saw a gray dog come down this alley."

"So?"

The kid's attention drifted up the stairwell and landed on the door to Conor's apartment. Under the roof overhang, the steps were dry. Red spots dotted the wood. "You got blood on your hand."

"Rough night." Conor took a step forward.

"I don't let people take what's mine." The kid hesitated, obviously surprised when Conor didn't back off. The teen couldn't be from the neighborhood or he'd have known better.

"Look, kid. This isn't a good idea," Conor said.

"That's not the way I see it." The kid shook water from his face. "I want my dog, and you're a fucking liar." He pulled a switchblade from his pocket and flicked his wrist. The blade clicked open, the metal shining in the yellow light.

Tonight it seemed stupidity and youth were eternal soul mates.

"You're making a mistake." Conor raised his open hands in front of his chest. Talk about idiotic. He'd done some ridiculous things in his life, but risking a knife in the gut for a dog had to top the list.

"Fuck you. You're the one making a mistake, stealing my dog. I'm gonna cut you. Then I'm going upstairs to see your old lady." He made a thrusting motion with his pelvis. The kid couldn't have been more than fifteen, and his baby face made the gesture more vulgar.

He lunged with the knife, right at Conor's face. Expecting a chest or belly attack, Conor's parry was a fraction of a second slow. The knife point grazed his cheek as he jerked his head out of the way. He grabbed the kid's wrist and twisted it backward. Then he plowed a hard right cross into the teen's nose. The kid's head snapped back. He dropped the blade and ass-planted in a puddle. Blood spurted from his nose and soaked the front of his white tank.

Conor shook his hand. His already-bruised knuckles smarted, he had spatters of blood on his shirt, and his face stung. "Get out of here. Next time I see you, I'm calling the cops."

"You'll be sorry for that." Holding one hand to his face, the kid snatched his knife from the pavement and got to his feet. "I'm not afraid of the fucking cops. I'll be back."

"What you need to do is go home, ice your face, and reevaluate your life."

The kid flipped him a bloody middle finger as he staggered away. Conor waited until the teen had disappeared from the alley. He went in the back door and detoured to the supply closet for the first-aid kit. He should call the cops and fill out a report. But the kid was long gone, and Conor hated paperwork. Besides, there was always the slim possibility this young teen would actually learn a lesson. The pope was tweeting. Anything could happen.

Back upstairs, he used an antiseptic wipe on the tiny nick on his cheekbone. *Damn. That had been close.* He settled on the floor next to the dog. "Don't bite me, OK?"

The dog trembled and looked away as he dried her coat and cleaned the dirt from her wounds.

"I think that's as good as it's going to get."

Sensing the worst was over, the dog stretched out on her belly, nose resting on her outstretched paws. She blinked up at him with dark, liquid eyes. Conor packed up his first-aid supplies and washed his hands. "You won't destroy the place, will you?"

Not that there was much to destroy. Conor lived a spartan life. He'd never been one to accumulate stuff. His younger brother, Danny, had moved out last spring, leaving the place emptier than ever. But the dog seemed content.

"Are you hungry?" A few slices of cheese didn't seem like enough for a dog of her size. He pulled a carton of eggs out of the fridge and scrambled a half dozen. While they cooled, he checked the dog's cuts. "Better. Most of them aren't bleeding anymore."

He served up dinner. The dog shuffled over, sniffed, and nibbled at the food while keeping one skittish eye fixed on Conor. Maybe she'd eat when she relaxed.

"Maybe I should block you in here for the night." Not that he thought the dog would hurt him. In general, pit bulls didn't deserve the bad reputation they'd acquired, and this one acted downright submissive. No doubt she'd been on the losing end of whatever fight she'd been forced into. But the dog probably had fleas.

"OK, then I'm going to bed. You stay here in the kitchen." He blocked the doorway with a low bookcase. "Don't give me that face. You're fed, and you have a roof over your head. You should be happy."

He stripped off his clothes and took a quick shower. As he eased onto the bed, he checked his phone on his nightstand. No call from Zoe. Maybe she wouldn't even bother. Maybe she'd just toss his card in the nearest trash can. A faint whine sounded from the kitchen. Conor rolled over and pulled the pillow over his ear. Would the teen with the knife be back, or would he write off the dog and pick up another, since there was no shortage of stray pit bulls in the city?

Tonight had been a disaster. He'd had to intervene between the girl and her drunken boyfriend, but risking his life for a stray dog hadn't been his smartest move.

He must have dozed off, because a shift in the mattress startled him awake. A hot waft of air crossed his face. Wait. Half-asleep, confusion ruled. He'd driven the brunette home, right?

He rolled over. Three inches from his nose, the skinny dog stared down at him, panting.

"You were supposed to sleep in the kitchen. Guess my barricade wasn't high enough."

His phone vibrated on the nightstand. He picked it up and read the unfamiliar number on the screen. Zoe? "Hello."

"Um, I'm almost at my place. Thanks."

"You're welcome." The line went dead. Conor set it back on the nightstand, relieved. He hadn't thought she'd actually call.

The dog licked his face. He put a hand up and scratched behind one of her missing ears. A scab had opened up on the side of her face during the night, and blood matted the fur under her eye. "You're not the kind of girl I usually go for, but I guess we have that rough-around-the-edges thing in common."

The stub of her tail swept back and forth across the sheets. She moved to the other side of his king-size bed, turned around three times, and curled up with her head on his extra pillow.

"Ah, the hell with it." Reaching across the bed, he rested a hand on the dog's side. She sighed contentedly and closed her eyes, her protruding ribs rising and falling under his bruised fingers. He'd avoided two potentially dangerous situations tonight. Risking a few fleas seemed minor in comparison. One of these days, his hero complex was going to get him in trouble.

CHAPTER
4

My mother always justified my curfew by saying nothing good ever happened after midnight. A clichéd but accurate statement. Take tonight. I knew what was going to happen, but the slim brunette on the sidewalk, shoulders hunched against the October rain, didn't know that her life was nearly over.

I pulled up to the curb, lowered the passenger window, and leaned across the seat. "Need a ride?"

Startled, she pivoted, bending at the waist to look into the car. Recognition crossed her face. "OK."

She got into the car—and sealed her fate.

"Where are you going?" I asked.

"Home," she said.

"I have to make a stop to pick up some weed." I made a right. "Want to come along?"

"Sure."

I knew she would. We'd gotten high together the week before.

I drove to the carefully selected location, a brick row home in North Kensington. The units on either side had been demolished. This one should have been razed as well. Its blackened brick exterior flaked. Tall weeds and strewn garbage covered the yard. Before stopping, I cruised the neighborhood. The surrounding blocks were more of a war zone than a place where people lived. I checked the dark street in both directions. There was no one in sight. Below evenly spaced streetlamps, yellow puddles of light glittered on wet blacktop. Drizzle coated my windshield in a light but continuous film.

So far, so good.

I parked at the curb, not worried about the car being seen. The vehicle was a nondescript sedan, and I changed the license plates often, picking from a pool of stolen plates accumulated just for the purpose. Flipping up the hood of my jacket and tugging on gloves, I reached for the door handle.

She hesitated, her eyes sweeping the darkness. "Are you sure this is safe?"

I shrugged. "I've picked up stuff here before, and there isn't anybody around who looks dangerous."

Except me.

Still she didn't move.

"Fine. Wait out here all by yourself if you want. I'm going inside." I got out of the car. As I predicted, the girl was beside me in a few seconds.

She followed me up the cement steps. On a nearby street, dogs barked over the soft patter of rain. Other than the distant wail of a siren, the neighborhood was quiet. No one here wanted to draw attention to what he was doing. On the crumbling stoop, I nudged the sagging door open with my foot and eased into the dark interior. The floorboards in the center of the living room had collapsed into the basement, but the biggest risk here was that someone else had decided to use this particular abandoned building for his own nefarious purposes.

I switched on my flashlight and gave the space a quick sweep. Dirt, rodent droppings, and pieces of bricks littered the interior. "All clear. I'm sure he'll be here in a minute. Stay on the edges of the room."

Gaze darting into the shadows, she went to the boarded-up window and peered through a gap between the sheets of plywood.

"No one will bother us here." I was the only thing she had to fear.

Still staring out the gap, she hugged her torso, rubbing her biceps. "Will this take long?"

"No. Not long at all." I walked up behind her and put one hand in my pocket. Pressing the button on my homemade stun gun, I gave it a few seconds to charge before pulling it out. The wires hit her skin with the soft blue pop of electricity. Her body jolted and collapsed to the floor, stiff-legged. I grabbed her ankles and dragged her down the stairwell into the basement, her body thudding on the old wooden steps. I dragged her into place and rolled her onto her side. Zip ties secured her hands behind her back. Another set bound her ankles. I connected both with a fat nylon rope to the water pipe that ran through the wall and down into the basement. Its foundation was solid. I'd already checked. She wouldn't be able to pull it loose.

As her body stopped twitching, I slapped a long piece of duct tape over her mouth. Even on this bombed-out block, a woman screaming was bound to attract attention. I couldn't have that.

I'd been watching this building for weeks and felt reasonably certain no one would be tempted to use it for anything. Even the crack addicts recognized the structural risks. But to be on the safe side, I rigged a trip wire and an explosive surprise on the basement stairwell. If anyone went down into the cellar—*kaboom*—no witnesses.

"I'll be back." I went outside. I'd let her marinate in fear for a few days, like an alligator stuffs large prey under a submerged log to soften underwater. Consistency was important, as was sticking as closely as possible to my plan. Plus, I'd prefer the effects of the stun gun to wear off before I killed her. This time, I wanted the culmination of my plan to be less of a disappointment and more of a proper climax.

CHAPTER
5

It was eleven o'clock before Conor ducked his head under the shower spray. Lathering up, he examined his black-and-blue fingers. A hard hour on the heavy bag this morning hadn't helped his bruised knuckles, even in heavy boxing gloves.

But the gym had been exactly what his soul had needed. There were no TVs at his gym. No fancy cardio machines. Just the thump of mitts on pads, the yelling of trainers, the grunts of physical exertion, broken up with the occasional metallic clang of weights stacked on a barbell. Conor's gym was full of hard-core fighters, and it was perfect for working out his frustrations—or punishing himself. No more fighting for him though. It was a young man's sport, and Conor had seen too many boxers with permanent brain damage. A human skull could only take so much abuse.

He should have ignored the young brunette—and the whimpering dog in the alley—last night. He needed to learn to mind his own damned business instead of honing in on the defenseless like a GPS tracker.

What if that dumbass kid had a gun?

He dragged his sorry butt out of the shower and toweled off, ignoring the ache in his abused muscles. Of course he'd been unable to dump the dog at the pound. He'd dropped her off at the vet earlier that morning. Now his apartment felt so empty, it practically echoed. Conor dressed in a T-shirt, jeans, and boots. Time to go downstairs to work.

Sullivan's had occupied a corner in South Philadelphia for over three decades. The bar was established and run by his parents until they'd been killed in a car accident when Conor was twenty. With Danny and Jayne both in junior high when it happened, Pat and Conor had spent the next ten years struggling to raise their young siblings and keeping the bar afloat. Things had gotten rocky again when Danny came home from Iraq two years ago with PTSD. His medical bills had nearly bankrupted them. They'd gotten through some more tough patches, like the deranged killer in Maine who had targeted Jayne and, later, Danny's fiancée. But things were smoothing out again. The Sullivans were a resilient bunch.

The kitchen staff was gearing up for the lunch crowd. His older brother, Pat, was behind the bar with a clipboard, taking inventory. In the light streaming through the plate glass that fronted the bar, Conor could see a few white hairs threaded through Pat's once solid-red head.

He smoothed his features. "Sorry I'm late."

All four of the Sullivan siblings had inherited their dad's distinctive turquoise eyes. This morning, Pat's saw right through Conor's game face. "Rough night?"

Putting an arm across his chest, he stretched his too-tight triceps. "You wouldn't believe it. How's your back?"

Pat grinned. At forty, two years older than Conor, half of his brother's life had been nothing but hard work and responsibility, but Pat's sense of humor was as solid as the inch-thick oak bar that wrapped around them. "Feels like someone used me as a trampoline while I slept."

"Hey, in your house, that's a real possibility."

Pat's three kids ranged in age from four to nine, and they were a wild bunch, true Sullivans down to their pint-size souls.

"No kidding." Pat laughed. "But next time I decide to break up a concrete patio solo, remind me that my back is too old for heavy labor."

"Will do."

Pat counted bottles of Absolut and wrote a number on his sheet. Conor pitched in, and together, they finished taking inventory. The bell on the door jingled.

"And here comes the lunch crowd," Pat said.

They spent the next couple of hours serving sandwiches. At night, orders of beer and wings ruled, but the lunch crowd preferred french fries and burgers. The crowd thinned to stragglers around two o'clock.

"Well, look at that."

Hefting a new case of beer, Conor paused, tracking Pat's gaze to the door. In the dim entryway, a slim blonde smoothed a hand over her sleek, fancy updo.

Oh, snap.

Conor wouldn't have been more shocked if the pope walked through the door and ordered a boilermaker. Louisa Hancock, PhD, didn't belong in his bar or his life, regardless of how many times she'd sneaked into his thoughts—and dreams—over the past six months. Besides her cool and prickly nature, which he perversely found to be a huge turn-on, he and Louisa were as different as NASCAR and yacht racing.

But she was here. In his bar. Every perfect, polished inch of her, as if his earlier thoughts had conjured her.

Like the first time they'd met, she was dressed in a conservative suit. The feminine cut of her skirt was just snug enough to give him plenty of ideas, and the silky drape of the fabric made him wonder if she wore fancy lingerie underneath. The less she showed, the more his hopeless imagination ran with the images. Where were the glasses that gave her that hot librarian look?

"Earth to Conor." Pat nudged him, whispering, "Who is that?"

"That is the museum curator I met in Maine when I was helping Danny out."

"She doesn't look much like a curator."

"No shit." Conor dumped the beer on the counter.

Pat poked him in the back. "Well, don't just stand there. Go see the lady."

"Going." Conor dusted his hands on his jeans. "You got the bar covered for now?" he asked.

Pat motioned to the nearly empty barroom. "You're joking, right?" He nodded toward Louisa. "Get the hell over there and talk to her."

Without further urging, Conor crossed the worn, old floor in a few long strides. Wishing he'd taken the time to shave this morning, or even yesterday morning, he held out a hand. "Louisa, it's nice to see you."

Sure, he'd known she'd moved to Philly.

Not that he was keeping track of her.

OK. He *had* been keeping track of her. *Ugh.* He even went to the Livingston Museum a few weeks ago, but he'd left without asking to see her. They had nothing in common, and despite the fun he'd had teasing the hell out of her, his acute and inexplicable attraction to Louisa was irritating.

Close-up, she wasn't quite as perfectly presented as usual. A few locks had escaped the uptight bun his fingers always itched to unravel. What would she look like with all that hair down, tumbling over her shoulders?

—

"Louisa?"

Conor's voice yanked Louisa from her daze. She blinked. Perhaps coming here was a mistake. She'd underestimated the impact seeing him would have on her. Maybe it was the strange and terrible circumstances that had first put them together in Maine, or the uncomfortably similar connection that had brought her here today, but Conor Sullivan had unsettled her from the moment she first saw him. She looked away.

Louisa studied the tavern, taking a few seconds to rein in her composure. Deeper than it appeared from the street, the interior of Sullivan's was dominated by a rectangular bar. Three flatscreen TVs, tuned to different muted sporting events, hung from the walls. A few dozen tables and booths crowded most of the remaining area. A scratched and dented piano occupied the far corner. Duct-taped to the floor, electrical cords snaked across the ten-by-ten empty space next to it. They likely hosted a band on busy nights.

"Aren't you going to introduce me to the lovely lady?" a deep voice asked.

Conor led her to the bar and introduced the burly redheaded bartender as his older brother, Pat. She knew he had a younger brother and sister as well. Louisa gave Pat a distracted smile and said, "Hello."

But her attention returned immediately to Conor as if pulled by an elephant-size magnet. An ancient gray Rolling Stones T-shirt clung to his sculpted torso. Equally worn jeans and motorcycle boots showcased lean hips and long legs. She'd come here for answers, not to gawk, but the worn fabric clung to the sculpted muscles of his chest. *Look him in the eye.* She raised her gaze.

Well, that didn't help. Under shaggy black hair, his turquoise eyes were sharp with the intelligence and humor that disconcerted her more than his impressive physical attributes. Lines fanned out from his eyes. As usual, his strong jaw was shadowed with several days' beard growth. Did the man own a razor? The overall effect was lean, utterly masculine, and completely different from any man she'd ever known.

She blinked.

"Why don't we sit down?" He guided her to a corner booth. "Are you hungry?" His words were serious, but his eyes were practically grinning at her. Did he find her reaction to him amusing?

"No, but thank you." She saw the pictures of that poor girl's corpse every time she closed her eyes. She doubted she could swallow food.

The comparison of his courteous manners against his edgy appearance threw her further off-kilter. There was an old-world, knightly honor about Conor Sullivan.

Oh Lord, all that romantic nonsense was ridiculous. An overactive imagination was a hazard of spending hours alone with artifacts and contemplating their origins. She should have pulled her nose out of her books now and then and spent more time with people in her youth.

Focus!

"Coffee, soda, beer?"

"Coffee would be fine." She removed her jacket and slid into the booth. Bordeaux-colored leather glided smoothly under the silk of her skirt. She folded her jacket over her purse on the seat beside her.

He went into the back and returned a few minutes later with a tray. Setting the edge on the table, he transferred two thick mugs of coffee, a thermal carafe, and a small ceramic pitcher of cream to the table. He might be the owner of the bar, but he'd obviously waited plenty of tables. Setting the empty tray aside, he sank into the seat opposite her. "I want to thank you again for helping me in Maine."

"I didn't actually do anything, and my intentions were entirely selfish." He'd helped her as much as she'd helped him. "I simply wanted to recover my exhibit."

Humor glinted in eyes the color of the sunny Mediterranean. "You could just say, 'You're welcome.'"

Heat flushed her cheeks. "You're welcome."

"What brings you here?" Conor sipped his coffee.

She added a drop of cream to her mug. "I took a job with the Livingston Museum."

"Congratulations." No surprise registered on his face. Had he known?

"Thank you." Being let go still stung.

"They shouldn't have fired you." His head tilted. Was he reading her mind? "None of what happened was your fault."

"It's complicated."

He let it go, but the tightness of his mouth suggested he didn't want to. "How do you like your new job?"

"It's good." Louisa stirred her coffee. Last time he'd come to her for help, and he'd pursued her with dogged determination until she'd complied. This time she was the one who needed something from him.

"Where are you staying?"

"I'm renting a condo at the Rittenhouse."

He whistled. "Nice."

"It's only temporary. I didn't know what I wanted, and it's convenient to work."

He sat back and studied her, and she suddenly wished she hadn't removed her jacket. The thin silk of her blouse wasn't enough of a barrier. She felt almost naked under his scrutiny.

Louisa watched the swirl of cream in her coffee, but she could feel his gaze on her skin.

Conor set his mug on the table, his intense focus threatening to blank out her brain again. "So what brings you into my bar this afternoon?"

It was a good thing one of them was functioning with all his brain synapses. "I'm looking for a girl."

Conor's head snapped up. "A girl?"

"Yes, one of my graduate student interns at the museum didn't show up for work today. But that's not the whole story." Louisa explained about Riki, the missing dagger, and the visit from the police the day before.

Conor leaned back against his booth. "I can't believe it. Someone stole a dagger from the museum and committed murder with it."

"That's certainly what the evidence suggests." Louisa set down her cup. Enough acid already churned through her stomach to dissolve metal.

"Haven't we been here before?" His tone held no amusement.

"Unfortunately."

Conor's head tilted. "The situation is awful, but none of this explains why you're here today."

Louisa toyed with her pearls. "Zoe's boyfriend said he left her here."

"Her name is Zoe?" Conor swept both hands through his overgrown black hair. "I bounced a loudmouth last night. His girlfriend chose not to go home with him. Her name was Zoe too. Long, dark hair. Freckles. Thin."

"That sounds like her. What time did she leave?"

"I drove her to the subway station a little after midnight."

"You drove her?" Louisa smiled, remembering how he'd shielded her from the media.

"It was late, and there was a lowlife hanging on the corner." Regret darkened Conor's eyes. "I should have driven her home. Are the police looking for her?"

"When I left the museum, the director was calling them. I'm not sure how they'll treat the report. If it weren't for Riki's disappearance, the situation would be more irritating than alarming. However, no one has been able to locate her all morning, which is definitely not normal behavior for Zoe. She might run a habitual thirty minutes late, but she always shows up. Did she act strangely last night?"

"It's hard to say. I don't know how she acts normally," he answered. "You've tried her friends and family?"

"Not exactly. Director Cusack was looking for a report she was working on for him. I didn't want her to get into trouble. She's already been written up for lateness. I tried her cell, but she didn't answer. When I called her apartment, her roommate answered and told me Zoe never came home last night. I thought, fine, she slept at her boyfriend's place. Her roommate gave me his number—"

Conor lowered his coffee cup. "Tell me you didn't call her boyfriend looking for her."

"I wanted to spare her the humiliation of being fired." Louisa's face burned with indignation. "Internships are very competitive. There are other students who would love her position. Trust me. It was one of the most embarrassing phone calls I've ever made."

"I believe you." He held up a defensive hand, but his lips were twitching again.

Louisa huffed. Why did he enjoy provoking her? And why did she react to his every jibe? She wasn't this snappish with anyone else. "Anyway, her boyfriend told me they'd had an argument, and he'd left her here. That's when I got worried." Not to mention shocked that Sullivan's was involved. The coincidence just didn't seem possible.

Conor rubbed his temples with a forefinger and thumb. "It was too late for a woman to take the subway alone."

"I might be getting way ahead of the situation. Zoe could be fine." Was Louisa's concern more guilt-driven than logical? The stolen dagger was her responsibility.

A buzz sounded from his pocket.

"Excuse me." He pulled out a cell phone and read the display. "I need to run an errand. If you want to keep talking, you'll have to walk with me."

She checked her watch. She'd taken a late lunch and was due back at work by three. "Will it take long?"

He shook his head. "Ten minutes. Come on. The fresh air will clear your head."

She half wanted to run from Conor at full speed. But questions about the previous evening still lingered in her mind. "All right."

As she followed him from the bar, she wondered if her agreement was based solely on her concern for her intern or if she was bowing to the part of her that *didn't* want to bolt.

CHAPTER
6

An afternoon breeze swept down Oregon Avenue as they set off down the sidewalk through elongating shadows. Louisa buttoned her jacket and clutched her purse tightly under her arm.

"This way." Conor's hand brushed her shoulder as he pointed left.

Though warm enough, Louisa shivered all the way down to her aching toes.

"Where are we going?" Her fingers cramped, and she loosened her grip on her purse.

"Just a few blocks. Can you walk in those shoes? Do you want to wait in the bar?"

"No. Tell me about Zoe's boyfriend. What did he do last night that was so awful?"

They stopped at the corner. Other pedestrians bunched around them as they waited for the light to change.

"He wouldn't take no for an answer." Conor angled his body between her and the crowd. "So, you've been at the museum for two months. An intern was kidnapped and murdered with a stolen knife, and now a second intern has vanished."

"That's how it seems."

"How many people in the museum know what happened in Maine?"

"Apparently, everyone. Why?"

"It's too much of a coincidence, especially now that I'm part of it too."

The light changed, traffic stopped, and the crowd moved en masse across the intersection.

"There were numerous newspaper articles." She thought of April's statement. "Evidently, the staff was passing them around in the weeks between my hire and my move down here."

"So our connection is public knowledge, even though we haven't seen each other for six months."

"Yes." She stepped up on the opposite curb. "I almost called you," she blurted out before she could stop herself.

A lazy smile tugged at his mouth. "Really?"

Louisa's hand was halfway to her pearls before she stopped it in front of her chest. Conor reached over and took her hand in his. They'd shaken hands before, but this felt different. This felt possessive, almost intimate. She tensed, her instincts urging her to break his grip, not because the contact was unpleasant, but because she liked it. Their gazes met. His was brazen, as if daring her to admit the attraction between them.

She took the challenge. Old habits needed to be broken. New city, new life. Heat soaked into her cold fingers and made her forget all about her fidgeting. And about letting go. "So . . . the group Zoe was with. Which one of them wanted to come here last night?"

"That's what I'd like to know. We're not part of the hip and happening club scene, and we're too far from University City for overflow." He steered her around a large crack in the sidewalk. "But her date was a Flyers fan, and we get plenty of postgame traffic. Still feels like too much of a coincidence, though."

"Coincidences do happen."

"True." He squeezed her hand. "I'm sad your intern is missing, but I'm happy to see you."

Nerve endings prickled over her skin at the genuine warmth in his words. Why did he have this effect on her? It wasn't in her nature to simmer under a man's attention. She dated and had had several short-term relationships. None had been serious. But then, none of her former boyfriends had been as intense or demanding as Conor.

He stopped in front of a white-brick building. The words VET-ERINARY CLINIC were stamped on the glass. "This is it."

When he let go of her hand to open the door, she missed the contact. When was the last time a man had held her hand?

Never?

The men she usually dated didn't lend themselves to intimate romantic gestures. They sent her expensive roses and bought her jewelry, all lovely but impersonal. None of those gifts had made her feel raw and edgy and hot. Even her silk blouse felt scratchy.

A bell mounted on the door jingled as they went into the clinic. The air smelled of animals and antiseptic. The scrub-clad technician at the reception counter greeted them with a smile. Her hair was braided in small cornrows that lay flat against her scalp, setting off sharp, exotic cheekbones.

"I'm here for my dog." Conor gave his name.

"I'm glad you're here. She won't eat for us. I hate to see such a sweet dog scared." The tech grabbed a file and presented Conor with a bill. "I know it's a lot, but you wanted her up-to-date on her shots. On the bright side, her injuries are superficial."

"It's OK." He winced at the total and paid with a credit card.

The vet tech brought the dog into the waiting room. The animal's head and tail hung low.

"Oh no. That poor thing. She's so thin. Are those bite marks? Did she get into a fight?"

"More likely she was put in a fight." Conor described how he'd found the dog the night before. "She looks better than when I dropped her off this morning."

At the sound of his voice, the dog's mangled ears pricked up. Her gaze landed on Conor. The stubby tail lifted and wagged back and forth.

"What horrible person would do that to an animal?" Louisa asked.

"The cops have been cracking down, but dog fighting is still a real problem in this city." Conor took the leash from the technician. "A pink collar and leash?"

The vet tech laughed. "We thought she needed something girly. The way they butchered her ears gives people the wrong impression. Consider it a gift for not dumping her at the shelter."

"Anything special I should do for her?" he asked.

"No." The tech handed him a sheet of paper. "She's been starved for a while, so reintroduce food slowly. If her appetite doesn't pick up in a week or so after she settles in, then bring her back. We'll also want to spay her, but I'd like to wait a couple of weeks and let her get stronger first."

"Thanks." Conor folded the paper and stuffed it into the back pocket of his jeans. He led the dog outside. On the sidewalk, he squatted and rubbed her head. "Bet you're glad to be out of there."

Louisa bent down. "Can I pet her?"

"You're not afraid of her? Some people might find her scary."

"Should I be? She looks pathetic."

"She is pathetic." Conor sighed. "Let her smell your hand first."

The dog gave Louisa's hand a sniff, then licked her fingers.

"She likes you."

Louisa stroked the animal's neck, being careful not to touch the healing wounds. Except for the scarred areas, her fur was silky soft, like crushed velvet. Her mother had been allergic to animals. After her death, the aunt who'd raised Louisa had forbidden animals in the house. "I've never had a dog."

"Would you like this one?"

"I wouldn't know what to do with her." But the thought was strangely appealing. Louisa gave the dog one more gentle pat before straightening. How hard was it to take care of a dog? "And I work all day." Though she could easily go home at lunchtime most days, and she'd seen the Rittenhouse staff walking other residents' dogs.

"You keep thinking about it. For now, let's see if we can get her to eat." Conor headed back toward the bar. The dog practically plastered herself to his legs.

"She's very attached to you."

"I don't know how that happened."

"I imagine it's because you were kind to her." Louisa fell into step beside him, her interest in the dog a welcome distraction from her acute reaction to Conor. "What's her name?"

"I don't know. I haven't really thought about it. I have a confession. I actually did take her to the pound this morning, but I couldn't leave her there. She was terrified, and the place was already full of pit bulls." Conor took her hand again. "Do you want to name her?"

This time Louisa barely hesitated before wrapping her fingers around his palm. "You'd let me name your dog?"

He lifted a shoulder. "Sure. Why not?"

"Seems like a big responsibility."

"Let me put it in perspective. We had a dog named Sneezes once because my parents let Jaynie name him. She was three, and it was her turn to name a pet. I assure you that Sneezes didn't care what we called her as long as we slipped her scraps of food under the dinner table. The dog was so fat, she waddled."

Hearty laughter bubbled out of Louisa's throat. The kind of laughter she hadn't felt in a long, long time. "All right. I'll try to do better than Sneezes."

"You're so serious most of the time. I like to hear you laugh." Conor stopped walking. His gaze dropped to her mouth. He leaned closer. Did he want to kiss her? She licked her lips. A little heat in his eyes completely disarmed her, and holding his hand short-circuited her brain. What would the taste of his mouth do?

As much as Louisa wanted him to kiss her, she couldn't stop the slight backward shift of her body weight.

He noticed. Suspicion narrowed his eyes as he straightened.

Oh no. She'd ruined it already.

"I'm sorry." She squeezed her eyes shut for a second and breathed in and out. Opening her lids again, she forced herself to make eye contact, expecting to see irritation on his face, but his eyes held only concern. How could she explain she was afraid of the way she responded to him? "I need to take things slowly."

He smiled. Was that relief in his expression?

"No worries. I'm a slow mover myself these days." Turning, he continued down the sidewalk, his pace easy and unhurried.

These days? What did that mean?

They walked in companionable silence for a few minutes, crossing an intersection and skirting an elderly man playing a violin on the sidewalk. A tattered coat hung to his knees. Under a fedora, long gray hair fell in a curtain over the side of his face. Conor tossed a dollar into the open instrument case at the musician's feet. When they reached the bar, he opened the door for her.

They went back to the booth. Conor brought the dog a cooked hamburger patty from the kitchen. She ate a few bites and then curled up under the table.

Conor picked up her bowl and set it aside. "So your intern was here last night, and no one has seen her since. Now what?"

"Now I grab a cab and hope I'm not late getting back to work. Maybe this is a misunderstanding. Maybe Zoe's boyfriend's behavior upset her, and she went to see an old friend. I know her hometown isn't far from here. If she wasn't thinking clearly, she could have made a mistake with her schedule." But a twinge of doubt lingered in the pit of Louisa's belly.

"What's your number?" Conor pulled his phone from his pocket.

Louisa gave it to him, and he punched the numbers on his keypad. Her purse vibrated.

"I sent you a text. Would you let me know what happens with your intern?"

"I will."

Light spilled into the bar, its brightness reminding her it was only late afternoon. The darkness of the interior, all scuffed wooden floors and red leather, suggested nighttime.

Two figures walked into the entryway, stopped, and scanned the room with purpose. Louisa stiffened. Detectives Jackson and Ianelli. Several policemen in uniform followed them inside.

"Conor Sullivan?" the older man asked.

Conor stood. "That's me. What can I do for you?"

"I'm Detective Jackson." The African American detective gestured to his associate. "This is Detective Ianelli. We'd like to ask you some questions."

—✦—

Not entirely surprised to see the police, Conor turned to Louisa. "Bye, Louisa."

"Dr. Hancock?" Jackson's eyebrows shot toward the ceiling. "What are you doing here?"

"Hello." Louisa shook the detectives' hands. "I was asking Conor about Zoe. I'm glad you're looking for her."

"We're just making a few inquiries." The detective sighed. "I'll probably have additional questions for you, Doctor."

"I'm already late getting back to work," Louisa said. "I'll be at the museum all day, and you have my cell number." She pivoted and strode from the bar.

Conor waved a hand toward the rear of the bar. "Please come back to my office, Detectives."

"Everything OK, Conor?" From behind the bar, Pat flicked a curious gaze at the cops.

"It's fine, Pat." Conor led the way down a short hall. Ahead was the kitchen; on the left, the restrooms. He turned right into a small office and took his place behind the scarred oak desk that had belonged to his father. The old wooden chair squeaked. The seat was hard and uncomfortable, but neither Conor nor Pat would ever replace it. Dad had been gone eighteen years, but if Conor closed his eyes, he could still smell the faint hint of cherry pipe tobacco. The detectives followed him in. Jackson took the plastic chair next to the desk. Ianelli leaned against the wall and crossed his arms over his gut.

"We're looking for a young woman." Jackson pulled a photo from the chest pocket of his jacket and handed it to Conor. It was a snapshot of Zoe. "Have you seen her?"

"Yes. Her name is Zoe. She was in the bar last night. Her boyfriend got drunk and started pushing her around. I had to bounce him."

"What did Zoe do?"

"She couldn't get ahold of her roommate for a ride, so I drove her down to the subway station." Conor paused, still kicking himself for not taking her all the way home. "It was late. I didn't want her to walk alone."

Jackson took notes. "Which station did you drop her at?"

"Pattison Ave."

"She didn't indicate that she was going anywhere else?"

Conor thought back, then shook his head. "I don't think so. She said she was going home."

"I assume you have surveillance cameras in the barroom?"

"We do."

"Could we have a copy of last night's tape?"

"Of course," Conor said. "I can have that for you in about an hour."

"I'll send someone over to pick it up." Jackson stood. "Thanks for your help."

The cops left, and Conor went back to the bar.

Pat popped the tops off two bottles of Heineken and served them to a couple of guys on the other side of the bar. Turning to Conor, he wiped his hands on his black apron. "Want to tell me what that was all about?"

"It's a long story." Conor filled him in.

Pat frowned. "That doesn't sound good."

"No. It doesn't." The police interview had been quick and painless, but Conor had a nagging feeling in his gut that they'd be back.

"Your curator is hot, though. So the day wasn't a total loss."

"She's not *my* curator."

Pat shrugged. Under the concern, a spark of humor glinted in his eyes. "If you say so."

Ignoring his brother, Conor went back to the office to copy the previous night's surveillance footage. Despite his protest, seeing Louisa had revved him. But the simultaneous disappearances of the replica knife and two young women tainted his pleasure. There were too many twisted connections in the events with Louisa, her intern, and the museum for Conor's comfort. Something was brewing.

CHAPTER
7

Though no one had noticed her slightly extended lunch, Louisa stayed an extra half hour to make up for the lost time. Walking home on Eighteenth Street, she turned right onto Walnut into Rittenhouse Square. Her phone buzzed, and she fished it out of her purse. Her father? Though they spoke once a week, she always initiated the calls. She couldn't even remember the last time *he'd* phoned *her*. Something must be wrong.

She answered, crossing the street and entering the park. "Daddy?"

"Louisa." Her father sounded nervous—and more importantly—sober. Since her mother's death, if Wade Hancock wasn't working, he was numbing his pain with scotch.

Heart attack and accident scenarios rolled through her mind. "Is something wrong?"

"No." He hesitated. "I just wanted to talk to you and let you know I'll be coming to the States for the holidays. I'm thinking of staying for a while."

"You're going back to Maine?"

"Why would I go to Maine when you're in Philadelphia?" he asked. "Anyway, I called to see if I should arrange hotel accommodations"—he paused, nerves hitching in his breath—"or if you might have room for me there."

Shock silenced her for a minute.

"Are you still there?"

"Yes. I'm here. Is there something wrong, Daddy?" *Oh my God.* He must be sick. Or dying. Had his liver finally given out under the onslaught of alcohol?

"I'd rather talk in person," he said. "I haven't been to your new apartment. I didn't know how big it is."

"Of course you can stay with me. I have plenty of room." She'd chosen the larger available condo based on the premium views. That way, in case her new plan to be more social didn't work out and she was sitting home alone, at least she'd have something to look at. Thank goodness.

"Great. I'll e-mail you my itinerary." Relief edged his voice, and something else she couldn't identify over the four thousand miles, and the equally large span of grief, that separated them. "Love you."

"Love you too."

He ended the call.

A stranger's arm bumped her, and Louisa realized she'd stopped in the center of the path. Around her, the park teemed with activity. The trees and shrubs gleamed green, the setting sun catching the sporadic gold of leaves just beginning to turn. She rarely saw her father, but knowing he was out there gave her a connection to someone, no matter how thin. Despite the steady stream of pedestrians, she'd never felt more alone.

She moved to a nearby bench and dropped onto the seat. Suddenly, she had no desire to go back to her huge, empty apartment and stare out the glass at the bustle of life she never quite felt part of. Her phone vibrated in her clenched fingers. Almost afraid to see her father's number and hear the bad news she knew was coming, she read the caller ID.

Conor.

"Come see me," he said. "I'll tell you what the cops wanted."

"You could tell me now," she offered.

"I'll tell you in person."

"All right," she said with no hesitation. Despite reservations about renewing their involvement, she was curious about the policemen's visit to the bar. She hadn't heard from the detectives. Had Conor learned anything about Zoe's case? But she couldn't fool herself. Her concern for Zoe wasn't the only reason she ended the call, walked to the garage, and retrieved her car.

The sound of his voice eased her loneliness.

Sullivan's bustled at happy hour. Louisa threaded her way through the tables and clusters of patrons. Laughter and conversation buzzed around her. Pat and Conor worked the bar. Pat smiled at her and gave his brother's arm an elbow nudge. Conor's eyes brightened when he saw her walking toward him. He set a tumbler of clear liquid on a cocktail napkin, tossed in a lime wedge, and slid it across the bar to a customer. He motioned her toward a stool at the rear of the bar. A bearded man of about thirty on the next seat looked her up and down. Conor narrowed his eyes at the man until he shrugged and turned back to his buddy.

Conor leaned over the bar. "Hi there, what can I get you?"

"Club soda." She claimed the stool, the snugness of her skirt making the effort more of an undignified hop than the smooth slide she'd intended.

"Are you sure? We have a decent wine list and a few really good craft beers."

"Club soda is fine."

He reached for a glass. "Everything all right? I mean, except for your missing friend."

She nodded, unwilling and unable to articulate her distress over her father's call.

Setting her soda on a napkin in front of her, he scanned her face. "Dinner?"

"No, thank you."

He frowned. His attention flickered to another customer. "I'll be back. The crowd'll thin in an hour or so. Then we'll have some time to talk. Are you sure I can't get you something to eat while you wait?"

"I'm OK." She watched him and sipped her soda. She envied his ease with people, the comfortable way he conversed as he worked. People responded to him. Women flirted. Men joked.

A petite but voluptuous young waitress set a plate in front of Louisa.

"I'm sorry. I didn't order anything," she protested.

The waitress shrugged. "Conor said to bring you a club sandwich."

She turned to catch his gaze, but he ignored her, seemingly on purpose.

She hadn't wanted food, but the scents of french fries and bacon tantalized her nostrils. She ate a fry, then another, then bit into the sandwich. Her mouth was full when Conor drifted over and refilled her glass. *He'd timed that well.* He glanced at the plate, gave her a know-it-all smirk, and sauntered away.

By seven thirty, the work crowd had thinned. The bar was still busy, but the waitress's trips back and forth to the kitchen slowed. Sports fans clustered around the hockey game that played on hanging TVs.

Conor propped an elbow on the bar and rested his chin in one palm. "So how was your day?"

The indelicate snort that burst from her lips shocked her. She covered her mouth with a knuckle. "Long. Yours?"

He gave her a small, wry smile. "Same here."

She was tempted to tell him about her father's call. What would it be like to have someone to confide in at the end of the day? But she couldn't get the words out. Face it. Sharing her emotions was a new endeavor. She'd have to start slowly. "How did it go with the police?"

He lifted a shoulder. "OK, I guess. They weren't here long. Asked for a copy of the surveillance tapes and left."

"Is that good?"

"Beats me." But suspicion lingered in his eyes. "You didn't hear from them?"

"No. I haven't heard anything about Zoe." She chewed her lip. "God, I hope she's all right."

Conor reached across the bar and rested his hand over hers. "I know."

A shadow fell across Louisa. Conor straightened. She twisted on the stool. Detectives Jackson and Ianelli were behind her.

Jackson presented Conor with a stack of folded papers. "Conor Sullivan, we have a search warrant for the bar, your apartment, and your car. We're also taking you to the police station for questioning."

They couldn't think he . . .

But Conor could see in Jackson's eyes that they did.

Conor was a suspect. They thought he did something to Zoe.

He focused on the senior detective, meeting his shrewd brown eyes with a direct stare.

The cop motioned to the uniforms behind him. "Get started." More cops flooded into the bar. Jackson turned to Conor. "We'll need the keys to your apartment and car."

Conor flipped through the search warrant. There was a basic description of Zoe. *Fingerprints, blood, fibers, DNA, weapons, other trace evidence, weapons,* the list went on. He skimmed through the legalese. In summary, the cops were looking for Zoe or evidence that might lead to a possible suspect in her abduction. Seeing no options, he handed the keys over.

"Before you go into the apartment, I'd like to get my dog out," Conor said. "I haven't had her long. I'm not sure if she'll bite if she feels threatened." He doubted it, but he didn't want her frightened.

The cop nodded.

Conor turned to Louisa. "Would you hold on to her? Pat can't take her to his house."

"Of course," she said.

"Dr. Hancock." Jackson's gaze darted between Conor and Louisa with suspicion.

Pat hurried over. "What's going on?"

"I'm not sure, but I think it'd be best to close up." Conor walked toward the back door with Jackson right on his tail. Upstairs, the cop watched him open his door, grab the leash, and snap it to the dog's collar. He led her downstairs and handed the leash to Louisa. "Thank you."

The dog cowered against Louisa's calves.

Jackson pulled a set of handcuffs from his pocket. "Now we're going to the police station."

Conor swallowed his shock and found his voice. "Would you find me a lawyer, Pat?"

White-faced, Pat pulled out his phone. "I'll call Jaynie. Maybe Reed can help."

Jayne's fiancé was a former cop.

The cop pushed Conor through the doorway by the elbow and paraded him through the bar.

The cop marched him out onto the sidewalk. A patrol cruiser was double-parked next to an unmarked car at the curb. Three more vehicles lined up behind them. Jackson steered him toward the black-and-white. Two uniforms waited by the vehicle. The cop shoved his head down, and Conor dropped onto the seat with an awkward side shuffle.

He looked out the window. Pat was standing in the doorway, cell phone against his ear, lips pressed into a bloodless line. Louisa, and everyone else who'd been in the bar, clustered behind him. Humiliation buddied up to Conor's discomfort.

The car smelled like the cold, stale grease of fast food. A wire cage separated the front and back seats. Conor was enveloped with a surreal sense of claustrophobia.

What could the police possibly have discovered?

CHAPTER
8

Stunned into paralysis, Louisa stared out the glass doors.

The police took Conor? That was impossible. She couldn't believe he would have hurt Zoe, not after the lengths he'd gone to in Maine to stop a killer, not after he'd rescued the dog and stepped in to defend Zoe the night before. She'd witnessed his devotion to his family.

Also, Conor was an intelligent man. The police found something in their search. If he *had* committed a crime, he wouldn't have left evidence in his apartment.

"What just happened?" Pat was standing in front of her, his jaw hanging open, his face shockingly pale.

Alarmed, she went to his side. The dog stayed close. "Don't worry. We'll get this straightened out."

"I know my brother. The last thing on earth that Conor would do is hurt a young girl." Pat scrubbed his red buzz cut with a huge, shaking palm, his eyes confused. "This can't be happening."

"Maybe you should sit down."

Pat didn't move. She wasn't sure he even heard her. His face was drawn as if he'd aged ten years in the last ten minutes. Louisa took his thick biceps in her hands, steered him to a table, and backed him into a chair. "Sit."

His legs folded obediently. The chair creaked.

"Dr. Hancock?" Detective Jackson summoned her from the open door. The triumph in his eyes sent a wave of anger rushing through her. Zoe was missing, and the police were pursuing the wrong person.

Louisa lifted her chin and steeled her spine. "I'll be with you in a moment, Detective."

His eyes narrowed. She turned back to Pat. "Do you have a lawyer?"

He frowned at her. "We haven't needed that kind of lawyer in ten years, not since Danny was young. My sister's husband might be able to help, but they didn't answer their phones."

"We'll take up a collection for a retainer," a man's voice said.

Louisa startled. She'd been so focused on the situation that she hadn't noticed the bar's handful of customers gathering around them. Voices murmured, and heads nodded in agreement.

She turned her attention back to Pat. "I know someone who might be able to help."

"Thank you."

The small crowd filled in the space, surrounding Pat with support and emphasizing her own solitude, while Jackson waited in the doorway, his arms crossed over his chest, his stare impatient.

"What's the best number to reach you?" she asked Pat.

"I got it." Another customer wrote on a cocktail napkin. "Here's Pat's cell number."

These people weren't just the Sullivans' customers. They were friends and neighbors. How did it feel to have a group of people who would stand by one's side? The intimacy spotlighted her outsider status, but then she should be used to being alone.

"I'll call you when I know something." Looping the leash over her wrist, she went back to the barstool for her jacket and purse.

At the exit, Louisa stopped for a deep breath before walking out onto the sidewalk. The balmy day had turned cool and damp.

Detective Jackson was waiting at the curb, his foot tapping on the cement. Louisa crossed the sidewalk.

"I need you to come down to the station as well." He gestured toward a scratched sedan with a floodlight attached to the side mirror.

"I'd prefer to drive my own car. I'm parked just down the block."

"Parking is a hassle. It's easier if you come with us. We'll bring you back here afterward." He opened the rear door.

She couldn't make phone calls to defense attorneys from the back of the police car. Louisa gathered her nerve. "Then I'll meet you at the police station. I need to drop the dog off at my apartment. I shouldn't be more than thirty minutes."

He considered her for a minute. Then he dropped his arms to his side. "Yes, ma'am." He wasn't pleased, but there was nothing she could do about that. She needed privacy.

She had the Rittenhouse valet hold her car while she dropped the dog at her apartment. Back in her car, she scrolled through her phone contacts for the number of the only attorney she knew in Philadelphia. Could Damian even help? He primarily worked with juveniles, which was how they'd met. Shortly after Louisa moved to town, Damian introduced himself and asked her for a donation to fund a shelter for teenagers. His sincerity had impressed her, and she agreed not only to write a check but to give her time as well, tutoring at the shelter. He answered his cell, and she was relieved when he agreed to go to the station immediately. If the case turned out to be more than he could handle, he'd give her a referral.

A half hour later, Louisa waited in a small, windowless room at the police precinct. Worried but feigning calm, she folded her hands across her lap and let her mind do the racing. Questions dominated her thoughts: Where was Conor? Why was the detective so convinced he was guilty that they searched his apartment and brought him here? What had they found?

The door opened, and Detectives Jackson and Ianelli came in.

Jackson sat across from her. "Sorry for keeping you waiting, Dr. Hancock." He didn't look sorry.

Ianelli took the seat next to his partner.

"How do you know Conor Sullivan?" Jackson asked.

"We'd met on one previous occasion, last spring in Maine. I consulted on a case involving Mr. Sullivan's brother."

Jackson's brows lifted. "So your relationship with him is entirely professional?"

"For the most part, yes."

"And you haven't seen him since?" Pen in hand, Jackson tilted his head. "Because you two looked awfully friendly tonight in his bar."

"Before today, I hadn't seen him since last spring."

He made a note. "Yet you moved from Maine to Philadelphia, Conor's hometown."

"Coincidence. The position at the Livingston Museum was the only one I could find after being let go from the museum in Maine."

Jackson's eyes brightened, putting her on guard. "We have proof Conor visited the museum three weeks ago. He showed up on footage from multiple security cameras."

"I didn't know he was there." Had he come looking for her? The thought was a small bright spot in the bleak room.

"He hasn't called you or kept in touch in any way? No e-mails or messages?"

Louisa shook her head. "No. We've had no contact until today."

"You finished college early, right, just like Zoe?" Ianelli jumped in. "Zoe is pretty smart too, isn't she? That's why she's in a doctoral program at twenty-one."

"That's correct," Louisa answered.

"You wrote her up for lateness." Jackson scrutinized her through the cover of his lashes. "Aren't you happy with her performance as your intern?"

"I didn't have any choice. She missed a staff meeting. The director wasn't happy." Louisa paused. "Zoe needs to work on her time-management skills. Other than that, she's an excellent intern. She's ambitious, smart, and confident about her work. I'm sure she'll be very successful." Louisa's breath caught. Zoe might not have a future. Louisa wiped an escaped tear from under her eye.

"Is there anything else you can tell us about Zoe? Friends or family we can check with, any particular places she liked to hang out?" Ianelli asked.

"As far as I know, she spends the majority of her time in class, the museum, and the library. Zoe's class schedule was considered when setting her internship hours. It doesn't allow her an abundance of leisure time." Louisa pictured the coffee cup Zoe usually had in her hand first thing in the morning and the bag she sometimes carried in after lunch. "On her way to the museum, she often stopped at Joe's Coffee Shop and frequented Fresh Deli at lunchtime. Both are within a block."

Ianelli leaned back in his chair and crossed his arms over his round belly. "How much do you know about her social life?"

"Our relationship was primarily professional, and I've only been a curator here for two months. I know her parents live about an hour away and that she's a bit shy."

"What about boys?"

"The boy she dated the other night is the first she's mentioned. She said he was new, so I assume they hadn't been together long."

Jackson lifted a page and read the underlying paper. "Let's talk about your last job. You were fired after several artifacts were stolen and used in an elaborate murder ritual?"

"Yes." Louisa braced herself.

"And soon after you started your new job here in Philadelphia, an intern and the dagger that killed her went missing."

Louisa inhaled. Fresh sorrow gathered in her chest. "So you're sure the victim is Riki? You weren't yesterday."

Irritation flickered in Jackson's eyes for a nanosecond before he smoothed it away. He hadn't meant to give that away. "DNA will take weeks to come back, but we were able to confirm her identity through medical records."

Louisa swallowed the burn of nausea in her throat. She blocked the images of Riki's smile and the photos of her wounds, but snatches of pictures leaked through.

Oh my God, Zoe could suffer the same fate.

Red tunneled Louisa's vision. She closed her mouth and breathed through her nose.

Jackson leaned forward and steepled his fingers. "Conor Sullivan was the last person to see Zoe alive. Are you sure you haven't seen him since last spring?"

"Quite." She needed to get out of this airless room, and it seemed the police were going to rehash the same material, so . . . "I'm done answering questions."

Jackson's jaw moved back and forth, as if he were grinding wheat to flour with his molars. "If we find out you've lied about your relationship with Conor Sullivan or that you've withheld information . . ." His partner's hand on his forearm cut Jackson off.

"I'm leaving now." Louisa rose, praying her legs held her frame upright. Images of Riki's ruined body flashed in an endless reel. "If you have any more questions, I'll need time to notify my attorney."

If the police were interested in finding Zoe, Louisa would be the first person in line to assist them. But Jackson actually implied *she* was involved in or knew about her intern's disappearance and Riki's death.

"One more thing." Ianelli frowned at his partner. "For a ritual killing, would there be some kind of complicated setup?"

"I don't know." Louisa gripped the edge of the table. Could Zoe still be alive? Had she been tortured? Set on fire? "Probably. The ones in Maine did. You should check with the state police detective there."

"We already have," Ianelli said. His dark gaze was intent on her face and seemed to recognize her distress. He stood and offered Louisa his hand. "I think we have everything we need for now. Thank you for your time. Do you need some water?"

Shaking her head, Louisa accepted his handshake. His warm palm nearly burned her icy hand. She directed her parting comment to Jackson. "I hope you're not so focused on Conor that you've stopped looking for Zoe."

"Every cop on duty is looking for her. If the killer has a pattern, then she might still be alive. Riki wasn't killed right away. She was tied up and tortured for a few days first."

Louisa's head spun. She fought the dizziness. Under her jacket, a chilly line of sweat dripped between her shoulder blades and soaked her blouse.

Ianelli shot Jackson a disturbed glance. Ianelli might want to pursue every lead, but the dynamics of the partnership were easily identifiable. Jackson was in charge, and he appeared to be concentrating his efforts on Conor.

She left the room on wobbly legs, her high heels seeming narrower. A few minutes later, she found herself standing next to her car with no recollection of walking to it. She opened the door and slid behind the wheel. The vehicle still smelled faintly of dog. Although cool, the interior felt suffocating. She lowered the windows and rested her head on the back of the seat.

The police detectives thought she could be collaborating with Conor, as if either of them could do what had been done to Riki. Those images would be forever branded into Louisa's brain. She would see them until the day she died. To think the police suspected her of collaborating or covering up such a deed was truly abhorrent.

Louisa knew *she* was innocent, and she couldn't believe Conor would do anything as horrible as they'd described. How would the police ever find Zoe if they weren't looking for other suspects?

—

A uniformed cop led Conor into a small interview room at the police station and locked him inside. He paced the linoleum for a few minutes, then dropped into a metal chair. He propped his elbows on the stainless-steel table and let his head fall into his hands.

His entire body felt like someone had beaten him with a stick. He'd spent the last hour perched on the edge of a metal bunk, staring at the moldy walls of a holding cell. With no empty interview rooms, he'd been briefly caged with two drunks, a couple of gangbangers, and one seriously crazy fucker who sat in the middle of the floor and banged his forehead on the concrete. The single toilet was clogged. Obvious stains covered the floors. The odors of vomit, human waste, and sweaty bodies were permanently infused into his nostrils.

When he got home, he was going to delouse himself. With bleach. His clothes were going directly into the Dumpster. He refused to think of spending the next twenty years of his life in a cinderblock-and-steel tomb. It couldn't happen.

The small interview room had no windows and no clock, but it was a vast improvement. Conor shifted his weight, then sat up and rolled his shoulders. His decision to wait for an attorney had slowed the entire process. They hadn't said anything, but that announcement had probably solidified his guilt in the cops' eyes, but he could practically see the railroad tracks spanning his body. There was no way he was talking to Jackson or anyone else without a lawyer in the room. His younger brother had gotten in enough trouble in his youth. Conor had learned the basics of the legal system keeping Danny out of juvenile detention.

The door swung open, and a thin, blond man strode in. Gold cuff links winked in the glare of the overhead light as he held out a hand. "Damian Grant. I'm your attorney."

Conor shook it. Everything about the young lawyer, from his short, edgy haircut to his slim suit pants, looked expensive. Where had Pat found this guy? "Thanks for coming."

"It's my job. Right now, I need you to tell me everything. Don't leave anything out."

"I didn't do anything." Panic sliced through the numb sensation in Conor's gut as he related the events of the night Zoe disappeared. "The police will investigate. They'll find whoever's responsible, right?"

"You've been watching too much TV." Damian slid into the seat opposite Conor, linked his fingers, and leaned on his forearms. The gel on his wavy hair gleamed in the light. "There are several extenuating factors in this investigation. First of all, the police would love to find this girl alive. Every minute she is still missing decreases the chances of that happening. They already have one dead girl. They don't want another. Secondly, if you're here, then they think you're responsible."

Conor opened his mouth to protest, but Damian cut him off with a raised palm. "I know. You're innocent. Let me finish. As always, political issues come into play as well. Jackson wants to close this case as quickly as possible. His boss is breathing down his neck. The captain wants to be mayor, and a string of murdered college girls isn't on the road to office.

"Lastly, the university's board members will apply their own pressure. Parents don't want to send their little girls off to a college where they won't be safe. This girl is pretty and young. They're going to trot out her fucking baby pictures for the media. Grade-school snapshots of Zoe Finch in pigtails will be all over the news and Internet. Her parents will go on the nightly news to plead for their daughter's return. You, on the other hand, had better never have been convicted of so much as a parking ticket. The media will find the worst shots of you possible to bombard the public. If there's anything resembling a mug shot anywhere in the universe, they will find it."

"This is all wrong."

"Conor, snap out of it. This is real. You are caught in the middle of an emotionally volatile situation. You have to deal with it. The detectives will be in here any minute. Answer their questions as succinctly as possible. If I think a question is loaded, I'll stop you from answering. Don't volunteer information. Do not refer to this girl in the past tense. Not even once. As far as you know, she is alive and well and spent the night at a friend's beach house. And Conor, pay attention, because the questions they ask will tell us about the evidence they've found."

Light-headed, Conor dropped his head into his hands. Blood rushed in his ears.

The door opened, and Detectives Jackson and Ianelli came

in. Damian moved to the chair next to Conor, leaving the cops to sit across the table.

Damian held up a hand. "Before we get started, Mr. Sullivan needs a glass of water."

Ianelli slipped out the door. He returned in a couple of minutes and set a paper cup in front of Conor.

He drank the cool liquid and used the minute to get his shit together. They read him his Miranda rights and handed him a paper to sign confirming he understood them.

Jackson rested his forearms on the table. "Let's start with a recap of Monday night."

"You have the surveillance video," Conor said.

Jackson nodded. "We'd like to hear what happened in your words."

"A group of Flyers fans came in after the game. One girl and four guys. The guys were drinking pretty hard. One of the guys grabs his girl. She protests, but he won't let her go. I interceded. The guy took a swing at me, so I popped him. Then I bounced him. The other three guys took him and left. The girl stayed behind. I offered to call her a cab. She declined, saying she'd call her roommate for a ride, but when closing time came, she was still there. I asked her how she was getting home, and she said the subway. I locked up, gave her a ride to the station, and went home."

"That's it?"

"Yes."

The cop stared. "Why did you give her a ride to the station? It's only a few blocks from your bar."

"I didn't want anything bad to happen to the girl," Conor said. As soon as the words were out of his mouth, he regretted them.

Jackson pounced. "Why would you think anything bad would happen to her?"

But the damage was done. "My little sister was attacked in a parking garage when she was in college. So I'm well aware that this city isn't as safe as it should be. Young girls shouldn't trust anybody."

The cop stared. Conor stared back.

Jackson switched gears. "How'd you get that scratch on your face?"

Oh shit. Conor had forgotten about that. "After I got home, I found an injured pit bull in the alley behind the bar. A kid came looking for her. Considering she looked like she'd been in a dogfight, I declined to give her back. He pulled a knife on me. I disarmed him, but he managed to nick my face."

Jackson tilted his head. "What happened to him?"

"I punched him in the nose, and he left."

"Two fights in one night?" Jackson's brow rose. "Do you have a history of violent behavior, Conor?"

The question felt loaded, and Conor didn't respond.

Damian cut in. "Both the incidents my client described were clearly self-defense."

Jackson nodded. "But you were a fighter at one time?"

"Amateur boxer," Conor clarified. "But I've been out of that for years."

"Detective," Damian said. "I don't see how my client's sporting activity is in any way related to the events of Monday night."

"She called your cell," Jackson said.

"I asked her to call me when she got home," Conor answered.

"Let me summarize the situation for you." Detective Jackson raised a fist. "You were the last person to be seen with Zoe Finch. We have a witness who saw an altercation between you two in front of the station. The transit surveillance videos do not show Zoe entering the station. You have a scratch on your face. The last call on Zoe's phone records is to your cell." He ticked off each point by extending a finger until he ran out of digits.

Altercation? Oh no. Someone had seen him startle Zoe with that tap on the shoulder and misinterpreted the act.

Damian waved a hand in the air. "All of that evidence is circumstantial."

Ianelli didn't blink. "Now let's get down to what was seized during the search. We found a bloody T-shirt in your hamper and long dark hairs both in your car and in your apartment. Was Zoe in your apartment, Conor?"

Conor reeled. How could this be happening? His voice sounded far away when he answered. "Just for a minute. I had to run up to get my keys. It was raining, so she followed me."

No one spoke for two long breaths.

"Did you hurt Zoe Finch?" Jackson shot questions at him rapid-fire. "What did you do with her, Conor? Is she still alive?"

"I didn't hurt anybody. The blood on my shirt is from the kid who attacked me."

"How do you know Riki LaSanta?"

"I didn't." Conor leaned forward to press the pads of his fingertips to his throbbing eyes. "Louisa told me about her today. That's the first time I heard her name."

"Why were you at the museum three weeks ago?"

Conor lifted his head.

Jackson's smile was predatory. "We spotted you on the surveillance videos at the museum."

"I'd read that Louisa had taken a job there. I thought about asking for her, but I changed my mind." Conor scrubbed his face with both hands. He wouldn't buy his own lame story.

"Why?" Jackson leaned in.

"I don't know," Conor answered flatly. That was the honest truth.

"How did you know Dr. Hancock had been hired by the museum? I doubt an assistant curator made the Lifestyle section of the *Inquirer.*"

Conor sighed. "I googled her."

"How often did you perform Internet searches on Dr. Hancock?"

"A few times since I met her last spring." Conor answered.

"Why?"

Conor chose his words carefully. *I couldn't get her out of my head* made him sound like a stalker. "I was curious."

"That's it?"

"Yes." Conor was not admitting he had a *thing* for Louisa. The cops would no doubt turn his attraction for her into something perverted.

"I'm surprised. You have nice, neat answers for everything else." Jackson gestured with his cup. "Almost like you planned every detail."

Conor groaned.

"Detective, my client has answered every question you've asked him." Damian pressed his forefinger into the table. "Are you prepared to charge him with a crime?"

Jackson scowled but didn't answer his question. Instead, he reached into his file and slid a photo onto the table. For the first few seconds, Conor's eyes and brain refused to register what he was seeing. But the image clarified all too quickly: a charred body. Conor closed his eyes, but it was too late. He couldn't unsee the horror on the stainless-steel table that had once been a young girl. It took all his strength not to hurl everything he'd eaten in the past three weeks onto the floor.

Louisa had mentioned the picture at the bar earlier. He knew it was going to be disturbing, and he was even sorrier that she had seen it.

"What the hell?" Damian's palms hit the table. "Was that really necessary?"

Conor rested his head in his hands. Damian pushed the water cup at him, but Conor shook his head.

"That's it. My client is done answering questions. Unless you're prepared to charge him with a crime, we're leaving."

Conor agreed. He was done answering questions. If the detectives thought he could do what had been done to that young woman, it was hopeless to try and convince them otherwise.

The cords of Jackson's neck went tight as steel cables, and his lips compressed into a bloodless line.

Ianelli stood up. "Your client will have to sit tight for a few more minutes." He left the room. Jackson followed without speaking.

"Just breathe for a minute. I didn't even get a good look at the picture, and I nearly lost it." Damian put a hand on Conor's shoulder. "On the bright side, if I hadn't already been convinced of your innocence, your reaction sealed the deal for me."

Conor raised his head. Acid burned up the back of his throat into his nasal passages. He needed to get out of this claustrophobic room. But the holding cell had been worse. What were they going to do with him?

Damian leaned close to his ear. "They're obviously checking with the DA to see if he's willing to file charges."

"Will he?"

"Frankly, Conor, it could go either way. They've gathered the perfect storm of circumstantial evidence."

CHAPTER
9

Louisa found a metered parking spot across the street from the museum. The exterior design of the Livingston Museum mirrored the exhibits within. Renovations over the years had given the old building a modern flare, a slide down the timeline of history from present to past.

The streetlight behind her reflected on the dark glass, casting her own image back at her. It was past closing time. She stepped closer and shielded her eyes with her cupped hands. She couldn't see any movement inside. But she knew people were in there. The night security guard would be on duty. He was likely making his rounds. The cleaners worked at least until midnight. She didn't have a key to the front door, and there was no one in sight. Heels ringing on the concrete, she slipped down the narrow alley that led to the rear of the building. She pulled her key ring from her purse and opened the back door. In the corridor, a tiny green light on the alarm panel blinked. She swiped her card through the reader and entered the four-digit security code, and the light stilled.

She flipped on the light switch in the rear corridor. The floor gleamed with fresh wax. The faint hum of a floor cleaning machine placed the cleaning crew in the exhibit part of the museum. She walked down the hall.

Why was she here?

Because she couldn't go home. Once she'd left the police station, she'd thought of one other spot the knife could have been placed by accident. If she could just find the reproduction, the museum could be absolved. She could be absolved.

Poor Riki's death wouldn't be her fault. She wouldn't lose her job—and disappoint her father again. All she had to do was find the knife and prove it wasn't the murder weapon.

She bypassed her office, then stopped. A light shone from under her door. Puzzled, she checked the doorknob. Locked. She took out her key and went inside. Nothing seemed amiss. The janitor must have forgotten to turn off the light. She switched it off, locked up, and went back into the hall. At the end of the corridor, the elevators banked the left wall.

Louisa and April had double-checked the entire *Celtic Warrior* exhibit. Other curatorial staff had been asked to inventory the other museum collections, and Director Cusack had assigned the search of miscellaneous prop and costume rooms to office employees. She was sure the office workers had done their best, but the extra storage room was the junk drawer of the museum. A second search couldn't hurt.

She scanned the packed shelves. Everything from fake rocks to urns to rubber insects was stored up here. Props supplied the details that brought the past to life. Could someone have put the replica knife up here? She sighed. In the back of the room were drawer units to hold smaller pieces. Shelves and drawers were labeled and ordered alphabetically. But she was looking for a misplaced item. It could be anywhere.

She started searching nearest the door, moving methodically from bottom to top, left to right. The shelving units contained the larger pieces, and she moved through them steadily with no sign of the missing knife. Something glittered at the back of a shelf. On her knees, she brushed the fronds of an artificial fern aside. Not the knife. Just a small gold-toned pedestal that might be used to display a piece of pottery or a sculpture. She sat on a step stool, took off a shoe, and rubbed her aching toes. She should have stopped at home to change before beginning her search. But she'd been consumed by the thought that the knife could still be here somewhere.

She'd need to leave soon, though. The dog would have to be walked.

She pulled her phone from her purse and checked the display. She'd been searching the museum for hours. She'd missed a call from Damian, but he'd sent a text: CONOR BEING RELEASED. CALL U TOMORROW.

What did that mean? Were the police charging him? Did he have to post bail?

She dialed Damian back, but the call went to voice mail. She left a message.

A metallic ping rang through the room. Louisa's head swiveled toward the open door, hidden behind the tall rows of shelves. A musket ball rolled past the aisle. Her heart skipped. Had her search knocked the small metal ball from its container? Slipping off her remaining pump, she climbed to her feet, heels dangling from her fingertips. The lights went out, leaving the windowless room black.

She froze.

The lights were on an energy-saving motion timer. Had she been too still?

Fabric rustled in the hallway. One of the cleaning staff? Another employee? She hadn't seen anyone else when she'd come in, but that didn't mean another curator hadn't decided to put in some overtime. Every department head wanted his or her exhibit to be perfect for the fund-raiser on Saturday night.

She opened her mouth to call out, then closed it, instinct and fear constricting her voice box.

She was being ridiculous. There were a number of people in the building at night, including cleaning and security staff, but seeing those pictures of Riki had sent her imagination into overdrive. Regardless, it was time to go.

Her grip tensed on her phone. She pointed it at the floor and sidled toward the door. Her elbow bumped something solid. She whirled. A face and bald head stared back at her. Louisa staggered backward, terror clogging her throat, locking her scream behind her sternum. She tripped and fell on her butt. Primal fear sent her bare feet out into a solid kick. The figure toppled, landing on top of her. She pushed at it. Her hands encountered plastic instead of skin or fabric.

A mannequin.

She shoved it away and skittered backward, crab-fashion. Panting, she pressed a hand to her chest. Beneath her breastbone, her heart banged against her palm, and her lungs worked like bellows. Facedown on the linoleum, the mannequin's arms were bent at grotesque, unnatural angles. Louisa climbed to her feet. She stepped around the figure and crept to the door, as if it were possible that anyone on the floor hadn't heard the scuffle.

She was acting like a child who'd imagined a monster under her bed.

Maybe one of the cleaning staff had simply turned out the light on their way out. Except she hadn't seen or heard anyone on the third floor in the time she'd been here. Had she been so absorbed in her search she didn't hear another person? It wouldn't be the first time that work had drowned out the normal sounds around her. She tended to hyperfocus on a task.

But the primitive warning wouldn't fade. She clenched clammy fingers around her phone and peered out of the storage room. She saw no one in the small beam of light. The corridor light switch was at the end of the hall, near the doors that led to the elevators and stairwell. All the doors on either side of the hall were dark and closed, just as they'd been when she went into the prop room. But none of them were locked. Anyone could be inside.

She moved faster, her imagination conjuring images of hands reaching out to grab her. By the time she reached the stairwell, she was nearly running. She paused at the door. Something whispered behind her, another soft brush of fabric on fabric. Louisa pushed through the door into the stairwell. She switched on the light and ran down two flights of stairs, bursting into the first-floor hallway sweaty and breathless. The hum of a machine drew her to the main corridor. A janitor pushed a floor cleaner slowly across the tiles, the path behind his machine clean and shiny with moisture. Glancing at the shoes in her hand, he raised a brow. She smiled and stopped to put on her heels.

Trekking down the main corridor, she spotted the security guard behind the reception desk near the front door.

The guard raised his gaze from his paperback. "Dr. Hancock." He greeted her in his slight Slavic accent and a curt nod of his white-haired head. "Is everything all right?"

"Good evening, Serge." Louisa took a deliberate breath to slow her racing pulse. "Are any of the other curators here tonight?"

He squinted. His head tilted as he studied her. "I haven't seen anyone come in, but then, I didn't know you were here. I was making my rounds until a few minutes ago."

"You weren't here when I came in," she admitted. "I used the back door."

"What is wrong?"

"I thought I heard someone on the third floor."

"Probably the cleaners. Dr. Cusack is also here." Standing with a wince, he came out from behind the desk, his posture painful and bent with arthritis.

Cusack didn't frequent the storage rooms.

Serge cracked his neck. "Why don't I go up and take a look?"

"I'd appreciate that."

She followed him to the rear corridor. They passed the public restroom. A janitorial cart propped the door open. The sound of running water echoed on tile and steel. Serge's jerky gait covered ground faster than Louisa expected, but he chose the elevators over the stairs.

On the third floor, he flipped on the hall lights. They moved from room to room in a cursory inspection. Thirty minutes later, after finding no one and nothing suspicious, Serge turned off the last light, and they returned to the elevator.

"Probably one of the cleaners," he said. "Or a rat."

Louisa hadn't thought of vermin when she'd been kneeling on the floor. The thought lifted the hairs on the back of her neck, and she suddenly wanted to go home. "Thank you, Serge."

"Anytime, Dr. Hancock." His spine bent in a curt bow. "Next time you need to wander around the museum at night, I'd be happy to accompany you. This building is frightening in the dark."

The elevator stopped, and they got out. Serge paused, staring at the end of the long hallway where a light shone from under her boss's door. He clucked his tongue. "You all work too much."

She smiled at Serge. "We're just trying to get ready for the big fund-raiser on Saturday night." Which sounded like a good reason for her to be in the museum late as well. But Director Cusack didn't do much of the actual physical work anymore. His job was more administrative, political even. She supposed he had plenty of last-minute details to organize for the big event.

"Do you need to see Dr. Cusack, or are you leaving?" Serge asked.

"I'm going home." She had no desire to explain her presence to the director. "I'm sure Dr. Cusack is here late so he can get work done undisturbed." Which could actually be true.

"Good. You look tired." Serge walked her to the front door and let her out.

Louisa hurried to her car and drove to the Rittenhouse. She'd had enough wandering around in the dark for one night. Despite evidence to the contrary, her nerves were still convinced she'd been in danger.

CHAPTER
10

Conor's jaw clenched hard enough to loosen the fillings in his molars. He rubbed the corner of his eye. "I need to find that kid I punched in the alley."

Damian snorted. "Yeah. Good luck with that. Even if you do find him *and* get him to talk to the cops, do you really think, after you broke his nose, that he'll give you an alibi?"

Ugh.

"But I suppose his broken nose *would* support your statement."

The door opened. Ianelli came back in. His smile was thinner than paper. "The DA is not willing to press charges at this time."

Conor was too damned exhausted to say anything. Being questioned in a murder case was like going five rounds with the defending champ. Every muscle in his body hurt, and his head felt like it weighed a hundred pounds. He felt like he had the flu. Or bubonic plague. He turned to Damian. "What now?"

Damian smiled. "Now you go home."

The detective left the room. The wide-open door was the best sight Conor had seen in hours.

"Come on. Let's get out of here." Damian led him from the room. They followed the guard through the maze of hallways.

Conor felt eyes on him the whole way through the building. "Is it my imagination, or are they all staring?"

"Better get used to it. They're going to be watching you."

Outside, Conor let the city air waft over him. A SEPTA bus chugged past. Diesel exhaust never smelled so sweet.

Damian nodded toward the parking lot. "I'll give you a ride home. I'm sure you want fresh clothes and a shower."

"Yeah. I want to bleach everything, including my skin."

They settled in Damian's Lexus sedan.

Conor leaned back on the headrest and closed his eyes. "So what happens next? Be honest."

"They have all the circumstantial evidence we discussed, and don't discount that. Enough of it can get a conviction, depending on the DA. But my thoughts are that they have the trace evidence from your apartment: the hair, the blood. They will send those for expedited DNA testing, which will take anywhere from three days to a week. In the meantime, they will be watching you."

"Too bad they don't seem interested in finding the truth, the girl, or the real criminal."

"That's the thing, Conor. They think you are the real criminal."

They turned down Oregon Avenue. Damian found a parking spot at the curb half a block from the bar. Only four hours had passed since Conor was taken to the police station, but he felt like weeks had gone by when they walked inside. The bar was quiet. The sound of a hockey game, voices, and the clink of glasses on tables welcomed him home.

Pat was behind the bar, and Jaynie was waiting tables. Her face was pale, her eyes worried. Spotting him, she tossed her empty tray on the bar and rushed to him. She threw her arms around his neck. "Conor, we were so worried. They showed an awful picture of you on the news from when you used to box, and they said you'd been in two fights last night."

Exactly as Damian had predicted.

Her curly, red hair smelled like strawberries, and he was reminded that he was filthy. "Jaynie, honey." He gently pushed her away. "Don't touch me. I'm disgusting. I'm going upstairs to decontaminate. I'll be right back. Then I'll tell you everything."

Well, maybe not everything. He'd give her the PG version. His sister had been through enough. "Where's Reed? I want to thank him for sending Damian to my rescue." Jayne's fiancé, now a wealthy artist, had once been a homicide detective.

Tears glittered in her eyes. "Reed didn't send anyone. He isn't even in town. He got a call yesterday morning that Scott got sick at school. He jumped on the first flight to Denver." Reed's son had started at the University of Denver in the middle of August.

"Is Scott OK?"

"His appendix burst." Jayne sniffed. "I'm waiting for Reed to call when he's out of surgery."

"Oh, honey. I'm sorry." He squeezed her hand. "Do you want to go home?"

"Reed wouldn't let me go with him because I wasn't feeling well."

"You were sick?" Conor put a hand to her forehead. "Why are you here?"

"Not that kind of sick." She blushed, the pink fever-bright on her pale face. "I'm pregnant."

Oh. The news just about took Conor out at the knees. Why was he so surprised? He kissed her on the cheek. "Well, congratulations. Are you all right? It's late. You should be home in bed."

"I'm fine now. I need to keep busy." She swiped a knuckle under one eye. "What happened at the police station?"

"I wasn't charged with anything. It's all good." He wasn't exactly lying. OK, he was, but Jayne had enough to deal with. She didn't need to worry about him. As a former cop, Reed would have been enormously useful, but since he was out of town and no doubt frantic over his son, there was no point distressing Jayne.

He introduced her to Damian. "Jaynie, would you please bring Damian a drink if he wants one?"

"Of course. What can I get you?" she asked Damian.

Damian perked up and smiled at her. "Please. I'd love a Guinness."

Conor led the lawyer to an empty corner booth they usually kept available for family use. "She's pregnant and engaged to a former homicide cop."

"OK." Shrugging, Damian slid into the seat. "Go clean up. I'll be here when you come down."

Conor took the back exit. He left his boots outside on the steps and went inside. The scene shocked him. His house looked like it had been ransacked. Drawers were hanging open, their contents bulging out. Sofa cushions listed on their sides. Everything that was even slightly out of place seemed like a violation. A fine layer of dust coated every surface.

Averting his eyes, he walked into the bedroom and stopped short.

Holy shit. *They'd taken the sheets and blanket from his bed.* The enormity of what the police suspected him of committing flattened him like a commuter bus.

They thought he'd murdered Zoe Finch right here in his bed. Trembles started in his knees and worked their way up until his whole body was shaking.

He reached for the back of a chair, then stopped himself a few inches short of the seat. No sitting on any of his furniture in these clothes.

Clenching his fists at his sides, he gathered his strength. He had other sheets. He didn't want the old ones back when the cops were through with them. Stripping off his clothes, he stuffed them in a plastic garbage bag and tied it closed. He'd never truly appreciated antibacterial soap until today. By the time he finished, he'd washed his hair three times and scrubbed his skin raw. He tugged on a pair of jeans and a T-shirt.

Was Zoe Finch dead? What happened to her after he dropped her off at the subway station? Both were questions he couldn't possibly answer tonight.

He finger-combed his hair and brushed his teeth with the diligence of an obsessive-compulsive. The second he finished, his stomach growled. He hadn't eaten since lunch. He stomped into an old pair of running shoes and went downstairs. Conor joined Damian at the booth, but he didn't sit down. The lawyer was digging into a plate of wings.

Pat walked up behind him. He wrapped an arm around Conor's shoulder and handed him a burger. "I'm damned glad to have you back."

"I'm glad to be back." Conor ate the hamburger in a few bites. "Thanks for springing me."

"Wasn't me." Pat shook his head.

Setting the plate on the table, Conor glanced from Pat to Damian. "Then who—?"

"Louisa hooked you up," Pat said. "You should go see her."

"It's late." But he knew he'd never sleep until he talked to her.

Damian nodded toward the door. "Really, she'll want to see you. She was worried."

"She was?" Conor asked.

"Yes. We'll talk tomorrow." Damian sipped his Guinness. "Go."

Conor was already out the door, car keys in hand. Louisa had saved his ass tonight. Why? Sure, he'd thought they'd had a couple of *moments* earlier, but he could never tell where he stood with her. She seemed confident about her professional abilities, but personally aloof and alone. He had to work to get a hint of the real person underneath all that expensive silk. But the glimpses he'd seen were a fascinating combination of strength and vulnerability. Reading her was like trying to see through frosted glass. After being skewered by Barbara's lies, lack of transparency made him wary. Louisa was definitely holding back on him.

Yet two minutes later, he was in his car and driving toward Rittenhouse Square.

CHAPTER
11

Louisa removed the tea ball from the ceramic pot and breathed in the jasmine-scented steam. Would Conor call? He was home. She'd talked to Damian earlier. The police hadn't pressed charges. Though Damian warned Conor was still in jeopardy.

The phone on the counter rang, and Louisa jumped to answer it. Only the front desk called on the landline. Everyone else used her cell number.

"Dr. Hancock, Conor Sullivan is here to see you," the doorman said.

"Please send him up." She hung up the phone and turned to the dog sleeping on the sofa. "See? I told you everything would be all right."

The soft knock on the door a few minutes later brought the dog off the couch. Louisa opened the door. Conor stood in the hall. She wanted to say hello, but she wasn't prepared for the flood of relief into her throat at the sight of him. His hair was still damp from a shower, and he smelled like soap. She inhaled. No fancy cologne, just the scent of clean skin.

He held out a takeout bag. "The doorman asked me to bring this up to you."

She swallowed. "Thank you. Come in."

In the foyer, he handed her the bag and crouched down on the tile floor to greet the dog. "Nice place."

Louisa led the way into the kitchen. The scent of grilled steak wafted from the bag, and her stomach rumbled. "The lease is short-term. Really it's more than I need, but I didn't know the city when I moved here. I didn't want to buy until I decided where I wanted to live." Though she loved the sleek kitchen, the gas fireplace, and the view of the city.

"Hey, I'm damned glad you're staying here." He followed her across the black-and-white porcelain tile. "Looks nice and secure."

"I prefer a building with a doorman and twenty-four-hour security." Louisa set the takeout on the black granite counter next to an assortment of designer dog food. She pulled the Styrofoam cartons from the bag. "Please sit down. You look tired. Are you hungry? I have green tea and coffee."

"Whatever you're having is fine." He slid onto a stool. "Thank you for sending Damian. How do you know him?"

"When I first moved here, he recruited me to help out in his teen shelter. I was impressed with what he's doing trying to get kids off the street and encourage them to stay out of gangs."

Louisa took a second china mug from the overhead cabinet and poured tea for both of them. "With Zoe's disappearance tied to the museum, I feel like your involvement is my fault."

Conor gave the steam a suspicious sniff, then tasted it. He set the cup down. "You didn't do anything wrong."

Opening the food carton, she lifted the steak onto a plate and sliced off a large chunk, which she cut into bite-size pieces. "I had my reservations about using Damian. He works mostly with juveniles. But I didn't know whom else to call. I haven't lived here long, and he's the only lawyer I know. Your brother was frantic."

"Damian was great. I don't know how to thank you. We'll find a way to pay you back."

She heaped French-cut string beans onto the plate and cut them into inch-long strips. "No need. He owes me."

Louisa slid the pile of cut-up meat and vegetables into a bowl and set it on the floor.

Conor stared. "What are you doing?"

"I can't get Kirra to eat dog food."

"So you ordered her a rib eye?"

"We were splitting it. The portions are enormous. Would you like some?"

"No, I just ate."

"I haven't shopped this week." Heat flooded Louisa's cheeks. "I researched dog nutrition on the Internet. An assortment of meat and vegetables is recommended for a balanced diet."

Conor dropped his head onto his crossed arms on the counter. His shoulders shook.

"Did I do something wrong?"

"No." He lifted his head. A grin tugged at his mouth.

"You're laughing at me." Relieved, she set the bowl on the floor. Kirra gave the food a wary sniff and a nibble but ate only a few bites before wandering away.

"I'm sorry." He stood up and rounded the kitchen island. "It's been a long day."

Louisa followed his glance to the corner of the room where she'd stowed a dog bed, a large chew bone, and several squeaky toys. "The woman in the store said Kirra would like her own bed, but she doesn't seem interested."

"You named her Kirra?" He stopped in front of her. His eyes, though red-rimmed and shadowed with fatigue, were bright with humor. How could he be laughing when he'd just been questioned by the police?

"It's Celtic for 'dark lady.'" She wanted to take a step back. No, she wanted to take a step closer. What did she want? "Is that all right?"

"I love it." He leaned in. "I love that you took my dog in at a moment's notice. I love that you ordered her a fifty-dollar steak."

"We were splitting it," she murmured.

"Thank you."

Her nerves hummed with anticipation. Even though she expected—and wanted—the kiss, the muscles in her body went rigid when he pressed his lips to hers. The kiss was tender and unhurried, and a surge of longing shot all the way to the arches of her bare feet. Her toes curled on the cold tile. He lifted his head, and her body protested. The lip-to-lip contact had lasted barely three seconds, not nearly long enough for her to relax.

He lifted his head, and his brow furrowed in concern. "Are you all right?"

"Yes." Louisa nodded, wishing she could explain. But she couldn't. She wasn't ready to trust him yet.

"You're sure?"

She was more than all right. He'd kissed her, and she'd enjoyed it. The tension in her body had been pure shock at how much she'd enjoyed it. She licked her still-tingling lips. A simple yes wasn't enough. He was still staring at her with that worried look.

"Definitely." A smile pulled at the corners of her mouth.

"Will you tell me something?"

She tensed. "Yes."

"Why did you hire Damian? Why are you so sure I didn't do anything?"

She could hardly tell him she just knew he hadn't done it. Although it was the truth, her gut reaction didn't make any sense, not even to her. "It's not logical."

"Excuse me?"

"I put that badly. I'm sorry." Louisa studied the small Flyers logo in the center of his gray shirt. "I often say the wrong thing when I get nervous."

"It's not a test." Conor put a finger under her chin and lifted her face. "Just say what you're thinking."

He had the most beautiful eyes. When he focused intently on her, like now, her skin warmed and her muscles loosened, remembering that gentle kiss. Yet the tension rising in her belly was anything but relaxed. She was simultaneously comfortable and aroused in the strangest juxtaposition of sensations, like she'd washed a muscle relaxer down with a triple espresso.

But he wanted her to talk, and she was going to ruin everything with her nerdy analysis. There was no yield in his gaze, just patient determination. Should she risk it?

New life. New attitude.

Here goes.

"You're an intelligent man. If you killed Zoe and intended to get away with your crime, you wouldn't have left a bloody T-shirt where the police could find it, nor would you have driven off with her in front of witnesses."

"What if it was an accident?" Conor reasoned.

"If you simply intended to sleep with her, why would you drive her anywhere? Your apartment is right upstairs. Plus, that doesn't explain the connection to Riki's murder. The police have based their case on an argument that isn't logical."

"Maybe you should be my lawyer." Conor grinned. "I think I should call you Spock."

"Spock?"

"You know, from *Star Trek.*"

"Oh, I've heard of it, but I've never seen it." Louisa sighed. "We didn't have a television growing up."

"No shit!" Conor cleared his throat. "I mean, that's a shame."

"Since you're joking with me, can I assume you aren't angry?"

"Why would I be angry?" Conor tilted his head. "You kept me out of jail."

"Because I didn't send Damian solely because I believed in you." Louisa blinked away. "Although that was part of it," she admitted. Heat flushed the back of her neck.

He paused, and his usually open expression closed down. "That would be foolish. We don't know each other well enough for blind loyalty."

But *she* wanted that deep-seated faith. She didn't want to believe this kindhearted man who was devoted to his family and made her laugh and took in a pathetic stray dog would hurt a young girl. She wanted him to be her knight, which probably wasn't fair to either of them. Life had taught her that no one could be that good. Even Lancelot betrayed his king.

From the shuttered look in his eyes, he knew that too.

This time Louisa chose her words carefully. "I've learned the hard way to be careful."

"Noted. If it helps, so have I." His admission wiped away the reservation in his eyes and left them full of empathy. "A few years ago, I was involved with a woman who neglected to tell me she was married. We'd been together for three months when her husband showed up at the bar. Apparently, he traveled a lot, and she got bored easily. I was just her plaything when he was away."

Betrayal thickened his voice. He'd had feelings for that woman.

"Oh, I'm sorry."

"So I know all about moving slowly. Whatever you have in your past, you can tell me."

She should. He'd shared something personal with her, but her story was long and complicated. Zoe's disappearance and Riki's death had left her spent. She didn't have the energy to put the words together, let alone deal with the emotional fallout talking about that pivotal night from her past would unleash. "Not now."

Doubt swirled in her lungs, shortening her breaths. Enough psychoanalysis. Riki was dead. Zoe was missing. "Tomorrow, I'm going to keep looking for Zoe. It seems as though the police are convinced she's already dead, and they don't see beyond you as a suspect."

"No kidding." Conor sighed. "Where are you going to start?"

Good question. "Her boyfriend, Heath, seems like the logical starting point. He was with her the night she disappeared. He claims to have gone home and passed out immediately after his encounter with you, but his alibi rests entirely on his friends' statements. Not the most reliable, in my opinion. How intoxicated was he that night?"

Conor considered. "Drunk enough to make him stupid, but unfortunately, not drunk enough to render him incapable of acting on it."

"Some people can't handle any alcohol." Discomfort welled inside her. She pushed the memory back into the dark corner of her mind where it belonged.

Conor snorted. "This wasn't Heath's first night out."

"When I spoke to him this morning, I suspected he might be lying, but I couldn't be sure over the phone."

"I don't like the thought of you alone with that arrogant jerk." Conor squeezed her hand.

"Would you like to come along?" Though their mission was somber, Louisa couldn't stem the rush of pleasure that accompanied the idea of spending time with him.

"That'd be a surprise to Heath." Conor laughed.

"It might be interesting to see Heath thrown off guard." In hindsight, Zoe's boyfriend had been entirely too composed when she'd spoken with him. He'd seemed barely concerned about his girlfriend's whereabouts. Was it because he was a self-centered, uncaring jerk or because he already knew what happened to Zoe? Or both?

"I like the way you think." Conor's eyes sparkled with shared mischief. "Count me in."

"I'd planned on talking with Zoe's roommate tomorrow as well. They lived together for a month. She must know some details about Zoe's personal life."

"Good idea. Now how about I walk the dog while you eat some dinner?"

"I'm not hungry yet." She went to the closet for a pair of athletic shoes and the dog's leash. "I'd rather we walk her together. I wish she'd eat more."

"The vet said to give her a week or so. She's had a rough time."

"I suppose you're right."

They took the elevator downstairs to the lobby.

Gerome, the Rittenhouse doorman, stooped to pet Kirra. "I want all the dogs in the building to like me. If you ever run late or need her walked during the day, just let me know."

Thinking about Conor's dog and the possibility of future dog-sitting, Louisa put Conor on her approved guest list. With a pat on Kirra's head, Gerome opened the door for them.

Conor took her hand as they crossed the street and followed the dog into the small park. A cool breeze swept through the neatly trimmed azaleas and wrought-iron fence that edged Rittenhouse Square. They strode along the circular walkway that ringed the park and turned onto one of the diagonal paths that ran from each corner and met at a rectangular reflecting pool in the center plaza. Old-fashioned lampposts flooded the paths and highlighted the Greek statues interspersed throughout the green space. It was nearly midnight, and the park was empty, except for a man walking a corgi on the other side of the square. Kirra led them down the walk, sniffing her way toward the center of the green space.

Louisa shivered.

"Are you cold?"

"No." She glanced around. A cluster of people lingered on the sidewalk in front of a restaurant. She didn't recognize anyone. No one was paying them undue attention, but Louisa couldn't shake the creepy feeling. Next to her, the dog abruptly stopped sniffing and pressed against Louisa's calves.

"What's wrong?" Conor moved a step closer, scanning the area. The dog hunkered between them.

"I don't know. Probably nothing."

"Come on. She's done." He took Louisa's elbow and steered her back toward the Rittenhouse.

She followed Conor back into the building, but she couldn't shake the cramping sensation deep in her belly, the feeling that someone was watching.

CHAPTER
12

In the shadow of a building on the west side of Rittenhouse Square, I pulled the hood of my sweatshirt over my head. I leaned a shoulder against the worn brick, the rough texture catching on the cotton fibers of my shirt like Velcro. Taking in the cool fall night outdoors was no hardship. The small patch of green was mostly empty, except for a man walking his dog. At the end of a retractable leash, the corgi sniffed the curb with unabashed enthusiasm. Some straggling late diners spilled out of a closing restaurant, two couples that walked slowly, as if digesting too much food and alcohol was requiring all their concentration.

Winter and its long, frigid nights were coming. This week's mild weather was merely a temporary reprieve, a delay of the unpleasant and inevitable months of cold darkness breathing down Philadelphia's neck.

I wasn't the only one watching the square. From my corner location with its clear view of the Rittenhouse, I could also see the unmarked police car parked in front of Smith & Wollensky's.

I'd observed Conor Sullivan walk into the hotel earlier. My prediction had come true. He'd gone to see Louisa almost immediately after being released. What did the police think of that? Did they question the nature of their relationship? I certainly hoped so. I'd all but written it down for them.

Across the street, Conor Sullivan and Dr. Hancock came out of the hotel. He was holding a pink leash connected to that ugly dog he'd taken in. He took Dr. Hancock's hand.

As soon as the dog had done its business, they hurried back inside. Sullivan's protective stance didn't escape my notice. Echoing the old newspaper clipping from last spring, he kept his body between Dr. Hancock and the park, as if shielding her from danger. Were the cops watching? Yes, they were.

Perfect.

CHAPTER
13

Ugh. A heavy weight settled on Conor's chest. He opened his eyes. Kirra stared down at him, front paws planted on his solar plexus, tongue lolling.

"Good morning."

She wagged her tail stub.

He squinted at the brightness pouring in through the huge expanse of windows in Louisa's living room. He was on her sofa. After their walk and Louisa's sudden attack of anxiety, they'd returned to her apartment. Her building was as secure as possible, but he hadn't wanted to leave until she'd calmed down. He must have fallen asleep while she ate her dinner.

Nudging the dog aside, he sat up and stretched. A cotton blanket fell down to his waist. She'd tucked a pillow behind his head too.

He got to his feet and used the convenient half bath off the foyer. His socks were silent on the tile as he returned to the kitchen. The open floor plan flowed right into the living room, taking advantage of the expansive windows with their stunning views of Rittenhouse Square and the city beyond. Her apartment was twice the size of Pat's house, and it was fitted out like a magazine spread in granite, leather, and gleaming wood. He ran a hand across the smooth, black counter and spotted an empty wine cooler underneath.

The Rittenhouse was one of the most exclusive residences in the city, with condominiums that provided all the amenities of the attached luxury hotel. He couldn't even imagine what this three-bedroom unit cost. Just how wealthy was she? Conor brushed his unease aside. It wasn't like he could ask her for a bank statement, but the *House Beautiful* decor was one more example of the fundamental difference between them. Not that her income should affect their relationship, but putting the dollars aside, their lifestyles highlighted that they lived in different worlds.

A short hallway branched off the kitchen. The closed door at the end must be Louisa's room. Last night he'd seen her more relaxed than ever in snug yoga pants and a loose sweater instead of one of her suits. A blast of need zoomed through him. He wanted to see her wake up. All that blond hair would be down on her shoulders, her eyes sleepy, her body warm . . .

The dog whined at the door. Conor turned around. He'd walk the dog before he left, and maybe bring Louisa coffee.

He slipped into his shoes, grabbed her apartment key from the bowl in the hall, and opened the hall closet. Kirra's leash hung on the back of the door. He walked the dog through the square to Nineteenth Street and ducked into La Colombe for two large coffees and muffins. When he let himself back in, the condo was still quiet. Last night, Louisa had eaten the baked potato and salad for dinner. She'd chopped the remaining steak and green beans and left them in the fridge.

Conor put the bowl on the floor for the dog. "You wouldn't be getting this kind of service at my place. Hamburger is high-end on my budget."

A door opened, and a bleary-eyed Louisa shuffled into the kitchen. She was still wearing the snug yoga pants from the night before, but a heavy sweatshirt covered her to midthigh. Her tou-sled, just-out-of-bed hair tumbled onto her shoulders and made Conor want to take her right back to bed.

She blinked at him in surprise. "Oh, you're still here. I thought I heard you leave."

Had she purposefully waited to come out until she thought he was gone? Had he overstayed his welcome? Sleeping over, even innocently, was a huge step considering that before yester-day, they hadn't seen each other for six months. "Do you want me to go?"

"No."

"Good." Because no matter how many reasons his brain came up with to walk out the door, he didn't want to. He crossed the tiles and handed her a coffee. "I walked the dog. We went for coffee."

"Thank you." She stared at the cardboard cup in her hand. Her gaze fell to the fuzzy slippers on her feet. "I should change."

A worried hand touched her neck, but her throat was bare. No pearls to play with this morning. She wrapped the other hand around her middle, and the vulnerability in her posture cracked his resolve to keep his distance.

"Don't." He let a hint of desire heat his eyes. "I like the casual you."

Her hand fell. She stood in the middle of her kitchen, lost. Allowing Louisa a few minutes to compose herself, he filled Kirra's bowl with fresh water. The dog hadn't eaten much of her breakfast. The vet had said to give her appetite a week. But if she wasn't eating by Monday, she was going back.

"Sit down." His hand brushed her arm as he passed her in the narrow space between the counter and the island. "Where are your plates?"

She pointed toward an upper cabinet.

"Blueberry or cranberry?"

"I don't usually eat breakfast." She slid onto a stool.

"I'm not usually awake for breakfast." He put the muffins on plates and set them on the shiny, black granite. "I close the bar most nights. I don't usually get to bed before three."

She selected the cranberry nut muffin and picked at it. "Your siblings don't take turns?"

"Pat takes a couple nights, but Danny moved to Maine, and we don't let Jaynie close the place alone."

"So you assume the bulk of the responsibility."

"I live alone. It's easier for me." Conor shifted on his stool. "You've met most of my family. Tell me about yours."

Sadness filled her eyes. She abandoned the muffin. "There isn't much to say. I'm an only child."

"Are you close to your parents? Do you miss them?" he prodded. Her reluctance to talk about her family was a red flag. After Barbara, the fact that Louisa wasn't being totally up front with him should be a deal breaker.

"My mother died when I was ten."

"I'm sorry. I lost my parents when I was twenty. Jayne and Danny were younger. It was much harder on them."

"You and Pat raised them, right?" She neatly turned the conversation back to him. No surprise.

"Pat did most of the work. I was in college at the time. Pat had been running the bar with my dad, but he couldn't raise Danny and Jayne and take care of the business solo."

"You left school."

"That wasn't a big deal." He shrugged it off. At the time, he didn't have the time or the desire to return to college.

"What was your major?"

"I was doubling in education and history."

"You were going to be a teacher." Louisa set down her coffee.

"I was."

"Weren't you disappointed?" she asked.

"Not at all." That level of grief was all-consuming and didn't leave room for much else. "My parents' deaths changed my whole perception of the world. It was like someone took a Technicolor film and made it black-and-white. All that mattered was getting Danny and Jayne through it. They were just kids."

Like Louisa. So maybe he could cut her a break for holding back on him.

"That was a long time ago," he said. "It wasn't my original plan, and there were some lean years, but I'm a successful businessman. I like the way my life turned out. After being my own boss for all these years, working for someone else isn't that appealing." He got up, put his plate in the dishwasher, and tossed his cup in the trash. "What's the plan for today?"

"I'm due at work at nine. I'd like to stop by Zoe's apartment to speak with her roommate, then swing by the boyfriend's before they both head off to classes or work. If you're available . . ."

"Kind of early for visiting."

"Yes, it is." Determination flattened her close-lipped smile. "But there's no time to waste with social niceties." Her eyes strayed to the clock on the microwave. "Zoe has been missing for thirty-two hours."

"In that case, I'm available." Ugh. He hadn't meant for that to sound like a double entendre.

"I'm glad," she said. "Then I'll go get dressed."

I'm glad? What did that mean? "Could I use your shower?"

She pointed to the other end of the apartment. "There's a guest suite through that doorway."

Her guest room was stocked with toiletry essentials. Conor liberated a toothbrush from its packaging. He scratched his jaw.

He should find a razor, but the small cut on his cheek was nearly gone. Shaving would just irritate it.

As he stripped down and stepped naked under the hot spray, he quelled a mental image of Louisa doing the same, but the vision of her willowy figure, slick and wet, wouldn't stay gone. He turned the spigot to cold. In his head he ticked off the reasons this undefined *thing*, whatever it was, between them wouldn't work. They had nothing in common. Their entire relationship was based on time shared during bizarre and terrible circumstances and his inexplicable compulsion to peel away the layers of Louisa's personal defenses. They hadn't spent a normal five minutes together. They hardly knew anything about each other, and every time he tried to get a glimpse of what lay beneath her perfect exterior, she put up a wall.

But his brain was definitely not running the show. He was operating on instinct, on a gut feeling that when he finally got to her core, what he discovered would be worth all the work.

And he didn't mean *core* in a sexual way. OK, he did, but it wasn't his primary motivation. He'd learned his lesson. Sex wasn't enough.

Thirty minutes later, they walked a block to the parking garage where Conor had left his car. He opened the passenger door for Louisa.

With a graceful twist, she lowered her body into the passenger seat. Conor slid behind the wheel.

"Your car looks wonderful." Louisa ran a hand across the leather dashboard. "I wouldn't know it was the same vehicle you were driving last spring."

"Thanks." He shifted the Porsche into gear and pulled out into traffic on Eighteenth Street. "It's a hobby. I buy beat-up old cars and restore them."

"Will you sell this one now that it's done?"

"Probably. I like a project." He stroked the steering wheel.

A bicyclist shot out from between two parked cars. Conor braked. Louisa gripped the armrest.

"What's wrong?" He steered around a double-parked delivery truck. The taxi driver in the next lane blew his horn and flipped them a middle finger. Conor waved him off.

Louisa gasped, her body stiffening in the seat. "I haven't adjusted to the traffic."

"It is rush hour." Conor turned onto Walnut Street and made his way to the ramp that led onto I-76 East. Less than a mile later, he exited onto University Avenue. They drove through the main campus, and Louisa directed him toward blocks of row homes that had been converted into student housing. "Where to first?"

Louisa gave him the address of the off-campus apartment Zoe and Isa shared. Conor wove through the city streets and parked at the curb near the converted row home. They rang the buzzer for Isa's apartment, but she didn't answer. They returned to the car, and Louisa left a voice message for Isa.

"I asked Zoe to call me when she got home." Conor stared down the quiet tree-lined street. "But when she did, she said, 'I'm almost at my place.' At the time I assumed she was calling from outside because her roommate was asleep inside, and Zoe didn't want to wake her up." Conor closed his eyes and tried to replay the call in his head. He'd been half-asleep. "To make a call, she had to be aboveground. It must have happened between her house and the subway station. Except the police said she never got on the subway."

"Maybe she took a bus or the camera just missed her some-how. What about campus security?"

"Timing would be key," Conor agreed. "Unless she got into

a car willingly. Maybe Zoe was walking home in the dark. She was tired and upset. It's six or seven blocks from the subway station or bus stop. She calls me just to get that out of the way. She just wants to be home. It's been a crappy night, and she wants to go to bed. She hangs up the phone. A car pulls alongside her and offers her a lift."

"Heath would fit that scenario," Louisa mused. "He'd be apologizing, asking her to forgive him."

They looked at each other. The night could have played out just like that.

"Right. Let's go talk to Heath." Conor pulled out into traffic.

Louisa gave him the address.

"How did you find out where he lives?"

"I paid for an Internet search," Louisa said. "If he lived in student housing, we'd be out of luck, but he lives off campus in a private residence."

Conor found the street, circled the block until he saw a spot, and shoehorned the Porsche between a Ford Escape and a Nissan Maxima parallel parked at the curb.

Heath lived in a stately three-story town house. Though renovated, the building's age showed in the slight tilt to the stoop and the blackened patina of the bricks. In Philadelphia tradition, a waist-high black wrought-iron fence encircled the tiny front yard. The gate was propped open with a fist-size rock. They went up the wide cement steps to the covered porch, and Louisa pressed the doorbell.

Conor leaned a shoulder against the side of the building and watched Louisa slide into the mask of stiff formality she'd worn back in Maine. She'd used that attitude on him when they first met. Why had he thought it was hot? What was it about that haughty profile that sent his engine into overdrive? Most women flirted with him. Why did he want the one who required effort?

"You'd better stay out of sight. He might not open the door if he sees you." The grin and the conspiratorial tone behind it were damned sexy.

Conor stepped to the side of the door, out of the peephole's view. The door opened.

"I'm Dr. Hancock. I'm looking for Heath Yeager."

"I'm Heath."

"Do you have time to talk?" she asked.

"I guess, but I only have a few minutes until I have to leave." Heath opened the screen door.

The door opened inward, and Louisa stepped over the threshold into a small foyer. "Thank you."

Conor followed. "Good morning, Heath." He echoed Louisa's overly cheerful inflection.

Heath took a surprised step back. The side of his jaw where Conor had popped him was puffed out and bruised. "Hey, what's he doing here?"

"Mr. Sullivan and I are trying to find Zoe." Louisa tilted her head at Heath. "Surely you'd like to do the same."

"I guess." Heath looked doubtful. "I mean, yes. I want to find Zoe. But why him?" He jerked a thumb at Conor. "I heard he's the prime suspect."

"So you remember me? I thought maybe you were too drunk." Conor kept his distance, slouching against the far wall.

Heath's face went blank, but thoughts churned in his eyes. Would he throw a fit about Conor's presence or play it cool? "I remember you."

What was the kid hiding?

Apparently choosing to be cooperative, Heath led them down a short, narrow hallway into the living room. The house was tall and narrow, with an open kitchen and living space on the first floor and probably four or five bedrooms and a couple of baths on the two upper floors. High ceilings were set off by fat architectural molding. The corner fireplace appeared original. Aged pine floor gleamed with a smooth matte finish.

Heath didn't lack for any of the amenities. A large flat-screen TV hung on the living area wall. Electronic tablets, a cell phone, a laptop, and game controllers were scattered on a round table in front of a leather sectional sofa. Stainless-steel appliances equipped the adjoined kitchen. Three pizza boxes were stacked on the black granite counter. Next to them, someone had erected an impressive four-tier beer can pyramid.

"Nice place," Conor said. "How many of you live here?"

"Four."

"The same guys you were with Monday night?"

"Yes."

"What else do you remember about that night?" Louisa asked.

Heath turned around and retreated behind the L-shaped counter. "Coffee?"

Conor shook his head.

"No, thank you," Louisa said.

Heath filled a steel travel mug. "The night is sketchy. I drank way too much, and I'm well aware that I acted like a jerk."

Conor played along. "Alcohol makes lots of guys act like assholes."

Heath nodded. "I feel terrible about what happened. I never thought . . ." He swallowed and pinched the bridge of his nose. "I never thought anything would happen to her. I figured she'd take the subway or bus home."

"No one could have expected her to disappear." Louisa placated him. "We just want to find her. Did you hear from her at all after you left her at the bar?"

Heath's eyes darted sideways. With jerky movements he opened the refrigerator and pulled out a gallon of milk. "Um.

Apparently I texted her after I got back here, but I don't remember doing that. I was pretty wasted."

"What did you say to her?" Louisa asked.

He over-tilted the jug, splattering milk down the side of his mug and onto the counter. "I called her a bitch and some other names." He lifted his chin to let them see his misty eyes. "I'm not proud of it."

Though Heath gave a soap opera–worthy performance, Conor wasn't buying into the sad act. This guy didn't need alcohol to be an asshole.

Louisa pressed. "Did she answer you?"

He shook his head. "No. I guess whatever happened to her had already happened." He swiped a finger under his eye.

"I have to go." Heath picked up his backpack.

"One more question," Conor said. "Who picked Sullivan's?"

Heath's brow wrinkled. "I don't remember. We'd already been to two bars. We didn't really have a plan."

Escorting them outside, Heath locked the front door and jogged down the steps.

"Thanks for talking with us," Louisa said as Heath went through the gate and turned down the sidewalk.

Conor and Louisa walked back to the car.

"He's playing us." Conor opened the door for Louisa.

"Probably." With a graceful body twist, she slid into the leather bucket seat, a feat that should have been awkward given the snugness of her skirt.

Conor watched her long legs swing under the dashboard. This morning's suit was a pale, practically colorless gray. The tailored cut showed off her slim form, and the forest-green blouse made her eyes greener. She didn't put anything on display, but her prim and proper suits made him more eager to get a glimpse of what lay beneath all that silk. He was hopeless.

He rounded the car and climbed into the driver's seat. She shifted her legs and crossed her ankles. Her skirt rode a few inches past her knees. His glance drifted sideways, and he was rewarded with a flash of pale thigh.

How could a scant two inches of skin make him drool? He saw a lot more than that every night of the week. Half the women who came into the bar wore skirts a scant inch shy of indecent, and he was hung up on Louisa's hot librarian getup.

Louisa looked at him expectantly. He ripped his gaze off her legs. What had she asked him? Oh, yeah. Heath.

"Sleep texting?" He started the engine. "That's just lame. If he was awake enough to text her, he was awake enough to snatch her."

"I'd love to get a look at the texts he sent."

Conor waited for traffic to clear. He checked his rearview mirror as he pulled into traffic. A big sedan pulled away from the curb right behind him. He went around the next block.

"What are you doing?" she asked.

"I think we're being followed."

Louisa turned her head to look out the back window. "The dark-blue sedan?"

"Yes." Conor made a right onto South Street. "Cops."

"How do you know?"

He glanced in the rearview mirror. The sedan dropped back, letting a couple of cars get between them. "I just do."

A few minutes later he pulled to the curb in front of the museum. "Let me know if you hear from Isa."

"I will." Louisa got out of the car and went inside.

Conor drove toward home, and his police escort stayed a few cars behind him. The bar didn't open for hours. He stopped for his gym clothes. The heavy bag was the best place to vent all his frustrations. The unmarked car crept along at the curb as Conor walked to the gym. How would the police ever find Zoe if they wasted limited manpower babysitting him instead of expanding the investigation to include someone who might actually be guilty?

CHAPTER
14

Louisa settled at her desk to catch up on messages, return e-mails, and check on the shipment of a sword and scabbard she'd purchased at auction the week before. She also put a call in to Zoe's mentor, Xavier English, in case he had any insight on Zoe's behavior. Professor English wasn't in, and she left a message. Then she reviewed the details for the fund-raiser scheduled for Saturday and checked on the progress of the renovations in the exhibit space. She needed to fill one of the new glass cases for the event.

When she returned to her office, April was pressing a crumpled tissue to her eye.

Louisa's heart stammered. "What happened?"

"Zoe's father called." April handed Louisa a pink message slip. "He wants you to call him back."

Louisa's vision blurred with moisture as she closed her door. She dialed Mr. Finch with shaky fingers. How could the Finches possibly cope with their daughter being missing?

"Dr. Hancock. Thank you for returning my call." Mr. Finch's voice was strained.

"Is there anything I can do for you?" Louisa asked.

"My wife and I would like to talk to you." Over the phone line, the sound of a woman crying filled the background.

"Of course."

Zoe had mentioned her parents lived close to the city.

"Is there any way you could come here?" he asked. "We don't want to be far from our phone."

"I understand." Louisa input their address into her phone and allowed the GPS to calculate directions. "I can be there in about forty-five minutes."

"Thank you."

Louisa took her purse from her desk. She didn't have time for another extended lunch hour, but how could she turn Mr. Finch down? His daughter was missing.

She slipped out without seeing her boss. Ten minutes later, she pulled out of her parking garage and turned her BMW toward the Ben Franklin Bridge, battling lunchtime traffic up Broad Street, and followed I-676 across the bridge.

Forty minutes later, she turned into a driveway marked by a rusted mailbox.

The Finches were rural poor. On the edge of a farming community, their one-story house occupied a large tract of weedy land. The roof sagged, wire fencing corralled a dozen goats, and peeling pickets protected a tidy vegetable garden. In a city-block-size cleared area behind the house, the brown remains of plants lined up in neat rows. Six cows grazed in a small, weedy pasture next to a listing barn and a scattering of ragged outbuildings.

She parked the car in a dirt rectangle next to a rusty pickup truck. Louisa opened her door and stepped out. Her heels sank in the sandy soil. A clucking sound came from the rear of the house. Chickens? Walking on her toes, she picked her way to the cracked concrete walkway that led up to the front stoop.

The door opened. The Finches stood side by side, presenting a solid front of grief.

"Please come in." Mrs. Finch clutched a tissue in her fist. She pressed it to her nose and sniffed.

Mr. Finch, a short, balding man in his sixties, put an arm around his wife's shoulders and ushered them into a formal living room. A flowered couch and two blue chairs surrounded a coffee table covered with papers.

Pictures of the smiling, young Zoe were everywhere. Louisa leaned over the piano and scanned a row of school pictures. She had no trouble picking Zoe out of the crowd. She was years younger and inches shorter than all of her classmates, just as Louisa had been through most of her school years.

The Finches perched on the worn couch. On his knee, Zoe's dad held his wife's hand between his palms. Though sick about the reason, Louisa envied the unity that emanated from the couple.

"We want to thank you for caring enough to look for Zoe, Dr. Hancock," Mr. Finch said. "Dr. Cusack mentioned it was you who raised the alarm about Zoe being missing."

"Please, call me Louisa." She took one of the chairs on the opposite side of the coffee table. She leaned forward and folded her hands in her lap. "Have you heard anything from the police?"

A flash of anger brightened Zoe's father's bleak, brown eyes. "We're frustrated with the police. They say they have a suspect, but they won't arrest him. If they don't have enough evidence, how do they know it's him? I don't understand why they aren't leaning on Heath Yeager." He picked up a paper and handed it to her. "What if this bartender isn't the right person? It's as if they're more concerned with a possible trial than they are with finding her before . . ."

He inhaled sharply, as if the thought of his daughter's unknown fate stole his breath.

Louisa scanned a printout of Zoe's texts. All were from the night of her disappearance, and all flowed one way: from Heath's number to Zoe's.

U FUCKING BITCH

WHR R U?

DON'T U DARE SAY ANYTHING

U CAN'T HIDE FROM ME

I'LL FIND YOU

Louisa set the paper down. Heath's texts painted a more damaging picture than he'd led her to believe. Why were the police so convinced of Conor's guilt when they had threatening texts from Heath to Zoe?

"How can they ignore all this"—Mr. Finch waved his hand at the list of texts—"because his friends say he was with them? Of course they would lie for their buddy."

Louisa read the texts again. Heath's messages went beyond what she'd imagined. Had Zoe been afraid of Heath? Is that why she didn't text him back? "Maybe she was afraid to go back to her apartment alone." Louisa reached up to her necklace and rolled a pearl between her fingertips. "Did she talk to you about Heath?"

Mrs. Finch sniffed. "She mentioned him, but she never brought him home. We never met him."

"Did she bring other kids home to meet you?" Louisa asked.

"No." Mrs. Finch stared at her clasped hands. "She didn't come home unless school was out. She helped out with chores when she lived here, but farming wasn't for her. We were so hoping that she'd finally found a place where she fit in. Somewhere she would be happy."

"Zoe was desperate to have a social life. She never had many friends." Mr. Finch rubbed his wife's hand, as if her fingers were cold and he was trying to warm them.

"It must have been hard on her, being so smart, so different from the other kids." Louisa knew exactly how that felt.

Mr. Finch nodded. "We had her late in life. We never thought we'd have a child, let alone be gifted with one as special as Zoe. By the time she was three, she'd taught herself to read. We knew she was different from other kids. The school here couldn't accommodate her, so we took out a second mortgage to send her to private school. But even there, she was in classes with kids so much older than her. Socially, she was always an outsider."

Mrs. Finch dabbed her eye with the crumpled tissue. "She was excited when he asked her out. She hadn't been out on many dates. I was worried, but I thought the university was so nice. All the kids seemed to have good manners. I worried about strangers hurting her. I never thought I'd have to worry about her friends."

"Now we know better." Mr. Finch's lips compressed with despair. "We've researched all the statistics. Most girls are harmed by people they know, not strangers. Did her boyfriend hang around the museum?"

"No, I'd never seen him before," Louisa answered. "Have you met any of Zoe's other friends?"

Mr. Finch's head bobbed in a tight, strained nod. "Her roommate, Isa. We've seen her a couple of times when we stopped by to visit Zoe. Frankly, we were going to ask you the same thing."

Louisa sighed. "I'm afraid not. Has she mentioned anyone else to you lately? Any difficulties with her courses? Any problems with other students?"

"No," Mr. Finch said quietly. "She seemed excited about her classes. She loves the museum and was very pleased to be working with you."

Louisa swallowed a lump of sadness. "She's a terrific student." She didn't want to believe that Zoe would never bounce into her office again.

"I thought she'd finally found somewhere she belonged, a place where she could find other people like her. She was supposed to make friends and have a normal life." A sob slipped past Mrs. Finch's tight lips. "She wasn't supposed to—"

Her control broke. Her shoulders shook, and tears streamed down her face. Her husband turned her into his chest and rubbed her back. The look he cast over his wife's shoulder was full of anger and sorrow. "Please let us know if you can think of anyone else that Zoe spent time with. The police act like there's no point in even trying. They won't say it, but I can tell they're convinced she's dead, but I can't believe it. I keep thinking that I'd feel different if she was gone. That I'd *know*. That something inside of me would have died right along with her."

"I'll call you if I learn anything." Louisa stood. She let herself out, leaving Zoe's parents alone with their grief and fear. On the drive back to Philadelphia, she turned up the volume on the stereo and tried to drown out all her thoughts, but one question refused to be silenced. Was Zoe still alive?

Back at work, her butt didn't spend two minutes in her desk chair before her phone rang with a summons to Cusack's office. She reported with none of her usual nervousness. The discussion with Zoe's parents had changed her perspective.

"Where have you been?" Cusack rose as she entered his office, his ingrained manners unaffected by his obvious irritation.

"Zoe's parents called me." She eased into the chair facing his desk.

Cusack smoothed his tie as he sank into his seat. "And?"

"And they asked me to come to their house."

His entire face sagged with a frown. "So you just left?"

"Yes. I took a long lunch hour. I'll be sure to stay later this evening. I won't fall behind."

"You could have asked me."

121

"What would your answer have been?"

"I would have said no."

"So you would have preferred I refuse Zoe's parents?"

Cusack leaned back in his chair and crossed his arms over his chest. "This is a matter for the police. I would prefer you to leave the investigation to them."

"*The Finches* called *me*," Louisa clarified. "I didn't initiate the contact, but I also didn't have the heart to say no. They're heartbroken. I work hard for this museum. I put in many extra hours. I fulfill my responsibilities and more." Her teeth clamped together with frustration.

They both knew he'd taken advantage of the situation at the Maine museum. She was doing a full curator's job at half the salary.

"Louisa, you are missing the point." Exasperation sharpened his clipped accent. "You cannot drive off without letting anyone know where you are."

"No matter how much I love working here, I can't put my career ahead of Zoe's life." Louisa lifted her chin and prepared to be fired.

"I wouldn't ask you to put your job ahead of Zoe." Cusack crossed his arms over his chest. "But two museum employees have disappeared. I do not want you to be number three."

Oh. Could Cusack have been worried about her?

"The museum can't take any more scandal." Of course. He was only protecting the museum. "You need to stay out of the investigation."

"I can't." Louisa met his gaze.

"Why not?"

"Because I'm not giving up on Zoe. She's been missing for thirty-eight hours."

———

Conor begged off the dinner rush to pick Louisa up after work. He texted her and waited a half block from the museum. She climbed into the car.

"How was your day?"

She rested her head against the passenger window. "I went to see Zoe's parents on my lunch hour. Her father showed me the texts Heath sent to Zoe Monday night." She summed up her meeting with the Finches. "Why aren't the police investigating Heath?"

"We don't know that they aren't." Conor scraped a hand down his chin. "But I think we need some background information on Heath."

He glanced sideways. Her face was drawn and tired. The encounter with the Finches had clearly taken a lot out of her. If she'd spent her lunch hour driving, then she hadn't eaten. "I have a late night. How about stopping for a sandwich and coffee?"

"OK," she answered, distracted.

He found a lucky spot at the curb, parked, and swiped his credit card at the parking meter kiosk. They walked a block down Eighteenth Street and ducked into a café.

Conor chose a dark, high-backed booth in the back for privacy. The bistro café catered mainly to the lunch crowd. Half the tables were empty. The waitress arrived, and Conor ordered coffee and a club sandwich.

Louisa asked for green tea.

When the waitress left, she told him about her heartbreaking visit to the Finches' house. He reached across the table and took her hand. "You were like Zoe, weren't you? Ahead of your class, separate from the other kids?"

"Yes." Louisa studied their intertwined fingers. "I earned my PhD at nineteen."

His thumb rubbed a slow circle on the back of her hand. "Is that why you need to find her so badly? Because she's like you?"

Was Louisa like Zoe's parents, simply refusing to accept the girl's death because the truth would be too painful?

"Maybe." Tears glistened in her eyes. "I know what it's like to be alone in a room full of people, to be an academic success and not have friends, to be desperate to fit in. My father traveled. My mother was dead. My aunt wasn't interested."

"And you were alone." His fingers tightened around hers. "I'm sorry."

"It was a long time ago."

But she hadn't gotten over it, and Conor thanked God for his three siblings. As crazy as his life could be, the Sullivans always had each other.

"That time-heals-all-wounds saying is total bullshit. Cuts that deep never go away, no matter how many years pass. I still miss my parents." Conor's sandwich arrived. He pushed the plate to the middle of the table, but she didn't seem interested. Had she eaten anything since the muffin he'd brought her that morning?

The setting sun elongated shadows on the sidewalk outside. For the first time, she'd opened up to him. She'd given him a glimpse of the wounded soul beneath her mask.

Now, staring out the window, her profile had frozen again, all evidence of her grief smoothed away. She was a swan gliding at the edge of the Schuylkill River, for all appearances elegant, quiet, and still. All the motion occurred beneath the surface, hidden from view. He wondered for the hundredth time how many layers he'd have to uncover to find the real her.

She fascinated and challenged him.

With a sinking sensation, he realized getting closer to her would require more touchy-feely type discussions. And dear God, *he* was going to have to be the one to initiate them, which was the complete opposite of the natural order of the universe.

Louisa's phone buzzed. "Excuse me."

She got up from the table, went outside, and answered the call on the sidewalk.

She returned a few moments later and slid her phone into her purse. "Xavier English is the professor of Celtic studies. He comes to the museum frequently. He's also Zoe's mentor. Professor English will talk to us if we meet him off campus. He doesn't want us to let anyone know he's speaking with you."

"I can understand that. Where does he want to meet?"

"He's coming here. It's dark enough, and he can always claim I didn't tell him you were here," Louisa said.

"How did you convince him to come?"

"I told him I thought you were innocent."

"And that was enough?"

She raised a shoulder. "He said he wants to decide for himself."

Ten minutes later, the door opened. Louisa half stood and waved to a man in the doorway. With a nod, he threaded through the tables to their booth. Professor English wasn't the old geek Conor expected. Fiftyish, the professor was six feet tall and athlete-fit. His salt-and-pepper hair was thick and cut short. He wore jeans and a button-up shirt.

He greeted Louisa with a warm smile and a handshake.

She introduced him to Conor. "Thanks for coming all the way over here, Xavier."

He sat next to her. "I'm worried about Zoe too. Punctuality might not be her strength, but running a little behind isn't the same thing as missing classes and her work at the museum.

That's not like her. But do you really think she's been abducted? It seems so unreal. The police have been all over campus the last two days." Xavier's eyes flickered to Conor. "The picture of you on the news doesn't look much like you."

Conor shrugged. "It's old, and my face was beat to shit."

"Why should I believe you're not guilty?" Xavier asked.

"I never met Zoe before Monday night," Conor said. "And isn't that backward? What happened to innocent until proven guilty?"

"The police think they have enough evidence to make you the lead suspect," Xavier said. "They're showing your picture around the college and asking everyone if they've seen you."

"What if Conor didn't do it, Xavier?" Louisa twisted in her seat to face him. "And the police are focusing their investigation on him? They won't find Zoe."

Xavier's eyes weren't 100 percent persuaded, but enough doubt lingered for Conor to plow ahead.

"When was the last time you saw Zoe?" he asked.

"Monday morning. I mentor four students. Zoe, her roommate, Isa, plus two undergraduates." Xavier laced his fingers. "I like to meet with the graduate students every couple of weeks. Both Zoe and Isa have a lot going on this year."

"Isa received the Pendleworth grant, is that correct?"

"Yes, and she's my teaching assistant as well this year." Xavier's casual smile faded. "I'd hoped to groom Zoe for the job next year."

"Zoe's young for a TA position," Louisa said.

"Young, yes, but dedicated to her studies. Frankly, she's one of the brightest students I've ever taught." He frowned. "I sometimes wonder, though, about the pressure she's under."

"What do you mean?" Conor asked.

"Well, Zoe is only twenty-one. She doesn't have many close friends. Most of her classmates are at least three years her senior.

Socially, that's a large gap. Even though I've only been mentoring her since the start of the term, I've gotten glimpses that she isn't always happy." Xavier rested his forearms on the table. "I think she's lonely. Until recently, her age kept her from joining the others when they would go out for beers after class."

Louisa nodded. "She was very excited about her birthday. I got the feeling she thought it would be a magic 'in' to the social scene."

"That's not very realistic," Conor said.

Xavier shrugged. "Their IQs don't make them more emotionally mature. In fact, I find it's often quite the opposite. Frequently, other children have shunned them from a young age. Plus, if they've been allowed to skip grades, like Zoe, their age is a definite detriment. Three years doesn't seem like a big deal at twenty-four, but in the lower grades, the gap might as well be the social Grand Canyon. What high school senior is going to invite a fifteen-year-old to her graduation party? Some of the brightest kids haven't had close friendships. They aren't good at reading social cues, and they have little experience interacting with their peers. They are easily taken advantage of. Frankly, Zoe would be an obvious target for a predator."

"How mature is she?" Conor asked.

"She's just as emotionally volatile as any other twenty-one-year-old girl. In fact, on Monday, she was distracted, a very unusual state for her. I was concerned. Part of a mentor's job is to make sure the kids haven't overextended themselves. When I asked if everything was all right, she mentioned that she had a date, but she seemed nervous about it. I could be wrong. Maybe she was just excited. We didn't discuss it beyond me making sure it wasn't a school-related issue." Xavier put his hands on his knees and pushed to his feet. "I have to get back. I hope someone finds her. I hope she's not . . ." He let the implication trail off.

Conor stood and shook his hand. "Did you know Riki LaSanta?"

"Not well," Xavier said. "She was in one of my classes last year, before she changed her graduate major from European history to Egyptian."

"Thank you." Louisa touched Xavier's wrist.

"Be careful, Louisa." Xavier covered her hand with his for a brief moment, just long enough to irritate Conor. "I'll see you Saturday night at the fund-raiser."

Conor bristled as Xavier left the café. Did Louisa have a date with the professor?

Louisa sipped her tea. "I wonder how Zoe felt when the date she'd been anticipating went horribly wrong."

Conor thought back to Monday night. "She was upset, even more so when she couldn't get her roommate on the phone."

"I wonder if Isa really didn't get the messages or if she ignored Zoe's calls," Louisa mused. "There's a lot of competition between graduate students." She checked her phone. "She hasn't called me back."

"Do you think Isa could feel Zoe breathing down her neck, academically speaking?"

"It's a possibility. I know Zoe was a close second for the Pendleworth grant."

"Did you know Riki was a European history major until this year?"

"No. I wonder if the police know." Slipping one foot out of its high heel, she absently rubbed her toes before stuffing her foot back in with a grimace.

Conor nodded toward her feet. "Why do you wear those if they hurt?"

Looking up at him, she cocked her head. "What else would I wear?"

"Something that doesn't hurt?" Conor suggested with a grin and a glance at the beaten running shoes on his feet.

"Oh, I'm sure *those* would go over well with my boss." Louisa chuckled. Her phone buzzed on the table. "I'm sorry. I have to get this."

"No problem. Go ahead. I'll pay the check and meet you outside."

Her face tightened as she walked toward the door and answered the call. "Hello, Aunt Margaret."

He joined her on the sidewalk as she pressed END and stared at her phone.

"Everything all right?"

She exhaled, forcing a smile to her compressed lips. "Yes. My aunt will be in town for a charity event. She wants to have dinner with me on Friday." Louisa rubbed the spot between her eyebrows.

"Is that bad?"

"I don't know. I don't talk to her very often." Louisa's hand drifted to her pearls. There was more to that story. "The situation is complicated. My father passed me off to his sister because he didn't know what to do with a daughter he barely knew. Unfortunately, Aunt Margaret wasn't suited to the role. Not that I was easy. Frankly, I resented her intrusion. I wanted my father."

He took her elbow and steered her toward her building. "None of that was your fault. You were a kid. Jayne and Danny had plenty of resentment."

Hope lit her eyes. "Would you like to join us? Aunt Margaret is staying at the Ritz Carlton, and we're dining at the Capital Grille. I'm sure I can extend the reservation to three."

Let's see, would he like to have a long, awkward, and fancy dinner with two women in a strained relationship? Not really. Besides, he'd promised Pat he'd cover the bar. "Tomorrow Pat has some open house thing at the kids' school on Friday. Jaynie's pregnant and tired. I hate to see her up late."

"Jayne is pregnant?" Louisa's mouth turned in a wistful smile. "I couldn't tell."

"It's early." He glanced sideways. "Tell me about this fundraiser on Saturday night."

"It's a silent auction. There'll be drinks and hors d'oeuvres. It's part of my job to help loosen wallets. Damian is coming, most of the museum staff, plus some of the university's history professors who work with the museum."

"Sounds interesting," Conor lied. He'd taken plenty of side jobs tending bar at charity events. The long line at the bar was all about numbing the boredom. But he wished he could be there to get a feel for the people involved in the case, and he'd also like to keep an eye on Damian and Xavier. Jealous much?

"Then it sounds more interesting than it will be." Louisa's tone turned wry. "Now that I think about it, the attendees will include several people who knew both Zoe and Riki. I'll be sure to keep my ears open. I'm sure the case will be one of the major topics of conversation."

Conor didn't like the idea of Louisa spending the evening in a roomful of potential suspects. But what could he do? He could hardly charm his way into an invitation. He stopped in front of the Rittenhouse. "I should probably go."

"Thank you for your help today." Louisa stood. In her heels, she was only a few inches shorter than him, a very kissable distance. But not here. Too public. He followed her into the lobby and tugged her away from the door. He leaned forward and put his lips to hers. This time she responded with no hesitation, her lips yielding slightly, then pressing back at his. Pleasure at the progress flourished in his chest, which was ludicrous considering the chaste nature of the kiss.

Conor's hand twitched at his side. He wanted to hold her, to pull her against his body. Visions of soft skin under silk drained the blood from his head and sent it shooting south. Slowly, he raised a hand and cupped her jaw, gently stroking her chin with his thumb.

He lifted her head. Her green eyes had gone dark. Desire zinged through his belly and landed in his balls. Yeah. Time to go. Sex clouded his judgment, and he wanted his mind clear.

"I'll call you tomorrow."

Louisa smiled. "Don't you want to collect your dog?"

Conor thought of the hooded teen in the alley. "Would you mind holding on to her for a couple of days?"

"Not at all." Her smile widened.

The dog would just be lonely in his apartment. If Kirra stayed with Louisa, they could keep each other company. He suspected they both had spent enough time alone.

"I have to go. Pat is running the bar solo. Be careful." Leaving Louisa at the elevator, he exited. On the sidewalk, the discussion with Xavier replayed in his head. He didn't blame the professor for doubting Conor's innocence. The amount of circumstantial evidence against him was staggering. Was Conor's involvement in Zoe's disappearance a coincidence or a setup? If someone planned to frame him, he'd have spent a lot of time watching both Conor and Louisa.

He glanced back at her building. In that light, her secure condo didn't look as safe.

CHAPTER
15

Louisa fed Kirra and took her outside for a quick walk. Having a dog was more pleasant than she'd imagined. The sun dipped behind the buildings, casting cool shadows across the sidewalk. As usual, the green space was busy with people determined to enjoy the last of the pleasant weather. Conor's kiss still tingled on her lips, but her joy was darkened by the forty-two hours that Zoe had been missing. The impending dinner with her aunt further blackened her mood.

"I should have said no to Aunt Margaret," Louisa said as they strolled past the reflecting pool. Kirra looked up and cocked her head. She was an excellent listener, and Louisa found herself telling the dog things she'd never share with another person. "But the minute I saw her number on my phone, all I could think was that she must know what's wrong with Daddy and that's why she wants to meet with me."

The possibilities raced through her head. Cancer? Heart attack? Liver disease? Was he dying? What would Aunt Margaret tell her Friday night?

On the way back into the building, the young doorman gave her a wide smile. "Someone left a package for you, Miss Hancock. It's at the desk."

"Thank you, Gerome." Louisa followed him to the small reception desk in the lobby. He handed her a distinctive teal-blue gift bag. Tiffany's. She peeked inside. Below a spray of tissue paper was a small box. "And thanks for walking Kirra this afternoon."

"Anytime, Dr. Hancock. She's sweet."

Gift bag in hand, Louisa took the elevator up to her apartment. What could it be? The only person who sent her jewelry these days was her father, but her birthday wasn't for months. He hadn't been in the States to say good-bye when she'd left Maine, and he'd seemed distracted when he'd visited last spring. But then, she'd just been fired and had assumed his disappointment in her professional failure had sent him away. Maybe he missed her. With a lighter step, she went into the bedroom to change out of her work clothes.

In yoga pants and a sweatshirt, she settled on the living room sofa. The pillow and blanket Conor had used last night were stacked next to her. She lifted the pillow to her face and inhaled. It smelled like him. She tucked it behind her. With reminders of Conor, and the dog at her feet, the large apartment didn't seem as empty. Perhaps she'd buy it after all.

Placing the gift bag in her lap, she removed the delicate, white tissue paper and reached in for the present. TIFFANY & CO. was printed on the top of the teal box. She gently slid off the white ribbon and lifted the lid. It must be from Daddy.

She opened the lid. Gold caught the light. It was a charm shaped like a sailboat. Louisa dropped the box.

No.

It couldn't be.

The box had landed right-side up on the rug at her feet. The golden sailboat gleamed in the light from the end table. Bracing herself, she tipped the gift bag and peered inside. A small white envelope sat on the bottom. She opened it, hoping she was wrong.

Dear Louisa,

A small token to show how much I miss you. I hope you'll reconsider your recent move and come home. You are the only one for me. I need you. I've always needed you. Please forgive me.

Yours always,

Blaine

Her stomach cramped as she read his signature. Of course she'd been right. Who else but the yacht-racing Blaine would send her a sailboat?

But how did he find her? She supposed finding a museum curator who specialized in European history wasn't all that difficult. As private as she'd kept her personal life, her professional life was unavoidably public. But he'd sent this to her home, not the museum. She'd been able to pay an Internet information provider for Heath's address. The same personal data was likely available on her. Hands shaking, she reached for the phone, dialed the doorman's line, and asked for Gerome.

"Yes, ma'am?"

Louisa gathered her voice. "Gerome, did you see the man who left the package for me?"

"Yes, ma'am. He was blond, a little taller than me, very well-dressed. I asked for his name. He said you would know who he was when you opened the box. He wanted to surprise you."

"Thank you, Gerome." Louisa swallowed her rising nausea at the thought that Blaine had been here. "If he comes again, please don't let him up or accept any more packages. Just call me immediately."

"Yes, ma'am." Gerome's tone flattened, telling Louisa he understood.

Louisa hung up the phone. Kirra pressed against her legs.

"It's all right, girl." She stuffed the gift box and card back into the bag and went into the kitchen. For a moment, she held it over the trash receptacle, then reconsidered. Perhaps sending it back to him would be a better move. Blaine needed to get it through his arrogant, thick head that she wanted nothing to do with him. He'd been pursuing her for years, and it needed to stop. She would never be his.

Not after what he'd done to her.

She opened the hall closet and put the bag on the top shelf. As soon as she had time, she'd mail it back to him. Ignoring him hadn't worked in the past. This time she would be more forceful. After checking the door locks, she swallowed two aspirin and went into the bedroom. A hot shower helped relax her, but sleep was going to be elusive tonight.

She settled on the couch and turned on the television. Kirra jumped up beside her, curled up, and rested her head on her leg. Grateful for the company, Louisa settled a hand on the dog's back.

Her mind whirled with Blaine's unwanted gift, grief for Riki, and worrying about Zoe. Where was her intern? The police seemed certain she was dead, but Louisa refused to believe it. But with Riki already murdered, how long could she hope that Zoe hadn't been killed?

Pat's red head drooped over his glass.

"Come on. Let's get you home." Conor grabbed his brother's arm and hoisted it across his shoulders.

Pat stood and swayed. "Okeydokey."

Conor staggered as Pat leaned on him. "Steady. If you fall down, that's where you'll stay for the night." He steered Pat out the back door and toward the waiting car.

"Watch your head." Conor opened the door and folded Pat into the passenger seat. He stuffed his brother's long legs under the dash. Twenty-year-old Porsche 911s were not designed to transport men the size of Pat.

"We raised them right." Pat's voice was thick and slurred.

"We did, Pat. We did a damned good job." Conor slid behind the wheel and took a couple of seconds to admire all the shiny new leather in the interior. His brother let out a massive burp, and Conor shot him a look. "Do not hurl in my car."

Pat thumped his chest. "I'm insulted. I can hold my liquor with the best of them."

Conor covered his snicker with a cough. Pat's tolerance for liquor was ridiculously low for his size.

He started the car. The engine fired with a sweet roar. He should think about selling her and looking for another project. He took one whole day off a week. What would he do without a car to fix?

But damn, this one had turned out to be one fine ride.

"I can't believe Jaynie's having a baby." Pat sniffed. "And she's getting married at Christmastime."

"Me either." Conor drove onto Oregon Avenue. The two cops who'd been sitting in the bar all night got into their unmarked car and followed him. "Maybe they should move the wedding date up. Be nice if she were married before she starts to look pregnant." He wasn't sure why that popped into his head and out of his mouth. Conor wasn't exactly fixated on propriety. But there'd been a time when appearances mattered, like when the social worker showed up for a home visit to make sure Pat and Conor had a good handle on their younger siblings. Most of the time they hadn't, but they'd faked it pretty well. All four of the Sullivan siblings were decent liars, which probably shouldn't be considered an attribute.

Pat waved off his comment. "Aw, she's happy. Who the hell cares?"

"As usual, you're right." Conor laughed, but he didn't feel the humor. An inexplicable sadness lodged in his bones tonight, a torrent of dissatisfaction that had been building to a crescendo inside him for months.

It felt disturbingly like self-pity.

Was he jealous of his three siblings' happiness? Because if he was, that was just lame. Lame and inexcusable. He really needed to get his own life. He and his siblings had suffered the same tragedy. They'd moved on. Why hadn't he?

"She's all grown up. She has Reed. She doesn't need us anymore."

"That's the way it's supposed to be, Pat." Did parents feel this jumble of emotions when their kids got married and had kids? How could he be sad and happy at the same time?

"And Danny's all settled up in Maine with Mandy." Pat sighed heavily. Alcohol made his brother emotional. "You're the last hold-out, Conor."

"Uh-huh." *Do not engage.*

"I'm serious." Pat hiccupped. "You need a wife."

Conor made another noncommittal sound and made a mental note that his brother's new cutoff was three drinks, two if he was rolling out the scotch like he had tonight to celebrate Jayne's news.

"How's your curator?" Pat asked.

"Fine." Conor wasn't going anywhere near a conversation about Louisa with a drunken and sentimental Pat.

Pat glanced in the side mirror. "The cops are behind us. It's a fucking parade. Have you heard from Damian?"

"He says they're waiting for the DNA test results." Conor turned down a narrow side street and navigated the sports car around a fallen garbage can. "I've seen them following me." Conor assumed they were always nearby, even if he couldn't see them.

"The test results will prove you're innocent," Pat said.

Conor didn't respond. The long hair they'd found in his apartment was Zoe's, but the blood wasn't hers. How would that play out?

He was glad to pull up in front of Pat and Leena's small piece of urban bliss. Like the family it housed, the brick row home exuded chaos and contentedness. The narrow front yard held a driveway barely big enough for a minivan and an equal-size strip of grass. A Big Wheel was upended on the walk, its tires in the air like a dog that wanted its belly rubbed.

"We're here." *Thank God.* Conor parked at the curb.

Pat sobered. "Leena's going to be pissed."

"Probably," Conor said just to make Pat sweat and hopefully take his mind off Conor's life. Pat might have a foot of height and a hundred pounds on his wife, but Leena ran the show. No question. Though she wouldn't give his brother a hard time. Not tonight. She knew how deeply Jayne's news had affected him. If Pat were sober, he'd know Leena had his back when it mattered, but those shots of scotch had warped his perspective, as liquor tended to do.

Pat wove his way up the walk. Following him, Conor grabbed the plastic trike, righted it, and set it on the porch under the eave. Leena already had the door open. A toy guitar dangled from her fingertips, and wet patches covered the front of her shorts and T-shirt. Bath time had been recently completed, and she was still in the clutter-clearing phase of the evening that followed what she called lockdown rather than bedtime.

She propped a hand on her hip and gave her husband a mock admonishment. "Celebrate much?"

Hoisting himself off the white wrought-iron railing, Pat mumbled something that sounded like "love you" and leaned over to give his wife a kiss.

"Love you too. Get inside before you fall down." Leena waved her hand in front of her face. "Oh geez, Conor, you let him drink scotch?"

"Sorry, Leena." Conor steered Pat over the threshold and into the living room. Pat took three crooked steps across the Berber and stretched out on the living room sofa as if he couldn't possibly walk another step.

Conor gave his sister-in-law a peck on the cheek. "He's all yours."

"Gee, thanks." Grinning, Leena closed the front door. Strands of her dark hair had escaped its ponytail. A damp lock fell over her eye, and she pushed it behind her ear. A wiggly mass of chocolate-colored fur, their new Labrador puppy, yapped and wagged from the other side of a gate across the doorway to the kitchen.

"How's Killer?"

"He's a good boy. Thankfully, crayons aren't toxic." Leena went to the gate and scratched the pup's head. "Are you sure you don't want a puppy? There are still two left."

"Positive." Conor thought of the dog currently sleeping in Louisa's bed. Kirra should stay there. "My apartment's too small, and I'm never in it."

"A dog would be good company. You spend too much time alone."

"Alone? I'm never alone. I'm always in the bar."

"You know what I mean."

A giggle drifted down the stairwell that ran along the living room wall. Someone was still up.

Leena dropped the plastic guitar into an open bin in the corner, walked to the base of the steps, and cupped a hand around her mouth. "Don't make me come up there."

Silence.

Yep. No question. Leena was the boss.

"You need help getting him upstairs?"

"Like we could get him up those steps." Leena laughed. "He's fine where he is." She had a point. The stairwell was narrow and steep, barely enough room for Pat when he was steady on his feet. "Tomorrow's backache will remind him why he isn't much of a drinker," Leena said without the faintest trace of pity.

"No doubt."

"The kids are obviously still awake if you want to pop up and say good night." She pulled an afghan off the back of the couch and tucked it around her husband. Her hand gave his square jaw a quick, loving stroke. A snore ripped through the room.

Normally, Conor would like nothing better than a round of hugs from his niece and nephews, but tonight the thought of their energetic affection hollowed out his chest. Why? What had changed? Why did Jayne's pregnancy make Conor nostalgic? Did it have something to do with Louisa?

The only thing he knew for certain tonight was that he was too tired and too strung out about the missing girl and the police investigation to analyze his love life.

"I really have to get back to the bar." Conor turned toward the door, then paused, his gaze drifting toward his brother. "Is Pat OK?"

"Yeah, why?"

"He got all choked up at Jayne's news."

"He's happy, but at the same time, the news made him feel older, less needed, like that chapter in his life is closed. You and Pat spent the last two decades acting more like parents than siblings." Leena's dark eyes zeroed in on Conor's like X-ray vision. "How are you dealing with Jayne's news? You raised her as much as Pat did."

"Fine. Pat did most of the parenting."

"You always do that."

"Do what?" Conor eased backward, toward the door. He should have kept his mouth shut.

"Brush off the credit." Leena closed the distance between them and poked him in the chest with one finger. She might as well have used a knife. "He couldn't have done it without you, and you know it."

Yeah. Leena saw right through him. Conor took a step sideways. "I'm thrilled for Jaynie."

"Conor . . ." She shook her head. "You haven't been yourself all summer. Talk to me. Pat said you have a new girlfriend?"

"She's not really a girlfriend."

"What is she?"

Good question. "I don't know. She's wrapped up in the police investigation."

Leena put her hand on his biceps. "How are you holding up?"

"I'm innocent."

"Duh." Leena rolled her eyes. "That isn't what I asked you."

"Everything will be OK." He leaned over and gave his sister-in-law a quick kiss on the cheek. "Good luck with Snorezilla. Love ya, Leena." Conor bolted, closing the door behind him. The last thing he wanted to do was talk to Leena or anyone else about his mood. He wanted what Pat currently had—oblivion, at least for a short time. But he had a business to run. Only one Sullivan could be incapacitated at a time.

He strode out on the sidewalk, his boot heels ringing on concrete covered with chalk drawings of rainbows. Walking promoted thinking, another thing he was avoiding, and he was glad to slide back into the Porsche.

Conor lucked out and found a spot at the curb around the corner from the bar. He cut through the alley toward the back door. Back to the bar. Back to work. But his mind was on Pat's family.

All Conor wanted was a simple life. He'd always thought he'd end up like Pat, with a wife and kids and a cramped but happy house.

Barbara's betrayal had floored him.

She'd come into the bar and pursued him with the single-minded focus of an alley cat chasing a rat. Why hadn't he seen her true predatory nature? She'd been sexy, wild, and always eager for him. They'd spent most of that summer in his bed. Probably if the relationship had gone on, he'd have realized it was nothing but sex. But at the time, the overabundance of sex hadn't promoted deep introspection.

Even more shocking than the husband walking into the bar and calmly informing Conor that he was sleeping with his wife was her reaction. Unwilling to compromise the lifestyle her wealthy husband provided, Barbara had broken it off with Conor with barely an *it was fun while it lasted* shrug.

Looking back on it now, with the perspective of time and distance, everything they'd had suddenly looked cheap and sleazy.

Conor hadn't been tempted to start a new relationship since, until he'd met Louisa. Unfortunately, he might not have the time to find out what could happen between them. The police would get the test results back in a few more days. What would happen then? Would they arrest him? Did they even have any other serious suspects? And more importantly, was Zoe still alive?

CHAPTER
16

At this point in the game, my biggest concern was that someone would discover my captive. Though I'd have heard about it. An explosion would likely make the evening news.

After a careful cruise through the neighborhood, I parked the old sedan in front of the building. The streetlamp overhead was out, but the harvest moon shone from a clear sky, its faint orange tint casting a sepia glow over the desolate block. I hadn't seen a single soul on my reconnaissance. The area was so empty the streets could be used as the set for an urban apocalypse film.

With gloved hands, I took my tool bag from the trunk and went inside, careful of the footing. After clicking on my flashlight, I edged my way to the stairwell. A board gave way under my shoe. With a quick grab, I spared myself an ankle-breaking plunge into the basement. At the top of the steps, I examined my trip wire. The booby trap was undisturbed. Removing the trip wire was delicate business. Finished, I descended.

The only inhabitant was the one I'd left there. I played the beam of my flashlight over her face. Naked, she lay curled on her side on the floor against the back wall, her hands cuffed behind her back and fastened to a pipe. Her eyes and nose had leaked all over the duct tape on her mouth, the tears and snot drying to a cracked white film on her skin. Blood crusted across the wounds on her thighs. The puddle of urine had dried to a brown stain on the concrete.

I was definitely done with her.

Over the mess on her face, her gaze still pleaded. But as I stood in the doorway, truth overtook the faint glimmer of hope and stomped it into the ground.

She knew this was it.

Dropping the bag at my feet, I knelt and pulled out the knife. Moving behind her to avoid the initial gush, I raised the weapon. She slid sideways, making the angle difficult.

"Don't make this harder than it has to be," I said, though secretly wishing she would do just that.

I reached for her chin to hold her head and neck still. She thrashed hard for someone dehydrated and weak. After the last experience, I'd only allowed ten minutes for the actual death. But she fought considerably harder than my first, using her bound legs as a counterweight to fling her body sideways.

I stepped on her head to pin it to the concrete. She twisted, but my weight immobilized her. I slashed the knife across the stretched, white skin of her neck. A low moan seeped from her lips as blood spurted in even pulses across the concrete. Her body twitched; fear clouded her eyes.

I moved my foot from her head. Her eyes met mine. Life faded from her gaze slowly, as if her soul clung with desperate fingertips to its physical embodiment.

I had caused this. I was in control. A strange and powerful surge of energy flooded me. *This* was a proper climax. No failure, no disappointment. I watched the blood drain until her chest deflated and her opaque, dead eyes lost focus, all because of me.

Note to self: the will to live is variable, and adequate time must be allowed even if it might not always be needed.

But what if the killing took longer? How would that feel? To draw out the experience, to watch the panic flutter in her pupils? What if she begged for death and I withheld it?

All interesting questions that could be explored at another time. For now, I'd stick to my predetermined schedule. But maybe I could experiment a little with the next one.

After carving the spiral on her abdomen, I lined up the rest of my supplies. Paper, kindling, gasoline, matches. Right on schedule. Paying close attention to detail, I proceeded to the next step.

CHAPTER
17

Louisa waited just inside the door, watching raindrops roll down the glass. Conor's Porsche pulled up to the curb. She went out, popping up her umbrella as she ran for the street. A fine drizzle amplified the scent of falling leaves. She climbed into the passenger seat, shook the umbrella, and closed the car door.

"How do you run in those shoes?" Conor eyed her pumps.

"It isn't easy." Her toes had felt the quick jog across the sidewalk.

"I still don't get why you wear shoes that aren't comfortable."

She looked down at the pretty, nude, patent leather Pradas. "Because I like them."

Shaking his head, Conor eased into traffic.

A tractor-trailer rattled past as he took the ramp for the Schuylkill Expressway, nicknamed the Sure Kill Expressway by Philadelphia residents for a reason. A bus driver blew his horn as Conor merged into traffic and drove toward University City. He reached behind the seat and handed her a Styrofoam box.

She lifted the lid. He'd brought her a sandwich. "What's this?"

"Turkey club. This is the third lunch you've missed this week."

"Thank you." She took a small bite. Her stomach approved.

"You're welcome. Now eat," he ordered.

She raised a brow at his bossy tone, but he ignored her. She finished the sandwich in a few impolitely large bites. She opened the bottle of water he handed her. "Are the police following you today?"

"Probably. Black-and-whites stand out, but sometimes the unmarked cars are hard to spot." Conor sighed. "I just assume they're there all the time."

He parked at the curb a few units away from Zoe and Isa's apartment. "Be careful."

"I'll be fine." Louisa opened the car door and popped her umbrella as she stepped out onto the sidewalk. She hurried to the covered front porch and scanned the list of names. She rang the intercom for apartment 3B. Nothing. She pressed the buzzer again.

"Who is it?" a sleepy and slightly testy voice asked.

Gotcha. "Hello, Isa. It's Dr. Hancock."

After a few seconds of silence, the voice mumbled something incoherent. With a faint buzz, the door lock clicked. Louisa went into the foyer and went up the two flights of dark, wooden steps to the third-floor landing. A girl in pajamas and a camisole held the door open. Her brown hair was pulled back in a sloppy tail, her face devoid of makeup, her eyes wary and irritated. She hadn't expected Louisa's visit, and she wasn't happy about it.

Louisa stepped inside. "I'm Dr. Hancock."

"I'm Isa." She rubbed a hand over her face.

"I'm sorry I woke you." Louisa crossed the threshold. The door opened into a cramped living room and kitchenette combination. Squeezed between the couch and the kitchen counter was a round laminate table covered with books and papers.

"It's OK." Isa yawned. "I have a ton of research to do anyway."

"Late night?"

"Yeah. I'm working on a project for the Pendleton grant."

"Congratulations," Louisa said. "That's a lot of work."

Isa smiled. "It is, but I'll power through it."

"Good attitude."

"What did you want to talk to me about?"

"Zoe."

"I don't know what else I can tell you. The police were already here. I told them everything I knew. They searched her room and everything." Isa nodded toward a closed door off the living room.

"Would you mind if I took a look?"

She lifted a shoulder. "I guess not. They took a bunch of stuff."

Louisa walked to the doorway and peered inside Zoe's closet-size bedroom. The bed was made. A small desk in the corner held books and papers stacked in neat piles. Zoe's backpack hung by the straps over the back of her chair. "You're sure she didn't come home Monday night?"

"Yeah, I pulled an all-nighter." Isa walked to the fridge and poured Diet Coke into a glass. "Want a Coke?"

"No, thanks. Is that normal for her not to come home?"

"We've only been rooming together since the beginning of the semester. So we really haven't established norms yet."

Louisa rephrased the question. "Had she ever not come home before?"

"No. Not that I'm aware of."

"You were here all night? You didn't run out to the library or to grab a pizza?"

"I said I was here all night." Isa's voice grew irritable.

"Why didn't you answer Zoe's texts Monday night?"

"My phone battery was dead." The words were flat, as practiced as a child reading a memorized line in the school play. "I'm terrible about keeping it charged."

Louisa could hear Conor in her mind. *Lame.* Charging a cell phone was as second nature to twentysomethings as brushing their teeth.

"I feel terrible about it. If I had picked her up . . ." Isa's eyes watered. She brushed at the corner of one.

Real or fake tears? Louisa scanned the apartment. No boxes of tissues. No tissues in the trash can. Isa's eyes didn't show any signs of previous crying. Louisa just couldn't shake the sense that something wasn't right.

Isa returned the two-liter soda bottle to the refrigerator. "I fell asleep around eleven."

"How long had she been dating Heath?" Louisa's gaze swept the cluttered surfaces. "She said he was new, but how new?"

"Maybe a few weeks?" Isa opened a white box emblazoned with the pink-and-orange Dunkin' Donuts logo. She held it out to Louisa. "Doughnut?"

"I'm fine. Thank you."

"When she didn't come home, I thought maybe she spent the night at Heath's."

"Had their relationship progressed that far?" Louisa hated to think Heath had taken advantage of the younger Zoe. But Zoe was naive, a perfect target for a handsome, popular guy like Heath.

"I'm not sure. We aren't really close." Isa shrugged. "Zoe's a lot younger than the rest of us. She doesn't really fit in."

Louisa switched topics. "How well do you know Heath?"

"Not well at all. I've seen him around, but he's in the business program. We don't have any classes together." Isa bit into the doughnut and chewed. Her appetite appeared to be solid.

"How did Zoe meet him?"

"I don't really remember." Isa looked away. "I have to get in the shower. I have a class soon."

"Sure. I'll get out of your way." Louisa headed for the door. "Thanks for talking to me."

Outside, she went back to the car.

"Well?" Conor asked as she slid into the passenger side.

"I think she was lying or hiding something." She slouched down in the seat and recited her conversation with Isa back to Conor. "I could be wrong. She said they weren't that close, but Zoe was still her roommate. Maybe I expect too much, but her demeanor just felt . . . off. Can we wait a while? I'd like to follow her."

Isa came out in less than two minutes, not nearly enough time to have showered.

"You'd better wait here."

"Why? I want to follow her," Louisa protested.

He grinned and gave her a deliberate once-over. "Dressed like that, you aren't going to blend. Plus she already knows what you look like. She may not recognize me."

The after-the-boxing-match picture the media had shown of Conor was chosen to make him appear rough, but the bruised and swollen face in the photo barely resembled him.

Conor flipped up the hood of his sweatshirt to conceal his face. With his jeans, boots, and lean body, he could pass for a student. But he was right. In her suit and pumps, *she* did not blend in with the student population.

"All right," she sighed.

"I'll text you if anything interesting happens," Conor said. "Lock the doors."

Louisa slid farther down in the seat. Where was Isa going?

———

Conor shoved his hands in the kangaroo pocket of his shirt and strode down the sidewalk. Even at a seemingly casual pace, his long legs kept pace with the girl hurrying a block ahead.

Two blocks later, Isa turned at the corner and broke into a jog as the rain increased. Conor followed as she cut through a service alley. Three houses down the next street, she was running up onto the porch to ring the buzzer of Heath Yeager's place.

There was a bus stop at the corner. Conor ducked into the clear three-sided shelter. He sat down on the bench and pulled out his cell phone. Pretending to text, he kept one eye on the door to Heath's building.

Isa wasn't long. In barely ten minutes, she retraced her steps.

Conor texted Louisa: WATCH FOR ISA.

A few minutes later, she texted back: SHE'S HERE.

He watched Heath's apartment another half hour, but the door didn't open. He returned to the car and slid into the driver's seat.

"She's still inside," Louisa said.

Conor brushed the hood off his head. His shirt was damp. "Heath hasn't gone anywhere either."

"What now?"

"I'll take you back to work." Conor started the car and pulled away from the curb. "At least we know they're both lying. They know each other much better than they'll admit."

"What could they be lying about?"

"They're up to something." Conor turned back toward Center City. "I'd love to get inside Heath's apartment."

"That's illegal."

"Yes, it is. And I have to work tonight anyway."

Louisa chewed on her lip. "I'd hate for you to get into more trouble with the police."

"OK. We'll shelve that idea for now." But eventually he might need to get into Heath's apartment and find out why he and Isa were lying. He glanced in the rearview mirror and picked out a dark-blue American sedan four cars back. He was probably already in more trouble with the police. But what choice did he have? Even when the DNA results came back on the blood and confirmed it wasn't Zoe's, Damian had flat-out told him he could still be arrested and convicted. The hair was hers, and Conor had admitted she'd been in his apartment. Either he solved his own case, or he went on trial for murder.

CHAPTER
18

"Have a nice evening, Dr. Hancock."

"Thank you, Gerome." Friday evening, Louisa walked through the open door to meet her aunt. She hadn't seen Conor since lunchtime the day before, but he'd texted her a few times. They'd both been busy with work. She'd spent the day moving artifacts into the *Celtic Warrior* exhibit cases. The exhibit wasn't finished, but guests at tomorrow night's fund-raiser would get a sense of how the display would come together. Conor had been tied up at the bar handling deliveries.

Neither of them had any ideas on how to look for Zoe. The Finches had done several heart-wrenching interviews begging for their daughter's return. The DNA tests had not come in. Did the labs work on the weekend, or would Conor be safe until Monday?

"You'll call if you need the car later?" the doorman asked with a polite smile.

"I will. Thank you."

A cool wind sent dead leaves scurrying in the gutter, and the moon shone with spectacular clarity through a few wisps of thin clouds. If only Aunt Margaret's intentions were as clear as the night sky. Would her aunt give her news that would unravel her life? Louisa pulled her cashmere wrap tighter around her shoulders as she crossed the pavement. A black town car waited at the curb. It seemed silly to ask for a car to drive her the half mile from the Rittenhouse to her aunt's hotel, but she'd had too many creepy *being watched* sensations in the past couple of days. Walking alone at night didn't appeal.

The driver stood by the open rear door. Louisa eased into the back. The silk of her simple black sheath dress slid across the seat, the leather chilling the backs of her thighs.

The car dropped her in front of the Ritz Carlton. Louisa climbed the granite steps and went through the glass doors. Situated on the prestigious Avenue of the Arts section of Broad Street, the hotel was located in the former historic Girard Bank building. The rotunda building was modeled after the Pantheon in Rome, complete with a soaring domed ceiling and neoclassical columns. More than a hundred feet in the air, the night sky darkened the glass oculus in the dome's apex. Voices and utensils echoed in the cavernous space as Louisa crossed the white marble floor.

Margaret would not be lingering by the door. She would wait for Louisa to come to her.

Louisa circled the space, admiring the red-and-purple color scheme, strings of beaded glass, and art deco accents popped against a backdrop of gleaming white marble. She spiraled inward, spotting Margaret in a high-backed chair by the bar. A long-sleeved belted column of deep crimson hugged her aunt's thin frame to just below the knee. Her platinum-blond bob was freshly colored, and a flute of pale, sparkling liquid dangled from her bony fingers. At fifty-five, Margaret fought aging with military ruthlessness, but her obsession with maintaining the slimness of her youth had left her skin crepe-papery and her limbs skeletal.

"Louisa." She set her glass down, stood, and extended both veiny hands.

"Hello, Aunt Margaret." Louisa briefly clasped her aunt's fingers and turned her face for an air kiss. Margaret didn't come from wealth, but she'd learned to appreciate—and spend—her brother's income.

"Sit." Margaret waved to the chair next to her, then signaled the waitress. "Would you like a glass of champagne?"

"No, thank you." Perching on the edge of the chair, Louisa held her clutch on her lap and ordered a sparkling water.

Her aunt frowned but recovered quickly. "How are you, dear?"

"I'm well. Thank you."

"Your new job?" Margaret asked, but what did she really want?

"Satisfying." Louisa would rather they went to dinner without the cocktail-hour delay. Unless her aunt got to the point early, which was doubtful. "What time is dinner?"

"We have an eight-thirty reservation." Irritation thinned Margaret's gaze. "Are you in a rush?"

Louisa checked her watch. Eight ten. The Capital Grille was right across the street from the hotel. They had fifteen minutes to kill. *Damn.* "Of course not. I'm simply hungry. How was your charity event?"

"The usual." Margaret's eyes sparkled. "I have a surprise for you."

Louisa's spine tensed as the server set a tumbler of ice and a small bottle of Perrier on the table. "Oh?"

"Yes." Margaret drained her flute and handed it off to the waitress. She clasped her hands together. "We aren't dining alone."

There was only one person Margaret could have brought with her. Warmth flooded her. Maybe her father had changed his mind about waiting till the holidays to visit. Or maybe his news couldn't wait. "But I thought Daddy was in Stockholm."

Margaret craned her neck and waved discreetly. Louisa turned in her chair.

"Your father is still in Sweden," Margaret said. "This is even better."

"This isn't about Daddy?" Confused, Louisa scanned the lobby but saw no one she recognized. Maybe it was one of Margaret's friends. Could her aunt have a man? Why she'd never married was a mystery. Margaret was an attractive woman, if a little predatory looking.

"And here he is." Her aunt's eyes gleamed with mischief.

"Hello, Louisa," a man said from behind the high back of her chair.

No. Louisa stood and whirled.

"Did you get my gift?" Blaine stepped around the chair. He was holding two flutes of champagne. He extended a glass toward her. His gaze pleaded with hers. "Please, don't make a scene. Have a drink. Let's put our past behind us. I miss you. I'm sorry we surprised you, but I had to see you. There didn't seem to be any other way."

Louisa stepped back. Shock and anger rippled through her like an avalanche. She turned to Margaret. "How could you?"

Margaret was the only person who knew. The only one she'd trusted all those years ago.

Her aunt's eyes steeled. "Nonsense. You need to get over yourself." Her voice dropped to a reptilian hiss. "You both made a mistake. Blaine loves you."

Louisa backed away. "I'm leaving."

"Oh, enough with the drama," Margaret snapped, closing in on her. "You were both young, and young people do foolish things. I don't know why you can't see that he's the perfect man for you. It's not like you have men lined up waiting to marry you.

He's the only one who's still interested. You have the personality of a textbook."

"Don't call me again. Either of you." Louisa's lungs tightened as if a heavy weight lay on top of her, crushing her chest, constricting her breathing. She turned away, barely hearing Margaret calling after her.

"Don't blame me if you spend your whole life alone."

"Louisa, wait!" Blaine called. "I love you."

Blood rushed in her ears. She rounded the corner that led to the lobby. Her heels slid on the slick marble. Catching her balance, she covered her mouth, suppressing the sob trapped in her throat.

"Are you all right, miss?" The doorman held the door for her.

She didn't answer as she escaped the building onto the sidewalk. The cool evening air rushed over her clammy skin. Swallowing the salty wedge in her throat, she walked and breathed. A block later, the sounds of traffic gradually drowned out the rush of blood in her ears. Her heart slowed. Of all the terrible things she'd expected of tonight, this hadn't made the list.

How could Margaret have invited Blaine to dinner? Even for her, that seemed excessively cruel. Granted, she didn't believe Louisa's story, but still . . .

Her toes protested her rapid pace. She slowed her strides, letting her heart rate return to normal, but the pressure beneath her sternum didn't abate. In ten minutes, Margaret had wiped out all the progress Louisa had made in the months since she'd moved to Philadelphia. Margaret was wrong about Blaine, but her assessment of Louisa was painfully accurate. She dated but never got close to anyone.

Conor's face flashed into her head. The piercing gaze that elicited emotions she didn't know she possessed. The need to see him welled inside her. But if she went to him in this state, he'd demand to know what had happened. Conor would see right through any excuse she could imagine. She'd go home. Kirra wouldn't ask for an explanation.

She stopped at the corner. She'd walked farther than she'd thought. She skirted a news crew giving a report outside the Academy of Music. A show had just let out, and people poured from the nearby Kimmel Center. She threaded through the theater crowd, working her way to the curb where pedestrians queued up for taxis.

She stepped into the line. A hand shoved in the center of her back. Her body was flung forward, and she sprawled into the street. Her knees and palms burned as bare skin skidded across asphalt. On her hands and knees, she raised her head and froze. Bearing down on her was the front end of a SEPTA bus.

—◆—

Ears still ringing from the band's last set, Conor set a Guinness in front of a regular. Patrons turned back to the hockey game playing on all three TVs. The Flyers were winning, and a celebration was in full swing. Two plainclothes cops sat in a corner booth drinking Diet Coke and watching the game, forced inside because they couldn't see both exits of the bar from the street. Conor didn't mind. In case anything else happened, he couldn't get a better alibi.

Jayne swung by, a tray loaded with beer, hot wings, and nachos balanced on her hip. Her face was whiter than its usual Irish pale, setting off dark shadows under her eyes.

"You shouldn't be carrying anything that heavy. Where does this go?" Slipping out from behind the bar, he took the tray from her hands and delivered it to the table she indicated.

"I'm fine, Conor," she said without enthusiasm.

"Have you heard from Reed?"

"Yes, Scott is out of surgery, but they put him in intensive care."

"I'm sorry, honey." Conor wrapped an arm around his sister. "Why don't you go home? Or go take pictures. That always takes your mind off your troubles."

Jayne was also a freelance photographer.

"I don't want to be alone." She rested her head on his shoulder.

He kissed the top of her head. "OK. Then you can help Ernie behind the bar, and I'll take care of the tables."

At least she wouldn't have to carry trays. Conor made a mental note to hire another waitress. He turned to take an order. A buzz from the TV overhead signaled another goal. Conor glanced up. The Flyers scored again.

"Whoot!" Phil, the cable repairman, leaped from his seat and high-fived the guy next to him. He turned, tripped, and dumped his beer on Conor. The nearly full glass soaked him from neck to knees.

"Oh, man. I'm sorry, Conor." Phil grabbed a handful of napkins and pushed them at Conor.

"It's cool." He backed away. "I'll just go change."

"Be back in a few minutes," he called out to Jayne and Ernie. He hurried toward the back door, dropping the order ticket in the kitchen on his way through. He jogged up the stairs into his apartment. Coming home to his empty place last night had sucked. He'd slept better the night before on Louisa's couch, and he could get used to the whole breakfast together thing. He'd kissed her—twice. Yes, despite being a murder suspect, things were looking up, and Conor was in a pretty damned good mood. If only the cops could find Zoe alive. Then maybe he and Louisa could spend some real time together, time not overshadowed by worry and death.

He pulled out his key and moved his hand toward the lock, but his door wasn't quite closed. Scratches marred the jamb, and the frame was splintered around the deadbolt. The hairs on the back of his neck prickled as he gave the door a two-finger push. It swung inward with a squeak.

Trashed didn't come close to describing his apartment.

His couch was turned on its back. Slashed cushions spilled their guts across the area rug. His glass coffee table was smashed. Graffiti—and what might be feces, judging from the smell—covered the walls. Conor didn't go beyond the foyer, but he could see the kitchen drawers had been pulled out, dumped, and broken. The cabinet doors had been pulled off the frames. Splintered wood, utensils, and broken dishes were heaped on the tile.

No point looking for clean clothes. From what he could see through the open bedroom door, the contents of his closet had been shredded. He pulled his phone out of his pocket to call the police. Then he remembered there were two cops downstairs.

Shock gave way to relief that Kirra hadn't been inside the apartment when the looters had broken in.

The odor overwhelmed his nostrils. He went back outside and jogged down the stairs. The streetlight cast deep shadows over the alley.

Two forms stepped out of the darkness behind the Dumpster. Conor recognized one of them as the kid from Monday night. He scanned the alley. Of course, the cops who'd tailed him all day were nowhere in sight. Surely they'd notice when he didn't come back.

Anger simmered in Conor's belly. "Did you destroy my place?"

His answer was a whir of a revolver cylinder spinning. The metallic sound echoed between the brick buildings. "I know you got my dog."

Well, that wasn't good. One kid with a knife he'd handled. Two kids with a gun was a whole different story. The .38 in the kid's small hand looked like a cannon.

The friend stepped sideways. Conor mirrored him, keeping the wall at his back. There was no way he'd let these kids flank him.

"I'm not leaving without my property." Kid number one raised the gun, turned it on its side, and pointed the muzzle at Conor's face gangsta style.

"Really?" Conor kept one eye on the gun and the other on the buddy. Was the friend armed? His eyes adjusted to the fading light. The pair pressed closer. They sported matching tattoos on their necks, some sort of spider encircled with words in Spanish. Great. Gang tats. He'd pissed off a junior gangbanger, and the irony of all ironies had to be that this little scumbag was Conor's alibi for Zoe's disappearance.

Way. To. Go.

"I don't have your dog," Conor said.

Kirra was at Louisa's apartment, where these two scumbags wouldn't get past the lobby. Thank God. If Louisa had been here tonight, Conor had no doubt these two would have raped and killed her. The bar was noisy on Friday nights, and with the volume of the band earlier, Conor hadn't heard them busting up his furniture. Would he have heard a woman scream? Probably not.

"You're a fucking liar," the kid snapped.

Where were the cops? They should come looking for him if he was gone more than a couple of minutes.

"There are thousands of pit bulls in this city. Why don't you just go find another one?"

"It's a matter of principal. If I let one person take what's mine, word gets out." The kid's statement was 100 percent bullshit. There was something he wasn't saying. "A man has to protect what's his."

The *man* was about fifteen. Conor searched the kid's face. The eyes that stared back were cold, dark, and mean. Nope. No compassion there. This kid would kill him without remorse. He'd have no trouble pulling the trigger and watching the bullet rip through Conor's head. These two would go through Conor's pockets and use his cash to hit Popeye's on the way home for a chicken sandwich.

Sweat broke out between Conor's shoulder blades and dripped down his back. His alibi was the least of his worries. "There are better ways to make a buck. I could give you a job." But he knew the answer to his question before disgust uglied up the kid's already busted face.

"What, you want me to wash dishes or some shit?"

"It's honest work." Conor had washed plenty of dishes and worse.

"Fuck you. I ain't cleaning up nobody else's mess." The kid pulled back the hammer. The click was as loud as a firecracker and sent a wave of bowel-loosening fear ripping through Conor. His pulse jumped. The door behind him opened, and he caught a glimpse of the cops. The kid's eyes widened. He pulled the trigger. The gun bucked in his hand, the bullet ricocheting off the steel door and hitting the back of the building. Pieces of brick scattered. The cops ducked behind the door. Conor dove to the asphalt and covered his head with his arms. He heard the slap of feet running away.

The cops came out from behind the door, guns drawn. They swept the narrow space.

Still prone, Conor pointed down the alley to the exit one block over on Johnston Street. "They went that way."

The cops ran down the alley. Conor got to his feet and brushed the dirt off his jeans. He picked a few bits of gravel out of the skin on his arm.

A black-and-white pulled in. Conor's friend since high school, Officer Terry Moran, got out. "I got a report of a shooting. What the hell is going on?"

Conor's heart recovered. "Thanks, man, but you missed all the action." He gave Terry a rundown and a description of the teenagers. "Be great if you could find him. He's my alibi."

"About that." Terry leaned closer. "Let me get this description out, call a crime scene tech to go over your apartment, and talk with those two. Then we need to talk."

The plainclothes cops returned. "They're gone."

"Meet you inside." Conor went in the back door. Customers gawked and gossiped at the police activity. Conor detoured to the bar. With shaky hands he grabbed the bottle of twelve-year-old Glenfiddich. For the first time ever, he broke his own rule about not drinking while working. Having a gun pointed in the dead center of his face justified the one-time exception.

"Oh my God. Are you all right?" Jaynie hugged him.

"You're going to spill that." Ernie took the bottle from Conor's hand and poured him a short glass. "All this over a dog? It doesn't make sense."

"No. It doesn't." Conor sipped. The single malt heated his throat and cleared his sinus passages. As a side benny, it also wiped the nasty stench from his nostrils. "I have to go talk to Terry. I'll fill you in when I'm done."

Terry was waiting for him in the office. Conor closed the door. "Where are your pals?"

"Outside. I told them I'd get your statement. Since we know each other, I'll stay away from any evidence. They're calling Detective Jackson."

"Oh goody. Hold on a second then." Conor picked up his cell and called Damian, who promised to drive over. Conor set his phone down and gestured with his glass to Terry. "OK. Go."

Terry pulled out a small notebook. "Let's get your statement for tonight out of the way."

Conor slid into his dad's chair and gave him the details.

"I'll write this up and bring a report by tomorrow for you to sign." Terry closed his notebook. "I want you to look at mug shots too. Chances are these scumbags have been arrested before."

"Great." Conor took a long pull of scotch, letting the fiery liquid numb a path through his gut.

"Now about that missing girl." Terry sat forward and leaned his forearms on his thighs.

Conor leaned forward and rubbed his forehead. "You know I didn't have anything to do with the girl's disappearance."

"Damned straight, but what I know doesn't mean squat. Detective Jackson is seriously jonesing for you on this case." Terry rubbed both hands down his face. "I wish I knew why."

"Me too." Conor leaned back in the chair.

"Jackson pulled me out into the parking lot to ask me if I had any dirt on you."

"What'd you tell him?"

"What do you think I told him? That you're a serial killer?" Terry rolled his eyes. "I told him I've known you since high school, and you wouldn't do anything like that."

"And?" Conor took another small sip.

Terry's grim face wasn't promising. "They have a shitload of circumstantial evidence on you."

"I'm afraid they aren't even looking for anyone else." Conor tossed the rest of the scotch back. "I'm going to have to find this girl myself."

"You aren't without friends at the precinct," Terry said. "But this case goes beyond us."

"I know there isn't anything you can do." Nerves steadied,

Conor stood. "I need to get back to work. We're shorthanded tonight."

"Watch your back, Conor." Terry pointed at him with his pen. "I'm serious. Jackson's got a rep as a determined motherfucker. Don't get in his way."

Conor ushered his friend out of the office. "I'm not arguing, but if I don't find out who did it, I'm still the number-one suspect."

Both Damian and Jackson arrived within the next half hour. They all went out back, where Jackson viewed the damage to Conor's apartment and reviewed his statement. Standing in the alley, Conor watched a uniform with a camera jog up the steps and enter his apartment.

Jackson squinted at Conor. "Did you set this up?"

Conor leaned against the brick and crossed his arms over his chest. Following the warm trail of scotch, anger was burning a path through his chest.

"You know that isn't true," Damian said. "Mr. Sullivan has been under police surveillance 24/7 since Monday night."

Jackson frowned. "I'm not convinced. Maybe you hired someone else to do it. You're a smart guy. There are ways."

Terry was right. Jackson was one determined motherfucker.

"This is ridiculous. Conor, don't answer any more questions," Damian retorted. His phone chirped. "Excuse me." He stepped away and glanced at the screen. "Louisa?" He stilled. "What's wrong?" Concern sharpened his voice. "I'll be right there."

Conor pushed off the wall. "What?"

"There's been an accident." Damian raised a hand. "She's OK. She just needs a ride home from the ER."

"What the—?" Conor was already moving.

"Conor, she didn't call you. She called me." Damian's palm hit him square in the chest. "I'll take her home. She said it was all scrapes and bruises. You need to stay here until they're done with you." He nodded toward Conor's apartment, where a couple of cops were taking photos and detailing the damage. "I'll call you. Or better yet, come to Louisa's when you're done."

Damian and Jackson went to their cars, leaving Conor to watch over his ruined apartment and think about Louisa injured, hurt, frightened, and choosing to call Damian instead of him.

Tonight, Louisa was in an accident, and Conor's place was trashed. How could either or both of these events be tied to Zoe's disappearance?

He looked down at his cell. Zoe had been missing for nearly four entire days.

CHAPTER
19

Horns blared and tires squealed. Louisa's knees skidded on the pavement. A loud bang and crash sounded close by. Then another. She lay in the street, her face burning. The smells of burnt rubber, tar, and diesel exhaust filled her nose.

"Miss?" She blinked hard. Her vision sharpened. She rolled onto her back. A circle of faces looked down at her.

A cop knelt next to her. "Don't move. An ambulance is on the way."

But his eyes were scanning the crowd, not Louisa.

She swallowed and cleared her throat. "I don't need an ambulance."

"You took a pretty hard tumble." The cop loomed over her. "I want you to get checked out."

Another policeman cleared the crowd. "All right, everyone. Move along. Show's over. Give the lady some room to breathe."

Beyond him, the bus that nearly hit her had swerved up over the curb and hit a streetlight. In the street lane next to her, a Tastykake delivery truck had rear-ended a taxi. Both southbound lanes of Broad Street were effectively blocked.

"Was anyone else hurt?" She struggled to sit up, bringing her splayed legs into a more ladylike position. Her dress was hiked up nearly to her crotch. She tugged at her hem as dizziness whirled in her head.

"Except for your fall, I don't think so. We got lucky."

"I didn't fall."

The cop frowned.

Her head settled, and Louisa surveyed the damage. The skin of both knees was torn, bleeding, and coated with dirt. She raised her hands. Abrasions on her palms didn't match the size of those on her knees, but they were just as filthy. As if seeing the injuries prompted her brain to recognize them, the first echoes of pain pulsed through her legs and hands. Her face throbbed. She touched her chin. Her fingers came away covered in blood. All in all, her wounds appeared superficial, messy but not serious.

"I doubt anything is broken." She stirred, absorbing the humiliating stares of onlookers. "I should get up."

Her purse and cell phone had skittered across the street. The cop handed both items to her. He put a hand on her forearm. "Here comes the ambulance. Better safe than sorry."

"I suppose you're right."

An ambulance pulled up. With a surge of whole-body ache that suggested her brain hadn't yet processed all her physical damage, Louisa was transferred to a gurney and loaded into the back.

Two hours later, the ER physician confirmed her injuries were minor. Distracted and hurried, he scribbled on her chart. "The nurse will be in with discharge papers in a few minutes. Do you have a ride home?"

"I called a friend." Damian was on his way. She'd also called the hotel and asked Gerome to walk Kirra.

"Keep the abrasions clean. Ice will help any swelling. You can take ibuprofen for pain." And he was gone.

Sitting on the gurney, she ran a finger over a scratch on the silver case of her cell phone. The night didn't seem real.

"Dr. Hancock."

She startled at the familiar voice. "Yes."

Detective Jackson parted the privacy curtain.

Why was he here?

"I heard about your nosedive into Broad Street. Traffic was backed up for an hour." He took a few steps to stand next to the bed. Instead of a suit, he was dressed in jeans and a loose blue sweater that didn't quite conceal the bulge of his weapon at his hip. Was he off duty? The mocha tint of his skin didn't completely camouflage dark smudges under his eyes. Perhaps he didn't take much time off in the middle of an urgent case.

His gaze moved over her, pausing on the gauze taped to her hands, knees, and chin.

She rubbed her temple with her fingertips.

"What happened?" Jackson's voice was less hostile than it had been in the police station. Was his change of tone part of an attempt to gain her confidence, or was he sincere?

"I felt a hand push into my back, but I hoped someone knocked into me by accident. The sidewalk was very crowded."

"Maybe." Jackson shrugged. "But maybe not. There's already one museum employee dead and another missing. I think you should be more careful."

"I wasn't expecting hailing a cab to be dangerous."

Jackson changed his angle. "I know you went to talk to Heath Yeager the other day."

"I did."

"Why?"

"Because I'm afraid for Zoe." Louisa met his flat gaze. "Are you making any progress on her case?"

"Some."

Which told her nothing.

Movement on the other side of the curtain interrupted the interview.

"Louisa!" A male voice sent a wave of sickening panic through Louisa. The curtain parted again, and Blaine stepped through. "Oh my God. I saw them load you into the ambulance, but no one would tell me where they took you."

He moved closer.

Louisa recovered her voice. She'd also recovered from the shock of seeing him earlier. In fact, the impact with the street seemed to have knocked the self-pity right out of her. She was done with Blaine. She wouldn't allow him to hold any more sway over her. He'd done enough damage. "Get out, Blaine."

Resentment flickered in his eyes, and his lips compressed. "I wanted to make sure you were all right. Let me take you home. Let me take care of you."

Louisa forgot the cop standing next to her. She forgot her injuries. The hospital cubicle faded around her. Anger and turmoil steamrolled over her physical pain. "Get out."

Blaine smoothed out his irritation. "You aren't well—"

Her voice rose. "Get. Out."

"Look, buddy." Jackson showed Blaine his badge. "The lady asked you to leave."

Blaine gave the detective his best aristocratic glare. "I don't think you know who you're talking to."

"Why don't you educate me?" The detective was not intimidated. "Were you with Dr. Hancock this evening?"

"I was."

The detective pulled a notebook out of his back pocket. "Your name?"

"Blaine Delancey."

"And why were you with Dr. Hancock?"

"We were supposed to have dinner, but we had an argument. Louisa ran off. Apparently, right into traffic. She obviously needs someone to look after her."

Argument? Ambush was a better description of the evening. Jackson ignored Blaine's attitude. "You didn't see the accident?"

"No."

"Where were you when the accident occurred?"

"On the steps outside the Ritz Carlton. I was looking for Louisa."

Blaine had been coming after her? Had he pushed her? Louisa's fingers tightened around her cell phone. Why would he do that? But then why would he send her a gift? Why wouldn't he leave her alone? Why wouldn't he take no for an answer?

"You're sure you didn't see it happen?" Jackson's pen hovered over the paper as he sized up both Blaine and his answers.

"Positive." Blaine scowled at the cop.

"I'll need your contact information," Jackson said.

Blaine complied, crossing his arms over his chest and switching his attention to Louisa. She clutched her phone until her bruised fingers cramped, but she would not back down. Not this time. Moving to Philadelphia was her fresh start. She would not let Blaine ruin it for her.

The cop studied Blaine's face. "The accident investigators will be checking the traffic cams on Broad Street. If we get lucky, we might have the whole thing on video."

If Jackson was hoping that, if guilty, Blaine would flinch at this news, Louisa could have saved him the effort. Blaine was an accomplished liar.

"I'll check in with you tomorrow, Louisa." His nod at her was superior and arrogant. "Someday you'll see that we were meant to be together."

"Don't." Louisa clamped her molars together.

"I'm done with you now, Mr. Delancey, and it sounds like Dr. Hancock is also." Jackson inclined his head. "Don't let the door hit you in the ass on the way out."

Blaine gave her an *it's not over* look as he exited.

"Your friend's an asshole," Jackson said.

"He's not my friend."

"Yeah. I got that. You want to tell me about the argument?"

"No." Louisa's stomach turned at the thought of sharing her conflict with Blaine. "It's old news." But Blaine's visit wasn't. Why tonight? And what did he really want? Come to think of it, what did Aunt Margaret really want? The stunt with Blaine didn't make sense. It had to be about money, but Louisa couldn't see the angle.

Jackson stared, clearly not buying Louisa's story.

She sighed. "When you have a lot of money, there are always people trying to get some of it."

Her jaw ached from its impact with the pavement, and from the thoughts and suspicions turning in her mind. She wanted to go home, get into bed, and pull the covers over her head.

Jackson shoved the notebook and pen back in his pocket. "Do you have a ride home?"

The question surprised her. Was he offering assistance? "I called a friend."

"Sweetie, what have you done to yourself?" Damian's arrival ended the interview. He frowned at the cop. "How did you get here so fast?"

Jackson didn't blink. "I can double-park."

Louisa looked from Jackson to Damian. "Did I miss something?"

"Have you talked to Sullivan tonight?" Jackson asked.

"No. Why?" She swung her feet over the edge of the gurney. *Ouch.* "Is there something wrong?"

"He had some trouble tonight too." Jackson watched her face. She was likely more transparent than Blaine.

"What happened?" Louisa's gaze swung from Jackson, who wouldn't give anything away, to Damian.

Her friend shrugged. "You'll have to ask Conor."

With a nod, Detective Jackson moved toward the door. "Be careful, Doctor. No more playing detective. You had a close call tonight. Next time, you might not be so lucky."

CHAPTER
20

Conor paced the alley. The police were finishing up in his apartment. Damian had said Louisa was all right, but Conor wanted to see her with his own eyes.

Terry pulled up in his cruiser. Conor hadn't seen him since the break-in a few hours ago. The cop was still in uniform, and his face was all business.

Conor walked over to the police car. "What's going on?" He gave Terry's partner riding shotgun a hello nod.

Terry lowered the window and handed Conor a picture. "Is this the kid who broke into your apartment?"

Conor looked down at a mug shot. "Yeah. That's him."

"His name is Hector Torres." Terry tucked the photo back into the chest pocket of his uniform.

"Who is he?"

"A little piece of garbage, but a dangerous one." Terry tapped a finger on the wheel. "He's been in and out of juvenile detention a few times, mostly petty shit. But the word on the street is that Hector's running with the Big K. That's how we found him, from your description of the tattoo on his neck."

"Damn, that's not good." Conor rubbed his scalp. The Big K was a gang that claimed a hunk of North Kensington as its territory.

"No. It's definitely not good." Terry shifted his weight. "The Big K is bad news."

"All gangs are bad news. What's the kid doing down here? This isn't North Kensington."

Terry shook his head. "I don't know."

"This can't be over a dog."

"It doesn't make any sense. We're trying to find Hector, but you better be extra careful, Conor," Terry said. "You should be glad you have cops watching you."

"Thanks." He stepped back from the car. The idea of the bar—and Conor's family—making any gang's radar sent terror skittering across his skin.

The two cops came out of his apartment. "We're done," the one holding the camera said. "You're going to want to call a professional cleaner."

"Thanks." Conor went back inside the bar and scanned the room for his sister. The kitchen was closed this late. Behind the bar, Jayne was popping the top off a couple of bottles of beer.

"No word from Reed?"

She shook her head. "Not since dinnertime. Scott is still in ICU."

"I'm sorry, honey. I haven't been there for you this week, and now I have to leave again." He explained about Louisa. "I called Pat. He's on his way over. He'll help you close up."

She put her hands on her hips. "I don't need Pat to close the bar."

"I know," he said. It might tweak Jayne's pride, but there was no way he was letting pregnant Jayne and old Ernie handle any potential rowdies.

Jayne heaved an exasperated sigh. "You and Pat are overprotective, but I guess you're too old to change your ways. Now go see Louisa." Jayne turned Conor around and pushed him toward the door. "Call me or text me. Let me know what's going on."

"You let me know if you hear from Reed."

"'Kay. Love you," Jayne called after him.

Philadelphia nightlife ended early. The drive took ten minutes. Why did Louisa choose to call Damian over him?

He parked in the garage at the Rittenhouse and gave his name at the desk in the lobby.

"Go on up," the doorman said.

Two minutes later, Conor knocked softly on her door. It opened. Damian and Kirra greeted him in the foyer.

Damian waved Conor inside.

"I'm glad you're here." The lawyer grabbed his keys from the counter. "I was just on my way out, and I really didn't want to leave her alone."

"How is she?" Conor stooped to pet the dog. She wagged her tail and then bolted for the master bedroom. The door was ajar, and the dog slipped through the opening. Conor could hear the sound of water running.

"Physically, just a little banged up, but it shook her." Damian snatched his suit jacket from the back of a stool. "She's changing her clothes. I don't think she had dinner. She could probably use something to eat."

"What the hell happened?"

"I'm sorry, Conor. I have a teenager in big trouble waiting for me." Folding his jacket over his arm, Damian headed for the door. "Louisa will have to fill you in on the details. I'll call you tomorrow."

Conor paced the kitchen. The rushing water sound ceased. He froze, the breath tightening in his lungs as the door opened.

"Damian, I can't get this zipper." Louisa stopped short. The dog sat next to her feet and looked up at her. "Conor."

She stood barefoot in the entry to the kitchen. His gaze snapped to the bruise on her chin and the stark white bandages on her hands and knees. Her hair tumbled down her back in a wild blond tangle. The slim black dress left her arms bare. Her face was pale, her eyes exhausted, and her dress torn.

He wanted to rush to her, to fold her in his arms, but he couldn't. She hadn't called for him, and that fact stung even as relief at seeing her whole and minimally injured swept through him.

"What are you doing here?" she asked.

He stuffed his hands in his front pockets. "I was with Damian when you called him. What happened?"

"While I was waiting for a cab, someone shoved or bumped me in front of a bus."

"Which one was it?"

"I don't know." Louisa didn't move forward either. "The sidewalk was crowded. Detective Jackson showed up at the hospital. He said he'd look into it."

"But you're all right?"

"Yes." Her throat moved as she swallowed. She winced and reflexively touched her swollen jaw.

"Let me get you some ice for that."

She exhaled as if she'd made a decision. Then she limped closer and turned around. "Would you unzip me?" She lifted her hair over her head with both hands.

Being careful to not pinch her skin, Conor drew the zipper down slowly from her neck to the small of her back. Inch by inch, the fabric parted, revealing the straps of her bra and a whole lot of soft skin. His hands itched with the need to strip the dress from her body and check every inch of her skin for injury. He lowered his head and kissed the back of her neck. The dimples at the base of her spine tempted him to press his lips there, but he resisted. "I wish you'd have called me."

She leaned against him and dropped her hair. Her body deflated with a slow exhalation of breath and tension.

"Me too," she whispered.

Enjoying the weight of her body, he rested his temple against the side of her head. His hands stroked up her arms. "Why did you call Damian instead of me?"

"Less risk."

"I don't understand."

"Damian is just a friend."

"So what am I?"

"More." She turned around. Her eyes misted. Behind the unshed tears, conflict lurked. "What I feel for you scares me. I'm not sure I can give you what you want. What you need. What you deserve. I just might not have it in me."

"Don't shut me out. Talk to me." Conor wiped the pad of his thumb under her eye, catching a tear before it rolled down her cheek. "Don't be afraid to tell me anything."

Doubt and fear flickered in her eyes.

"I mean it."

"I know you do." She stared at the center of his chest for a minute, her blond lashes concealing any change in her emotions. "I'll try, but it's not going to happen overnight. I'm used to being alone." Her voice was hoarse, as if her words were sandpaper in her throat.

Conor took the admission as progress—and accepted it as enough for one night.

"OK. Baby steps then." He grinned. "Do you need help getting the rest of your clothes off? Please say yes."

The corner of her mouth tilted upward. "I think I can manage."

"Too bad." He let out a long-suffering sigh. Her eyes didn't look so bleak. "What can I do for you?"

"I could use some ibuprofen and ice."

"Have you eaten?"

She hesitated, her eyelids dropping like shutters. "No."

"Do you want to tell me what happened to dinner?"

"Not right now."

"OK. Later then, but you're not getting out of talking to me." He kissed her forehead. "Why don't you change, and I'll see what I can rustle up in your kitchen."

She backed away. "There's not much in there."

"I like a challenge."

Kirra followed Louisa into the bedroom. Conor went into the kitchen, which was mostly empty. He sniffed a quart of skim milk. Sour. He emptied it in the sink and tossed the carton in the trash. Two containers of moldy Chinese takeout followed. He set cheese and bread on the counter and rooted through the cabinets until he found a frying pan. A few minutes later, butter sizzled around a grilled cheese sandwich, and the kitchen filled with the scent. In the pantry, he found a can of tomato soup.

He put the soup and sandwich out on the island. With the dog trailing behind, Louisa returned in a baggy sweatshirt, yoga pants, and thick socks. She eased onto a stool. Conor watched, pleased, as she ate half the sandwich. Chewing looked painful, and she moved on to the soup. She consumed most of it before she pushed the bowl aside.

He handed her two tablets and a glass of water. "You should get into bed."

"Good idea." She took the ice pack he offered next.

Conor and Kirra followed her into the bedroom. A king-size platform bed took center stage. Folding back the ice-blue comforter, she climbed between the hotel-white sheets with a low groan and settled the ice pack on her jaw. Kirra jumped onto the bed and curled up with her head on Louisa's hip. "She hasn't left my side since I got home."

"Dogs know."

"Know what?"

"They know when something's wrong."

"I've never had a pet." She stroked the dog's head. "It's nice."

"So I guess you're still considering keeping her?"

"I couldn't do that. She's your dog."

"Doesn't look that way from where I'm standing," Conor said as Kirra closed her eyes and heaved a contented sigh. "Besides, she's not safe in my apartment."

Louisa sat up, wincing. "Jackson said he was with you tonight. What happened?"

"Someone broke in tonight and busted up the place."

The ice pack dropped from her face. "That's terrible! You think it's Kirra's former owner?"

"I'm sure. He was waiting for me." Conor didn't mention the gun. She had enough to worry about.

Her eyes scraped over him. "But you're all right?"

"I'm fine." He touched her hand. "But I'd feel better if Kirra stayed with you."

"If you're sure, then I'd be happy to keep her." Louisa's smile was lopsided, but her pleasure shone through her eyes.

Conor's chest swelled at her pleasure. "Do you mind if I sit in here with you for a while?"

"I guess not." But Louisa's eyes narrowed in suspicion when he stretched on top of the covers next to her.

He ignored her look and puffed the giant pillows behind his back. A flat-screen hung on the wall opposite the bed. "Want to watch a movie?"

"Sure." She handed him a remote control. "You pick. I don't watch much TV."

Looking for something relaxing, Conor flipped through the

channels until he found an old movie network showing *Bringing Up Baby*. He tossed the remote on the bed next to him. "How's this?"

"I love Cary Grant." Louisa snuggled deeper into the pillows.

"Me too. My parents used to watch his old black-and-whites when I was a kid." Conor remembered crawling into bed with them on Saturday mornings.

"Were they happy?"

"Very. I never doubted they loved each other. That's what I always thought I'd have someday." Conor glanced over. The soft light of the television played on her delicate features, spurring an ache deep in his chest. "What was it like before your mother died? Were your parents happy?"

"I think so." She sniffed. "He's never gotten over her death. After she died, he started drinking and spending most of his time in Europe."

"Did he ever take you with him?"

"Once in a while. Most of the time he left me with his sister."

"The one you saw tonight?" Suspicion bloomed in Conor's chest. Louisa's aunt had upset her tonight.

"Yes." Her voice faltered.

Wanting a connection with her, Conor reached across the comforter and put his hand over hers, careful not to touch her bandaged palm. "Want to tell me what happened?"

"Tomorrow." She pulled the covers up to her neck. "Tell me about your brothers and sister."

"Jayne and Danny were a handful, that's for sure." He told her about some of the trouble they got into, including the time they stole a car. He talked until her eyes closed and her breaths evened out.

Conor, used to being awake until the early hours, waited fifteen minutes before he gently lifted the ice pack from her face and returned it to the freezer. He eased back onto the bed and adjusted the pillow behind his head.

Louisa sighed. Still asleep, she rolled toward him. Her temple settled against his shoulder, the intimacy of the weight of her head on his body spurring an urge to gather her closer, but he didn't want to disturb her. How would she react when she found him in her bed tomorrow morning?

Didn't matter.

No matter how secure her building, there was no way he was leaving her alone. Not after she could have been killed. Conor rested his temple against her hair and breathed in the scent of her shampoo. He was staying right here, all night.

CHAPTER
21

Why hadn't she drawn the shades? Sunlight burned Louisa's eyeballs right through her closed lids. She tried to go back to sleep, but pain pulsed through her face. The ibuprofen had worn off. Her knees protested with stiffness and fire as she rolled away from the glare, opened her eyes, and stared at a man's rib cage.

She jolted. *Ow.* Straightening her leg, she eased her left knee into a more comfortable position. Then she turned her attention back to the half-naked man in her bed.

Next to her, Conor reclined on two pillows. He was still dressed in his jeans, but he'd removed his shirt and shoes during the night. His eyes were closed, and his jaw was shadowed, as usual. Her gaze drifted down. After all, she knew what his face looked like, but she'd never seen him without a shirt. *Oh my.* The arm flung over his head stretched his torso taut. His body was all about understated power. A scattering of dark hair swirled across his pectorals. Firm muscle expanded his broad chest and shoulders and defined a lean abdomen. She swallowed, the sight of his body stirring a primal need inside her. Her eyes followed the line of dark hair that swirled into the waistband of his jeans and led to—

"Good morning." His throaty voice startled her.

Her cheeks heated. She blinked away from admiring his flat belly, and then some. "I'm sorry. I was staring."

"Yes. Men hate it when women ogle their muscles." Conor rolled his eyes. "Do you want me to put my shirt back on?"

How could she answer that question? "It's not necessary."

The turquoise in his eyes brightened with roguishness. "Necessary isn't a factor. What do you *want*?" He dropped his voice to a husky whisper.

Oh Lord. Warmth flushed her torso. She pushed the covers back. *Was the heat on?*

"If you took off your shirt, then we'd be even," he teased.

"Doesn't the dog need to be fed or walked or something?"

He rolled on his side to face her. "Kirra was fed and walked at seven."

At the sound of her name, Kirra, lounging at the foot of the bed, raised her head and wagged the stump of her tail.

Touched by his thoughtfulness, she said, "Thank you. Did she eat?"

"Not much. I'll give her until Monday to start eating, then it's back to the vet."

He was studying her face. *Oh my God.* Her face. She raised a hand to her jaw. The skin was puffy under her fingers. She could only imagine . . .

He took her hand and kissed her knuckles. "You look beautiful."

"How do you always know what I'm thinking?"

"I have a sister, remember? That bruise looks like it hurts. I'll get you some ice." Muscles rippled as he sat up.

She tried not to stare, without success.

"Kirra and I bought breakfast while we were walking. Let me bring you food so you can take an aspirin." He moved to the edge of the bed, stretched, and stood. Glancing back, he caught her staring again. "I'll leave the shirt off." He left the room grinning—and still half-naked, giving Louisa an eyeful of hard and powerful back that made parts of her sing through the soreness of her bruises.

She fell back on the pillows. He wasn't the first man she'd seen without a shirt, but none had affected her this way. The hardness of his body concealed kindness that made her heart do a triple-espresso flutter. But she had to admit, though it felt superficial, she wouldn't complain about the hot body attached to his generous soul.

If she wasn't hurt . . .

What? She'd have him instead of her breakfast?

Why not? Clearly, he was interested. Neither of them was attached. Though she hadn't had a relationship for some time, she enjoyed sex. Sex had never been her issue. It was the emotional expectation generated by physical intimacy that had always been her problem. Typically, she was one who preferred to keep sex and her relationships casual. But eventually, most men wanted to see a relationship progress. They wanted marriage and children and all the associated connections that Louisa was unable to make.

Something warned her that sex with Conor would be more intense than any she'd experienced in the past. Could she handle it? Or would he end up joining her short list of failures? Even worse, was she ready to risk hurting both of them?

On that depressing note, she pushed to a sitting position. Her limbs were achy and stiff. Pain throbbed through her jaw, but she felt better than she'd expected. Today was Saturday. No work. She could stay in bed all day . . .

Saturday.

Oh no.

"What's wrong?" Conor walked back into the bedroom carrying two cups of coffee and a white bakery bag.

"The museum fund-raiser is tonight." She pressed a bandaged palm to her forehead.

"I think they'll expect you to cancel." He set the coffee on her nightstand.

Louisa swung her legs over the side of the bed. "We have a lot riding on tonight."

"Take it slow." He took her hand as she got to her feet, his grip solid and steadying as the floor pitched beneath her feet like a cruise ship in high seas. His gaze assessed her, doubtful and worried. "Dizzy?"

"Not at all," Louisa lied as she limped toward the bathroom, her equilibrium steadying. She switched on the light and looked in the mirror. *Ugh.* Her jaw was puffy, and a bruise extended from her chin nearly to her ear. She was lucky she hadn't knocked out any teeth.

Her palms weren't so bad, and her black-and-blue, scabbed-up knees could easily be covered with slacks. But her face . . . Major concealer work to be done there.

"Considering you took a swan dive into pavement last night, you look pretty good." Conor leaned on the doorframe. "Why don't you just call your boss and explain? I'm sure he'd understand."

"The museum is largely dependent on donations." She brushed her teeth. "This is the first big fund-raiser since I started. The opening of the new *Celtic Warrior* exhibit is the biggest event this autumn. I have to be there to talk about my qualifications and the new exhibit. Patrons want to see where their money is being spent." Plus, she didn't trust her boss. What would he say in her absence?

Conor shook his head. "So you still intend to go?"

"I don't have a choice." She shooed him out of the bathroom and closed the door to use the toilet. When she emerged, he was lounging on the bed drinking coffee, as relaxed as if he spent every morning in her bedroom. "I don't want to lose this job."

Conor looked around the apartment. "Do you really *need* it?"

"I don't need the job in the financial sense, no. But I love what I do." Losing another job would no doubt disappoint her father again. What would he think if Louisa didn't work? If she just managed her trust fund and spent her time organizing charity events? Could she even do that? Her entire life had been focused on this career. It was a major part of her identity. The thought of leaving it behind was disconcerting.

Louisa pointed at her chin. "Do you think I can get this swelling down at all before tonight?"

"Maybe. Keep your head elevated and be diligent with the ice pack."

"That'll help?"

"It should. Back in my boxing days, I used to pack my face in ice after every fight. It wasn't pretty." He reached for his shirt.

Too bad. "I saw the picture the media released. It looked painful." Though even battered, he'd been attractive in a virile, primal way. "And they tied in the fight you had with Kirra's owner with your altercation with Heath. They succeeded in making you seem violent."

"Which is exactly what Damian said they would do." He grimaced. "I have to run by Jayne's house and pick up the laundry I left there. Everything in my apartment was ruined. Are you all right here by yourself?"

"I'm fine."

"OK then. I'll bring lunch back with me. Anything special you want?"

Louisa moved her aching jaw. "Something soft."

"I'll be quick." Conor kissed her gently on the uninjured side of her face before leaving.

Louisa put an ice pack on her face for twenty minutes, then grabbed her laptop and brought it back to bed. Turning it on, she propped a pillow against the headboard. Kirra jumped onto the duvet and stretched out next to Louisa.

She skimmed through her e-mails. Twenty messages into her inbox, she spotted a message from her father, the subject line: "Itinerary." She clicked on it and copied the details of his upcoming holiday visit to her calendar. Nerves rattled in her belly. What was he going to tell her? She glanced at the clock. Nine a.m., three p.m. in Stockholm. It was time for their weekly phone call. Ward Hancock kept a strict routine. Saturday afternoons were spent in his study, working. If she was lucky, and she phoned early, she'd catch him still relatively sober.

She wasn't the luckiest soul in the world.

She picked up her cell and speed-dialed his number, her stomach knotting as the line rang again and again. Where was he? She left a message and set her phone aside.

"Something's wrong, Kirra."

The dog rolled closer and flipped Louisa's hand with her nose. Louisa settled a hand on the dog's head. "Something is definitely wrong."

———

The phone rang as Conor emerged from the shower in Louisa's guest room. After toweling himself off, he pulled jeans from the duffel bag on the dresser. The basket of laundry he'd retrieved from Jayne's house was all the clothes he had left. Almost everything else Conor owned was destroyed. He sat down on the edge of the bed and caught his breath. Renter's insurance would cover most of the damage, and he didn't have many personal possessions that couldn't be replaced, except the photographs the scumbags had piled up and pissed on.

He'd hired professional cleaners to strip the place bare. Then what? Would these kids ever leave him alone? Why the hell were they so determined to have Kirra? The streets were teeming with pit bulls, and Kirra wasn't much of a fighter. Why did they want her back so badly?

And how could his life have gone to complete crap in the course of a week?

He'd been questioned for murder, attacked with a knife *and* a gun, and his apartment had been ransacked.

Someone knocked on the bedroom door.

"Conor?" Louisa called.

He stepped into the jeans, walked into the bedroom, and opened the door. Her eyes blinked on his bare chest.

Conor grinned. Not everything about his week had been bad. "Can I help you?"

The pretty green of her eyes sobered. "The police are on their way up."

"Be out in a minute." He went back into the bathroom, tugged on the T-shirt, and brushed his teeth. He didn't want Louisa to have to face the two cops alone. Jackson and Ianelli were walking into the foyer when Conor emerged. Louisa led them into the living room. The detectives eased onto the overstuffed couch.

"Coffee?" Louisa asked.

"No, thanks." Jackson pulled his notebook from his pocket. "You might want to sit down."

She chose an overstuffed club chair on the other side of the coffee table. Conor perched on the arm.

Jackson leaned forward, resting his elbows on his knees. "Just a short while ago, the body of a young woman was found in an abandoned building in North Kensington. The cause of death and disposal were similar to Riki LaSanta's murder." He took a breath. "If you turn on the TV, I'm sure you'll see the story. The news crews were at the scene when we left."

Louisa sagged. "Is it Zoe?" Her voice was barely a whisper.

Conor put an arm around her shoulders. Her body was stiff, unyielding, prepared for the blow.

"We can't confirm the body's identification at this time." The detective clenched and unclenched his hand on his knee.

Louisa let out a breath. Her frame trembled. "But?"

Jackson broke eye contact. He examined his fist for a few seconds before meeting Louisa's gaze. "Her identity hasn't been determined by the medical examiner."

"But you're here," Conor said. "So you think the remains might be Zoe." In fact, if the cops had a body, why weren't they slapping cuffs on him?

Jackson deadpanned. "We have reasons to consider Zoe as a possible identity of the dead woman."

"So it *might* be Zoe." Louisa interlocked her fingers on her lap. Her knuckles blanched. "You're not sure it's her."

"No. Not yet," Jackson said.

"So there's hope." Louisa took a shaky breath.

Jackson didn't respond. His lips thinned to a bloodless line. Conor's heart squeezed. Louisa didn't want to believe Zoe was dead, but Detective Jackson was convinced. Otherwise, why were the cops here?

"Was she burned?" Louisa's tone matched Jackson's with its lack of inflection.

The cops exchanged a glance.

Jackson nodded. "Yes, she was burned. Dr. Hancock, where were you on Wednesday evening between six p.m. and midnight?"

Louisa recoiled as if his words had struck her. Conor squeezed her shoulders. All this time, they'd been hoping Zoe would be found alive, but the poor girl had been lying in an abandoned basement, murdered. "That's when she was killed?"

Jackson leaned forward. "Where were you, Dr. Hancock?"

"I was here." Louisa's face drained of color, her pallor adding contrast to the darkening bruise on her jaw.

Jackson pulled out his notebook and wrote something down. "Can the doorman verify that?"

"Yes." Louisa's hand twisted in her lap.

Jackson looked at Conor.

"Hey, you know I was at the bar." He raised his palms. "You had a cop watching me all night." He stiffened. "Does this mean I'm no longer a suspect?"

"No," Jackson said. "We don't even have an official ID on the body. Until we do, you are on my short list."

But if the body was Zoe, Conor couldn't have killed her. It was hard to do better than two cops for an alibi. "So you have other suspects?"

Jackson ignored his question.

"Can you think of anyone who would want both of these girls dead?" Jackson asked.

"Why would anyone want to kill two young women? It's sick. It's crazy." Two bright spots of pink flushed on Louisa's cheeks, and her voice rose with an edge of hysteria. Conor rubbed her arm.

"But the stolen knife suggests the association is with the museum." Ianelli tilted his head. "Has anyone been acting strangely this week?"

"No." She stared down at her clasped hands. "Was this woman killed with the same knife as Riki?"

"That will be up to the medical examiner to decide," Jackson said. "What would you expect to see in an ancient Celtic ritual murder?"

Louisa leaned back and breathed through her nose as if she was nauseous. "Sometimes the Celts killed a victim with multiple methods to appease more than one god. They would likely have made offerings with the sacrifice. There might be symbols to indicate which gods were being targeted."

Unable to sit still any longer, Conor got to his feet and paced. He dragged a hand through his hair. He turned to Louisa. She was too quiet, too still. Her face and body were frozen. Even her eyes looked empty. But he'd spent enough time with her now to understand that her ice-queen facade meant the opposite of her appearance. Her emotions were escalating faster than she could process.

Jackson stood. "If you think of anything else, please give us a call," he said to Louisa.

She gave him an almost imperceptible nod.

Ianelli turned to Conor. "You're not off the hook yet, Sullivan."

Jackson tucked his notebook into his pocket. "By the way, the DNA report just came back positive on Riki LaSanta. The results will be made public today."

Louisa flinched.

Conor showed the detectives out. He closed the door. Silence blanketed the air like August humidity. He returned to Louisa and knelt down in front of her.

"I won't believe Zoe is dead." Louisa's bruised chin lifted. "The police don't even have confirmation that the body is hers, and they've stopped searching for her."

"They didn't say they'd stopped looking." Conor moved to the chair and wrapped an arm around her.

She leaned into him. "They have, because they think Zoe is dead."

CHAPTER
22

Through the glass facade of the museum's entrance, Louisa scanned the street and sidewalk. Vehicle and pedestrian traffic flowed with the usual rhythm. A taxi pulled up to the curb. A couple in cocktail attire climbed out, walked into the museum, and passed through the metal detector. Cool, damp air followed them, sweeping through the atrium lobby and ruffling the hem of the woman's black A-line dress. On the black-and-white tiled floor, well-dressed people congregated. Conversations echoed on metal, glass, and marble. A waiter circled, extending a tray loaded with glasses of champagne to any guest with an empty hand. In small groups, patrons drifted toward the arch that led to the exhibit rooms. Everything appeared normal.

But it wasn't.

Could Riki's killer be part of this group mingling in the lobby right now? Holding a flute of champagne and smiling, making polite conversation about the exhibits, leaning close and gossiping about the murdered girl in hushed whispers?

"Welcome." Louisa greeted the newly arrived couple with a smile and nod, then checked their names off her guest list. The pen and clipboard in her hands saved her from handshakes. She'd worn a white silk poet blouse with a ruffled cuff that extended over her palms. Black dress slacks covered her bandaged knees, and Ferragamo ballet flats were a concession to her overall soreness. Concealer dimmed the bruise on her jaw. The overall effect was acceptable but more casual than she would have preferred for such an event.

On her right, April plucked two name tags from the small table and handed them to the couple.

April leaned close and turned her face away from the crowd. "Are you sure you don't want me to get you a chair?"

"I'm sure." Louisa shifted her weight to ease her aching knees. "Now that the initial crush seems to be over, I should move inside anyway."

"Go ahead." April took the clipboard. "I got this."

Louisa followed the plaintive sound of a string quartet to the wide central corridor. Tuxedo-clad waitstaff circled, offering guests glasses of champagne and hors d'oeuvres. Curators and other museum staff mingled with the guests, encouraging conversation and answering questions. Louisa spotted a few university professors and board members, some of whom overlapped. Interns and some borrowed university students manned the long tables that displayed auction items on either side of the space. Louisa saw Isa selling raffle tickets. Technically, the museum wasn't attached to the school, but the relationship was incestuous.

A dozen guests lined up at the bar in the corner. Louisa's eyes roamed and nearly bugged out of their sockets when she spotted a clean-shaven, devastatingly handsome Conor mixing drinks behind the bar.

Oh. My. God.

What was he doing here? A fresh haircut sharpened his angular features. His broad shoulders filled out a classic black tuxedo that looked more than a cut above the rest of the waitstaff's attire. Louisa took a deep breath. No one appeared to be giving him undue attention, except for the admiring second glances from female guests. As Xavier had pointed out Wednesday evening, the image of Conor circulated by the media wasn't an accurate representation.

He caught her staring and pointedly looked away.

Right. She could hardly talk to him here. Louisa smoothed her features and walked in the opposite direction.

She crossed the gleaming tile floor and went through a wide arch into the *Celtic Warrior* exhibit room. Three long glass cases sparkled in the center of the space. The middle display was filled with ancient and brittle-looking weapons: spears, swords, and knives. The remaining cases were still empty. On the three long walls behind the cases, murals of life-size warriors engaged in battle depicted their original use in vivid color. The murals and cases were sectioned off with velvet theater roping to protect them from possible spills at tonight's gathering. Normally, the prohibition on food and drink was strictly enforced.

Patrons wandered in, drinks in hand, and Louisa answered their questions.

She leaned over a row of Iron Age swords. Above the rusted weapons, a new and shiny sword gleamed in the spotlight.

"Is that one of the replicas?" a familiar male voice asked.

Louisa turned. Xavier walked toward her.

"It's stunning. And looks lethal." The professor set his empty champagne glass on a nearby tray and stopped just a little too close to her. His slurred speech and pirate-eye told her he'd already had too much to drink.

"If it were sharp, it would be. The artisan tried to mimic the original process as closely as possible." Louisa resisted the urge to check on Conor. Other than Damian and Louisa, Xavier was the only other person at the fund-raiser who'd met Conor in person. Would Xavier give him away? Thankfully, it appeared he was drinking champagne rather than mixed drinks. She doubted Xavier would want to admit any association with Conor, but she didn't want to test that theory and hoped Xavier wouldn't make a trip to the bar, not in this unstable, unpredictable condition.

"The police came to my office today," Xavier said. "Did you know they found a body? They won't speculate, of course, but I know they think it's Zoe."

"Yes. I know about the body." Sadness coated Louisa's throat.

He leaned closer to the display case. "Which one was the model for the stolen replica?"

"I didn't put it out." His callous question reminded her that someone at this event could be a killer. But who? The girl had been killed Wednesday evening. Where had Xavier gone after he'd stopped at the café to speak with her and Conor? Was Xavier on the list of suspects?

"Tactful as always." Xavier's tone dripped with uncharacteristic resentment. He signaled a circling server and plucked a full flute of champagne from the tray. "I heard about your accident."

"It was unfortunate, but as you can see, I'm fine."

"Your beautiful face." He reached out and touched her chin.

So much for the expensive color-correcting concealer the saleswoman at the cosmetics counter had sold her.

"It looks worse than it is." Louisa removed his hand with a deliberate motion. She took a slight step back, reclaiming her personal boundary.

Xavier's eyes narrowed to piggish slits.

"Look, there's Damian." Louisa waved at the lawyer, who was chatting up an elegant white-haired woman draped with diamonds and gold.

"I really should say hello." Louisa smiled. "Excuse me, Xavier."

She escaped before the professor could utter another word.

"Louisa!" Damian greeted Louisa with a gentle peck on the cheek of the uninjured side of her face. "How do you feel?"

"I'm fine, considering."

"Yes, you could have been flattened." Damian touched her forearm. He leaned close to her ear and whispered through gritted teeth. "What is you-know-who doing manning the bar?"

Louisa's cover smile was tense enough to make her chin throb. "I have no idea."

"We need to talk after the auction." Damian flagged down a waiter and plucked a glass of champagne from a tray.

"Definitely."

Damian looked over her shoulder. "Here comes your boss. Poker up."

"Damian." Dr. Cusack nodded politely at Damian before turning to Louisa. "I need to borrow Dr. Hancock."

"Of course." Louisa smiled at Damian. "I'll talk to you later."

"How are you?" Cusack asked as he steered her away.

"I'm fine."

"Then there are several important guests I'd like you to meet." Cusack leaned closer and lowered his voice. "But there will be no discussion of death, and if you want to keep this job, you'll stop questioning people."

Louisa stopped. "I won't stop looking for Zoe."

"I mean it, Louisa. I'll fire you if I have to. This matter is police business, and I wouldn't want to see you hurt again," he said in a *discussion over* tone. He steered her through the crowd, introducing her to VIPs.

An elderly woman rapped her cane on the tile next to the exhibit case. "Have you gotten those murders straightened out yet?"

Louisa bobbled.

"The police have the situation in hand." Cusack's smooth voice steadied her. "Have you met our newest assistant curator, Dr. Louisa Hancock?"

"What a lovely brooch." Louisa bent her head to examine a cameo pinned to the woman's jacket. "Is it an antique?"

For the next two hours, Louisa deflected gossip about the murders, talked about the new exhibit, and charmed museum patrons while the throbbing in her knees grew to a crescendo. The auction topped off the night's agenda. The evening had been a success, in spite of the negative publicity hovering around the museum, or maybe because of it. Louisa overheard too many fascinated whispers speculating about the murders. She surveyed the thinning crowd. Her gaze settled on Xavier. He was Zoe's mentor, and Riki had been one of his students. He'd shown her a different, unflattering side of his personality tonight. Where had he been during the murder?

—

Conor mixed drinks and watched Louisa work the crowd. A few hours into the event, the line at the bar dissipated.

Damian approached. "Club soda." He glanced around. No one was close by.

Conor flipped a glass and scooped ice.

"How did you get in here?" Damian asked in a low tone.

"I blackmailed the caterer." Conor twisted the cap off the soda bottle. "If you don't want people to know you're messing around on your wife, don't take your mistress to bars."

"I'll keep that in mind," Damian said. "But seriously, what made you think this was a good idea?"

Conor squeezed a lime wedge into the drink and placed it on a cocktail napkin. "Because Louisa was coming, and one of these people could be a killer."

"What will the cops think of you butting into the fund-raiser?"

"I don't know. We could ask the one who followed me over here. He's probably parked outside."

Damian shot him a *bad idea* glare. "We need to talk after this. Louisa's place."

"You and Louisa are close?" Conor forced the words out of lips tight enough to crack.

Damian's eyes sparked. "Oh my God. You're jealous." He covered his laughing mouth with his fist.

"Why is that so hilarious?" Conor grimaced.

Damian spun around and scanned the crowd. He raised a finger in the air, motioning to a tall, blond man. "Mark?" Damian turned back to Conor.

The blond extricated himself from a conversation with three well-jeweled elderly women and walked over. He gave Conor a critical once-over and raised an approving eyebrow at Damian. "You called?"

Damian gestured. "My *partner*, Mark, will have a Johnny Walker on the rocks."

"And I'm not his law partner." Mark smiled.

Cheered, Conor poured whiskey over ice. "Nice to meet you."

"You too." Taking the drink, Mark gave Damian a nod. "If you'll excuse me, I'll just go back to charming those very wealthy widows into making fat donations."

"You didn't know I was gay?" Damian asked after Mark returned to his conversation.

"I've never felt so clueless in my life."

"You've been preoccupied." Damian handed over his empty glass for a refill. "Does it bother you?"

Conor laughed. "Damian, you have no idea how happy I am that you're gay."

"I didn't realize you thought there was something going on

between me and Louisa. She's just a friend. A good friend. So if you hurt her, I'll let you rot in jail."

"Noted." Conor nodded.

Damian took his refill and wandered off. Guests drifted toward the lobby. The room emptied out. At a signal from the caterer, Conor started breaking down the bar. He was hoisting a case of glassware onto a rolling cart when he spotted Louisa out of the corner of his eye. She was heading down a corridor. Alone.

He put the box on the cart, glanced around, and set off after her. He caught up with her easily. Her pace was slow and deliberate, as if she was masking pain. "Where are you going?"

"I locked my purse in my office." She turned and stopped him with a raised hand. "You can't come back here."

"Well I don't want you to go back there by yourself."

"It's my office." She propped a hand on her hip.

Conor crossed his arms over his chest. "It's dark and empty." Impasse.

Louisa *humphed*. "Fine. I'll get April to come with me. Go back to your *job* before someone sees you back here."

An angry whisper from around the corner stopped them. "I'm warning you."

Conor held a finger to his lips and pushed Louisa behind him. He peered around the corner. Halfway down the corridor, a door was ajar. He motioned for Louisa to look.

She stuck her head into the hall and pulled it back. "Copy room," she whispered.

Conor motioned her to stay put. He crept to the open door and listened.

"I'm done with you."

The slurred male voice sounded familiar. Conor pulled out his cell phone and turned it over. He used the silver back of the case as a mirror, angling it to see inside the doorway. Two figures faced each other in front of an industrial copier. Both presented profiles to Conor. Xavier English and Isa Dumont.

Xavier was swaying on his feet.

Isa stood a few feet away from him, her arms akimbo, her attitude petulant. "Is that a threat?"

"Yes," Xavier spat. "We're through."

"How much do you want to keep your job?"

Xavier's face darkened to impending-stroke red. "You're a bitch."

"Yes, but I'm the bitch in charge." Isa sneered.

"You took advantage of me."

"*I* took advantage of *you*?" She pointed at his chest. Fury radiated from her eyes, her anger hot enough to scorch the reams of paper stacked on shelves behind them. "How can you even say that with a straight face? From my perspective, this is karma. You got yourself into this mess. Try to exercise a little self-control in the future. In the meantime, you'll do exactly as I say."

Xavier's eyes bugged with rage. Isa brushed past him toward the door.

Conor hustled back to Louisa. He held up an *in a minute* finger and pulled her into the shadowed alcove that led to the restrooms. Isa blew past. A few minutes later, Xavier followed, his steps rushed and uneven. After he passed, at Louisa's insistence, Conor waited in the alcove while she hurried back to her office for her purse. She returned a minute later, her purse and a file tucked under one arm.

"Come back to my house when you're finished here," she said.

"How are you getting home?"

"Damian and his partner are waiting for me in the lobby."

"OK."

They returned to the foyer separately. Louisa headed for the lobby while Conor helped the caterer load the truck parked in the alley before walking down to Rittenhouse Square. Louisa must have been waylaid along the way, because he arrived at her apartment right behind the threesome.

In the kitchen, Louisa gave Damian and Mark each a quick hug. "Thanks for the escort home."

"Anytime."

Conor took off his jacket and draped it over the back of an island stool. "Is it normal for Xavier to get that drunk?" Conor steered her across the floor.

"No." Louisa shook her head. "That's the first time I've ever seen him act like anything less than a gentleman."

"Same here," Damian said. "Not that we're besties or anything, but I've run into him at other functions. His behavior is usually professional."

Conor snorted. "Alcohol turns some people into asses." Of course, sometimes booze simply lowered a man's ability to hide his true nature.

"It was appalling the way people were discussing the murders." Louisa's mouth tightened with disgust. "It was almost as if they found gossiping about the case exciting."

"People suck, honey." Mark rubbed her arm.

"You know what's really aggravating and pathetic?" Damian's eyes shifted to angry. "I reported a teen missing the same day as Zoe Finch disappeared. She was one of the kids in my after-school program. She didn't get a clip on the news. No one cares what happened to her."

The sudden burst of temper surprised Conor. "Louisa mentioned that you represent disadvantaged kids."

Mark wrapped an arm around Damian's shoulder. "He's trying to open a supervised after-school program for high schoolers in the neighborhood where he grew up. Some of these kids don't have a safe place to wait until their parents get home."

"That's great. Where did you grow up?" Conor asked.

"West Philly." Damian rattled off a crossroad.

Conor whistled. "Rough area."

"No kidding." Damian snorted. "Try being a geeky, under-sized teen in that neighborhood fifteen years ago. Every day, walking home from school was like running a gauntlet. Some-times I'm surprised I made it out alive."

"Well, I'm glad you did." Mark smiled.

"Time for us to go home." Damian gave Louisa a peck on the cheek. "You get off those feet and get some rest."

"Thanks again." Louisa showed them out and then turned to Conor. "I'm going to change. Once I sit down, I might not get up again." She limped down the hall.

The dog didn't follow her mistress back to the bedroom. Conor looked down at the pit bull. Big brown eyes stared up at him expectantly.

"I'll walk Kirra." He took her downstairs for a quick turn around the park. Returning, he checked the fridge. Nothing had appeared while they were gone.

"Did you eat anything tonight?" Conor filled two plastic bags with ice.

"No."

"Do you want another grilled cheese, or should I make a takeout run?"

"Grilled cheese would be great," she called from the bed-room. He heard drawers opening and closing, then the soft sound of a zipper. She hadn't closed the door. Another small sign of trust?

Trying not to picture Louisa undressing, Conor got busy making sandwiches. By the time he was done, the kitchen smelled like browned butter. She reappeared in plaid flannel pajama bot-toms and a sweatshirt. Her hair was down again, tumbling over her shoulders in a blond wave. Conor brought the food into the living room. He moved the coffee table over and pulled an ottoman up to the sofa. Louisa raised her feet and sighed as he settled the two ice packs on her knees.

"Eat before you fall asleep."

"What could be going on between Xavier and Isa?" She bit into her sandwich and groaned. "God, I could eat this for every meal."

Her groan made him think about . . . "Could it be sex?"

Louisa wiped her mouth with a napkin. "I guess it's possible. He wouldn't be the first professor to sleep with a student."

Conor finished his food and pushed his plate back. "If they're sleeping together, what's the conflict? Is she blackmailing him?"

"She's doing something." She shrugged. "But if she's sleeping with Xavier and blackmailing him, what is she doing with Heath?"

"Good question." Conor took the empty plates to the kitchen and loaded them into the dishwasher. Isa shared an apartment with Zoe. The police had searched their place. But what would a search of Heath's apartment yield? Inquiring minds wanted to know.

"Could you bring me that file on the counter?" Louisa asked.

He brought the file and the reading glasses she'd left on the counter back to the couch. She put the glasses on and pulled off hot librarian without the suit. Louisa settled back on the cushions, relaxed. She flipped through papers.

"What are you looking for?"

"I'm not sure. This is a list of museum employees. Anyone on this list could have stolen the dagger." Louisa sighed and closed the file. "But without more clues, the list doesn't mean much. I'll see what I can make of it in the morning. Xavier is definitely a suspect. He might not work for the museum, but he visits often enough that people are accustomed to seeing him there."

Conor sat next to her. Their bodies touched from hip to shoulder. "What about your boss?"

Louisa lowered her glasses to her lap. "Dr. Cusack?"

"Yes."

"I don't know." Louisa sighed. "Tonight he seemed more concerned with making the museum's budget than with Riki's murder, but that doesn't mean he actually feels that way. He's just doing his job. He did order me to stop asking questions. He threatened to fire me."

"And you said?"

She shrugged. "I said I wouldn't stop. But my *performance* tonight might bolster some support. This evening's donations were substantial. My skill at eliciting funds for the museum might balance my disagreement with Cusack over Zoe."

"I'm sorry your boss is a jerk, but I'm proud of you."

"He's not a jerk. He's a politician. OK, maybe he is a jerk. Regardless, I really don't want to lose my job, but I won't let fear for my career make me stop looking for Zoe. Her family deserves better." Louisa shivered.

Conor wrapped one arm around her. "Then it's a good thing she has you."

Her head fell onto his shoulder. "I'm tired."

"Should I leave?"

"Would you mind staying? I sleep better when you're here." Her voice was sleepy and soft.

"I'd love to stay." He sat up and turned to make eye contact. "Do you want me to take the couch?"

"No. I like sleeping with you." She blushed. "I actually mean sleeping."

"I know what you mean; I don't expect anything. In fact, I prefer to wait. To me, there's nothing casual about sex."

He stood and held out a hand. She took it and let him help her to her feet. Wrapping an arm around her, he took some of her weight as she hobbled to the bedroom. Her knees must have stiffened as she sat. "But I'm warning you now. I get hot. I'll probably end up taking off my shirt."

Her body shook in a silent laugh. "I'll try to control myself."

Kirra beat them to the bed, curling up in the exact center of the duvet.

Conor stretched out on the bed and picked up the remote. "If you get too warm, feel free to take yours off. I won't be offended."

"That's kind of you to offer." She chuckled, easing onto the mattress.

"Yeah, I'm considerate that way." He picked up the remote. "Mind if I put on the TV for a while? I'm not used to sleeping this early."

"It won't bother me. I often sleep with the TV on for company. I find the Weather Channel the most conducive to sleep."

"I do that too." Conor settled on a hockey game and adjusted the volume to low.

"Do you think she's alive?"

He glanced at her profile, delicate in the flickering light from the TV. "I don't know."

"The police are convinced she's dead."

He reached across the bed and took her hand. He intertwined their fingers. "I know."

"It's not right. People can't just disappear." Her voice caught. The light played across her eyes, shining with moisture. She brushed a fingertip across her cheek.

"It's not your responsibility. It's up to the police to find out what happened to Zoe. There's only so much we can do."

"I just want her to be all right, but I know she probably isn't."

"Come here." Conor shifted sideways and tugged her closer. Kirra shot him a look, then scooted farther down on the mattress and rested her head on his foot. Louisa settled in his arms and put her head on his chest. A faint shudder passed through her body. He stroked her arm with a slow, rhythmic motion until her body relaxed.

Watching over her while she slept was no hardship. If only Zoe had had someone to look out for her. Louisa wanted to believe her intern was still alive, but Conor doubted it. He'd seen the pictures of Riki LaSanta's body. Whoever did that to a young woman enjoyed killing too much to stop. And Conor was going to make sure whoever it was didn't set his sights on Louisa.

CHAPTER
23

Sullivan's was busy on Sunday evening. From her seat at a booth, Louisa sipped her Diet Coke and watched Conor draw a tall glass of dark beer from a tap. For the last two hours, he'd served drinks and talked with customers. He seemed to know almost everyone on a first-name basis. But every time she'd glanced at him, those striking turquoise eyes were focused on her. Conor's eyes weren't the only ones she felt on her skin. Everyone seemed to be staring at her.

Even the plainclothes cop making a futile attempt to blend in at the back of the bar.

A shadow fell over the table. Conor's sister, Jayne, was tall and lovely, with eyes of the same shade as her brothers' and curly red hair that tumbled carelessly down her back.

"Do you mind if I join you?" Jayne set two plates loaded with burgers and fries on the table and slid into the booth.

"Not at all."

"Good. I brought you dinner." Jayne sipped a glass of water. "I hope you like burgers. Conor ordered me on dinner break. I thought we could eat together."

"I love burgers." Louisa took off the top bun and squirted ketchup on the meat. She added a puddle on the plate for her fries.

Jayne grinned, a dimple compressing a small scar on her cheek. "Good."

Louisa set down the bottle.

"I'm starving." Jayne picked it up and loaded her burger. "It's amazing a being the size of a peanut can make me this hungry. I've been either sick or starving every minute of the day since I got pregnant."

"Congratulations." Louisa bit into her sandwich. "You look excited."

Jayne beamed. "Thanks. I'm thrilled."

"When are you due?"

"Not till June, which is good. Reed and I are getting married at Christmas. I'm hoping to feel better by then. This morning sickness goes on till lunchtime."

"How's the burger?" Conor interrupted, sliding into the booth, bumping Louisa's hip to make room. He put one arm over her shoulders across the top of the booth. With the other hand, he stole a fry from her plate and popped it into his mouth.

"It's good. Aren't you going to eat?" Louisa asked.

"I'll get something later." He kept an eye on the bar. "No big games tonight. Things will slow down by seven." Conor turned to his sister. "How's Scott?" he asked Jayne.

"Better." She smiled. "He's out of ICU, but he'll need to stay in the hospital for a few more days. Reed wants to bring him home for a couple of weeks to recuperate, but Scott is arguing already. He said he's already behind in his classes."

"Arguing is a good sign," Conor said.

A scraping sound drew Louisa's attention to the corner of the room. Three young men gathered. Two held guitars. The third perched on the stool behind the drum set. Feedback squealed.

Conor leaned across the table toward his sister. "Who told them they could play tonight?"

Jayne blushed. "I did. I'm sorry."

"I thought we had a Friday-or-Saturday-night-only policy," he said, raising his voice over another ear-piercing screech.

"We do, but they asked really nicely." Jayne grinned.

"You're a softie." Conor shook his head and smiled at Louisa. "They're local boys, trying to catch a break. We let them play *once* a week." He shot his sister a lifted brow.

She raised an unconcerned shoulder. "They're nice kids."

He glanced at the bar, where customers were backing up in front of the older bartender. Giving Louisa a quick peck on the mouth, he slid out of the booth. "Break's over for me."

The band started playing. The music was decent, but the sheer volume curtailed any further conversation with Jayne. Louisa sat back, ate her burger, and enjoyed the atmosphere. Jayne went back to waiting tables. A set later, the crowd had thinned.

Conor took another break, joining Louisa in the booth to eat a meatball sandwich. He'd barely finished when the guitarist spoke into the microphone.

"Hey, Conor! How about getting up here and doing a song with us?"

Conor waved them off. "Not tonight, guys."

"Oh, come on. One song."

"I have a lady here," Conor protested.

The guy laughed. "Like picking up a guitar ever lessened a guy's chances of scoring with the ladies."

Conor glanced at Louisa. "Do you mind?"

She sipped her soda. "Not at all. I'm intrigued."

Sighing, Conor wiped his mouth with a napkin and stood. Someone handed him an acoustic guitar, and he stepped up behind the mic, more comfortable than Louisa expected. He was a quiet, unassuming man, not the type she'd associated with public performances.

"What are we playing tonight?" the drummer asked. "For the love of Pete, let's not go all melancholy and sad like you usually do."

"I can't help it. It's my Irish heritage. Be glad I don't make you play 'Danny Boy.'" Conor slipped the guitar strap over his head and settled the instrument against his hip. "I'm in a Black Keys sort of mood."

"Now you're talking." The drummer rested his sticks across his thigh. "Whenever you're ready."

As Conor picked up the first few notes, the bar went quiet. The melody was bluesy and, yes, melancholy, and his tone was surprisingly pleasant. He leaned into the microphone and closed his eyes, his body still except for the motions of his hands on the instrument. The rest of the room faded away until she could see only him. Emotion rolled through his voice, picking up strength as he hit the end of the first chorus.

As he sang about his blinded, broken heart, something melted inside of Louisa. The heat built to a slow simmer that thickened her blood. The band kicked in and the pace picked up, but those first two verses had done her in. Conor opened his eyes. His gaze locked with hers. For a few seconds, raw need poured from him. He blinked away, but her heart recognized he'd been holding back on her, as much as she'd been holding back from him.

And the way that she suddenly craved everything he had to offer made her hands shake when she reached for her soda.

The final notes of the song faded. He lifted the guitar strap from around his neck and handed the instrument back to another member of the band. Back-slapping and camaraderie from the other musicians followed.

Louisa lifted her glass and drank. Icy liquid slid down her throat but failed to cool the rest of her body. His emotional performance had left her both disconcerted and aroused. But in her defense, he'd definitely cheated. What girl could resist a man with a guitar? "Well, that just wasn't fair."

"You are not the first woman to say that."

Louisa jumped.

Jayne was standing next to her, a tray balanced on her hip. "Do you want another Diet Coke?"

"No, thank you." Louisa dabbed at her mouth with her napkin. "I'm sorry. I didn't mean to say that out loud."

Conor was working his way through the small crowd, but everyone stopped him. More than one woman slid a hand down his arm to get his attention as he passed.

Jayne laughed. "It's OK."

"Do they all have to touch him?"

"That's nothing." Jayne set the tray on the table. "Years ago they practically threw their panties at him when he'd sing."

"Thank goodness they're just pawing at him, then." Was that lick of heat in her belly jealousy? Yes, it was.

"No worries." Jayne smiled. "He's been hit on by every available woman in the neighborhood, and a fair number of the unavailable ones, come to think of it. But deep down, they all know the chase is pointless. Which is the reason they all keep staring at you."

Louisa choked. Coke dribbled down her chin. She mopped her face. "Me?"

"You're the first woman to catch his attention in years."

Louisa's eyes were drawn back to Conor, extricating himself from a woman's grasp on his forearm. A head above most of the crowd, he turned back to look at Louisa with apologetic eyes. Had he felt her gaze, or was he in a rush to get back to her?

He pried the woman's fingers from his wrist and squeezed through an opening like a fish slipping through a hole in a net.

"Sorry about that." He slid into the booth next to her.

She checked the time on her phone. Eight thirty. "Don't you close soon?"

"We'll close at nine." He leaned back and studied her face. "Do you feel OK?"

"I'm fine."

"OK, then." He scanned the bar. The band was packing up. People paid their checks and drifted toward the door. "I'll go help Ernie and Jayne so we can get out of here faster."

———

Conor turned the deadbolt in the front door of the bar, then led her past the EMPLOYEES ONLY sign into the back hallway. His police babysitter had moved from his booth to an unmarked car at the curb out front, where he would wait to follow Conor wherever he went for the night. The constant police presence was a reminder that the body still hadn't been confirmed as Zoe. Conor still headed the short list of suspects.

On the bright side, Louisa was safer with the cop hanging around. Since her pavement dive, Conor didn't want to leave her alone. Sure, it could have been an accident, but what if it wasn't? What if the killer didn't like the questions she'd been asking? What if the murderer was someone she knew and trusted enough to let into her apartment?

"Do you want me to stay with you tonight?" He hoped she did, and not just because his apartment was uninhabitable.

Louisa locked eyes with him. "Yes."

Her gaze was level and . . . hungry?

"I'll be finished in a few minutes." He lifted the cash register tray in his hand.

"All right." She followed him into the office, pacing impatiently while he sorted and filed the night's paperwork.

Something was up with Louisa. On autopilot, he counted cash and tallied the total with the computer-generated numbers.

Tucking the bills into a bank envelope, he closed the zipper. Nerves slid up his spine with the same deliberate zing.

"Ready?" he asked.

She pivoted and crossed the dented oak floor to stand in front of him. In slim jeans and a sweater, her legs seemed impossibly long. Her athletic shoes, worn as an accommodation to her bruised knees, made her a full head shorter than him. Despite the casual attire, she'd swept her hair into one of those fancy, uptight knots.

Her green eyes were fever-bright. "Yes."

For once, she didn't avoid his direct and searching gaze, but met him stare for stare. He leaned down and pressed his lips to hers. She opened with no hesitation. Her body pressed against his, making solid contact from thigh to chest. Her hands slid up his biceps, her fingers and nails digging into his flesh. A groan reverberated deep in her throat. Instead of the chaste, sweet kisses they'd shared in the past, this was tongue and teeth and heat. Need roared through him like a subway car, screeching in his bones and muscles with the harsh discord of steel wheels in an underground tunnel. He wanted more from her than this physical storm. But her need, pure and raw, rammed through his resolve and left it shattered.

He dropped the bag. It hit the desk with a soft thud. His hands cradled the back of her head, his fingers sliding into her thick mass of hair. Pins pinged to the floor as he unraveled the bun at the base of her neck. Hair tumbled over her shoulders in wild disarray.

"I need you." She tugged at the hem of his T-shirt. Her hands burrowed under the fabric. One splayed on his chest, right over his beating heart. She had the power to rip it to shreds. Her free hand slid down his belly toward the snap of his jeans.

"Easy." He lifted his head. Her eyes were dark, bright-green irises darkened by expanded pupils, emotion blurred by desire.

A finger delved into his waistband. A breath hissed out through his teeth.

His body screamed for more, while his heart insisted that a feral coupling on his desk wasn't enough.

He caught her wrists and pulled her hands to his chest. "Slow down."

"Don't want to." She pressed her hips against his. The pressure of her belly on his erection sent a wave of electric pleasure rippling from his balls to the base of his spine that nearly buckled his knees. His heart's voice telling him this wasn't enough grew dimmer, but he could still hear its whisper. Barely.

"We'll get there. I promise."

She shook her head. "Now."

A moan of frustration escaped her lips. He captured the sound with his mouth. He released her hands, bent down, and caught her by the backs of her thighs, picking her up. She wrapped her legs around his waist, her core creating more sweet friction. Her arms encircled his neck as he turned and set her on the desk. Brushing papers and a stapler aside, he lowered her to the wooden surface. She was pulling at his shirt. He reared up and tossed it off. Her body arched backward. Her head tilted back. The overhead light caught the bruise on her jaw as a purple shadow showing through her makeup.

Instead of allowing those busy hands to roam freely, he caught her by the wrists again. "I don't want to hurt you."

"I'm fine." Her lips trailed down his neck.

"You're not fine." He lifted his head, more concerned with her abrupt personality change than her physical injuries. "Look at me."

Her eyes blinked open and met his, and the gaze staring back at him shifted from raw sexual desire to more. Much more. The heat that filled his belly rose twenty degrees.

"Louisa." Yearning deepened his voice. "I don't want to do this here. It shouldn't be like this. Let's go back to your place—"

Louisa's eyes changed again. Fear clouded desire. Her body went rigid.

He released her wrists and backed off of her. Louisa didn't move for a few seconds. Conor reached a hand toward her face. He wanted to touch her, to comfort her, to help heal whatever was broken inside of her. But how?

She bolted upright. Standing next to the desk, she straightened her sweater and smoothed her hair, futilely trying to put her appearance in order when everything was in wild disarray.

"I'm sorry." She walked out of the office and went into the ladies' room. Water rushed through the pipes while he paced the worn oak floorboards just outside.

Five minutes later, she emerged. Her head was high, her face pale, her eyes wet and shining with unshed tears. "I have to go."

"Please don't." Panic filled his chest at the thought of her tossing him aside.

She snatched her purse from the floor where she'd dropped it. "It's all my fault. I should have known better. I should have known I couldn't have it all. I'm sorry if I hurt you, but what I feel for you is too much. I can't handle it."

Was she talking to him or herself? With a stiff, mechanical gait, she strode toward the door.

"Wait!" He grabbed his shirt off the floor and pulled it over his head as he followed her. "Let me take you home."

"I called for a car. It should be here in a minute." She bolted through the door, her rejection leaving him stranded.

The warmth inside his gut went cold. His skin went clammy, sweating like a glass of icy liquid on a hot day.

What just happened? Conor shook off his stunned paralysis and followed her out the back door. His booted feet hit the pavement just as she disappeared out of the alley. He jogged to the corner, emerging just as the hotel's car pulled up to the curb. Louisa didn't wait for the driver to open the door. She got in, and the car sped away.

Conor ran back to the bar and snatched his cell phone from the desk. He had to see Louisa. If she wanted to end their relationship, there wasn't anything he could do to prevent it. He couldn't make her talk to him. But he wasn't going to let it end like this. After all they'd been through, she owed him an explanation.

He couldn't let her run away from what had just happened between them. If he did, he'd have to live with being tossed away like garbage one more time. Barbara had done a number on him, and what he'd felt for her seemed like nothing compared to the staggering connection he'd just shared with Louisa.

He couldn't lose her. If she rejected him, it would take his heart down like a sweep to the ankles, and discarding the precious, fragile bond they'd formed felt like a sacrilege.

He climbed into his car and started the engine. Conor stopped for a few red lights, but Broad Street was quiet on a Sunday night. Ten minutes and three turns later, he pulled up to the Rittenhouse Hotel and tossed his keys to the valet.

Fear roiled in his gut as the elevator carried him toward Louisa's floor and the coming confrontation.

CHAPTER
24

Double-crossing should be an Olympic sport. I'd thought murder took planning and intelligence, but turning the tables on criminals was twice the work. The guilty were naturally wary, constantly suspecting others of doing the illegal and immoral deeds blooming to life in their own minds.

Guilty is as guilty does.

I watched Isa cross the library parking lot. The bitch. She wore her backpack by one strap. The glow from her cell phone illumined her features with an odd uplight, adding sinister shadows to her pretty face. I'd parked my nondescript sedan ten feet away from her car. Just out of range of the overhead light. I adjusted my hood, got out of the car, and slumped my way toward the entrance. I tilted my chin down. The university hoodie was excellent camouflage. At least 25 percent of the male student population was wearing a logo hoodie at any given time. Not that I had to worry about being seen. Not by Isa. Her head was down, and she was so entranced by her phone screen she saw nothing of her surroundings.

I slowed my steps. The library parking lot was backed by a small stand of trees, and the air smelled of a combination of molding leaves and exhaust. Over it all, the scent of burnt grease wafted from the McDonald's across the street. I wanted to take her near my car. There was no sense creating extra work for myself, and right now the lot was empty. Who knew how long it would stay that way? Plus, if I went too much closer to the building, the security camera mounted high on the light post would catch my next move. Tonight's venture was my riskiest feat yet. If this were a chess game, I would be putting my queen in jeopardy. Timing was everything. I tuned in to the faint sound of rumbling traffic. The only close-sounding noise was the clear, incessant chirp of a cricket in a nearby shrub.

It was time.

Shoving both hands in my kangaroo pocket, I pushed the button on the disposable camera.

We passed within a few feet of one another. Whipping out the camera, I struck. The two protruding wires zapped her in the ass. She went down fast, a confused jumble of limbs flopping to the ground. Her phone skittered across the pavement. I grabbed her ankles and dragged her across the blacktop to the rear of my car. Getting her into the trunk was a bit trickier. She was skinny, but 100 percent deadweight. The alternating twitching and stiffness in her limbs didn't make the job any easier. I hoisted her shoulders up and over. The sedan's trunk had a low clearance, something I'd checked before I'd stolen it. Her legs followed. A quick glance around ensured me that I hadn't been seen. I took an extra ten seconds to zip-tie her hands and feet, and slap a piece of duct tape over her mouth. The trunk closed with a solid thud. The electrical shock should keep her quiet for the next ten minutes, but it was nice to know I didn't have to worry about releasing a banshee when I opened the trunk. I tossed her backpack in the back seat, then retrieved her phone, removed the battery, and put it in my pocket.

Isa would disappear as cleanly as the others. The police would find her car abandoned in the lot. Inside they'd find a surprise.

She hadn't been carrying a purse. Where did she keep her keys? Not in her jeans pocket, I hoped. I really didn't want to open the trunk again until we'd reached our final destination. Well, technically, it was only Isa's final destination. I reached in the backseat and rummaged in the front pouch of her backpack. With a satisfying jingle of metal, I came up with her key ring. I dug in my own pocket for the Ziploc baggie. Inside it were a few of Conor Sullivan's hairs, taken from the comb in his bathroom. I walked to Isa's Nissan and pressed the fob. The door unlocked with a faint chirp. I sprinkled half of the hairs in the driver's seat. I saved the rest for later.

The crime scene technicians had better find my little gift.

I got back in my car and drove out of the lot. A glance at the dashboard clock told me the entire feat had taken six minutes. I smiled. I'd allowed eight, but Isa had gone down with no resistance. No time to waste, though. I had a schedule to keep.

The campus disappeared in my rearview mirror. I headed for West Philadelphia and the crumbling house I'd selected for the next stage in my plan. Isa was victim number three. After I finished with her, I had one more death on my agenda. I would need to pay close attention to detail for the next phase, and its execution would require finesse.

CHAPTER
25

Louisa clutched her purse in both hands as she hurried for the elevator. The fake smile she'd donned for the driver and doorman felt brittle as centuries-old metal. If she touched her face, her pleasant, composed veneer would crumble to dust. The elevator dinged at the eighteenth floor. The doors parted, and the hallway stretched out. She fumbled with her key, missing the lock several times, unable to hold her hand steady. Finally, she rushed into the foyer. Kirra met her in the hall and followed her into the kitchen. Louisa dropped her purse on the counter.

She'd expected to fall apart the second she was in the privacy of her home. Instead, numbness slid over her as if she'd wrapped her body in an ice pack. She leaned on the counter, the granite under her fingertips as cold and unyielding as her fear.

Kirra bumped her leg, and Louisa crouched to stroke the dog's head. Kirra had been hurt, and yet she trusted Conor instinctively. What did the dog know that Louisa didn't?

She'd hurt him too, wounded him in a way that would leave a scar. Guilt magnified her turmoil. She hadn't meant to reject him, but she hadn't been able to speak. Reflex had taken over. Her mind had shut out what it couldn't accept.

What she'd seen in his eyes—and felt in her heart—had terrified her. Now that she'd caught her breath, she missed him with the same intensity.

Would she ever be able to trust? He had the power to hurt her more than anyone she'd let into her life. Her mother had died, her father abandoned her, and her aunt betrayed her. Could she give anyone the power to wound her again?

A knock sounded on her door, firm, demanding.

She should have known he wouldn't let her off so easily. The next knock was louder. He wasn't leaving.

She gathered the courage to face him, but she hadn't moved when she heard him in the foyer. Had she forgotten to lock the door? She heard it shut. The deadbolt *clicked* into place. His boot heels rang on the tile until he was standing directly behind her body. His shadow fell over her.

"Louisa," he said with gentle insistence.

Her throat couldn't form words. Her lungs tightened, inelastic and unyielding. It felt as if her rib cage had turned to steel, refusing to expand. Light-headed, Louisa suddenly remembered to breathe.

His hands closed over her biceps. Warmth seeped through the cotton knit of her light sweater. With easy pressure, he turned her around to face him. She stared at the direct center of his chest. "I'll completely respect your decision if you want this to end between us, but I think you don't. I hope you don't."

Raising her chin, she searched his eyes. There was no sign of anger, just tenderness and worry.

"Talk to me." He rubbed his hands up and down her arms.

"I can't." Her voice was barely a whisper. But she took a step forward and pressed her face to his chest, turning her head to listen to the steady thump of his heartbeat.

A relieved sigh left his chest as he closed his arms around her. His wide palm stroked up and down her back.

"Why are you here?" she asked.

"Do you want me to leave?"

"No." She hesitated. Trusting him was frightening, but the thought of him leaving scared her more. Her life hadn't been great before she met him, but how could she go back to that cold, loveless existence now that she'd tasted what life could really offer? "But I need to understand why you're here. Why you came after me after I ran out on you in the middle of . . ." She waved a hand.

"Understand what? That I care about you? That I wanted to make sure you were all right?" His hand cupped the unbruised side of her jaw. He tilted her face up. A quick flash of anger blazed his eyes and heated her skin.

He cared about her enough to chase after her in the middle of the night.

"I'd hope you'd think more of me by now." His tone was annoyed. "I don't care about sex. Frankly, sex is easy to come by. You're not."

She remembered the taste of his mouth, the hardness of his body, the gentle stroking of his hands. "But I *do* care about sex. I wanted you. I still want you." She dropped her guard and let him see it in her eyes. "I need you." She needed the physical reassurance of his presence. The press of his body against her skin.

He hesitated.

"Please." Her hand curled in his shirt. "Unless you don't still want me."

"Oh, I want you. You have no idea how much I want to make love to you." He pressed a kiss to her temple. "But I also want you one hundred percent on board. I don't want our first time to be an impulsive, heat-of-the-moment act. Despite the way my body reacts to you, I'm no adolescent controlled by raging hormones. You mean more to me than a physical release. I could take care of that by myself. The whole point is that it's you. I can wait."

"I don't want to wait." If he rejected her now, she'd crawl in a hole and cry. She wouldn't be able to trust anyone else. No one else had ever worked this hard to connect with her. No one else had ever cared enough to persist. "Besides, I've gotten used to having you in my bed. I sleep better when you're there."

"That was my devious goal: to make you dependent on me as a sleep aid." Though his words were tinged with humor, his eyes were serious. His thumb stroked her chin. "We could just sleep."

She captured his hand in hers, turned, and led him into the bedroom. "I need you."

"You have to talk to me." His eyes were determined. "There's no getting out of it if we take this next step."

"I will. Just not now. I'm tired of overthinking everything. I need to *feel* you."

"That big brain of yours does get in the way." His eyes darkened. "But you have to promise you won't run away from me again. Afterward, we're going to have that long talk. I don't do *just sex.*"

"All right."

"I would never hurt you."

"I know." She reached for the hem of his shirt and tugged it over his head. Tossing it aside, she put her hands on the firm muscles of his shoulders. Her earlier desire had been a thunderstorm, all clash and noise. This was a steady summer rain, warm and gentle, soaking into her skin like a parched summer garden. She pulled her sweater off and dropped it at her feet. Her lace bra followed.

A soft masculine sound hummed in his throat. His hands slid up her sides, stroking her rib cage, sliding around to cup her breasts. "God, you're beautiful."

She drew his head closer and kissed him.

"Not enough." She backed him across the floor. When she pressed on his shoulders, he sat in the chair. His gaze was on her bare breasts as she pulled his boots off. They hit the floor with dual *thunks*. Standing, she unbuttoned her jeans and slid out of them. Her lace Brazilian bikini was pale blue. "Your turn."

He was quicker, shedding his pants and socks all in a few economical motions. He wasn't a boxer or brief man and was totally comfortable with his nudity.

"Come here." Gentle hands urged her to him. Sitting on his lap, she pressed her body to his, skin to warm skin. His tongue was in her mouth, his hands on her back, stroking her inside and out. The erection pressed between them assured her that he still wanted her.

Brushing her hair aside, his mouth cruised down her neck, tongue and teeth and lips setting her nerves on end as they traveled down her collarbone to her breast. He drew her nipple into his mouth, his tongue laving until she was hard as a pebble. Lifting his head, he slid his hands down her sides. He traced the lace edges of her panties, fingers dipping just under the elastic over her hips. One hand slid over her buttock, caressing, squeezing her flesh through the lace.

She reached between their bodies and palmed the hard length of him. He groaned, a deep and masculine sound of approval. His hips surged upward. Hands eased inside her panties, palms cupping her bare bottom. One finger slid around to stroke her core, testing. Pleasure surged inside her. Involuntarily, her hips moved.

She ground her aching center against his hand, but it wasn't enough contact. The heat was building. She had to quell it before the frenzied need returned. Before she lost control. "Now. Please."

He froze. "Are you sure?"

"Yes. Do you have a condom? Please say yes." She backed away to discard her panties.

He cleared his throat. "Wallet. Back pocket."

There were two. She tossed the spare onto the desk.

"There's no rush." But the cords of his neck were taut, and his erection bulged huge and hard beneath her touch.

She caught and held his gaze. "I want you now."

Turquoise irises darkened. He took the condom. His hands weren't entirely steady as he sheathed himself and waited for her to come to him. Her eyes raked over his lean, naked body, taking in his broad shoulders, defined abdominals, and powerful legs. He was the quintessential male, the ideal physical specimen. But ultimately, it was his kindness, his generosity, and his willingness to put his own needs aside for hers that sparked her desire. As he'd said, sex was easy to get. She'd had plenty of offers, but she wanted him.

She straddled his hips and took him into her body inch by inch. His body stiffened. His fingers dug into her hips as he allowed her to control the movement. She pressed down until he filled her completely. His hardness pressed against the soft ache inside of her. His body trembled beneath her.

Her head dropped backward. Her spine arched with pleasure. A moan started in her solar plexus, rippled up her throat, and slid from her lips. This was how it was supposed to be. Two bodies joined as one. Her core throbbed with the beat of her heart. Inside her, she felt the echoing pulse of his erection. Any movement would increase the sensation. Her body insisted, but her mind paused. Her control was spiderweb thin and just as fragile.

Conor's hands curled around the backs of her thighs, the fingers digging into her flesh. "Sweetheart, one of us is going to have to start moving." His voice was hoarse, his teeth clenched as if his movements were barely contained.

She rose, sliding to his tip in slow motion, then taking him deep again.

"Jesus," he hissed. "You're going to kill me."

She did it again. Her body bowed back farther, drawing pleasure from her nerve endings like the sweet friction of a violin bow on taut strings. Conor's hands slid up to her waist. His hips surged, matching the agonizingly slow pace she set.

"Louisa." He strained his head toward her, the effort tightening his abdominal muscles. His hand swept over her breast and collarbone to cup her jaw, urging her face closer. He kissed her, the motion of his tongue in her mouth mimicking the wet slide of their joined bodies.

She wrapped her arms around his shoulders. Their chests met, the coarse hair on his pectorals rubbing against her breasts.

His lips moved to her ear. "I can't get enough of you."

With one hand pressed to the small of her back, he thrust upward again.

She closed her eyes as sensations overwhelmed her, the tension spiraling tighter and tighter in a swirl of white light behind her eyelids. From head to toe, her muscles clenched, her body tensing to the point of pain. A whimper of frustration escaped her lips.

Conor's hand left her back to cradle her face. "Look at me."

She raised her lids. The turquoise of his irises was nearly eclipsed by expanded pupils. She saw both pleasure and possessiveness in his gaze. What did he see in hers?

"Stop thinking, Louisa. Give that busy mind a rest." His hand returned to the small of her back, his palm warm and sure. "Just let go. Relax. Trust me."

His eyes held her captive.

"Breathe," he whispered. "Feel."

She exhaled and drew fresh air into her lungs.

"That's it." His smile did her in. Another slow thrust of his body pierced her control. It exploded inside her, shattered through her in electric waves of heat and light, her senses plummeting in a wild free fall that left her reeling and limp.

She felt him tense and grind against her. He shuddered twice, then relaxed. Breathing hard, he scanned her face. Sweat gleamed on his skin, and his damp hair was tousled over his forehead. She reached up to smooth her own locks, but he caught her hand, brought it to his mouth, and kissed it. "Don't. I love knowing that I made you come undone. It makes me want to do it all over again."

Oh, he undid her all right. Her heart was as wrung out as every other muscle in her body.

He pulled her to his chest. His lips brushed her temple. "Geez, Louise. My heart just about exploded."

The giggle that sneaked from her lips felt foreign. Had she ever giggled before? Likely not since she was a child, maybe not even then. "Even for you, that was a bad joke."

"I have some other bad things I'd like to try." He smiled, his eyes glinting. "When I said I didn't care about sex, I lied."

Her soul felt lighter than before they'd made love. She'd had sex with other men, but she'd never made love with anyone else. She'd only thought she'd made love because she hadn't known better. There would never be *just sex* with Conor. He wouldn't allow it.

CHAPTER
26

"Be right back." He got up and went into the bathroom to deal with the condom. When he emerged, the room was empty.

"Louisa?"

The apartment wasn't that big. He wandered toward the kitchen.

Draped in a pale-blue silk robe that covered her from neck to feet, she was filling a glass with sparkling water. Her hair was a tousled fall of blond that reached nearly to her waist. "Would you like some water?"

Conor accepted the glass. Louisa picked up her cell phone from the counter. She unlocked it and frowned at the screen.

"Something wrong?"

"I've been trying to get in touch with my father since yesterday."

"He's in Sweden, right?"

"Yes." She set the phone down. "I call him every Saturday."

"Maybe he went away for the weekend."

"Why wouldn't he take his cell with him?" she asked, a line of concern creasing her brow. "I'm worried about him. He isn't stable."

"What do you mean by *not stable*?"

Her gaze dropped to the counter. "He drinks a lot."

Conor touched her hand. "I'm sorry."

"When we spoke last week, he told me he was coming here

for the holidays. I could tell something was wrong. I think it was the first time he sounded sober in years."

"Isn't that a good thing?"

"I guess." She pulled her lip between her teeth. "But he said he needs to talk to me, and it was something he couldn't tell me over the phone, and now I can't get hold of him."

Conor pulled her into a hug.

Woof.

Kirra was standing at the door.

Conor took a sip of water. "I'll be right back."

He pulled on clothes and grabbed the leash from the closet. He clipped on her leash and headed outside.

"That was bad timing," he said to the dog. "She was talking to me. Really talking. I was getting somewhere. So let's make this quick, OK?" He tugged Kirra toward the grass. "I have plans."

The dog cooperated, and he was back in the apartment in ten minutes without incident. Maybe he'd overreacted. He opened the closet to hang up the leash. A blue Tiffany bag fell from the shelf and landed at his feet. A card and a small box labeled TIFFANY & CO. slid across the tile. He picked them up.

"Are you back?" Louisa stood at the end of the hall, her eyes riveted on the gift in his hand.

"I'm sorry. I knocked these out of the closet." He held out the bag. "Do you want me to put it back?"

She backed up a step, the warmth in her eyes dimming. With trepidation, he opened the box. It was a pendant. A gold sailboat gleamed on a thin, elegant chain. He opened the envelope and read the note.

Dear Louisa,

A small token to show how much I miss you. I hope you'll reconsider your recent move and come home. You are the only one for me. I need you. I've always needed you. Please forgive me.

Yours always,

Blaine

"Who's Blaine?" Conor asked, but he knew. From the devastation on Louisa's face, Blaine was guilty of something. Conor dropped the bag on the hall table and crossed the tiles to her. She hadn't moved. He lifted his hands and gently took her by the shoulders. "Talk to me."

She shook her head, her face paling, anger brightening her eyes.

"It can't be that bad." He pulled her stiff body to his chest and kissed the top of her head, but her body still felt wooden.

He lifted her to sit on a kitchen stool. "Please, talk to me. Who is Blaine?"

She looked away. "Blaine is my aunt's godson, the child of her childhood friend who died young. After my mother died and Aunt Margaret came to live with us, Blaine visited her. He showed up at family parties. That sort of thing. He's six years older than me."

"Were you friends?"

A small shudder passed through her frame. "No. But I had a crush on him when I was a teen."

Conor stroked her arm. She inhaled, and he knew the story was coming.

"On my sixteenth birthday, my aunt threw a huge party. Of course, Blaine was there. It was noisy and crowded with people I didn't know. Most of the guests were Aunt Margaret's friends. My father had missed his flight home from Munich, and I was heartbroken. He'd been touring Europe, lecturing, and I hadn't seen him for several months. Blaine found me hiding in the library, crying. He grabbed a bottle of champagne and talked me into going down to the boathouse with him. My aunt was very strict, and I'd seen my father's drinking problem up close. I'd never had more than a sip of alcohol before. But I was so angry and hurt, I thought maybe I'd just follow in his footsteps." She paused, her eyelids falling to half-mast, disgust flattening her lips.

"It's OK," Conor encouraged. "You'll feel better if you get it out."

But she wouldn't meet his eyes. "The next thing I knew, it was morning and we were both naked. I didn't remember anything. I'd never had sex, but it was obvious that's what had happened."

Picturing a young and vulnerable Louisa, Conor clenched a fist and rapped it against his thigh. "What did Blaine say?"

"He was enthusiastic about doing it again." Two bright spots of color rose into her cheeks.

"How old was Blaine at the time?"

"Twenty-two."

Twenty-two-year-old boys generally knew how to drink. Conor had seen more than one guy try to get a girl wasted to get into her bed. "I assume he'd had alcohol before?"

"He was in a fraternity. Alcohol consumption seemed to be his major at the time."

"Not you, though." No, Louisa had *good girl* written all over her.

A sad smile twisted her lips. "I didn't have much of a social life. Like Zoe, I was years younger than my classmates. At sixteen, I'd just received my bachelor's degree, but I'd never been to a college party. Frankly, I was a pathetically obedient teen. The total trying-to-win-Daddy's-approval-by-being-perfect cliché. If I disappointed my aunt in any way, the first thing she did was call my father to tell him."

Conor's heart pinged. Louisa identified with her lonely young intern. Both had been preyed upon, but Zoe had likely ended up dead.

"Honey, Blaine took advantage of you. You can't beat yourself up for the rest of your life about it," Conor said. "How much did you drink?"

"A glass? I don't remember."

Conor froze. "You drank one glass of champagne and blacked out?"

"Yes. That's why I don't drink. Obviously, I have an adverse reaction to alcohol."

He straightened her shoulders, forcing her to look at him. "Louisa, no one passes out from one glass of champagne."

"What are you saying?"

"Health conditions exist where people have no tolerance for alcohol, but they're rare. Do you have any weird medical issues? Were you on medication?"

"No." Louisa's head tilted, and he could see her mind making connections. "Would you explain what you're thinking?"

But Conor thought he'd better prove his point. "The condos are connected to the hotel, right?"

"Yes."

"Do you get room service?"

"Yes. The number is on the base of the phone charger."

He reached for the handset, dialed the room service number, and ordered a bottle of champagne.

"You want to get me drunk?" she asked, one brow shooting upward.

"No, I want to do an experiment." He met her eyes. "Do you trust me?"

"I do." She didn't hesitate.

He went to the fridge and pulled out the cheese. He found an unopened pack of crackers in the pantry. A knock on the door signaled the arrival of room service. Conor opened the door. A young man in a white shirt and black slacks wheeled a cart into the living room. A champagne bottle sat in a bucket of ice. Two tall flutes flanked it.

The waiter opened the bottle and poured two glasses before bowing out.

Louisa sat down on the couch. She picked up a glass and fingered the stem. "I've tried alcohol a few times since that night, but I never got past the first sip. The taste triggered anxiety. I was afraid of what might happen."

"Look, I'm not saying it's impossible, but don't you think you should know?" Conor set the plate of crackers and cheese on the coffee table. He picked up the second glass. He tapped it to hers. "Here's to the truth."

Louisa sipped. Her free hand went to the base of her throat, but there were no pearls to rub. She needed a distraction.

"Does it taste all right?"

Worry clouded her eyes. "I'm never going to like it."

"That's OK." Conor scanned the living room tables. "Where's the remote?"

"In the drawer."

He turned on the flat-screen hanging opposite the couch and surfed until he found a classic movie channel. A whistling Ray Milland sauntered across a black-and-white seascape.

"Oh, I love this movie."

Conor set the remote control on the table. He leaned back on the sofa. "What is it?"

"*The Uninvited*. It's a ghost story." Taking minuscule sips of her drink, she settled in next to him.

He wrapped an arm around her shoulders. Fifteen minutes later, their glasses were empty.

"Should I have another?"

"How do you feel?"

"Fine. A bit relaxed."

"That's it?"

"Yes." Her forehead wrinkled. "Should I have another?"

"No. We have to preserve the integrity of the experiment and recreate your experience as closely as possible." Conor wheeled the cart into the hall and called room service for a pick up.

"What now?" She yawned.

"We go to bed." He took her hand and pulled her off the sofa. She went into the bathroom for a few minutes. When she came out, he went in to brush his teeth. The whole routine was normal and domestic. Warmth spread through his limbs as he took off his clothes and climbed into bed naked, pulling the sheet up to his waist. Louisa emerged from the closet with clothes in her hand. She paused, her eyes skimming over his bare chest.

He waggled his eyebrows. "What do you have?"

"Pajamas." She laughed.

"Pajamas?" He lifted the covers. "You don't need those."

"All right." She set them on a chair and smiled at him as she untied the sash of her robe. Blue silk slithered down her naked body and pooled at her feet.

Conor went hard in an instant.

She eased into bed and reached for him.

"Nope. No sex."

"But you're, you know . . ." She nodded at his obvious interest.

"Yes, I have a hard-on. I will survive." Putting a hand on her hip, he rolled her on her side and spooned. The pressure of her bare buttock against his erection urged him to do more. "We have to preserve the integrity of the experiment, remember? I want to make sure you have total recall tomorrow morning."

"I doubt I'll forget this." Her arm was halfway to the nightstand lamp when she tensed in his arms. "I'm obviously not unconscious."

"No. You are not."

"What does that mean?" She needed the truth.

"He put something in your champagne," he said. "A date rape drug like roofies can make girls—"

"I know what a date rape drug is," she snapped, sitting up in a jerky movement and drawing her knees close to her chest, withdrawing, moving away from him. "I just can't believe that could happen in my own house. I've known Blaine most of my life. That would be . . ."

"Despicable?" Conor finished, hating the look of betrayal and pain in her eyes. "Yes, any man who drugs a woman and has sex with her unconscious body is the lowest form of humanity. Doing that to a sixteen-year-old girl who's practically family makes Blaine a predator."

She wrapped her arms around her shins. "He's in town."

"What?"

"My aunt invited him to have dinner with us on Friday night." Her speech quickened as her mind worked.

"Did she know what he did?" She couldn't have, he thought.

Louisa sighed. "I went to her immediately. To be fair, I told her that Blaine and I had been drinking. I accepted my share of the responsibility, but I also knew that he'd taken advantage."

"What did she say?"

"That we were both at fault, and I could hardly blame him if I drank with him willingly. I shouldn't have told her, but I didn't know what else to do. I was afraid of getting pregnant."

"You might not have realized he'd drugged you, but him using alcohol and your emotional state to achieve the same ends is bad enough. The fact remains that you were upset that your father didn't show up, and Blaine took advantage of that. If a guy did that to my niece, I'd be plenty pissed off."

Louisa let out a hard breath. "I couldn't believe it when I went to her hotel and he walked into the lobby bar. She might not think it was all his fault, but she knows how I feel about him."

"What did you do?"

"I left."

Suspicion tightened Conor's gut. "Could he have followed you?"

"It's possible." Louisa raised questioning eyes. "Do *you* think Blaine pushed me?"

Conor was actually thinking Blaine could be guilty of much more than that. "Do you know how long he's been in Philly?"

"No." Louisa's eyes widened. "You don't think he had anything to do with the murders."

"He has a beef with you. He's here in Philadelphia. He knows your history. We've already established that he's a predator."

"But murder?"

"He could have killed you. He obviously gave you some sort of drug. How could he have known how your body would react? Girls have died from date rape drugs." Conor took Louisa's hand. "Do you think you can talk to the police about it tomorrow? You have no proof of what he did, but I think the cops should know about Blaine. They can find out where he's been for the past four weeks."

She didn't answer. Her hand was freezing. He rubbed it between his. "I'm not criticizing you, but why do you even speak to your aunt?"

Louisa sighed. "I thought she was going to tell me what's wrong with my father."

Conor heaved himself up on the bed next to her and pulled her into his arms. He was not letting her withdraw again.

Slowly, her muscles relaxed. "I can't believe Blaine would drug me, but you're right. The symptoms fit perfectly. It should have occurred to me before, but I don't like to think about that night."

"Are you afraid your aunt is going to cut you off financially?" Conor stroked her back. "You wouldn't be able to live in the Rittenhouse, but you could definitely survive on your own."

Louisa choked. "No, she can't cut me off from the family money. It's actually the opposite. The money is mine."

"What?" Shock pulled Conor back.

"All of my fortune comes from my mother's family." She studied their joined hands for a few seconds, breathing, seemingly gathering strength. "My mother loved my father very much, but she had no illusions about him. He is and has always been a pure academic. He comes from an old blue-blooded family with more pedigree than money. He has no interest in being rich. He makes enough lecturing and guest teaching in Europe to fund his travels. That's all he cares about. My mother died of cancer. She knew she was dying for several years, so she put the bulk of her estate in a trust. My father receives a generous annual allowance. He is more than happy about the arrangement. He has no desire to do any of the work involved with managing the funds, but his sister is a different story. When she agreed to move in with us and take charge of me, she assumed she'd have access to the money. She was furious with my mother for cutting Dad off. She carried that grudge over to me. Dad gives his sister most of his allowance. He doesn't need it, and he feels like he owes her for giving up her life to raise me." Louisa nestled closer. "She never married or had children of her own."

"Well, thank God for that." Conor hugged her tighter. "I'm sorry."

Louisa brushed a tear off her cheek. "I'm sorry for snapping at you."

Conor sat up and faced her. "Don't apologize for being sad or angry or try to cover it up with a fake smile. I don't want an act. I want you, however you're feeling. If your family makes you depressed, that's OK. Please don't ever *pretend* to be in a pleasant mood for me."

Though Conor couldn't help but wonder if she was truly capable of *not* covering up her emotions.

"Is there any way Blaine could benefit from your death?"

"Financially? I don't think so." Louisa shrugged. "If Blaine tried to kill me, it would have been pure anger. He doesn't like to take no for an answer, and he usually gets what he wants."

"You don't think he could have killed those two girls to emotionally destabilize you, to get you fired, and ultimately to force you to go back to Maine?" Conor asked.

"That would take a great deal of planning, and it'd be . . ."

"Evil?" Conor filled in.

"Yes. Killing two girls to force me back to Maine would be the ultimate self-centered act of evil." She straightened. "Blaine is both selfish and deviously intelligent, so yes, it's far-fetched but possible. But it is far more likely that he had a burst of temper over my rejection."

"If I can't have her, no one can?"

"Yes." Louisa nodded. "*That* I could believe." She took a long breath. "When we were children, Blaine had a small sailboat. As a punishment for some misdeed, his father took it away and gave it to Blaine's younger brother. Blaine sank it out of pure spite."

The fact that Blaine could be crazy jealous, emphasis on the *crazy*, scared Conor even more. "So you'll talk to the police again?"

"If you think Blaine could have killed Riki and Zoe, then I'll have to." But her discomfort was clear on her face. "They know who Blaine is because he showed up at the ER that night, but even though it's impossible to prove, they should hear what he did."

Probably not a good time to go to sleep. Conor located the remote and found the movie they'd been watching in the other room. But no amount of clever cinematography could possibly make an old ghost story as frightening as real-life murder.

His mind reeled with all of Louisa's revelations about her father, her aunt, and Blaine. Their relationship seemed to have turned a corner tonight, but how could he be sure she wouldn't hold back on him again? Was she even capable of being in a long-term relationship? And if she wasn't, what would it do to him?

CHAPTER
27

Louisa awoke in a cold, empty bed. Her hand automatically swept the sheets next to her, seeking him.

Where was Conor? She got up, picking up her robe from the floor and putting it on. She tied the sash, remembering the look of raw hunger on Conor's face when he viewed her naked body. Then his resignation when he refused to have sex with her a second time.

She remembered every moment of the previous night.

He'd been right. Blaine must have put something in her drink at the party. Why did that make her feel better? If anything, the truth made her more of a victim. But it also verified what she'd always known inside and never admitted, not even to herself. Blaine had done more than capitalize on her vulnerability and take advantage of her sadness at her father's absence, and he'd been lying about that night ever since.

But did Blaine's actions mean he could kill two young girls? The police hadn't said whether or not the girls were sexually assaulted. Blaine clearly didn't have a conscience, but was he a murderer? The theory felt like a huge stretch.

By the time she'd turned sixteen, she'd already fielded his advances numerous times. So Blaine obviously did whatever it took to get what he wanted. Was he doing that now?

Later this morning, she would call Detective Jackson and tell him everything. Perhaps the information, even unsubstantiated, might make the detective look at Blaine more closely.

Fortified by her resolve, she went into the kitchen and started a pot of coffee. Today was Monday. She had work, she had purpose, and she felt a lot less helpless than she had the night before.

The door opened, and Conor walked in with Kirra. He had a grocery bag in one hand. He unsnapped her leash, and the dog trotted to Louisa for a head rub.

"Has she eaten?" Louisa asked.

"No." Conor walked into the kitchen and kissed her. "We're going to have scrambled eggs." He unloaded eggs, milk, and bread onto the counter. Then he took out a frying pan and went to work on breakfast with the efficiency of a short-order cook. Ten minutes later they were eating eggs and toast at the island.

Kirra sniffed the eggs with little interest, went to the corner, and curled up in the dog bed.

"Her appetite doesn't seem to be improving." Louisa pushed her own breakfast away half-eaten, but she doubted the dog's appetite was affected by worry.

"I'm going to take her back to the vet today. She doesn't act sick, but she isn't behaving normally either." Conor frowned from the dog's nearly full plate to Louisa's. "You're not hungry?"

"Not really."

"How do you feel?" He turned her head to examine her jaw. "Your bruise is turning a nice shade of green."

"Terrific. I'm definitely less stiff today, and I think I can do without the Band-Aids on my hands." She paused. "I remember everything about last night."

"I knew you would." His eyes sparked with fierce possessiveness that heated her blood. "I want to track Blaine down and pummel his face."

"But you don't think less of me?"

"God, no. Why would I? What I feel for you has nothing to do with anything that happened to you in the past." He locked gazes with her. His was unyielding. "But I wish you would have told me earlier. I would have been more careful with you."

Frustration bubbled into Louisa's throat. "I don't want more care. I want normal. I want you to treat me like a normal, whole person. If you want to take me standing up against the elevator wall, then I want you to do that without worrying about hurting me."

"I wasn't talking about sex. I meant I would have understood why you find it hard to trust. But you are a normal, whole person." He swiveled his stool to face her squarely.

She didn't break eye contact. "I'm broken inside. I can't connect with people."

"Really?" He lifted an eyebrow. "Then what's happening between us? Is this all in my head?" He motioned between them.

Her heart skipped. "No."

"OK then. What Blaine did to you is in the past. It isn't a reflection on you, but I will keep it in the back of my head. I can't help that." He brushed a piece of hair off her cheek and tucked it behind her ear.

"What does that mean?"

"It means I care about you." He kissed her, sliding off his stool to stand in front of her. "You need to send your brain on vacation. You're overanalyzing everything. Just relax and let it happen."

"Let what happen?" She shifted, leaning back. Her robe gaped. Cool air washed over hot skin.

His gaze dropped to the opening. "I don't know. I can't predict the future." He splayed his hand on the center of her chest. Her heart thumped against his palm. "I feel things for you I've never felt before."

"I've never let anyone get this close. I've always kept relationships casual. Nothing about our lovemaking yesterday was casual." Her voice dropped to a whisper. "Does it make you uncomfortable?"

"Yes. Sometimes it's downright scary," he admitted. "But I'm brave. If we need to make love over and over until we get used to it, I'm willing to suffer through it."

"You'll take one for the team?"

He grinned. "Dozens if necessary."

She smacked him lightly on the shoulder. "This is serious."

"It doesn't have to be." His hand moved, brushing aside the fabric of her robe to reveal her breast. "Sex can be fun and intense at the same time."

His thumb teased her nipple. A yearning flared deep in her belly.

"Tell me. What set your hormones off in a sprint last night?" He moved closer, nudging her legs apart with his knee. Her robe fell fully open, her nudity exposed to him. His lips brushed her collarbone. "What turns you on?"

She tilted her head back to give him more room. "It was the guitar."

"It worked well for me in high school." He laughed. "But I never thought it would attract a genius and a scholar."

"Yes, the guitar is hot." Her brain synapses weren't firing well enough for long sentences.

"Does that make you my groupie?" He kissed her ear and sang softly. "I want you to want me."

His breath caressed her neck. Her hands burrowed into his thick hair. Her head fell back, wanting his mouth on the rest of her skin. "No matter what you sing, I'm not throwing my panties at you in public."

He chuckled. "Clearly, you've been talking to my siblings."

"Um. Yes." Louisa tilted her head.

"How about in private?" He nuzzled her neck, finding the sweet spot at the base of her throat. Where were his hands, and why weren't they on her skin?

Her legs parted, her bare core pressing against his hard, denim-clad thigh. How could her body respond to him again? "Maybe. I'm not wearing any now."

"I noticed," he moaned. "Next time you wear one of those fancy, uptight suits, I'm going to be thinking about you without panties."

"Maybe I won't wear any," she teased, shocked at the easy way the banter rolled between them. Perhaps he was right. Perhaps a relationship could be fun. With him she could imagine that possibility.

He froze and pulled his lips off her neck to stare down into her eyes. His pupils were large and dark, hunger eclipsing the bright color. "Do you want to know what I'm thinking now? Want to know my ultimate fantasy, what I've been thinking about doing since the first day I met you in that museum in Maine?"

She shivered. She couldn't look away from his eyes. His gaze raked over her. She followed its slow progress over her breasts and belly down to her spread thighs and back up again. He licked his lips.

"Here's my fantasy." His voice deepened. "You're wearing that gray suit, the super conservative one. And those black framed glasses that make you look smart." His hand snaked out and picked up her reading glasses from the counter. He set them on her nose. "You're at work, sitting in that executive chair, looking all smart and prissy and untouchable. Until I come in. I lock the door behind me. I kneel in front of you and unbutton your blouse. It's white and crisp and nerdy. You're wearing a white lace bra, which I open so I can tongue your nipples." His voice grew huskier, and his breath stroked over her ear like a caress, but he didn't touch her. She could see the scene playing out in her head. She went damp all over again just from the mental image. "Would you like me to do that?"

"Yes," she groaned, leaning back and straining her chest toward him.

He crouched lower. She watched, fascinated, as his tongue laved warm and wet over her nipple until it peaked into a stiff bud. Then he turned his mouth to the other breast. He looked up at her, his eyes totally wicked. "Wanna know what's next?"

"Yes." Which seemed to be the only word her brain could generate.

"I push your skirt up to your waist." His big hands curled around her thighs. He lifted one leg to rest her foot on the stool next to her. The other he put over his shoulder. "I spread your legs and put my mouth to you, and you lose it."

He slid down her body, his mouth cruising lower and lower. His tongue flicked in her belly button, then traced the contour of her hip, his eyes brightening with feral male interest. He pressed a tender kiss below the bandage on her knee. "This is what I'm going to do." His mouth was hot against her cool, swollen flesh. His tongue probing, testing, tasting. His fingers splayed on the insides of her thighs, pushing them wide open. With the slow, torturous onslaught of his lips and tongue, what else could she do but lose it? Pleasure coiled deep in her center and radiated through her pelvis. She rocked her hips toward him.

He lifted his head. "Anyway, that's what I'm going to do. So next time I call you and tell you I'll pick you up for lunch, I want you to be thinking of what I really want. And if you should be taking off those panties." He got to his feet.

She blinked at him.

He grinned. "Did you want something else?"

"Oh my God. Don't you dare stop."

"You're hot when you're bossy." He reached into the grocery bag still on the counter and withdrew a whole box of condoms. "But you have to keep the glasses on."

She reached forward, grabbing him by the waistband of his jeans and pulling him back to her. Her fingers worked the zipper, and she freed him. His erection pulsed in her hand. A groan slid out of his lips. His head fell back as she closed her hand around him. Then he had the condom open and was pushing her hands aside to sheath himself. His T-shirt fell in the way. He tugged it over his head and tossed it over his shoulder.

"Now who's in a rush," she said.

He shoved his jeans down a few inches. "This is how I want you, all naked skin. Eager. Hot." His eyes flicked to hers again. "Wet."

He cupped her buttocks with both hands and slid inside her. Pleasure pierced her. She wrapped her legs around his waist and pulled him deeper.

He stopped moving. "Does this work for you, or do we need to go out into the elevator?"

"Will. You. Please. Stop. Talking." She panted. *Almost there.*

"Yes, ma'am." He took her hard and fast, rocketing her to a climax. His body shuddered to a halt as she pulsed around him.

He brushed a quick kiss across her temple. "You're going to be thinking about that all day at work."

Work! She glanced at the clock. "I'm going to be late for work."

She ran for the bedroom, robe flapping around her bare legs. She showered in record time, then, because he'd tortured her into being his sex slave when she should have been getting ready, she put on her ultra conservative gray suit and pumps. Payback.

He was tugging his shirt on when she returned to the kitchen. His eyes brightened as he looked her up and down. "Tell me you're not wearing panties."

"Wouldn't you like to know?" She gave him a sensual look she didn't know she possessed. "You're going to be thinking about *that* all day while I'm at work."

"That's mean."

"I know." She smiled.

He followed her to the hall. "How about Kirra and I walk you to work?"

"That would be nice." She slid her purse strap over her shoulder.

"We can talk about the merits of fresh air on hot skin." Bending down, he snapped the leash onto the dog's collar.

"Are you working tonight?"

"I'm supposed to." He leaned close to her ear. "We can sext."

She laughed. "You may as well stay here, since your apartment is trashed. I'll let the hotel staff know. You might want to leave your cell number in case there's a problem with Kirra and they can't get in touch with me." She dropped her spare key into his open palm.

"OK. Thanks. Gerome seems protective."

"He's been very helpful with the dog." Louisa gathered her keys and purse from the hall table. Turning toward the door, she stopped.

Conor was staring at the key in his hand, an unusual furrow above the bridge of his nose.

"What's wrong?"

His mouth opened and closed. He wrapped his fingers tightly around the key. "Nothing. Let's go."

"Don't." Her muscles, loose from sex and laughter, contracted, bracing for bad news.

"Don't what?" He smoothed the tension from between his brows, but his eyes held on to their reservations.

"Don't pretend." She pulled her purse to her body and clutched it against her chest, but it wasn't enough to shield herself from the doubt in Conor's eyes. "No holding back, remember? You made me promise to talk to you when something is upsetting me. Don't you think I deserve the same consideration?"

—

Conor gripped the key, its small, insignificant weight heavy with implication. She'd given him the key to her apartment. He opened his fingers and stared at it. How could something so small come with such huge responsibility? Her decision was likely more practical than emotional, but the symbolism glared at him. He'd never gotten this far with Barbara. In one week, he and Louisa had already surpassed anything he'd experienced over an entire summer with Barbara. He'd started out determined to take this relationship slowly. What the hell happened?

His feelings for Louisa felt like hitting standing water on the expressway. The tires of his Porsche had lost traction. He was going too fast, just on the border of losing control, and he was pretty sure he couldn't stop even if he was driving straight into the river.

What if the next time she faced a traumatic event, he couldn't talk her down? What if she shut him out again? Could he take that? Last night had demonstrated how little he knew about her. She was about as open as a fire safe. His gaze traveled the long corridor. He didn't even know how much her apartment was worth.

And with his brain backfiring, all that came out of his mouth was a lame explanation. "We have nothing in common."

"What are you talking about?"

"I'm a regular guy. I work till three in the morning. I get one day off a week, and I usually spend it doing laundry and working on my car. What did you do for fun as a kid?"

"Before my mother died, we went sailing. I had a pony, and she used to take me to horse shows." Comprehension dawned in her eyes.

"Is this about money?"

"Not exactly."

"Is that what you think of me? That I'm superficial and only care about things like sailboats?" Louisa's face reddened with anger.

"I meant that we're fundamentally different—"

Her glare cut him off. Uh-oh. He could feel her anger, her hurt, sizzle through the air.

She held her purse against her body like armor, like a shield, protecting her from him. "I don't need you to be rich. Frankly, I have more than enough money of my own. I work for a living anyway. Do you know why?"

The question felt rhetorical, and Conor kept his mouth shut. He could barely move, but he bet he could still get his motorcycle boot into his mouth if he said a word.

"Because it isn't enough. I'm not going to deny I like having money. I've never appreciated my fortune more than this week. I'm grateful I can afford this very secure building. But money isn't everything."

Conor swallowed and croaked, "I just—"

"Seriously, I love to vacation in Europe. I'd love to share my favorite places with you. If your ego can stand it."

His ego had been given a good bitch slap, and a well-deserved one at that.

"I can't believe, after a lifetime of dodging men who are interested only in my money, I find the one man who doesn't want it."

"I didn't say—"

But she wasn't finished. "I'm falling for you, and if that isn't enough, then there's nothing I can do."

Falling for him? Was she implying the L word?

Stunned, Conor took two steps across the foyer. "It's more than enough. Look, I'm not perfect. I can't pretend I'm totally comfortable with our basic differences." He gestured between them. "I wasn't prepared for this."

"Oh." She let the purse drop to her side, but her posture remained tense. "I'm sorry I freaked out."

She leaned her forehead against his chest for a few seconds, then pushed away. "I need to get to work."

He opened the door for her. "Will you be all right here alone tonight while I'm at work?"

"It's a safe building."

"OK, but don't let that lower your guard. Don't let anyone in. Not even someone you know. Especially someone you know." Conor locked up behind them. "I won't make it back until about three a.m."

"You don't have to come back here if that's not what you want."

"It's what I want." He took her hand, but the tension in her muscles remained.

Of course, she had just made a major emotional revelation, and he'd totally backpedaled. What was his problem? It wasn't like him to be such a fucking coward.

They took the elevator to the ground floor and walked toward the door.

A dark sedan was parked illegally at the curb in front of her building. Detectives Ianelli and Jackson got out of the vehicle.

Jackson stepped in front of them, halting their progress. Kirra growled softly. Maybe the dog wasn't useless as a protector.

"We need to talk with you both." Jackson nodded at the building behind them.

Louisa's breakfast tumbled. "What's wrong?"

Jackson frowned. "Isa Dumont is missing."

CHAPTER
28

Louisa called April to let her know she'd be late. She didn't say why.

Back in her apartment, Detective Jackson didn't waste any time. He'd barely sat down when he started. "Isa Dumont was supposed to be at her parents' house for dinner last night. She didn't show up. Knowing everything that has been happening, her parents immediately started looking for her. No one has seen her since she left the university library at seven. Her car was found in the parking lot at nine o'clock."

"Oh no." Louisa sank onto a chair. Disappointment from her argument with Conor was swept aside with new grief. Standing next to her, grim-eyed, Conor squeezed her shoulder in a silent message. *Tell him.*

She clenched her hands in her lap. "I have something to tell you about Blaine Delancey."

Jackson's brow rose with interest. Ianelli leaned forward and rested his forearms on his thighs, his black eyes focused on her. He would miss nothing.

Telling her story was no easier than it had been last night. "I always assumed I simply couldn't tolerate alcohol, but now I know that isn't the case."

Ianelli cocked his head, his gaze unreadable. "You have no evidence he did anything."

"No. I have no proof. I understand that incident is over and done with from a legal perspective, but I thought you should know what Blaine is capable of."

"OK. We'll find out how long Blaine Delancey has been in town." Jackson unwrapped a square of gum and put it in his mouth. He chewed with aggressive, angry back-and-forth motions of his jaw. "Does Blaine inherit anything if you die?"

"Not directly, no." Louisa opened her hands. Blood rushed into her fingers with pinpricks of heat. She studied the fading bruises on her palms. "The way the trust is structured, if I die with no children, then the money goes to my father, but in reality, the trust is controlled. He'd receive both my annual trust income and his, but only a portion of the estate is accessible. If my father and I both pass with no heirs, the money is distributed among a number of charitable organizations. If I have children, then a portion of the principle is carved out for each of them, with them receiving an annual income, et cetera. The idea is to preserve the family money for future generations."

Jackson absorbed the information. "Are you on good terms with your father?"

A flash of anger brought Louisa's gaze to meet Jackson's. "First of all, my father has no interest in money, which is why he told my mother not to leave it to him."

"Everybody is interested in money."

"He's a hopeless academic. All he desires out of life is to spend his days with his books and research. My father has no interest in anything besides his work."

"When was the last time you saw him?" Ianelli asked.

"He came home in May. He stayed two weeks and returned to Stockholm." He couldn't wait to get away from her and her failure. "He's guest lecturing at a university in Sweden through next spring. My father has a generous allowance from the trust.

He gives most of it to his sister, Margaret, to run the house in Maine." Louisa stopped. "Margaret can never directly inherit, but she would likely have increased access to the trust income through him if I died. Blaine is her godchild, the son of her oldest friend. If she indirectly controlled the fortune, she would be very generous with Blaine."

"That feels like a pretty thin motive." Ianelli's mouth pursed. "Isn't this Blaine guy rich too?"

Louisa shivered. "I assure you Blaine is very shrewd. He's been kowtowing to Margaret for favors since he was a child. His father lost the family money in a series of bad business decisions. Blaine has been bitter about that his whole life. But honestly, what makes me more uncomfortable about Blaine is his insane jealousy regarding anything he perceives is his. This might include me."

Jackson made a few notes and tucked his pen back into his pocket. "We'll be sure to check Blaine Delancey out thoroughly." His tone didn't promise results.

"Now back to more plausible suspects." Ianelli refocused on Conor. "We have a witness who saw Conor following Isa Dumont the other morning."

Detective Jackson chimed in. "You were parked outside her residence, the one she used to share with Zoe Finch. She left the building, and you followed her."

"Isa had something going on with Heath," Conor said. "And I knew you were following me the whole time."

"Still doesn't look good."

Conor rolled his eyes. "You can't still think I'm your best suspect."

"Why not? Because you're a good liar?" Jackson's frown furrowed his whole face. "We found short dark hairs in the front seat of Isa's car and on the second body."

"And?" Conor crossed his arms over his chest.

"You have short dark hair." Jackson gave Conor's head a knowing look.

Conor snorted. "So does half the city."

"DNA will tell. It doesn't lie." Ianelli's piercing black eyes locked on Conor.

"You don't even have my DNA." Conor straightened.

"Don't we?" Ianelli shrugged.

Louisa put a hand on Conor's forearm. "I think we should call Damian before we answer any more questions."

Ianelli stood, brushing a wrinkle from his slacks. "Never mind. We're leaving. We just thought you should know Isa Dumont had disappeared."

"Wait. You didn't ask us where we were when Isa was taken." Louisa raised a finger. "You said she was last seen at seven, and her car was found at nine last night. You know Conor and I were both in the bar at that time. There was a policeman watching us all evening."

"And we're still watching you." Jackson picked a dog hair from his jacket sleeve.

"Isa was taken from the parking lot?"

"We believe she was grabbed on her way back to her car," Jackson answered. "But we're not sure."

"Then how would her attacker's hair get in the front seat of her car?" Louisa asked. Were the police so determined to pin these crimes on Conor that they would ignore logic and facts? Or did they just want general information and were trying to intimidate her and Conor to get it?

"Maybe that's where he waited for her." Ianelli shrugged, but his brows dropped lower, shadowing his eyes. "Or he grabbed her after she got into the car. Lots of possibilities."

"That makes no sense." Conor shook his head. "If he left her car there, he'd need to have his own vehicle. He could hardly toss her over his shoulder and fireman-carry her away. Someone would notice. So if he had his own car, why would he bother to break into hers? He'd nab her while she was digging her keys out of her purse or unlocking the door."

The police didn't offer an opinion on Conor's comment.

"Have you made any progress with Riki or Zoe's cases?" Louisa asked. "Are any of Zoe's DNA test results in yet?"

Originally, Damian had speculated the tests would be back within a week, which was tomorrow.

The police didn't answer. Instead, Jackson rose. "We're done here."

"I'll see you to the door." Louisa gestured toward the foyer. She didn't want Conor to say anything else until she'd firmly closed the door on the police.

She pressed her back against the cold steel. "I can't believe Isa is gone."

Conor paced the small foyer. "How can another girl go missing without anyone noticing?"

"I don't know." Dread swirled in Louisa's stomach. "He's very cunning."

He whirled, his face an angry mask of frustration. "More likely he's someone the girls knew—and trusted."

"Time to call Damian," Louisa said. "So he can inquire on the status of the DNA test results. With Riki the police didn't release that information to the public until her family had been notified. Maybe the same thing is happening with Zoe."

"Maybe. I don't want to be too optimistic, but it feels like their case against me is weakening. It's hard to beat cops for an alibi."

"Then why were they here?"

"I'm not sure." Conor scrubbed his scalp with his fingers.

"Looking for a new lead? Hopefully it wasn't because they don't have any other serious suspects."

—

The late morning October sun was warm on Conor's head as he sat on the bus stop bench across from Heath Yeager's town house. He'd parked his car a few blocks away and strolled over, a backpack slung over one shoulder. Back in his cell phone and hoodie disguise, he blended in with the male students, as long as he kept his face hooded. Two kids pedaled by on bikes. A trio of young women exited the converted row home next door and strode away, absorbed in conversation. Backpack between his feet, head bent down toward his phone, Conor watched.

He couldn't believe he'd blown it with Louisa. But how did he feel about a real, long-term relationship with a woman who kept secrets until he pried them from her with a metaphorical crow bar? And putting money aside, their backgrounds *were* polar opposites.

Movement snapped Conor out of his introspection. Heath came out of his front door and walked toward the campus. Two of his roommates had left a half hour before. Where was the fourth?

After Heath disappeared around the corner, Conor got up and ambled toward the building. On the front porch, he used his elbow to ring the doorbell, then pretended to wait to be let in. No one answered. Where was the fourth roommate?

Conor tried the doorknob. It turned in his hand. He pushed the door open. Heath hadn't even locked the door. The last roomie must be upstairs somewhere. Sticking his head inside, Conor listened. A shower was running on a higher floor.

He wavered. When would he get another shot at this? He'd have to be quick and hope the roomie liked long showers.

He made a quick sweep of the first floor but saw nothing obvious. Where would a guy like Heath keep his information? Conor's gaze landed on two laptops lying on the desk. Bingo. Young guys were all about their electronic toys. The first one belonged to some guy named Sam. But the second was marked with the initials HLY. Nice. About time some luck went Conor's way.

He opened the computer. It was already on and woke up from hibernation mode instantly. Unlike the old desktop in his office that Conor intended to replace as soon as he had time, Heath's powerhouse laptop was smooth and silent. No chugging or locking up when Conor inspected the folders. He skimmed through the photos. Some tasteless pics of Heath and his friends partying. Didn't these kids know not to take selfies while they were smoking pot? Drunken girls flashing their boobs *Girls Gone Wild–*style. Porn. Yeah. Heath was a classy guy.

Keeping one ear on the still-running shower, Conor started opening videos. More porn. Didn't Heath actually do any schoolwork? Conor opened the fifth video, labeled RS1. Another naked girl. But this video looked different. Homemade. The girl wasn't watching the camera. There was no canned dialogue. She didn't seem to know she was being filmed, which pushed Heath to a whole different level of skeeve. Did Heath secretly videotape his sexual exploits?

Feeling like a voyeur, Conor placed the cursor to close the window. Then he froze. The picture sharpened. He'd seen that girl before. Was that Riki LaSanta? It sure looked like her photo on the flyer. Had she slept with Heath? Had Heath slept with Isa or Zoe? Possibilities whirled through Conor's suspicious mind.

A naked man walked into the room, his back to the camera. He eased onto the bed with the girl. Conor blinked. That wasn't Heath. Professor Xavier English's profile came into focus. He stretched out on the bed next to the girl, and his eyes shifted to give the camera a quick glance. The professor knew the camera was there.

What. The. Fuck?

Why would Heath have videos of the professor with Riki LaSanta? How would he have gotten the vids?

Uh-oh. Upstairs, the shower cut off. He had to get moving. This wouldn't be a good time to be caught, not when the cops were still riding Conor's butt. But how to get the video to the cops? He opened Heath's e-mail and dug Detective Jackson's card out of his wallet. Bingo. He clicked NEW MAIL, typed in the cop's e-mail address, and attached the video. A nasty idea prodded the back of his mind. While the video uploaded, he searched for correspondence with Professor English. There it was, and the video was attached. Heath was blackmailing the professor. According to the e-mail, there were other videos. Who else had the professor slept with? Riki had been his student, so could inappropriate relations get him fired?

While he waited for the file to load, he browsed the rest of the files, stopping on one titled ID1. Knowing what he'd see, Conor opened the file. The bed was empty, but not for long. Professor English backed Isa Dumont to his bed and began taking off her clothes. The professor was two for three. If Conor kept looking, would he find a video of English with Zoe? He attached the second video file and hit UPLOAD.

Footsteps on the floorboards upstairs startled him. *Come on. Come on.* The upload bar turned green. He clicked SEND, closed the windows he'd opened, and lowered the laptop's lid. Footsteps thudded above his head. Grabbing his backpack, he checked the peephole. The porch was empty. Once outside, he slung the mostly empty backpack over his shoulder and crossed the street to the bus stop. The morning was cool but clear. The scent of damp, molding leaves filled the air and discoveries filled Conor's head.

A guy emerged from Heath's place, locked the door, and set off down the walk toward campus. Close one.

A horn gave two short beeps next to him. A dark sedan parked at the curb. Damn. Cops.

For a day that had started out pretty damned good, it sure had gone to hell in a hurry.

"Hey, Sullivan," Jackson said out the lowered window. "How about going for a little ride?"

"I'm kind of short on time," Conor answered. "How about a rain check?"

Jackson's eyes narrowed with impatience. "Get in the car."

Conor sighed. The cops hadn't immediately arrested him. Why not? Curious, he opened the rear door, tossed his backpack onto the seat, and climbed in after it. "So, what's up?"

Behind the wheel, Ianelli pulled into the street. He made a right-hand turn and drove away from the residential blocks. One thing about Philadelphia, you didn't have to drive far to go from a decent neighborhood to a rat hole. Six blocks away, the renovated row homes were replaced by boarded-up hovels. The decorating committee was big on spray cans, sledgehammers, and fire.

Ianelli eased to the curb. "I think we should be asking you that question." The cop met Conor's gaze in the rearview mirror. "Since we just watched you come out of Heath Yeager's apartment."

"Yeah. He wasn't home." Conor spoke the truth without hesitation. No need to elaborate.

"Enough with the games." Jackson turned and spoke through the cage separating the front and back seat. "We have you cold on breaking and entering. Tell me, why did you search Heath's place, and what did you find?"

"Technically, I didn't break in." Conor put a hand on his chest. "Are you asking for my help?"

Ianelli turned around. "Asking? No, we ain't asking."

Conor sized up the cops. Were they backing off him as a suspect? Or was this a trick of some sort? "Heath has been blackmailing someone at the university." It wasn't like Conor didn't want the cops to know. He'd e-mailed them the files. He just hated to be bullied.

Jackson's eyes brightened like a gutter rat that just caught sight of a discarded burger.

Ianelli didn't even raise an eyebrow. "Who?"

Conor waited a beat. "Professor Xavier English."

"What'd he do?" Ianelli asked, his dark eyes glittering with interest.

Conor spilled the rest about the videos of the professor with Riki and Isa. "I'm no expert, but the girls didn't seem to know they were being taped, and English looked right at the camera."

"So how did Heath get the copies?" Jackson asked.

Conor lifted a *no idea* shoulder. "You'll have to ask Heath."

Jackson chewed his lip in silence.

"Is sex with a student worth paying a blackmailer?" Ianelli mused.

"I'd think it could cost him his job," Conor said. "But one of those students has been murdered, and another has disappeared. *That* is worth paying someone to keep quiet."

"You didn't get a copy of those videos, did you?" Jackson asked.

"It's your lucky day." Conor grinned. "Check your e-mail."

CHAPTER
29

Louisa walked into the museum, late, in a daze. Conor had walked her to the front door and made her promise to call the hotel's town car at the end of the day. She checked in at the security desk. The security guard requested secondary identification, and Louisa dug her driver's license out of her wallet. In the wide corridor that divided the museum, an extra guard stood at attention, his eyes scanning the visitors.

In her office, she plunked her purse down on the blotter and sank into her chair. Out of habit, and because she needed to *do* something, Louisa booted up her computer. The monitor was off angle. Bumped by the cleaners while dusting her desk? She adjusted the tilt. When the screen came to life, an annoying window announced her operating system had crashed.

Louisa reached for her phone, stopping with her hand halfway across the desk. She was going to call Zoe—her go-to computer geek when she didn't want to wait for a visit from the museum computer tech—but Zoe was gone. Louisa pressed a fist to her mouth and squeezed her eyes shut. It took several minutes to regain control. With no energy to deal with the computer, she simply turned it off. She'd put in a request to tech support later.

April came in, closing the door behind her. "Did you hear about Isa?"

"Yes."

"I can't believe it." April dropped into the guest chair facing the desk. Her eyes were glazed, her usually chipper attitude deflated with shock. Leaning forward, she rested her elbows on the desk and tipped her forehead into her hands. "Riki, Zoe, Isa . . ." Her voice trailed off.

Louisa reached across the desk and grasped April's hand. "I'm sorry."

"I can't believe Zoe is dead." A small sob squeaked from April's chest.

Louisa squeezed her fingers and released them. "They haven't confirmed that."

"But it was on the news that the investigators believe the body they found could be Zoe."

"Believing isn't the same as knowing." Hope was crucial. Hope kept people going. When hope died, all that was left was despair. It was coming. Louisa could feel the truth shaking her control, the tiny quakes of sadness that would fracture her denial and leave her shattered.

April's head bobbed in a tight-lipped nod. "But Isa was taken from the library, right?"

Louisa choked on the sudden grip of grief around her throat. Even April believed Zoe was dead. She was just humoring Louisa. But what if the police were wrong? What if Zoe was out there, hurt, waiting to be rescued? Tears pressured Louisa's eyes. She blinked them back. "Yes. The police came to my apartment this morning to . . . tell me."

"Those poor girls." A tear slid down April's cheek.

Watching her gutsy assistant cry broke Louisa wide open. Tears poured down her cheeks as sorrow rattled her bones. She felt a strong arm around her shoulders. Sobbing, April stroked the back of her head. "Let it out. You'll feel better."

No, she wouldn't. She couldn't deny the fact any longer. Zoe was dead. She'd been abducted, tortured, and murdered. How could accepting *that* make her feel better?

Louisa straightened, sniffing hard. April brushed a hair from her cheek, a motherly gesture that almost made Louisa break down again. She yanked a tissue free and wiped her eyes and nose. She took three long, slow breaths and gathered her control around her like a shield. "I'm sorry."

"No reason to be."

"I hate being weak," Louisa admitted, realizing too late that the admittance was in itself weakness.

"Don't be ridiculous." April blew her nose. "I know you're tough. You've been through some rough patches, but nothing like this. You're not a robot. Our friend was horribly murdered. Anyone who doesn't react to that is lacking a heart. You're not weak; you're human."

Louisa looked up. She wasn't the tough one in the room. April took that credit. Living with sorrow was much harder than holding on to denial.

April pressed her fingers under her eyes. Anger glittered. "It has to be someone with the museum or university."

"Maybe."

"I guess there isn't anything we can do besides spread the word for the students to stay in groups and be extra careful." April sniffed.

"No." Louisa had never felt so helpless. Or useless. Or disorganized. "I haven't checked my calendar. What's going on here today?"

"Not much. Director Cusack scheduled a staff meeting this morning before we open. Attendance is mandatory." April's lips flattened. "God forbid anything interferes with the museum's schedule."

Louisa sighed. Her sinuses throbbed. She opened her desk drawer and searched for her small bottle of ibuprofen. "Have you seen my Advil?"

"No." April snatched a tissue from the box on Louisa's desk and wiped her wet cheeks. "I have some in my desk."

"Thanks."

April plucked a few more tissues from the box and stuffed them in her pocket. "We need to get to the staff meeting anyway."

Fifteen minutes later, two dozen employees packed the conference room, some sitting at the long table, the rest crowding behind chairs. Standing in the corner, leaning on a credenza, Louisa sipped coffee in a desperate bid to clear the sad ache behind her eyes, which three ibuprofen hadn't alleviated. Next to her, April dabbed puffy red eyes with a folded tissue. Most of the staff wore similar tear-streaked expressions of disbelief and sorrow.

Dr. Cusack cleared his throat. Hands laced behind his back, he paced the front of the room. "I'm sure you've all heard about Zoe and Isa."

A small sob punctuated his opening statement.

Cusack's frown deepened. "I've decided to move the opening of the *Celtic Warrior* exhibit back to December." His eyes sought Louisa's. "I'm sorry, Dr. Hancock, it can't be helped. Considering recent developments, hosting a big party would make the museum look callous, as if we didn't care."

Louisa tipped her head and spoke in a raspy voice. "I agree one hundred percent." Which sounded much better than what she was actually thinking: *I couldn't care less about the exhibit.*

"We'll be issuing a press release shortly, announcing that we'll be moving the date in respect of the victims and their families." Cusack's voice faded in her ears. Something shone in his eyes. Excitement? Frustration? Louisa's stomach pitched. Was he enthused about the prospect of more media attention, or could there be a more sinister reason behind the gleam in his eye? Or was he just frustrated and angry like the rest of the museum employees? She'd assumed Cusack hadn't been actively involved with the interns, but perhaps her judgment had been hasty. Cusack wasn't married. What if that cold, Teflon-like exterior was merely a cover for a sinister soul? Cusack had short, dark hair. He had access to the girls' personnel and student records, and he was brilliant enough to pull off an intricate crime. He knew about the incident in Maine and the relationship between Conor and Louisa, something he'd deliberately kept from her.

"Lastly, we're changing custodial services based on some nighttime thefts." He raised a hand to halt the murmurs. "Nothing of great value to the museum is missing, but between the theft of the dagger replica and the small personal items that have disappeared in the last few weeks, the change makes sense. Your office door locks will be changed. I'll let you know when new keys will be issued. Until then, I advise not leaving anything valuable in your offices. Any questions?"

Chairs scraped as people sensed the end and started to move.

"Then that's all for now," Cusack said in dismissal.

"One more thing." Ignoring the director's sharp glance, Louisa raised her voice. "Everyone needs to be careful. Please stick together. Don't go anywhere alone, especially at night."

"Yes," Cusack interrupted. "Dr. Hancock makes excellent points. Although I'm sure the police will solve these crimes quickly, the museum has already temporarily increased security. No one will be admitted without an employee badge. Don't be alarmed if you see additional guards patrolling the building. All employees, especially females, should ask for an escort to your car if leaving after dark and parked across the street. If you're using public transportation, try to coordinate your commutes.

Please don't take your safety for granted. You need to be just as careful when you aren't here. The police don't suspect any of the girls were taken from museum grounds."

He dismissed them with an authoritative nod.

Cusack approached, the momentary glimmer in his eye replaced with an appropriate level of solemnity. "Dr. Hancock, I hope you weren't blindsided by the announcement."

"Not at all. I'm relieved, in fact." Louisa held her coffee in front of her body as a personal boundary marker. "The staff should be focused on helping the police and keeping each other safe."

"I concur," he said, but his stern, tight mouth said he wasn't happy with her. "I'll meet with the board and finalize a new date for the opening."

"Thank you." Louisa waited until everyone else had left the room. "Why are employees being asked to show a second piece of identification?"

Cusack stepped closer and lowered his head. "According to security records, an employee on maternity leave used her ID several times over the last few weeks. When we called her at home, she denied coming to the museum and couldn't find her ID."

"So someone was using her card to gain access to the museum?"

"That's what the police think." Cusack's face pinched with displeasure. What were ordinarily small lapses in security were magnified in light of the three girls' disappearances. "And Dr. Hancock?"

"Yes."

"No more working late at night," Dr. Cusack said, his eyes flat. "I wouldn't want you to put yourself in danger."

Louisa took an instinctive step back at his tone. Had that been concern or a veiled threat? With an agreeable nod, she bolted for her office. Along with the weird encounter with Cusack, the morning's interview with the detectives lingered in her mind like the taste of burnt garlic. Who might know what was going on with the case? Damian. She'd called him earlier, but he hadn't called back with any news.

She picked up the phone and dialed Damian's number. "Are you free for lunch?"

Over the connection, she could hear papers shuffling. "I can shift some things around. Is it important?"

"Yes."

"Then I'm all yours," Damian said. "How about a picnic at Logan Square? I'll bring the food."

Louisa hesitated. Damian favored sandwiches from the grease trucks that parked in University City, but she doubted she'd have much of an appetite. Plus, outside in the middle of the square with its geyser of a fountain, it was unlikely that anyone would overhear their conversation. "That's great. Noon?"

"You're on."

"I'll meet you there."

"Let me pick you up," Damian objected. "I don't think anyone associated with the museum should be walking around alone."

She hung up the phone with Damian's warning echoing in her office. The director had sent around a press release, and using her smartphone, she busied herself sending out e-mails addressing the postponement of the exhibit opening.

At lunchtime, she picked up her purse, slipped into her jacket, and went into the outer office. April was slitting mail open with a letter opener with the efficiency of a butcher. Her eyes tracked to her monitor. Her mouth slacked open. "Oh my goodness."

Louisa went round the desk. A banner scrolled across the bottom of the screen. LIVE BREAKING NEWS ON THE MUSEUM MURDER.

"What happened?" April leaned over the desk.

Louisa swiveled the monitor toward her assistant and turned on the volume.

A reporter stood in front of the History Department building. "Dr. Xavier English, a history professor at Livingston University, was arrested in the museum murder."

Louisa and April listened, slack-mouthed with shock, as the reporter summed up the case.

"I can't believe it." The news channel moved on to another story, and April turned off the volume.

"Me either. Let me know if you hear anything else."

"You too."

Louisa went to the museum foyer. Damian was waiting just outside the glass doors. A brown bag dangled from one hand. She pushed through the glass doors into the not-so-fresh city air.

He kissed her cheek. "I can't believe Xavier was arrested."

"Do you know what evidence they found?" They walked toward the square. In the center, the dazzling autumn sunlight turned Swann Memorial Fountain into a spectacular display of sculpture and sparkling water. Two, possibly three young women were dead. She respected Xavier. Even after his obnoxious behavior at the fund-raiser, it had never occurred to her that he could be a killer. How could she not have known?

Damian lowered his head and his voice. "Rumor has it that he was sleeping with a bunch of his students and—wait for it—making sex tapes without their knowledge."

"That's so . . ." Louisa searched for the right word.

"Trite? Boring? Crass?"

"Awful." Louisa pictured young women fooled and duped by a charming professor. "They must feel so betrayed and humiliated." She could have been one of his victims. Before being put in Conor's path, she'd thought perhaps Xavier was working up to asking her out. She would have said yes.

"And let's not forget dead."

Louisa felt the blood drain from her face in a wash of chilly fall air. "Why would he kill them?"

"Apparently, someone got hold of some of the videos and was blackmailing him."

"Who?"

"Another student."

Louisa watched the wind blow water across the square. She picked a dry bench. The geyser in the center of the square spouted high in the air, often soaking visitors. "I can't believe it."

Damian's mouth twisted. "Why is it that everyone feels so damned much pity for smart college girls, but the world couldn't care less about my missing teen?"

"No word on your runaway?"

"Hard to find someone no one's looking for." Damian's voice turned bitter. "Here's a piece of advice, girls, don't be poor or uneducated. No one will care if you disappear."

"I'm sorry." Louisa touched his hand.

"I know you are." But Damian's smile was brittle, and she wondered again why he was her friend. She was wealthy, educated, and born to privilege, everything Damian despised.

"OK. I'm done ranting on the social injustices in the world." He jerked his chin up. "We need to be grateful for small successes. Today, a predator was stopped."

"Not soon enough." Louisa's skin felt raw with grief.

"The good news is that Conor is off the cops' radar." Damian handed her a sandwich. "Police surveillance is an irrefutable alibi."

Louisa set it on the bench next to her without unwrapping it.

Chewing, he nudged her sandwich toward her. "It's pulled pork. Eat it. The world is a terrible place full of terrible people. Starving yourself isn't going to change that."

She opened it and took a bite without tasting anything.

Damian lowered his lunch. "I know you're having trouble accepting all this, but those three girls aren't coming back."

Louisa's next breath hitched in her chest. She looked up at the sunshine glinting on water droplets in the fountain's spray like diamonds under a jeweler's loupe. The beauty of the afternoon felt like a sacrilege, as if all pleasure and beauty in the world should cease existing while parents mourned the deaths of their children. Even as one predator was stopped, all over the world, the wicked preyed on the innocent. There was no shortage of evil opportunists.

She gave up on her lunch. "I know. I just pray the police have the right man. I don't want any more young women to get killed."

Damian escorted her back to the museum. Louisa went back to her office but couldn't concentrate on her paperwork. Conor called to tell her about the videos he'd found in Heath's house. He'd been tied up with the police all morning. She decided to work on finishing out the *Celtic Warrior* exhibit. It didn't matter that the grand opening had been pushed back. The work needed to get done, and physical tasks took less focus. She headed to the third floor with a list of items still needed for the life-size diorama.

She got off the elevator and skirted a ladder in the hallway. A technician in a security company uniform was mounting a small camera to the ceiling. She spent an hour sorting through fake rocks and tufts of grass in the prop room. Then she went into the apparel room and started searching for a proper helmet for one of her warrior mannequins.

Louisa stifled a sob. She was going to miss her intern, and not just because of her superior knowledge of Celtic history. Zoe's youthful energy and drive would be sadly lacking in the office.

Her arms were full. Why hadn't she brought a box with her? Spying a large cardboard box behind the shelves, she rounded the unit and opened it. But it wasn't empty. Inside were a number of small personal items: a bottle of antacids, an iPod, a flashlight, a pen, mints, dental floss, and a bottle of ibuprofen that looked exactly like the one that had been in her desk drawer. A museum brochure was tucked under the jumble. Could she have found the museum thief's stash?

Forgetting about her 3-D scene, she hefted the box down to Director Cusack's office.

His secretary's desk was empty. Louisa knocked.

"Come in," Cusack's voice commanded.

She opened the door.

"What is it?" Cusack closed his desk drawer with a slam. His mouth was tight and his eyes annoyed.

Louisa hesitated. Fear prickled her nape. Was he hiding something? She left the door open as she crossed to his desk. "I found something upstairs you'll want to see."

His attention snapped to the box.

"I believe this is full of stolen personal items." Setting the box on the corner of the desk, Louisa explained how she found it. "Do you want to call the police?"

"Yes, I'll handle it," Cusack said.

"You should go home." Cusack scrutinized her face. "You look tired."

Louisa sighed. She *was* tired. "I just have a couple of things to finish before I leave for the day."

She hurried out of his office. Cusack was acting strangely. One minute he was irritated, the next he was uncharacteristically considerate. He knew all the girls. He had access to the replica knife. If the police hadn't already arrested Xavier, Louisa would be suspicious.

CHAPTER
30

"I think you're being a big idiot."

Leaning on the bar, Conor looked up from the stack of invoices in his hand. "What?"

Next to him, Pat dropped his reading glasses on the receipts he was tallying. The bar hadn't opened for the day, but there was plenty of work to be done. "Hey, you asked."

"I spill my guts, and that's what I get back?"

"A smart, gorgeous, sweet woman told you she's falling in love with you, and you didn't say it back, even though we both know you feel the same way. You can't commit because she has more money than you? That's the lamest thing I've ever heard." Pat pointed a finger straight into Conor's nose. "Danny's medical bills took us all by surprise. But we've paid off all the debt. We're not flat broke anymore. In fact, without those extra interest payments, the bar has been turning a nice profit lately."

"But—"

"I'm not finished." The flush was creeping up Pat's neck into his face. Pat didn't get angry often, but when he did, he went full out. "We spent all our lives sweating the lack of money, Conor. I still wake up with flashbacks of an empty fridge, a mailbox full of bills, and a social worker on the doorstep ready to take Jayne and Danny away. Now you're going to cry over the possibility of having too much money? Give me a fucking break."

"I always thought I'd end up with a simple life, like you." Conor stepped back to get out of the way as his brother paced to the end of the bar and back, his movements tense and jerky with anger. "Louisa and I have nothing in common. What do I know about yachts and ponies?"

"Simple? You think my life is simple?" Pat shook his head in wry amusement. "Let me tell you this. Nothing is simple. And it pisses me off when you say you're not good enough for her. What about Jayne and Danny and me? Are we unworthy? Because we all come from the same humble roots. Should Jayne not marry Reed because he's loaded and she's not? Maybe Leena should have left me years ago. It was her salary that fed us for a long time."

Guilt washed over Conor. Pat was the best man he knew. The thought that he'd just insulted him—a real insult, not their normal daily ball-busting—made him feel six inches tall. "I didn't mean—"

"I know you didn't." Pat rubbed his forehead as if it hurt. "What's the real reason you're running scared? Is it because of Barbara?"

Conor sighed.

"I know you got burned, but Jesus Christ, that was three years ago. Get over it," Pat said. "If I hadn't thrown my back out, I'd knock your ass down and sit on your chest like I did when you played hooky and I had to cover for you."

"I was twelve. This hardly compares."

"It compares because it was a stupid thing to do and you needed some sense knocked into your thick head," Pat retorted. "Do you love Louisa?"

Certainty engulfed him without warning, like a flash flood in Cobbs Creek, and the thought of spending the rest of his life without her hollowed his chest. "I do. How did you know?"

Pat rolled his eyes. "Because you're normally not such an idiot. Something had to be different."

"She's a lot of work. She has issues and enough baggage to need her own pack mule. She's been hurt and has trouble trusting people."

"In that case, you have more in common than you think." Pat picked up his glasses and gestured with them. "I've never known you to be afraid of work. Good things don't come easy. Besides, there's no such thing as an *easy* woman."

"Leena would kick your ass if she heard you say that."

"Exactly." Pat nodded. "But honestly, Conor, life doesn't come with any guarantees. You have to risk it to get the biscuit."

"And on that profound note," Conor laughed. "There's ten minutes until we open for lunch. I have to run upstairs and check a couple of things in the apartment so we can get moving on the renovation."

"Maybe you won't be needing the apartment for long." Pat waggled his eyebrows.

"Maybe not." The idea of waking up with Louisa every morning sparked hope inside Conor. After the turmoil of the past week, all he wanted was some quiet time to get to know her. If only the cops would find the killer, then everyone could begin the healing process, including Louisa. He hoped she'd give him a second chance to explain why he was such an idiot that morning.

"I'll be back in a few." Conor gathered up the invoices and receipts. "I'll drop these in the office on my way out."

"Take your time." Pat headed for the front door, keys jingling in his hand.

Conor hurried outside and jogged up the back stairs. Empty. That was the only word to describe the apartment. The professional cleaning crew had been forced to trash most of his belongings. The floors were scheduled for refinishing this week. Then the walls would be painted. An entire new kitchen had to be installed. Everything would be brand new, but Pat was right. Conor had no desire to live here alone any longer. Being with Louisa had changed his life. She'd changed him.

A distant woof from a neighborhood dog triggered a twinge of anxiety. He'd dropped Kirra off at the vet's office on his way to the bar. They were going to run some tests. He checked his phone display for the tenth time, but he hadn't missed any calls. If the vet didn't call in the next hour, Conor was going to give the office a ring.

Kirra shouldn't lose her second chance either.

With a last survey of the bare space assuring him that the apartment was ready for renovation, Conor let himself out and jogged down the wooden steps. Pat would need help with the lunch crush. Primitive instinct cramped his belly as his boots hit blacktop. Conor scanned the alley, the hairs on his nape quivering. No teens with guns or knives. Nothing at all. What the hell was wrong with him?

Something scraped. Conor froze, listening hard, but he heard nothing but the usual sounds of traffic and muffled voices. Conor started toward the door. A shuffling sound stopped him. He crouched and peered into the shadow under the stairwell. Oh shit.

He recoiled from the sight. Shaking his head, he leaned down again, just to make sure he hadn't imagined the grisly sight.

No. He hadn't. A body lay under the steps. A ragged gasp drew Conor closer.

It was the teen gangbanger who'd been after him, Hector Torres. He was still alive, but from the looks of him, just barely.

Conor whipped his cell phone from his back pocket and called 911. Then he crawled back under the steps. The kid's torso was covered in blood, and he'd leaked all over the pavement. Hector's eyes opened, and his gaze locked on Conor. The teen's glazed look was filled with fear, but also a shocking amount of hate, considering the shape he was in.

This was a bad day for the cops to stop tailing him.

"Don't move." Conor unzipped the hoodie and found the source of the bleeding, a stab wound just under Hector's ribs. Conor tugged off his own T-shirt, folded it, and pressed it against the wound. He leaned on his overlapped hands to apply pressure. It seemed like a long time until the thin wail of sirens announced the arrival of help. Two patrol cars and an ambulance crowded in the alley. Conor moved out of the way for paramedics to take over.

He gave a statement to the beat cops while the ambulance loaded Hector into the back and took off. The patrol cops left, and a familiar dark sedan pulled into the alley. Jackson and Ianelli got out.

"If you want to talk to me, you'll have to come inside." Conor walked to the back door and gestured toward it with a bloody hand. "Would you mind?"

Jackson opened the door. Conor led the way to the men's room. He opened the swinging door with his hip. Jackson turned on the spigot for him.

"Thanks." Conor lathered up his hands and forearms all the way to his elbows. He scrubbed the blood out from under his nails.

"You missed a spot." Ianelli pointed to Conor's ribs. A streak of blood had dried to rusty brown.

Conor scrubbed the spot with a soapy towel. He leaned on the sink with both hands.

"I hear your alibi is in pretty bad shape." Jackson leaned on the wall.

"You're kidding me, right?" Conor stared at the cop, whose gaze didn't flinch. He yanked a paper towel from the wall dispenser and dried his hands, arms, and ribs. Walking out of the restroom, he let the cops follow him to the office, where he dug out a clean Sullivan's Tavern T-shirt and tugged it over his head.

Jackson's eyes were roaming over the desktop. So what? Conor didn't have anything to hide.

The venom in the wounded kid's eyes was going to stick with him. Halfway to death, Hector still wanted to kill Conor. What bred that level of animosity? "You think he's going to make it?"

Jackson's frown deepened the lines in his face. "Didn't look good. You sure you didn't stab him?" Jackson popped a piece of chewing gum into his mouth and chewed voraciously.

Conor stared, exasperated. "Why the hell would I try to save him if I stabbed him?"

"I've seen weirder." Ianelli lifted his palms to the sky in a *who knows* gesture. "Maybe you just pretended to try and save him."

"I called 911." Conor gave up. "Whatever."

Wait. Was that almost a smile on Jackson's face?

"What's going on?" Conor dropped into a chair, exhaustion flooding him. He was tired of all of this.

Jackson shoved his hands into his pockets and stared at the floor. When he looked up, his eyes were gleaming. "Sorry. We were just fucking with you."

Conor looked from one cop to the other. In the middle of his stone-cold face, Ianelli's eyes laughed.

"What?"

"Don't you watch the news?" Jackson asked, shaking his head. "We arrested Professor English for the museum murder."

"You did?" Conor would have jumped to his feet if his legs had been steadier.

"Can't give you the deets, but we were on our way back to the station when this call came in. We thought you should know." Jackson stepped toward the door. "Excuse us, we have to go nail his ass."

"Good luck with that," Conor said.

Jackson turned back. "Oh, and we're bringing Blaine Delancey in. We think he might have been the one who pushed Dr. Hancock into the street."

"You'll let me know if the kid makes it, right?" Conor asked.

"Sure," Jackson said.

The cops walked out the door, leaving Conor in a state of disbelief. Even though he'd found evidence the professor was a pervert, and he'd considered the possibility of Xavier being the killer, the cop's confirmation of the professor's guilt was still a shock.

Was it really over?

His phone vibrated. He glanced at the screen, hoping it was Louisa. The vet's number popped onto the display.

He answered the call. "Hello?"

The vet didn't waste any time. "You need to come down here immediately."

———

Louisa checked her cell phone. Nothing from Conor. He'd promised to call her when he heard from the vet. Maybe the vet hadn't finished the tests or he'd gotten tied up at work. The bar could get insanely busy at dinnertime. He'd call when he could. She needed to be patient.

Did he even know about Xavier's arrest? She still couldn't believe the professor was a sexual deviant and a killer.

She collected her purse, shimmied into her jacket, and locked her office. April slumped at her desk, not looking any more productive or less miserable than Louisa had been all afternoon.

She stopped in front of her desk. "I'm heading out."

April sniffed. "Good idea."

"Are you going to be all right?" Louisa hesitated, unsure of how to proceed with the closer relationship that had sprung up with her assistant.

"Yeah." April gave her a watery smile. "We have to face one day at a time. That's all we can do."

Louisa took a deep breath. Her lungs ached with sadness, fighting tight ribs to expand. "I suppose you're right."

It was over, but it was going to take a long time for it to feel that way.

April wiped her nose and pulled her purse from her drawer. "I'll walk out with you."

Seeing April cry started Louisa all over again. She plucked a tissue from the box on her assistant's desk and dried the tender skin around her eyes.

April changed into athletic shoes. They walked toward the exit in silence and swiped their badges at the security desk. Outside on the concrete apron in front of the museum, April turned toward the bus stop with a sad wave. Louisa scanned the curb for the Rittenhouse town car.

The museum murderer had been caught. She could just walk home, but she'd arranged for the pickup that morning, and her limbs felt as if they had tripled in weight since then. Every step was a supreme effort. She was going to take a hot bath, put on yoga pants, and climb into bed. But without Kirra, the apartment would be empty. How could she have gotten so attached to the dog in less than a week?

An even better idea occurred to her. She would change her clothes, then go see Conor at work tonight and have dinner at the bar. Perhaps the crowd and noise would be better than her silent apartment. So what if he hadn't said he was falling for her too? Probably, she should have waited before springing that on him this soon. A week did not make a relationship.

Decision made, she suddenly craved his strong arms around her body. Just being with him would make her feel better. How could she have gotten so attached to *him* in such a short period of time? It suddenly seemed as if her life had started when she'd walked into his bar the week before. Prior to him, she'd been alive, but she hadn't really been living.

Everything had changed since that day. Riki and Zoe were dead, probably Isa too.

The wind blurred her watery vision. She spotted the sleek black vehicle fifty yards ahead. As she approached, the uniformed driver got out and opened the door for her. Blinking away her tears, she rooted through her purse for another tissue. She was blotting her eyes and running nose as she stepped into the vehicle. A jolt of pain struck her in the shoulder and blazed through her body. She stiffened and fell forward onto the back seat. Her twitching legs were shoved roughly into the vehicle.

What was happening?

A shadow loomed over her. A knee pressed into her back, shoving her face into the seat. The weight holding her down sparked a surge of brain-numbing panic. Before she could move, something bound her ankles. Her hands were pulled behind her back and fastened together. In seconds, she was effectively kidnapped.

The weight moved off her back. Unable to control her body enough to even turn her head, she caught the driver's back in her peripheral vision. She couldn't see his head, but the figure was too tall, too thin. It wasn't the short, stocky driver from the Rittenhouse. Then who was it?

The door closed. Her captor got into the driver's seat. The quiet *snick* of the door locks made everything fall into place.

Oh my God. Fear slammed through her with the same jolt of electricity as she realized the truth. The police had arrested the wrong person as the murderer.

CHAPTER
31

The back room at the veterinary clinic smelled like dogs and disinfectant. Conor stared at the plastic pouches of coffee-colored liquid spread on the stainless-steel tray. "What is that?"

Standing next to him in pale blue scrubs, the vet scratched her head. "We aren't positive, but we suspect drugs."

"Drugs." Events and information clicked into place like the tumblers in a lock. "And you took them out of Kirra's stomach?"

"Yes." The vet gestured to the packs. "There have been several other recent cases of liquid heroin and cocaine being transported inside animals."

"Liquid heroin." It made perfect sense. Hector had been way too determined to get Kirra back.

"Yes. Kirra is a lucky dog. If one of those pouches had burst, she would have died."

"But you said she's going to be OK."

"She is." The vet nodded. "The police are on the way. Since she's your dog, you'll need to stay and talk to them. Do you want to see her while you wait?"

"Yes." Relief coursed through Conor as his gaze swept over the pitiful dog. Her belly was shaved. A long row of stitches closed an eight-inch incision. An IV line was taped to her foreleg. The line snaked out of the metal cage and attached to the bag of fluids hanging on the bars above the door.

The vet opened the cage door. "You can pet her."

Conor reached in and stroked the dog's head. Her eyes opened. Her tail stub jerked in a weak wag the second she caught sight of him.

"I spayed her since she was under anesthesia anyway. She'll need to stay here overnight," the vet said.

"Thank you." Conor checked his messages but saw none from Louisa. A sliver of apprehension slid through his gut. She'd been waiting for word on Kirra.

The next hour was spent answering questions for the police report. The cops verified the pouches were likely full of liquid heroin. They'd had several other cases of drugs being transported in animals recently. It was seven o'clock before Conor finished. He left the vet's office. Pulling out his phone, he hurried toward the bar. He left a message on Louisa's cell phone and sent her another text. Something was wrong.

He went into Sullivan's.

Behind the bar, Pat set a freshly drawn draft in front of a customer. "Is everything all right?"

"The dog was full of heroin packets."

Pat's eyes widened. "Holy shit. No wonder that kid wanted her back so much."

"Yeah." Conor's gaze swept the bar. "Louisa hasn't been in?"

"No." Pat took an order and tilted a tall glass under the tap. "Was she supposed to come here?"

"No, but I haven't heard from her. She was worried about the dog. She should have called me right after work." Conor paced the length of the bar. "I'm going to drive over there."

"Go." Pat straightened the glass. A perfect head of foam topped the amber liquid. "Text me when you find her, all right?"

"Yeah." Conor headed out the back door. Was it just this

morning that he'd found Hector bleeding in the alley? Seemed like much longer. His Porsche was parked on the street at the end of the alley. He started the engine. His phone chirped as he pulled away from the curb. He didn't recognize the number.

"Hello."

"Mr. Sullivan?" a familiar voice asked.

"Yes."

"This is Gerome from the Rittenhouse."

Conor's heart double tapped.

"The police have already been notified, but I wanted you to know too," Gerome said. "You know Dr. Hancock arranged for the car to pick her up after work."

"Yeah. I was there."

"Right. When she didn't come home right after work, I thought maybe she wanted to stop somewhere. But we just found our driver in the men's room utility closet. He was tied up. Someone zapped him with a homemade stun gun. His uniform and the car are missing. Dr. Hancock isn't in her apartment."

Conor's heart dropped into his stomach. "Someone stole the town car?"

"Yes."

"Did you try Dr. Hancock at the museum?"

"She left two hours ago."

"I'll be right there." Conor floored the Porsche. Weaving in and out of traffic on Front Street, he dug Detective Jackson's card out of his wallet. He left his name and number on the cop's voice mail with a simple message. "Louisa is missing."

Two patrolmen were questioning the driver when Conor ran into the Rittenhouse.

Gerome paced the lobby.

"Does he remember anything?"

"No." Gerome stopped and shook his head. "Someone zapped him as he came out of the stall. Whoever it was dragged him into the utility closet, stole his clothes and keys, and tied him up."

One of the cops walked over. "Are you the boyfriend?"

"Yes." Conor gave him his personal information. "Do you have any clues? What about tracking the GPS in her cell phone?"

"The town car is fitted with a GPS. We're trying to get a position on it now." The cop looked grim. "Her purse was found in the street in front of the museum. Her phone was inside."

Pacing, Conor dialed the museum, but the after-hours message played. He tapped Gerome on the shoulder. "I'm going to the museum. Call me if anything happens here?"

"Will do," Gerome said.

A police cruiser was parked at the curb in front of the museum. An officer was in the foyer, talking to the guards and a tall man Conor recognized from the fund-raiser as Louisa's boss. Conor banged on the door. Cusack opened it.

Conor pushed his way inside and introduced himself. "Where's Louisa?"

Cusack crossed his arms over his chest. "The police are reviewing the security camera footage. The guard saw Dr. Hancock walking toward a black sedan about fifty yards down the street. That's all he saw. It was rush hour. Most of the office staff was heading out. We're not open on Monday nights."

A second cop hustled down the hall.

"Are you familiar with the museum murder case?" Conor asked.

"Every cop in the city knows about the case," the cop said and then turned to Cusack. "Did anything unusual happen here today?"

"The whole office was out of sorts. Between the news that Isa Dumont had disappeared and Professor English had been arrested, everyone was in shock." He paused. "I doubt that it's connected, but just before she left, Dr. Hancock brought a box to my office. She claimed to have found it in one of the third-floor storage rooms. We've had a petty thief in the museum over the past few weeks. The box contained some of the items the staff had reported missing. I called the detectives in charge of the case. They weren't available, so I left a message."

"Would you show us the box?" the cop asked.

"Of course." Cusack led them to his office. "We changed cleaning contractors this week in hopes that would solve the problem. The things seemed to go missing at night."

Conor and the cop looked into the box of random personal items.

The cop pulled gloves out of his pocket and lifted the museum brochure onto the desk. He opened it, and a pile of papers fell out, including what appeared to be a map printed off the Internet. "It's a map."

Conor pointed to a fat line on the map. "The expressway." He moved his finger to tap two wavy squiggles. "The Delaware and Schuylkill Rivers."

They identified other landmarks.

"I wonder what these stars mean?"

"They're numbered. One and two are in North Kensington. Number three is in West Philly. Number four is in Camden." Conor squinted at the tiny marks.

The cop looked over Conor's shoulder. "Those aren't the best neighborhoods."

"Wait. The first two bodies were found in North Kensington." Conor's heart clenched. The blood it pumped through his veins turned refrigerator cold. "Number three must be Isa. Louisa is the fourth victim. That means she's in Camden."

"I think you're right." The cop reached for his radio and turned toward the corridor.

Camden, New Jersey, then. It had to be.

But what if he was wrong?

"You need to talk to Detectives Jackson and Ianelli," Conor shouted after the officer. He grabbed the map, carried it out of the director's office, and ran off a copy at the machine next to the secretary's desk. He hit the hallway running before the cop turned around. He read the map as he bolted down the main corridor and through the lobby.

"Wait!"

Conor stopped and turned.

"They located the town car," the officer shouted down the hall. "In the Delaware River."

Conor paused, terror freezing his feet in place for a few long seconds. No. He couldn't believe she was dead. He wouldn't be able to function. She couldn't be gone. "Was anyone inside?"

"Not that they could see," the cop yelled. "They won't be able to open the trunk until it's pulled out of the water."

Conor ran out on the implication that Louisa could have been in the trunk. His Porsche was still illegally parked out front. He jumped in and roared away from the curb. Detective Jackson hadn't called back. Conor headed toward the Ben Franklin Bridge. He raced down Market and made a left onto Fifth Street. The bridge loomed bright in the night sky, its lighted frame spanning the Delaware River. Somewhere on the other side of that dark width of water, Louisa faced a killer.

The car door opened. Louisa lay on the seat. She'd managed to roll onto her side, but the ride had been short, not even long enough for her to regain complete use of her body after the electrical shock. She blinked, temporarily blinded by the vehicle's interior dome light. Outside, everything was dark.

Her captor leaned in. The light glittered on a knife. Louisa pulled her legs up and kicked out. Her feet connected, and she knocked the figure backward.

"You bitch."

Louisa froze. She knew that voice. But it was impossible.

A knife flicked out, severing the thin plastic tie that bound Louisa's ankles. A gun was pointed directly in Louisa's face. "Get out of the car."

Shock paralyzed Louisa. Had her ears been affected by the electricity?

"Now." The gun shook with erratic motions.

Louisa wiggled to the edge of the seat and sat up. A fiery pins-and-needles sensation burned through her feet as she flexed her ankles. Her bound hands behind her back impeded her movements. With an awkward heave, she lurched to her feet. Dizziness swirled in her head. She had to be wrong. She squinted into the darkness.

"Move." The figure motioned forward with the muzzle of the gun. Louisa looked up at a crumbling old row home. In the darkness, all she could see was the outline of the building against the sky. The roofline appeared to have significant gaps. A dog barked in the distance.

With a prod from the gun, Louisa stumbled into a narrow alley that ran between buildings. With the muzzle pressing hard into her back, she climbed three cement steps and pushed open a door. Her mind reeled. The stench of garbage and human waste assaulted her nostrils as she crossed an unstable floor, the wood creaking and shifting under her feet. She walked toward a faint glow. A doorway led to a wooden stairwell.

"Downstairs."

The shove sent her tumbling. She flipped once. Her head struck a tread, and the faint light faded to blackness.

Camden, New Jersey, jockeyed with Detroit and Flint, Michigan, for the highest per capita murder rate in the nation. With boarded-up factories, plenty of vacant row homes, and crack houses, Camden was a model of urban blight. After Conor passed the demolished Sears building, he exited Admiral Wilson Boulevard onto Martin Luther King Boulevard. Once he drove through the public facade of Camden, the refaced buildings and inset brick crosswalks that marked the new city center, he emerged into the heart of the city, a heart that could use a thousand-way coronary bypass.

Conor pulled over and turned on the dome light. He counted the streets past Broadway, drove through three more intersections, and turned right. Before he navigated the next two turns, he turned off his headlights and crawled forward in the dark. The Porsche bumped along. The paved-over backstreet was worn down in spots to its original cobblestones.

Boarded-up row houses lined the street. An occasional chain-link fence corralled God-knew-what. Buildings slated for eventual demolition were tagged with red-and-white signs. A house with fresh paint on the door and flowers in urns on the step was the saddest sight of all, a sign that someone cared. The streetlights were dark. Half the lots were vacant and knee-high with weeds. On the left, a six-foot rusted privacy fence ran the length of the street. Dogs barked behind it.

Several wrong turns wasted precious time. The star on the

map was just up the block. Conor pulled over behind a Dumpster.

He called Detective Jackson again, this time leaving a detailed message with the address of the mapped star. The Philly cops would have to coordinate with the Camden police. Conor didn't have time for any of that bullshit. If Louisa was here, he'd find her.

Then he got out of his car, opened the trunk for the tire iron, and headed toward the boarded-up brick row home halfway down the block. He paused, hiding behind a rusted Cadillac on blocks, and sized up the house. Bricks crumbled. Graffiti covered most of the surfaces.

Tire iron in hand, Conor crept toward the side of the house. Like all the others, the side window was boarded up.

Sweat trickled down his back, and his heart thudded, loud as a bass line. But now was his chance to check inside. Moving toward the rear of the building, he climbed the cracked cement stoop and checked the door. Unlocked. He pulled it open. The inside was beyond dark. No moonlight penetrated the boarded-up windows. He stepped to the side and listened, easing the door closed behind him. The inside of the house was dead silent. He didn't even hear any rats or insects rustling around.

He gave his eyes and ears a few minutes to adjust, but he still couldn't see six inches in front of his face. There was zero light for his desperate pupils to absorb. Conor pulled his phone out of his pocket, held it an arm's length away, and turned on the screen. Nothing attacked him. He let out his breath. He brightened the display and swept it around the space. More graffiti tags decorated the walls. Trash, a rotted mattress, and bottles littered the floor. The odors of feces and urine burned his nostrils. He shined his phone at the floor. Something had been dragged through the dirt. Stepping around a scattering of used needles,

Conor followed the path to a doorway. Stairs descended into the black cellar.

He turned up his phone's brightness to maximum and started down the steps.

———

Pain lanced behind Louisa's eyeballs and swelled in her temples, radiating downward through most of her body. She cracked an eyelid to total darkness. Judging from the hard coldness seeping through her clothes, she was lying on cement. A basement? Curled on her side, she wriggled, but she could barely move. Her hands and feet were bound and fastened to something solid behind her back. She tried to open her mouth but couldn't. She moved her lips. Something sticky tore at her skin. Tape.

Where was she? What had happened?

As she lay still, a memory pushed past the agony in her head. The museum. She'd gotten into the town car and . . .

The memory—and all its associated betrayal—clarified in her mind.

Fear and nausea rose in her throat. She closed her eyes and breathed through her nose, willing her stomach to settle and her panic to subside, but hysteria bubbled inside her chest. Perhaps choking on her own vomit would be preferable to what lay ahead: multiple stabbings, a knife slicing through her throat, fire eating at her flesh. The wounds on Riki's body played in her own private slideshow.

How much would it hurt to bleed to death?

A wave of grief spilled over her. Conor. She'd finally fallen in love, finally found a good man, only to die before they could enjoy any happiness. Before he even told her he loved her.

Did he? Would he be devastated by her death?

A scuffing sound prompted the involuntary reopening of her eyelids. A floorboard creaked overhead. She strained to see something, anything, in the darkness. A faint glow descended toward her. She blinked to clear her blurry vision. There were stairs on that side of the room. With another bout of queasiness, she remembered tumbling down, her head striking a tread, her vision blackening.

The light flickered over her. She closed her eyes and braced herself for more pain. Fear swept through her. Her numb, restrained limbs trembled.

"Louisa?"

Conor!

Relief rolled over the pain in her head. The glow crossed the cement toward her. He set his cell phone on the floor beside her and checked her binds.

"Hold still. The plastic ties are digging in." Keys jingled as he pulled them from his pocket and sawed at the zip ties. A few minutes later, her hands and feet were free. Conor gently peeled the tape from her mouth. She gulped air.

"Can you sit up?" he asked in a whisper, his hands running over her arms and legs. She winced at every movement of his fingers. Every inch of her body felt bruised from head to toe. "Do you think anything is broken?"

She tried to answer, but all she could do was cough. Her voice was an unintelligible rasp.

"I'm going to get you out of here." He lifted her upper body until she was sitting up.

Her head protested the change of position. Her stomach heaved. She twisted sideways and vomited on the cement. Conor's strong arm supported her until she was finished. His fingers went to her head, sweeping gently through her hair. When he touched a spot on the back of her scalp, her vision turned red. She nearly blacked out.

"I'm going to pick you up." He scooped her under the knees and back. Muscles strained as he stood.

Conor froze as footsteps thudded on wood.

CHAPTER
32

A bright flashlight beam blinded Conor. He set Louisa down on the cement and stepped in front of her. One flashlight. Did that mean one person? Was he armed?

"Drop the phone."

The familiar voice stunned Conor. He released his grip on his cell. It clattered to the cement.

"Now step on it. Hard."

Conor stomped a heel on the screen. The display went dark.

The flashlight beam dropped, playing over Louisa's still form. Then the light moved toward the wall. With the click of a switch, the soft light of a camp lantern illuminated the basement.

Six feet in front of him, Zoe stomped her foot. An oversize sweatshirt concealed her slight frame. A gun shook in one hand. A large duffel bag dangled from the other. "You can't have found me. It's impossible."

Conor didn't point out the obvious.

Zoe shook the flashlight. She was wearing the same miniskirt she'd been wearing the night of her disappearance. It was wrinkled and grimy. From the smell wafting across the space, Zoe hadn't showered that week. Her dark hair hung in a greasy ponytail. "I only needed twenty more minutes. That's it. Then everything would have been in place." She gestured toward Louisa. "*She* would be dead. The scene would be staged. You would walk right into my trap." She dropped the bag on the concrete. Metal clanged. She pulled what looked like a disposable camera from her pocket. Two wires protruded from one end. A home-made Taser. "A quick zap with this would render you immobile enough for me to get you into position to shoot yourself in the head."

He shifted his weight, judging the distance between them. Could he tackle her before she shot him?

Probably not. If Louisa were able to run, he'd try it. But the crack on the back of the head had rendered Louisa helpless. If Zoe killed him, Louisa would be next.

"Zoe, put the gun down," he said with authority. "It doesn't have to end like this."

"No way. And don't even try to tell me everything will be OK," Zoe spat. "Because it won't. You two screwed everything up. I was supposed to *escape* this week. I would be the sole survivor of *your* killing spree."

"So Isa is dead?" Conor asked, sadness rolling through the turmoil in his gut.

"Yes. Now there's no one in my way."

"What do you mean?"

"The Pendleworth grant," Louisa breathed.

No way. "You killed three women and planned to frame me for murder and suicide over a grant?"

Louisa had mentioned academic competition, but she'd had the players backward. Of course, the major assumption of her theory had been that Zoe was a victim.

Zoe rolled her eyes. The whites gleamed in the dim. "Of course. It was no accident I went to your apartment and the police found the evidence I left. It would have worked perfectly if the cops hadn't been completely incompetent. They should have arrested you that first night."

The police hadn't been totally incompetent, thought Conor. They hadn't charged him without physical evidence to corroborate the circumstantial. In the end they'd figured out the killer wasn't Conor. Not that he was going to point that out right now. Maybe she didn't even know. "Too bad you couldn't predict that."

"I gave them way too much credit." Her eyes went crazy wide. Her face twisted into an angry, animal-like snarl. The girl was freaking out, the gun in her hand trembling out of anger, not fear. "I'd thought they would follow the clues to the logical conclusion. You and Dr. Hancock were involved with that ritual killing in Maine together. You were the last person to see me. I left some strands of hair in your apartment and your car. It should have been airtight."

"It's been a rough day."

She waved the gun. "Oh well. I'll have to improvise. At the end of the night, it'll still look like you killed Louisa, then turned the gun on yourself."

Yeah, dying or letting Zoe kill Louisa were not items on his to-do list for the night.

Just behind Conor's boots, Louisa stirred. Without moving his head, he dropped his gaze. He could just see her in his peripheral vision. She was struggling to sit up. Even if she got to her feet, she couldn't run. Not with the concussion he suspected she'd suffered. Rage competed with panic in Conor's chest. Zoe had done that—and much, much worse. All because she wasn't the star of the university? No, there had to be more.

Conor needed to keep Zoe talking. The police had the address. It was only a matter of time until they showed up. "Isa was older than you and a year ahead in school. Why would Professor English give you the grant instead of her? She'd been working with him for a year already. Dr. Hancock told me you'd probably get the grant next year. Why not just wait?"

Zoe's eyes narrowed in anger. "Age has never been a factor for me. I've gotten everything I've set out to achieve, except the grant that bitch stole from me. Working with Dr. English? Is that how you think she got the grant? She was fucking him. She thought she was so smart, but he was fucking other girls too. Professor English isn't very discriminating."

"What about Riki and the other girl? Who is she? Why did you kill them?"

Zoe glared at Conor as if he was an idiot. "I killed the other two girls to cover my tracks. I threw Dr. Hancock in to cement your guilt, to make my plan a complete circle, and because she wrote me up for being late a few times. Tardiness. What the fuck does tardiness have to do with brilliance?"

Conor let the truth wash over him. Zoe had killed a fellow student over a grant. But not in a fit of jealousy. This had been cold, calculated, premeditated murder. Zoe had planned every detail. She'd taken opportunities to improve her scheme along the way, like adding additional killings and framing Conor for the deaths.

She'd done a bang-up job of it too. She might have gotten away with it if she hadn't gotten cocky and kidnapped Louisa. Actually, Conor thought, staring at the gun, she might still get away with it.

The threads of her twisted logic were unknotting in Conor's mind. "How are you going to win the grant if you're presumed dead?"

"I'll be found at another location, dehydrated but alive." She lifted her hands toward him. Plastic ties encircled each wrist. The too-tight binds had left bloody rings in her skin. "See? I have ligature marks on my wrists. They're on my ankles too." Pride beamed from her smile. "I won't know why you didn't kill me. Maybe you were driven to suicide when you killed Dr. Hancock.

I won't dwell on that. I'll consider myself lucky and not look back. I'll be the brave survivor of a crazed serial killer."

"What was my motivation for killing the girls and Dr. Hancock?"

Zoe lifted a hand in a *that's an easy one* gesture. "Before you blow your brains out, you'll write a note of apology to your siblings. You've always had a violent side. You've managed to keep it in check, but the killing in Maine whetted your appetite. And since Dr. Hancock was the only one who figured out the truth about what you were doing to her interns, she had to be killed too. But you also loved her and couldn't live without her."

"No one who knows me will believe that." As he argued, terror swept cold over Conor. She'd studied him.

"The opinions of your friends and family don't really matter. The police will buy it. You were a boxer. That implies a certain comfort level with violence. You've been in two physical altercations in the past two weeks. The media has blown them both out of proportion. Heath will attest to your bloodlust. If that gangbanger dies, I'm sure the police will try to hang his death on you too." She smiled as if she knew a secret. "I've been watching the news at night on my laptop. You've been on the top of the suspect list the whole time. Convincing them won't be hard."

No, it wouldn't. Jackson and Ianelli had wanted Conor so badly for these crimes. They'd jump on Zoe's explanation. Conor already thought he knew the answer to his next question, but he asked anyway. Anything to spin out some more time. "Did you stab Hector Torres?"

"Is that his name?" She lifted a *barely interested* shoulder. "I went to the alley behind your bar this morning. I tossed Isa's bloody clothes in the Dumpster. He was hiding and saw me. I couldn't risk any more variables."

Conor's stomach turned. "The cops didn't find Isa's clothes."

"I can't say how disappointed I am with the police."

"You really think you'll be able to pull off pretending to be a victim?" She wasn't just crazy. Zoe was evil. Her eyes glittered when she talked about her plan. She hadn't killed those girls just to get ahead. She'd enjoyed being smarter than everyone else, jerking the cops around—and Conor suspected she'd also enjoyed the killing.

"Yes. It's the perfect alibi." Her knowing smile faded. "Now, enough talking. It's time for you to die. Dr. Hancock will have to be next."

He had to admit, Zoe's plan was brilliant and devious. He'd never suspected she was the killer.

Suddenly a look of curiosity crossed her already crazed features. "How did you find me here?"

"Louisa found the map you hid in the museum."

"Those were supposed to go into the incinerator. But I'd planned out the buildings I was going to use in advance. I didn't want to make any mistakes. Then Cusack changed the cleaning crew and beefed up security. He screwed up my plan to return to the museum to destroy everything."

Thank you, Dr. Cusack.

"Enough questions." Zoe pointed the gun at Conor's chest. Her finger moved. He lunged sideways. At the same moment, Louisa launched her body at him from the ground. The gunshot reverberated on concrete. Louisa's body jerked. She hit the cement slab and didn't move. Conor rolled and kicked the camp lantern. The light shifted in crazy arcs.

The gun went off again. The shot went wild, pinging off the concrete and thudding into the wooden stairs. Conor rushed Zoe. His shoulder collided with her ribs. He felt the air whoosh from her body as they hit the ground. The gun skittered across the floor. She reached for it.

"Oh no you don't." He landed on top, sitting up and pinning her to the floor just as sirens sounded outside.

Footsteps thudded above. "Police."

"Down here," Conor yelled. "Call an ambulance."

"Hands up." Four uniformed cops came down the steps, guns and powerful flashlights sweeping the basement. The guns pointed at Conor. "Get off the girl."

Conor put his hands in the air.

Below him, Zoe sobbed. "He tried to kill me."

A cop tackled Conor and flipped him on his stomach. He knelt on his spine and snapped handcuffs around his wrists. Another uniform helped Zoe to her feet. "Are you all right, miss?"

"Don't take your eye off of her. She's a murderer." Conor's blood ran cold. Once again, the cops thought he was the killer. As long as they took care of Louisa, he'd deal with whatever happened later. "And get an ambulance!"

CHAPTER
33

Louisa's body bloomed with pain. Her lungs refused to inflate. She inhaled. Instead of air, her breath gurgled with liquid. It felt like a car was parked on her chest. A choking sensation filled her throat.

She opened her eyes. Bright lights and men in uniforms swept the basement. Someone came down the stairs with a hand-held floodlight. A policeman wrapped a blanket around Zoe's shoulders. Conor was on the floor, facedown and handcuffed, with two cops on top of him.

A policeman knelt at her side. "Hold on, ma'am. Help is just a few minutes away."

Louisa summoned all her strength. Her hand fisted in his pant leg. "Not him. Not Conor. *She* shot me."

The cop leaned closer to her mouth. "What?"

"She said the girl is the murderer." Detective Ianelli's voice boomed over the commotion.

Louisa used her last store of energy and oxygen to nod. "*She* shot me."

Silence fell over the basement. The last thing Louisa focused on before darkness descended over her vision was the sight of Detective Jackson taking the handcuffs off Conor's wrists. She let herself go into oblivion.

—

Conor skidded to his knees next to Louisa. Breath rattled in and out of her mouth with a wet sound. "Honey, stay with me."

"Ambulance is just around the corner." Jackson lowered himself to one knee. "Shit. Ianelli, get over here. She can't breathe."

"Move over." Ianelli dropped to the concrete. The Camden cops moved out of the way as the detective ripped Louisa's blouse open. The bullet wound was low on her left rib cage. "Her lung is punctured. Air is getting in. I need plastic."

Jackson searched his pockets and came up with a brand-new pack of gum. He tore the cellophane wrapper off and handed it to his partner, who used it to seal the bullet wound.

Louisa's breathing eased a little. A few dozen raspy breaths later, a new siren approached.

"Ambulance is here," a uniformed cop called from the stairwell.

Ianelli got up. The paramedics took over.

Jackson slapped his partner on the shoulder. "Ianelli was an army medic."

Conor rocked back on his heels, watching the paramedics work in silence. One punched a huge needle between Louisa's ribs. Conor flinched.

Ianelli's hand landed on Conor's shoulder. "He's just evening out the pressure." The cop helped him to his feet. "Come on. Let's get over to the hospital."

An IV line was started. Louisa was put on a backboard and transferred to a gurney.

Conor followed the gurney up the steps and into the cool night air. Jackson and Ianelli were right behind him.

"Don't you have to stay at the scene?"

Jackson popped a piece of gum into his mouth. "Nope. Not our jurisdiction."

Zoe was frog-marched to a patrol car and put in the back. As the cop pushed her head down, she turned and glared at Conor.

He shivered. Her eyes were pure evil.

CHAPTER
34

Conor paced the surgical waiting room. Three hours before, Louisa had been rushed through the ER into an operating room. Dropping into a chair, he reached into his jacket pocket and pulled out Louisa's pearls, given to him to hold by one of the ER nurses. Leaning forward, elbows on his knees, he stretched the strands between his hands. The beads were smooth under his fingers, but spots of Louisa's blood had dried to a rusty brown on the lustrous finish, the stains an insult to the necklace's perfection. His mind replayed images of Louisa's pale skin coated in red, the bullet wound in her side, her blood-soaked silk blouse. Her beauty and elegance magnified the violence and horror in the Camden basement.

She'd lost a lot of blood. She'd nearly drowned in it. Her lung had collapsed. She could die.

Fear and reality crowded his mind and his heart.

This morning, she'd said she loved him, and he'd withdrawn. Pat was right. He was a coward.

Had he lost his chance? Would she die never knowing she'd claimed his heart?

Pat and Jayne walked in. Jayne handed Conor a cardboard cup of coffee. "Sit down for a minute." She tugged him to a chair and pushed him into it. Sitting next to him, she wrapped an arm around his shoulders. "She's going to be all right."

"She's tougher than she looks," Damian said from another plastic chair.

Conor put the coffee on the laminate table untouched. He couldn't respond. The bullet had entered through Louisa's ribs and lodged in her lung. They'd intubated her in the ambulance. She wasn't even breathing on her own. How could she be all right?

Detectives Jackson and Ianelli had hung around. They sat across the room, occasionally ducking into the hallway to take a call.

Everyone stood when a grim, green-scrubbed surgeon walked into the room. A mask hung loose around his neck. "Who's here for Louisa Hancock?"

Conor stepped forward, his heart slamming into his rib cage until it felt bruised.

The doctor swept the cloth hat from his head. Sweat beaded his forehead. "She came through the surgery fine."

Conor didn't hear the details. The surgeon's voice was drowned out by the rush of blood in his ears. Pat's giant hand slapped him on the back. Conor stiffened his buckled knees. "No permanent damage?"

"Risk of infection aside, she should make a full recovery. We'll keep her in ICU for the next twenty-four hours as a precaution. You can see her as soon as she comes out of recovery." The doctor left the room.

Conor backed up to a chair and let his legs collapse. For the next hour, he was busy being grateful and counting his blessings. Jayne brought him fresh coffee and a candy bar from the vending machine. When the nurse escorted him to Louisa's bedside, he almost felt human.

She was pale and attached to a dozen wires and tubes, but her heartbeat was steady on the monitor next to the bed. Nice and strong and steady. He took her hand and held it for the allowed five minutes. It wasn't enough. It would never be enough.

—

Two days later, Louisa sipped water from a straw while Detectives Jackson and Ianelli asked her gentle questions. Conor took the cup from her hand and set it on the wheeled tray.

"Zoe really killed three women just to eliminate Isa as her academic competition?" Louisa shifted her position and winced.

Conor put a hand behind her back to support her weight while he adjusted her pillow.

"Not exactly." Jackson sighed. Since the case had come to a conclusion, disbelief and disgust were etched deeper in the lines on his already-craggy face. "She was used to getting everything she wanted. Her parents gave up their lives to educate her. She was always the number-one student in her class. She'd never been turned down for anything. Until she didn't get the Pendleworth grant. But it was clear when we interviewed her that she got off on the whole thing. So what started out as a plan to get the Pendleworth grant escalated as she developed a taste for murder."

"I can't believe it." Louisa let Conor fuss. Frankly, the pain in her chest made her more than OK with him taking care of her. "She was so smart, so talented."

"Don't forget crazy." Jackson stuffed a piece of gum into his mouth. "She put her smarts to use, that's for sure. She planned this entire operation down to the smallest detail."

"The cops at the museum found some other personal stuff of hers hidden in the museum storage rooms. Looked like she'd been sleeping there since she went 'missing.' We also found three small trinkets, one from each of the dead girls, in another box. There are fingerprints all over them. Plus notes, schedules, and observations about both of you and the three murder victims. She had a laptop and an air card. Apparently, she holed up in the museum attic like the Hunchback of Notre Dame," Ianelli explained. "So by the time we got your second text from the house in Camden, we already suspected it was Zoe."

Isa's body was found at the house marked by the third star on Zoe's map.

"I am totally creeped out." Ianelli shivered. "That is one evil girl."

"I can't believe she did the things she did to those girls." Louisa was still reeling from the discovery that Zoe was behind the murders. The medication was numbing her emotions as well as her pain, which was fine with her.

"She grew up on a farm," Ianelli said. "She'd slaughtered plenty of animals. She's physically strong."

"Who was the second victim?" Conor asked.

"A runaway who'd been hanging around the university. Zoe picked her because she fit her basic physical description," Jackson said.

"I still can't wrap my brain around it." Conor shook his head.

"She's been pretty cooperative in questioning," Ianelli said. "She also stole an ID from an employee out on leave and bought a stack of general admission passes to the museum to gain access in the daytime. She'd mapped out every surveillance camera. The guards' patrols were very routine. Working around their patrols wasn't difficult. Since she routinely helped coworkers with their computers, she knew several people's passwords and logins. She'd stashed changes of clothes in the apparel storage room, including a pair of coveralls from the cleaning service, and borrowed wigs from the museum's collection to use as disguises."

"What will happen to her now?" Louisa shivered. Conor tugged the white blanket up to her chin, took her hand in his, and rubbed her cold fingers.

"I'm not sure whether they'll play innocent or insane." Ianelli shoved his hands into his pockets.

"She's not insane." Jackson unwrapped a piece of gum. "And the evidence is piling up."

Louisa tried to concentrate, but the pain was reaching a crescendo. She wanted more answers before she tapped her morphine drip. "What about Professor English?"

Jackson's jaw sawed on his gum with determination. "He's up on charges, just not for murder. We're not sure how that will pan out. English didn't sell or distribute his home movie collection. The DA has to prove the girls weren't aware they were being filmed. Isa and Riki are both dead. They have to identify the other girls and get them to testify. The professor had dozens of videos on his computer, and it seems like he used grants and the teaching assistant position as rewards for sex. In the past twelve years, he's never had a male TA. He could end up serving a couple of years. Most likely, the case'll drag out until nobody cares."

"His career is over, regardless." Conor was watching her, his eyes intent, as if he could sense her increasing level of pain.

"Apparently, Isa was the one who found the camera," Jackson continued. "She didn't know what to do. She didn't want to lose the grant or her position as TA with her PhD right around the corner, or risk getting caught up in an ugly university scandal at that time, so reporting the professor was out. She found the videos on his computer, copied them, and went to Heath for advice. Heath had been chatting her up while he was dating Zoe. Heath is the one who suggested blackmail as revenge. Isa was angry enough to agree. Heath took care of the process, and they split the money. They'd already milked the professor out of twenty grand and had no plans to stop."

"She opted to use him instead of being used by him." In a way, Louisa thought that was apt. She took a deep breath, and pain cleaved her in two like a magician's saw. Conor put the morphine button in her hand. She pressed it. If there were any other loose ends, she'd have to hear about them another day. The medication slid through her veins, smoothing and blurring all the sharp, painful edges.

"Zoe saw the video on Isa's computer." Jackson's voice faded.

"What happened to Hector?" Conor asked.

Jackson shook his head. "He didn't make it."

"We're looking for Louisa Hancock," a woman's voice said from the hallway.

Dread contracted Louisa's muscles and amplified her pain. She fought the drug's effects and the vulnerability they produced.

Conor put down her hand. "I've got it."

———

Conor walked out of Louisa's room. A thin, older woman in an expensive-looking dress and coat clutched a small purse with manicured fingers. Next to her, a guy in a suit glanced around him. He looked worried. As he should.

Conor's feet took him to the desk. "Excuse me. You're looking for Louisa?"

The woman sized him up and arched a snooty brow. "What I'm doing here isn't any of your business."

"You must be Aunt Margaret," Conor said. He shifted his gaze to the blond man. "Does that make you Blaine Delancey?"

"Yes." Blaine tugged at a cuff. "And you are?"

Conor punched him dead center in the face. Blood spurted across the pale gray linoleum. Blaine fell backward, landing on his ass on the floor. With a stunned blink, he covered his bleeding nose with a hand.

"What the hell is wrong with you?" He climbed to his feet.

"Oh my goodness." Margaret rushed to Blaine's side and pushed tissues into his hand. "Someone call security."

Conor jabbed a finger in the air. "I know what you did."

"I have no idea what you're talking about." Blaine pressed the tissues against his nose.

"I know what you did to Louisa." Conor enunciated the words individually. "In the boathouse."

Blaine paled, then shook off his shock. "Everyone in here saw you assault me."

The detectives stood in the doorway.

"I didn't see anything." Detective Jackson shrugged. He back-knuckle tapped his partner on the arm. "Did you see anything?"

"Nope." Ianelli crossed his arms over his chest. "I was checking my e-mail. Sorry."

"Margaret." Blaine put a hand on her shoulder. "I hope you'll excuse me. Obviously, I'm not wanted here. I'm going back to the hotel."

"Wait, Blaine. I'm Louisa's next of kin. I have the right to make her medical decisions." Margaret cast a steely eye over Conor. A woman accustomed to getting her way. "I don't know who you are, but no one else gets in to see her except me. You don't need to leave, Blaine. They do."

"Aunt Margaret." Louisa's voice was weak but clear. "I'm fit to make my own decisions. You may come in. Blaine can go to hell."

Margaret hesitated before walking into the room with unsure steps.

"I think you'd better sit down," Conor heard Louisa say.

Blaine took the cue. Grabbing a fresh pile of tissues at the nurses' station, he walked toward the exit with hurried steps.

Jackson pushed away from the doorframe. "We'd better go."

"What are you going to do about him?" Conor jerked a thumb toward the elevator doors, which had just closed with Blaine inside the car.

"We found a traffic camera with a decent view of Broad Street in front of the Ritz." Ianelli's mouth twitched. "Old Blaine was right behind Dr. Hancock when she took her spill into traffic. Now let's go." Jackson headed for the elevator. "I want to keep him in sight. Soon as he crosses back into Philly, he's ours."

After the cops left, Conor turned an ear to Louisa's door. She and her aunt were talking in hushed tones. He leaned on the wall and waited. Fifteen minutes later, Margaret exited. She blew past Conor without stopping, her chin high, her mouth tight, angry tears shining in her eyes.

He went back into Louisa's room, expecting her to look worn. Instead, her expression was lighter. "Are you all right?"

"I am." Her voice and eyes were blurry. "She stands by Blaine. I decided I don't care. I told her never to call me again."

"Good for you." He reached into his pocket and pulled out her pearls. "Oh, I forgot. The nurse gave me these when you first came in."

"Would you hold on to them for me? They were my mother's. I don't want them to get lost."

"I will." He squeezed her hand lightly.

Her body relaxed, and her voice faded.

Conor picked up his book from the bedside table and sat in the chair next to the bed, prepared to keep watch. The threat to Louisa's life was over, but she'd need time to recover.

CHAPTER
35

One week later

Louisa opened her eyes. For the first few minutes she was surprised she was in her apartment. Sunlight streamed into the bedroom onto the dog lying next to her. A three-inch row of stitches tracked Kirra's pink belly. Louisa put her hand inside the plastic cone and scratched her head. The dog sighed.

"Are you all right? Do you need anything?"

She turned her head. Conor sat in an oversize chair he'd brought in from the living room. A book lay open on his lap. He hadn't left her side since he brought her home the day before.

"I'm fine." She shifted. Pain surrounded her rib cage, shortening her breaths, but she was content. Home, with her man and dog, was enough for today.

"Maybe you should have stayed in the hospital a few more days." He moved to the side of the bed and helped her adjust her pillows.

"No." She'd had quite enough of needles and tubes and IVs. "It felt so good to sleep in my own bed last night."

"I'll bet." Conor eased his weight onto the edge of the mattress. He patted the dog's flank. Her tail stub wagged.

"Are you sure you can stay here all the time? Don't you have to work?" Louisa reached for the glass of water on the nightstand.

Conor picked it up and handed it to her. "No. Jayne's fiancé is back. He'll fill in for me. I'm here until you're both back on your feet. We're hiring a new bartender, so I'll be cutting some of my hours back on a permanent basis."

Sipping through the straw, she settled back on the pillow. "How's your apartment?"

"The remodel is going to take at least a month." His hand rested on her thigh. "I was hoping I could stay here until it's done."

"You can stay here as long as you like." Forever would work for her. She squeezed his hand. "I love you."

"I love you too." He leaned forward and kissed her, then brushed a stray hair off her cheek. "Do you want me to close the curtains so you can sleep?"

"No. I don't want to sleep."

"You look exhausted."

She glanced at the clock. "How can I be this tired? My biggest feat for the day was walking to the bathroom a couple of times."

"Don't push yourself," he said. "The nurse is coming at three. If she gives you the all-clear, you can take a shower."

"Oh my God. I want to wash my hair more than anything right now."

"Then you should rest up." Conor stood. "How about some lunch?"

Louisa sniffed. Her stomach rumbled with the first twinges of hunger since she'd been shot. "What's that smell?"

"I put chicken and vegetables in the slow cooker this morning."

"I have a slow cooker?"

"No. I borrowed it from Jayne." Conor laughed. "What do you want for lunch?"

"Could I have a grilled cheese sandwich?"

"Coming right up." He handed her the remote control. The phone in the kitchen rang as he walked out. "I'll get it."

She flipped channels and stroked the dog's head. Her gaze drifted to the flower arrangements on the dresser and tables. The yellow-and-white daisy display on the nightstand was from April. Dr. Cusack had sent a pastel spray of roses and carnations. There were several more from her museum coworkers, plus flowers from Conor's family and Damian. She had lived in Philadelphia for just a few months, but she'd already made a home here.

"Do you like this apartment?" she called to Conor.

Conor came through the doorway with a plate in his hand. He gave the bank of windows overlooking Rittenhouse Square a pointed look. "What's not to like?"

"I'm thinking about buying it."

"Just don't tell me what it costs." He set her lunch on the nightstand, took her arms, and eased her more upright. "My head might explode."

"Deal." After a week of liquids and hospital food, the grilled cheese was the best thing she'd ever eaten.

At the sound of the doorbell, Conor ducked out of the room again. More flowers?

Conor poked his head in. "Louisa, do you feel up to some company?"

She swept an automatic hand over her limp hair. Dry shampoo was no substitute for the real thing.

"You look beautiful." Conor stepped aside.

Louisa gasped at the figure in the doorway. Her father wore the usual: beat-up work boots, a ragged sweater, and jeans, his face prematurely lined from depression and alcohol. Under a sloppy, unkempt mop of gray hair, green eyes stared at her. They were the same shade as her own, the one physical trait he'd passed on to her. No one would accuse Ward Hancock of being a slave to fashion. She let out her breath with a rush of pain and put a hand over the thick wad of bandages under her sweatshirt.

Conor looked over her dad's shoulder. "You all right?"

She nodded.

He walked to the bed and carefully lifted Kirra in his arms. "I'll take the dog for a limp around the park." He planted a kiss on her lips before leaving the room. After the door closed behind Conor and Kirra, her father walked to the side of the bed. He pulled Conor's chair closer and sat down hard. His gaze raked over her. Angry lines tightened around his mouth.

"I missed you," she said.

His mouth opened and closed. A line furrowed between his brows as if he were searching for words. "I can't believe my daughter was shot and didn't call me." His voice was steady with no trace of a slur. Was he sober?

"I'm sorry, Daddy." Guilt swamped Louisa.

"No. It's not your fault." Leaning forward, he took her hands between his and stared down at them. "The fault is all mine. I'm sorry. For everything."

"You haven't—"

"Louisa, when your mother died, I didn't handle it well. I didn't handle it at all. I used my work and scotch to put the whole situation out of my head. I didn't want to think about it. About her. About living without her for the next fifty years. The rest of my life felt so . . . long." He sighed. "Every time I looked at you, I saw her. You made me remember, and I was too much of a coward to face it."

A tear rolled down Louisa's cheek. Her throat clogged with the salt of sorrow. "I'm sorry."

"There's nothing for you to be sorry about." He glanced up at her, his eyes moist.

She should have called him. "How did you find out?"

"Conor called me right after you got out of surgery last week. I almost flew here that day, but I wanted to clear up a few things first."

Yes, work. Always his number-one priority. Disappointment pressed on Louisa's chest, as painful as her stitches. At least her gunshot wound was healing. "I'm sorry to drag you back to the States. I know you love Stockholm."

His head snapped up. "Oh no, I didn't mean that. I took a leave of absence."

"I don't understand."

"I'm staying." His smile was sad. "I've been a terrible father for a long time. I can't make it up to you. That's impossible. But I can do better. I sure as hell can't do worse." He looked away. "I'm not being entirely honest. I bottomed out last spring. Seeing you so sad . . ." He looked down at his hands and cleared his throat. "Anyway, instead of staying here and helping you, I rushed back to Sweden. I drank for a week straight. I showed up to a lecture drunk. The dean pulled me aside and *suggested* a leave of absence. I haven't worked in three months."

"What have you been doing?"

"At first, nothing except wallowing." He exhaled hard through his nose. "Then the dean paid me a visit. He dragged me to an AA meeting every day for a month. I've been sober for nine weeks."

"Is that what you were going to tell me on Thanksgiving?"

He nodded. "I need to start over. I don't want to go back to Maine or Stockholm. There are too many bad associations with both those places."

"I know all about needing a fresh start." Louisa took a deep breath. Despite the pain in her ribs, her lungs felt looser. Her father was going to be all right. "Where are you staying?"

"I don't know. I haven't had a chance to look for an apartment. Or a hotel. I came here right from the airport." He rubbed the back of her hand.

"You can stay in my guest room while you look." She smiled. "Kirra and I are pretty high-maintenance right now. Conor could use a hand. He can't be here all the time."

"Just until you're healthy. These last couple of months have been the hardest of my life. But I need to do this myself if the changes are going to be permanent." Her father handed her a tissue. "Conor seems like a good man."

"He is." Louisa sniffed.

"I talked to Margaret." Her father squeezed her hand.

Louisa stiffened. She wanted to crawl under the covers and hide.

"I wish you'd have felt comfortable enough to tell me."

Louisa picked at the edge of the sheet.

"But that's my fault, not yours." Her father exhaled. He released her hand and scrubbed both his palms down his face. "My sister is a bitch, which I didn't realize because I was hiding in Sweden."

Louisa's throat was too raw for words. She sipped her water and swallowed her discomfort. Dad was here. He was talking to her.

"I'd like to beat him senseless." Her father's hand clenched.

"Conor already did that."

"Did I tell you how much I liked him?" Despite the joke, he lightly punched his thigh.

"I'm glad you're here." Louisa put her hand over his fist. "What are you going to do?"

"My first order of business is to find an AA meeting. They'll hook me up with a sponsor. I still need daily meetings. It's too easy to slip up. I've done that once already."

The outer door opened. Dog tags jingled. Kirra trotted into the bedroom, dragging her pink leash.

"Get back here." Conor chased after her. "No jumping."

"I've got her." Louisa's father intercepted the dog at the bedside. Stroking her head, he set her gently on the mattress. Kirra padded to Louisa's side and stretched out beside her. The big head was heavy on her thigh, but she didn't care.

"She isn't allowed to jump up or down for another couple of weeks." Conor unsnapped her leash and coiled it in his hand. His eyes met Louisa's. His brows lifted, asking a silent question. *Are you all right?*

She nodded. "Dad is going to stay in the guest room."

"I'll put his bag in there." Conor had made himself comfortable in her bedroom—and in her bed—claiming to be there in case she needed anything during the night. Last night, she'd woken up and found him watching her sleep. The image was comforting. She closed her eyes, suddenly exhausted.

"You look tired. I'll let you get some rest." Her father stood.

He walked out with Conor. Content, Louisa closed her eyes and listened to the dog snore.

Two months later

She stared at her e-mail. She'd spent her first morning back at work sorting through her inbox. Dr. Cusack had stopped by twice to tell her not to tax herself and to leave early if necessary. Apparently, he'd been starstruck by her father, who had visited the museum several times and would be guest lecturing at the university. Cusack had even been reading Ward's latest book on the sly, which he'd been hiding from Louisa in his desk.

Her office door opened. "Honest, April, I'm fine."

"Do I look like April?" Conor walked in, a thermal lunch bag in his hand. He closed the door behind him and leaned on it. "I wanted to make sure you weren't working too hard."

"You drove me here this morning. I'm fine. The doctor cleared me for all normal activities."

His eyes glinted. "All normal activities?"

"Well, no triathlons, but other than that I can do whatever I feel up to."

He locked the door behind him. She swallowed, her mouth suddenly dry.

Conor stalked to the desk. He knelt in front of her.

She cupped his unshaven jaw. "I love you."

"I love you too." He turned his head into her palm. "I have two things for you."

"Two?" Louisa could only think of one thing at that moment.

He set the bag on her desk. "The first one is your lunch."

"Is that a grilled cheese sandwich?"

"It is, though you should be sick of those by now." Conor shook his head. "You've eaten one nearly every day for two months."

"Never." She kissed him hard on the mouth.

The renovations on Conor's apartment were finished weeks ago, but he'd never left Louisa's condo. Instead, he was renting out the unit over the bar to Sullivan's new bartender and parking his motorcycle boots next to her bed. He had a chunk of space in her closet—and her heart.

He kissed her back. His mouth tasted of coffee. Conor angled his head and deepened the kiss, his tongue stroking hers.

Tingles shot up Louisa's thighs. "You said you had two things for me."

"I do." He kissed her again. His face split in a wicked grin. His hands slid around her ankles and ran up her thighs. Desire warmed her. "Are you wearing panties?"

"I guess you'll have to find out."

"You're killing me." His voice was breathless, and as always, that sexy gleam in his turquoise eyes sent her pulse into a happy dance.

"It's your fantasy." She caressed his cheek with her thumb. "I already have more than I ever dreamed."

ACKNOWLEDGMENTS

My biggest thanks goes to my cousin Cris V. for providing key story elements that got me out of my plotting corner. I'd probably still be writing this book without your help.

Publishing a book is a team effort. More thanks go to my agent, Jill Marsal, and the entire team at Montlake Romance, especially my editor, JoVon Sotak, and chief author herder/technical goddess Jessica Poore. More thanks to developmental editor Shannon Godwin for helping to bring this story together.

ABOUT THE AUTHOR

Melinda Leigh abandoned her career in banking to raise her kids and never looked back. She started writing as a hobby and became addicted to creating characters and stories. Since then, she has won numerous writing awards for her paranormal romance and romantic-suspense fiction. Her debut novel, *She Can Run*, was a number-one bestseller in Kindle Romantic Suspense, a 2011 Best Book Finalist (*The Romance Reviews*), and a nominee for the 2012 International Thriller Award for Best First Book. *Midnight Exposure* was a 2013 Daphne du Maurier Award finalist. When she isn't writing, Melinda is an avid martial artist: she holds a second-degree black belt in Kenpo karate and teaches women's self-defense. She lives in a messy house with her husband, two teenagers, a couple of dogs, and two rescue cats.